THE MONSTROUS

heard of the writers it contains, and Ellen Datlow is at the top of that list. She has this crazy knack of consistently putting together stellar anthologies and *Hauntings* is no different."—*Horror Talk*

— PRAISE FOR LOVECRAFT'S MONSTERS —

"Ellen Datlow's second editorial outing into the realm of Lovecraft proves even more fruitful than the first. Focusing on Lovecraftian monsters, Datlow offers readers sixteen stories and two poems of a variety that should please any fans of the genre."—*Arkham Digest*

"[An] amazing and diverse treasure trove of stories. As an avid fan of Lovecraft's monstrous creations, THIS is the anthology I've been waiting for."—*Shattered Ravings*

"Editor Ellen Datlow has put together an anthology that will rock your liquid fantasies. Tachyon Publications has produced an excellent themed anthology. Lovecraft enthusiasts will plunge into the volume and be happily immersed in the content."—*Diabolique Magazine*

"[A]n entirely enjoyable read…For Mythos devotees I would highly recommend picking it up."— *Seattle Geekly*

"*Lovecraft's Monsters* will appeal to fans of Lovecraft's work, particularly his Mythos stories, and to readers of dark fiction everywhere."—*Lit Reactor*

"Datlow brings together some of the top SF/F and horror writers working today and has them play in Lovecraft's bizarre world. And that's a delight."—*January Magazine*

— PRAISE FOR THE CUTTING ROOM —

A Publishers Weekly **Book of the Week**
"Superstar editor Datlow makes no missteps in this reprint collection of dark tales involving movies and moviemaking…[T]he entire volume is outstanding."—*Publishers Weekly*, starred review

A Kirkus Excellent Horror Read for October
"What if, for example, the Wicked Witch of the West didn't stay in Oz? What if James Dean got a second chance at life? These are just some of the weird-but-cool ideas explored in this tempting volume of stories from renowned editor Ellen Datlow."—*Kirkus*

"This collection of 23 stories should appeal to fans of horror and SF primarily, though noir and hard-boiled-mystery readers should feel welcome too…Definitely worth checking out."—*Booklist*

"Horror cinephiles and bibliophiles will have extra cause to rejoice this Halloween: *The Cutting Room*, a literary anthology, is an October treat."—*Diabolique*

"When Datlow's name is on the cover, however, you know the collection will contain the highest-quality writing and arranging…*The Cutting Room* is a major success."—*Ensuing Chapters*

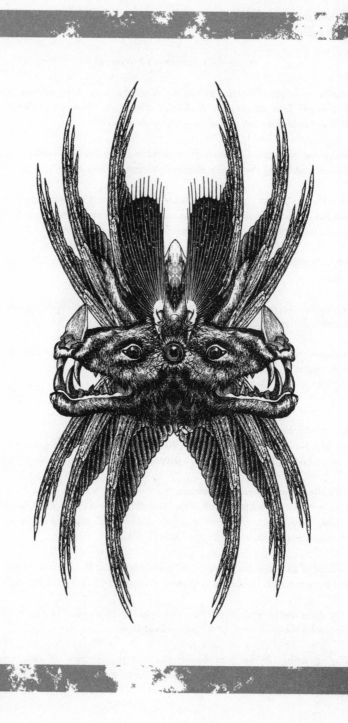

THE

MONSTROUS

edited by ELLEN DATLOW

TACHYON

Monstrous

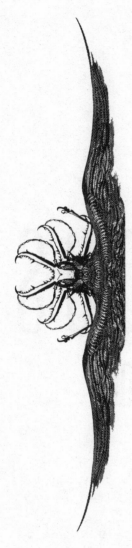

COVER ART © 2012 BY REIKO MURAKAMI.
COVER DESIGN BY ELIZABETH STORY.
INTERIOR ART AND DESIGN COPYRIGHT
© 2015 BY JOHN COULTHART.
VIGNETTE ILLUSTRATIONS FROM
'DE MONSTRIS' (1665) BY FORTUNIO LICETI.
CAPITALS ON CONTENTS PAGE
BY ROMAN CIEŚLEWICZ.

TACHYON PUBLICATIONS
1459 18TH STREET #139
SAN FRANCISCO, CA 94107
WWW.TACHYONPUBLICATIONS.COM
TACHYON@TACHYONPUBLICATIONS.COM

SERIES EDITOR: JACOB WEISMAN
PROJECT EDITOR: JILL ROBERTS

ISBN 13: 978-1-61696-206-7

PRINTED IN THE UNITED STATES
BY WORZALLA
FIRST EDITION: 2015

A Whisper of Blood
A Wolf at the Door (with Terri Windling)
After (with Terri Windling)
Alien Sex
Black Heart, Ivory Bones
   (with Terri Windling)
Black Swan, White Raven
   (with Terri Windling)
Black Thorn, White Rose
   (with Terri Windling)
Blood and Other Cravings
Blood Is Not Enough: 17 Stories of Vampirism
Darkness: Two Decades of Modern Horror
Digital Domains: A Decade of Science Fiction
   and Fantasy
Fearful Symmetries
Haunted Legends (with Nick Mamatas)
Hauntings
Inferno: New Tales of Terror
   and the Supernatural
Lethal Kisses
Little Deaths
Lovecraft Unbound
Lovecraft's Monsters
Naked City: Tales of Urban Fantasy
Nightmare Carnival
Off Limits: Tales of Alien Sex
Omni Best Science Fiction:
   Volumes One through Three
Omni Books of Science Fiction:
   Volumes One through Seven
OmniVisions One and Two
Poe: 19 New Tales Inspired by Edgar Allan Poe
Queen Victoria's Book of Spells
   (with Terri Windling)
Ruby Slippers, Golden Tears
   (with Terri Windling)

Salon Fantastique: Fifteen Original Tales
   of Fantasy (with Terri Windling)
Silver Birch, Blood Moon
   (with Terri Windling)
Sirens and Other Daemon Lovers
   (with Terri Windling)
Snow White, Blood Red
   (with Terri Windling)
Supernatural Noir
Swan Sister (with Terri Windling)
Tails of Wonder and Imagination: Cat Stories
Teeth: Vampire Tales (with Terri Windling)
Telling Tales: The Clarion West 30th
   Anniversary Anthology
The Beastly Bride: And Other Tales of
   the Animal People (with Terri Windling)
The Beastly Bride: Tales of the Animal People
The Best Horror of the Year:
   Volumes One through Seven
The Coyote Road: Trickster Tales
   (with Terri Windling)
The Cutting Room: Dark Reflections of the
   Silver Screen
The Dark: New Ghost Stories
The Del Rey Book of Science Fiction & Fantasy
The Doll Collection
The Faery Reel: Tales from the Twilight Realm
   (with Terri Windling)
The Green Man: Tales of the Mythic Forest
   (with Terri Windling)
The Nebula Awards Showcase 2009
The Year's Best Fantasy and Horror
   (with Terri Windling, Gavin J. Grant,
   and Kelly Link)
Troll's Eye View: A Book of Villainous Tales
   (with Terri Windling)
Twists of the Tale
Vanishing Acts

Introduction

ELLEN DATLOW

What's the first thing that comes to your mind when you hear the word "monster"? Giant, repulsive, lumbering nonhuman creatures intent on destruction? That's what most of us think of first, and yes monsters can be that, but the word *monster* and its etymology is complicated.

Monēre is the root of *monstrum* and means to warn and instruct. This benign interpretation was proposed by Saint Augustine, who saw monsters not as inherently evil but as part of the natural design of the world, deliberately created by God for His own reasons: spreading "abroad a multitude of those marvels which are called monsters, portents, prodigies, phenomena.... They say that they are called monsters, because they demonstrate or signify something; portents because they portend something, and so forth...ought to demonstrate, portend, predict that God will bring to pass what He has foretold regarding the bodies of men, no difficulty preventing Him, no law of nature prescribing to Him His limit."

A few centuries later, the Middle English word *monstre*, derived from Anglo-French and the Latin *monstrum*, came into use, referring to an aberrant occurrence, usually biological, that was taken as a sign that something was wrong within the natural order. So abnormal animals or humans were regarded as signs or omens of impending evil. It wasn't until the 1550s that the definition included "a person of inhuman cruelty or wickedness."

1

Over time, the usages of the concept became less subtle and more extreme, so that today most people consider a monster any creature—usually found in legends, horror fiction, or movies—that is often hideous-looking and/or produces fear or physical harm by its appearance and/or its actions. The word also usually connotes something wrong or evil; a monster is generally morally objectionable, in addition to being physically or psychologically hideous and/or a freak of nature. The word is also applied figuratively to a person with an overwhelming appetite (sexual in addition to culinary) or a person who does horrible things.

Since humans began telling stories, monsters have figured in them. There's a rich tradition of monsters in literature ranging from the Greek snake-haired Medusa and the one-eyed Cyclops to the Arabian fire demons known as Afrits and Ghuls (which became Ghouls, when Westernized). There are also Japanese fox maidens; the Mesopotamian Ekimmu, said to suck life force, energy, or sometimes, misery; the Inkanyamba, a huge carnivorous eel-like animal in the legends of the Zulu and Xhosa people of South Africa; and huge ogres that are a staple in African folktales. Bad fairies, evil witches, crafty wolves, and nasty trolls that terrorize and/or eat humans in fairy and folktales from Europe fit in perfectly with this crowd of international monsters.

What I said when I solicited stories: I am looking for unusual monster stories. Not your usual monster kills/destroys everything. The end. I also said "no human monsters." This I did because I wasn't looking for a host of serial killer stories. Yes, there are human monsters represented within, in that many of the characters have done or do monstrous things, but I was looking for something more. Sometimes finding a creature monstrous requires a shift in perspective. Who is the worse monster in Mary Shelley's *Frankenstein*? The creature abandoned to his own devices by his creator or the prideful Victor Frankenstein? Who is worse? A creature that destroys without conscious thought or those who exploit it? What are the ethics of being a vampire in a concentration camp? If a child is murderous and isn't aware of what she is doing, is she monstrous?

In addition to new monsters, you may find yourself encountering a Lovecraftian monster or two, at least one fairy tale villain, and, yes, even a serial killer. But what's most interesting to me as a reader, and in the stories herein, is how the humans react to the monstrosities they encounter.

So take a peek inside, and after you read the stories, you judge what or who are the monsters.

Never forget that monstrosity is in the eye of the beholder.

A Natural History of Autumn

JEFFREY FORD

On a blue afternoon in autumn, Riku and Michi drove south from Numazu in his silver convertible along the coast of the Izu Peninsula. The temperature was mild for the end of October, and the air was clear, the sun glinting off Suruga Bay. She wore sunglasses and, to protect her hair, a yellow scarf with a design of orange butterflies. He wore driving gloves, a black dress shirt, a loosened white tie. The car, the open road, the rush of the wind made it impossible to converse, and so for miles she watched the bay to their right and he the rising slopes of maple and pine to their left. Just outside the town of Dogashima, a song came on the radio, "Just You, Just Me," and they turned to look at each other. She waited for him to smile. He did. She smiled back, and then he headed inland to search for the hidden onsen, Inugami.

They'd met the previous night at The Limit, an upscale hostess bar. Riku's employer had a tab there and he was free to use it when in Numazu. He'd been once before, drunk and spent time with a hostess. Her conversation had sounded rote, like a script; her flattery grotesquely opulent and therefore flat. The instant he saw Michi, though, in her short black dress with a look of uncertainty in her eyes, he knew it would be a different experience. He ordered a bottle of Nikka Yoichi and two glasses. She introduced herself. He stood and bowed. They were in a private room at a polished table of blond wood. The chairs were high-backed and upholstered like thrones. To their right was an open-air view of pines and the coast. She waited for him to smile and eventually he did. She smiled back and told him, "I'm writing a book."

Riku said, "Aren't you supposed to tell me how handsome I am?"

"Your hair is perfect," she said.

He laughed. "I see."

"I'm writing a book," she said again. "I decided to make a study of something."

"You're a scientist?" he said.

"We're all scientists," she said. "We watch and listen, take in information, process it. We spin theories by which we live."

"What if they're false?"

"What if they're not?" she said.

He shook his head and took a drink.

They sat in silence for a time. She stared out past the pines, sipping her whisky. He stared at her.

"Tell me about your family," said Riku.

She told him about her dead father, her ill mother, her younger sister and brother, but when she inquired about his parents, he said, "Okay, tell me about your book."

"I decided to study a season, and since autumn is the season I'm in, it would be autumn. It's a natural history of autumn."

"You've obviously been to the university," he said.

She shook her head. "No, I read a lot to pass the time between clients."

"How much have you written?"

"Nothing yet. I'm researching now, taking notes."

"Do you go out to Thousand Tree Beach and stare at Fuji in the morning?"

"Your sarcasm is intoxicating," she said.

He filled her glass.

"No, I do my research here. I ask each client what autumn means to him."

"And they tell you?"

She nodded. "Some just want me to say how big their biceps are but most sit back and really think about it. The thought of it makes all the white-haired *ojiisans* smile, the businessmen cry, the young men a little scared. A lot of it is the same. Just images—the colorful leaves, the clear cold mornings by the bay, a certain pet dog, a childhood friend, a drunken night. But sometimes they tell me whole stories."

"What kind of stories?"

"A very powerful businessman—one of the other hostesses swore he was a master of the five elements—once told me his own love story, about a young woman he had an affair with. It began on the final day of summer, lasted only as long as the following season, and ended in the snow."

"What did you learn from that story? What did you put in your notes?"

"I recorded his story as he'd told it, and afterward wrote, 'The Story of a Ghost.'"

"Why a ghost?" he asked.

"I forget," she said. "And I lied—I attended Waseda University for two years before my father died."

"You didn't have to tell me," he said. "I knew when you told me you called the businessman's story 'The Story of a Ghost.'"

"Pretentious?" she asked.

He shrugged.

"Maybe," she said and smiled.

"Forget about that," said Riku. "I will top that make-inu businessman's exquisite melancholy by proposing a field trip." He sat forward in his chair and touched the tabletop with his index finger. "My employer recently rewarded me for a job well done and suggested I use, whenever I like, a private onsen he has an arrangement with down in Izu. I need only call a few hours in advance."

"A field trip?" she said. "What will we be researching?"

"Autumn. The red and yellow leaves. The place is out in the woods on a mountainside, hidden and very old-fashioned, no frills. I propose a dohan, an overnight journey to the onsen, Inugami."

"A date," she said. "And our attentions will only be on autumn, nothing else?"

"You can trust me when I say, that is entirely up to you."

"Your hair inspires confidence," she said. "You can arrange things with the house on the way out."

"I intend to be in your book," he said and prevented himself from smiling.

After hours of winding along the rims of steep cliffs and bumping down tight dirt paths through the woods, the silver car pulled to a stop in a clearing, in front of a large, slightly sagging farmhouse—minka style, built of logs with a thatched roof. Twenty yards to the left of the place there was a sizeable garden filled with dying sunflowers, ten-foot stalks, their heads bowed. To the right of the house there was a slate path that led away into the pines. The golden late-afternoon light slanted down on the clearing, shadows beginning to form at the tree line.

"We're losing the day," said Riku. "We'll have to hurry."

Michi got out of the car and stretched. She removed her sunglasses and stood still for a moment, taking in the cool air.

"I have your bag," said Riku and shut the trunk.

As they headed for the house, two figures appeared on the porch. One was a small old woman with white hair, wearing monpe pants and an indigo katazome jacket with a design of white flames. Next to her stood what Michi at first mistook for a pony. The sight of the animal surprised her and she stopped walking. Riku went on ahead. "Grandmother Chinatsu," he said and bowed.

"Your employer has arranged everything with me. Welcome," she said. A small, wrinkled hand with dirty nails appeared from within the sleeve of the jacket. She beckoned to Michi. "Come, my dear, don't be afraid of my pet, Ono. He doesn't bite." She smiled and waved her arm.

As Michi approached, she bowed to Grandmother Chinatsu, who only offered a nod. The instant the young woman's foot touched the first step of the porch, the dog gave a low growl. The old lady wagged a finger at the creature and snapped, "Yemeti!" Then she laughed, low and gruff, the sound at odds with her diminutive size. She extended her hand and helped Michi up onto the porch. "Come in," she said and led them into the farmhouse.

Michi was last in line. She turned to look at the dog. Its coat was more like curly human hair than fur. She winced in disgust. A large flattened pug face, no snout to speak of, black eyes, sharp ears, and a thick bottom lip bubbling with drool. "Ono," she said and bowed slightly in passing. As she stepped into the shadow beyond the doorway, she felt the dog's nose press momentarily against the back of her dress.

In the main room there was a rock fireplace within which a low flame licked two maple logs. Above hung a large paper lantern, orange with white blossoms, shedding a soft light in the center of the room. The place was rustic, wonderfully simple. All was wood: the walls, the ceiling, the floor. There were three ancient carved wooden chairs gathered around a low table off in an alcove at one side of the room. Grandmother led them down a hallway to the back of the place. They passed a room on the left, its screen shut. At the next room, the old lady slid open the panel and said, "The toilet." Farther on, they came to two rooms, one on either side of the hallway. She let them know who was to occupy which by mere nods of her head. "The bath is at the end of the hall," she said.

Their rooms were tatami-style, straw mats and a platform bed with a futon mattress in the far corner. They undressed, put on robes and sandals, and met in the hallway. As they passed through the main room of the house, Ono stirred from his spot by the fireplace, looked up at them, and snorted.

"Easy, easy," said Riku to the creature. He stepped aside and let Michi get in front of him. Once out on the porch, she said, "Ono is a little scary."

"Only a little?" he asked.

Grandmother appeared from within the plot of dying sunflowers and called that there were towels in the shed out by the spring. Riku waved to her as he and Michi took the slate path into the pines. Shadows were rising beneath the trees and the sky was losing its last blue to an orange glow. Leaves littered the path and the temperature had dropped. The scent of pine was everywhere. Curlews whistled from the branches above.

"Are you taking notes?" he called ahead to her.

She stopped and waited for him. "Which do you think is more autumnal—the leaves, the dying sunflowers, or Grandmother Chinatsu?"

"Too early to tell," he said. "I'm withholding judgment."

Another hundred yards down the winding path they came upon the spring, nearly surrounded by pines except for one spot with a view of a small meadow beyond. Steam rose from the natural pool, curling up in the air, reminding Michi of the white flames on the old lady's jacket. At the edge of the water, closest to the slate path, there was ancient stonework, a crude bench, a stacked rock wall covered with moss, six foot by four, from which a thin waterfall splashed down into the rising heat of the onsen.

"Lovely," said Michi.

Riku nodded.

She left him and moved down along the side of the spring. He looked away as she stepped out of her sandals and removed her robe, which she hung on a nearby branch. He heard her sigh as she entered the water. When he removed his robe, her face was turned away, as if she were taking in the last light on the meadow. Meanwhile, Riku was taking Michi in, her slender neck, her long black hair and how it lay on the curve of her shoulder, her breasts.

"Are you getting in?" she asked.

He silently eased down into the warmth.

When Michi turned to look at him, she immediately noticed the tattoo on his right shoulder, a vicious swamp eel with rippling fins and needle fangs and a long body that wrapped around Riku's back. It was the color of the moss on the rocks of the waterfall.

Riku noticed her glancing at it. He also noticed the smoothness of her skin and that her nipples were erect.

"Who is your employer?" she asked.

"He's a good man," he said and lowered himself into a crouch, so that only his head was above water. "Now, pay attention," he said and looked out at the meadow, which was already in twilight.

"To what?" she asked, also sinking down into the water.

He didn't respond and they remained immersed for a long time, just two heads floating on the surface, staring silently and listening, steam rising around them. At last light, when the air grew cold, the curlews lifted from their branches and headed for Australia. Riku stood, moved to a different spot in the spring, and crouched down again. Michi moved closer to him. A breeze blew through the pines, a cricket sang in the dark.

"Was there any inspiration?" he asked.

"I'm not sure," she said. "It's time for you to tell me your story of autumn." She drew closer to him and he backed up a step.

"I don't tell stories," he said.

"As brief as you want, but something," she said and smiled.

He closed his eyes and said, "Okay. The autumn I was seventeen, I worked on one of the fishing boats out of Numazu. We were out for horse mackerel. On one journey we were struck by a rogue wave, a giant that popped up out of nowhere. I was on deck when it hit and we were swamped. I managed to grab a rope and it took all my strength not to be drawn overboard, the water was so cold and powerful. I was sure I would die. Two men did get swept away and were never found. That's my Natural History of Autumn."

She moved forward and put her arms around him. They kissed. He drew his head back and whispered in her ear, "When I returned to shore that autumn, I quit fishing." She laughed and rested her head on his shoulder.

They dined by candlelight, in their robes, in the alcove off the main room of the farmhouse. Grandmother Chinatsu served, and Ono followed a step behind, so that every time she leaned forward to put a platter on the table, there was the dog's leering face, tongue drooping. The main course was thin slices of raw mackerel with grated ginger and chopped scallions. They drank sake. Michi remarked on the appearance of the mackerel after Riku's story.

"Most definitely a sign," he said.

They discussed the things they each saw and heard at the spring as the sake bottle emptied. It was well past midnight when the candle burned out and they went down the hall to his room.

Three hours later, Michi woke in the dark, still a little woozy from the sake. Riku woke when she sat up on the edge of the bed.

"Are you alright?" he asked.

"I have to use the toilet." She got off the bed and lifted her robe from the mat. Slipping into it, she crossed the room. When she slid back the panel, a dim light entered. A lantern hanging in the center of the hallway ceiling bathed the corridor in a dull glow. Michi left the panel open and headed up the hallway. Riku lay back and immediately dozed off. It seemed only a minute to him before Michi was back, shaking him by the shoulder to wake up. She'd left the panel open and he could see her face. Her eyes were wide, the muscles of her jaw tense, a vein visibly throbbing behind the pale skin of her forehead. She was breathing rapidly and he could feel the vibration of her heartbeat.

"Get me out of here," she said in a harsh whisper.

"What's wrong?" he said and moved quickly to the edge of the bed. She kneeled on the mattress next to him and grabbed his arm tightly with both hands.

"We've got to leave," she said.

He shook his head and ran his fingers through his hair. It wasn't perfect anymore. He carefully removed his arm from her grip and checked his watch. "It's three a.m.," he said. "You want to leave?"

"I demand you take me out of this place, now."

"What happened?" he asked.

"Either you take me now or I'll leave on foot."

He gave a long sigh and stood up. "I'll be ready in a minute," he said. She went across the corridor to her room and gathered her things together.

When they met in the hallway, bags in hand, he asked her, "Do you think I should let Grandmother Chinatsu know we're leaving?"

"Definitely not," she said, on the verge of tears. She grabbed him with her free hand and dragged him by the shirtsleeve down the hallway. As they reached the main room of the house, she stopped and looked warily around. "Was it the dog?" he whispered. The coast was apparently clear, for she then dragged him outside, down the porch steps, to the silver car.

"Get in," he said. "I have to put the top up. It's too cold to drive with it down."

"Just hurry," she said, stowing her overnight bag. She slid into the passenger seat just as the car top was closing. He got in behind the wheel and reached over to latch the top on her side before doing his.

Michi's window was down and she heard the creaking of planks from the porch. She leaned her head toward her shoulder and looked into the car's side mirror. There, in the full moonlight, she could see Grandmother Chinatsu and Ono. The old lady was waving and laughing.

"Drive," she shrieked.

Riku hit the start button, put the car in gear, and they were off into the night, racing down a rutted dirt road at 50. Once the farmhouse was out of sight, he let up on the gas. "You've got to tell me what happened," he said.

She was shivering. "Get us out of the woods first," she said. "To a highway."

"I can't see a thing and I don't remember all the roads," he said. "We might end up lost." He drove for more than an hour before he found a road made of asphalt. His car had been brutalized by the crude paths and branches jutting into the roadway. There would be a hundred scratches on his doors. During that entire time, Michi stared ahead through the windshield, breathing rapidly.

"We're on a main road. Tell me what happened," he said.

"I got up to use the toilet," she said. "And I did. But when I stepped back out into the hallway to return, I heard a horrible grunting noise. I swear it sounded like someone was choking Grandmother Chinatsu to death in her room. I moved along the wall to the entrance. The panel was partially open, and there was a light inside. The noise had stopped so I peered in, and there was the shriveled old lady on her hands and knees on the floor, naked. Her forearms were trembling, her face was bright red, and she began croaking. At first I thought she was ill, but then I looked up and realized she was engaged in sexual relations."

"Grandmother Chinatsu?" he said and laughed. "Who was the unlucky gentleman?"

"That disgusting dog."

"She was doing it with Ono?"

"I almost vomited," said Michi. "But I could have dealt with it. The worst thing was Ono saw me peering in and he smiled at me and nodded."

"Dogs don't smile," he said.

"Exactly," she said. "That place is haunted."

"Well, I'll figure out where we are eventually, and we'll make it back to Numazu by morning. I'm sorry you were so frightened. The field trip seemed a great success until then."

She took a few deep breaths to calm herself. "Perhaps that was the true spirit of autumn," she said.

"'The Story of a Ghost,'" he said.

The silver car sped along in the moonlight. Michi was leaning against the window, her eyes closed. Riku thought he was heading for the coast.

He took a tight turn on a narrow mountain road and something suddenly lunged out of the woods at the car. He felt an impact as he swerved, turning back just in time to avoid the drop beyond the lane he'd strayed into.

Michi woke at the impact and said, "What's happening?"

"I think I grazed a deer back there. I've got to pull over and check to see if the car is okay."

Michi leaned forward and adjusted the rearview mirror so she could look out the back window.

"Too late to see," he said. "It was a half-mile back." He eased down on the brake, slowing, and began to edge over toward the shoulder.

"There's something chasing us," she said. "I can see it in the moonlight. Keep going. Go faster."

He downshifted and took his foot off the brake. As he hit the gas, he reached up and moved the mirror out of her grasp so he could see what was following them.

"It's a dog," he said. "But it's the fastest dog I ever saw. I'm doing forty-five and it's gaining on us."

They passed through an area where overhanging trees blocked the moon.

"Watch the road," she said.

When the car moved again into the moonlight, he checked behind them and saw nothing. Then they heard a loud growling. Each searched frantically to see where the noise was coming from. Swerving out of his lane, Riku looked out his side window and down and saw the creature running alongside, the movement of its four legs a blur, its face perfectly human.

"Kuso," he said. "Open the glove compartment. There's a gun in there. Give it to me."

"A gun?"

"Hurry," he yelled. She did as he instructed, handing him the sleek 9 mm. "You were right," he said. "The place was haunted." He lowered his side window, switched hands between gun and wheel. Then, steadying himself, he hit the brake. The dog looked up as it sped past the car—a middle-aged woman's face, bitter, with a terrible underbite and a beauty mark beneath the left eye, riding atop the neck of a mangy gray mutt with a naked tail. As soon as it moved a foot ahead of the car, Riku thrust the gun out the window and fired. The creature suddenly exploded, turning instantly to a shower of salt.

"It had a face," he said, maneuvering the car out of its skid. "A woman's face."

"Don't stop," she said. "Please."

"Don't worry."

"Now," she said, "who is your employer? Why would he send you to such a place?"

"Maybe if I tell you the truth it'll lift whatever curse we're under."

"What is the truth?"

"My employer is a very powerful businessman, and I have heard it said that he is also an Onmyoji. You know him. In a moment of weakness he told you a story about an affair he had. Afterward, he worried that you might be inclined to blackmail him. If the story got out, it would be a grave embarrassment for him both at home and at the office. He told me, spend time with her. He wanted me to judge what type of person you are."

"And if I'm the wrong kind of person?"

"I'm to kill you and make it look like an accident," he said.

"Are you trying to scare me to death, you and the old woman?"

"No, I swear. I'm as frightened as you are. And I couldn't harm you. Believe me. I know you would never blackmail him."

She rested back against the car seat and closed her eyes. She could feel his hand grasp hers. "Do you believe me?" he said. In the instant she opened her eyes, she saw ahead through the windshield two enormous dogs step onto the highway thirty yards in front of the car.

"Watch out," she screamed. He'd been looking over at her. He hit the brake before even glancing to the windshield. The car locked up and skidded, the headlights illuminating two faces—a man with a thin black mustache and wire-frame glasses, whose mouth was gaping open, and a little girl, chubby, with black bangs, tongue sticking out. On impact, the front of the car crumpled, the air bags deployed, and the horrid dogs burst into salt. The car left the road and came to a stop on the right-hand side, just before the tree line.

Riku remained conscious through the accident. He undid his seatbelt and slid out of the car, brushing glass off his shirt. His forehead had struck the rearview mirror, and there was a gash on his right temple. He heard growling, and pushing himself away from the car, he headed around to Michi's side. A small pot-bellied dog with the face of an idiot, sunken eyes, and swollen lower lip was drooling and scratching at Michi's window. Riku aimed, pulled the trigger, and turned the monstrosity to salt.

He opened the passenger door. Michi was just coming around. He helped her out and leaned her against the car. Bending over, he reached into the glove compartment and found an extra clip for the gun. As he backed out of the car, he heard them coming up the road, a pack of them, speeding through the moonlight, howling and grunting. He grabbed her hand and they made for the tree line.

"Not the woods," she said and tried to free herself from his grasp.

"No, there's no place to hide on the road. Come on."

They fled into the darkness beneath the trees, Riku literally dragging her forward. Low branches whipped their faces and tangled Michi's hair. Although ruts tripped them, they miraculously never fell. The baying of the beasts sounded only steps behind them, but when he turned and lifted the gun, he saw nothing but night.

Eventually they broke from beneath the trees onto a dirt road. Both were heaving for breath, and neither could run another step. She'd twisted an ankle and was limping. He put one arm around her, to help her along. She was trembling; so was he.

"What are they?" she whispered.

"Jinmenken," he said.

"Impossible."

They walked slowly down the road, and stepping out from beneath the canopy of leaves, the moonlight showed them, a hundred yards off, a dilapidated building with boarded windows.

"I can't run anymore," he said. "We'll go in there and find a place to hide."

She said nothing.

They stood for a moment on the steps of the place, a concrete structure, some abandoned factory or warehouse, and he tried his cell phone. "No reception," he said after dialing three times and listening. He flipped to a new screen with his thumb and pressed an app icon. The screen became a flashlight. He turned it forward, held it at arm's length, and motioned with his head for Michi to get close behind him. With the gun at the ready, they moved slowly through the doorless entrance.

The place was freezing cold and pitch black. As far as he could tell there were hallways laid out in a square, with small rooms off it to either side.

"An office building in the middle of the woods," she said.

Each room had the remains of a Western-style door at its entrance, pieces of shattered wood hanging on by the hinges. When he shone the phone's light into the rooms, he saw a window opening boarded from within by a sheet of plywood, and an otherwise empty concrete expanse. They went down one hall and turned left into another. Michi remembered she had the same app on her phone and lit it. Halfway down that corridor, they found a room whose door was mostly intact but for a corner at the bottom where it appeared to have been kicked in. Riku inspected the knob and whispered, "There's a lock on this one."

They went in and he locked the door behind them and tested its strength. "Get in the corner under the window," he said. "If they find us, and the door won't hold, I can rip off the board above us and we might be able to escape outside." She joined him in the corner and they sat, shoulders touching, their backs against the cold concrete. "We're sure to be safe when the sun rises."

He put his arm around her and she leaned into him. Then neither said a word, nor made a sound. They turned off their phones and listened to the dark. Time passed, yet when Riku checked his watch, it read only 3:30. "All that in a half-hour?" he wondered. Then there came a sound, a light tapping, as if rain was falling outside. The noise slowly grew louder, and seconds later it became clear that it was the sound of claws on the concrete floor. That light tapping eventually became a clatter, as if a hundred of the creatures were circling impatiently in the hallway.

A strange guttural voice came from the hole at the bottom corner of the door. "Tomodachi," it said. "Let us in."

Riku flipped to the flashlight app and held the gun up. Across the room, the hole in the bottom of the door was filled with a fat, pale, bearded face.

One eye was swollen shut and something oozed from the corner of it. The forehead was too high to see a hairline. The thing snuffled and smiled.

"Shoot," said Michi.

Riku fired, but the face flinched away in an instant, and once the bullet went wide and drilled a neat hole in the door, the creature returned and said, "Tomodachi."

"What do you want?" said Riku, his voice cracking.

"We are hunting a spirit of the living," said the creature, the movement of its lips out of sync with the words it spoke.

"What have we done?" said Michi.

"Our hunger is great, but we only require one spirit. We only take what we need—the other person will be untouched. One spirit will feed us for a week."

Michi stood up and stepped away from Riku. He also got to his feet. "What are you doing?" she said. "Shoot them." She quickly lit her phone and shone it on him.

Instead of aiming the gun at the door, he aimed it at her. "I'm not having my spirit devoured," he said to her.

"You said you couldn't hurt me."

"It won't be me hurting you," he said. She saw there were tears in his eyes. The hand that held the gun was wobbling. "I'm giving you the girl," he called to the Jinmenken.

"A true benefactor," said the face at the hole.

"No," she said. "What have I done?"

"I'm going to shoot her in the leg so she can't run, then I'm going to let you all in. You will keep your distance from me or I'll shoot. I have an extra clip, and I'll turn as many of you to salt as I can before you get to me."

Turning to Michi, he said, "I'm so sorry. I did love you."

"But you're a coward. You don't have to shoot me in the leg," she said. "I'll go to them on my own. My spirit's tired of this world." She moved forward and gave him a kiss. Her actions disarmed him and he appeared confused. At the door, she slowly undid the lock on the knob. Then, with a graceful, fluid motion, she pulled the door open and stepped behind it against the wall. "Take him," he heard her call. The Jinmenken bounded in, dozens of them, small and large, stinking of rain, slobbering, snapping, clawing. He pulled the trigger till the gun clicked empty, and the room was filled with smoke and flying salt. His hands shook too much to change the clip. One of the creatures tore a bloody chunk from his left calf and he screamed. Another went for his groin. The face of Grandmother Chinatsu appeared before him and devoured his.

The following week, in a private room at The Limit, Michi sat at a blond-wood table, staring out the open panel across the room at the pines and the coast. Riku's employer sat across from her. "Ingenious, the Natural History of Autumn," he said. "And you knew this would draw him in?"

She turned to face the older man. "He was a unique person," she said. "He'd faced death."

"Too bad about Riku," he said. "I wanted to trust him."

"Really, the lengths to which you'll go to test the spirit of those you need to trust. He's gone because he was a coward?"

"A coward I can tolerate. But he said he loved you, and it proved he didn't understand love at all. A dangerous flaw." He took an envelope from within his suit jacket and laid it on the table. "A job well done," he said. She lifted the envelope and looked inside.

A cold breeze blew into the room. "You know," he said, "this season always reminds me of our time together."

As she spoke she never stopped counting the bills. "All I remember of that," she said, "is the snow."

Ashputtle

PETER STRAUB

People think that teaching little children has something to do with helping other people, something to do with service. People think that if you teach little children, you must love them. People get what they need from thoughts like this.

People think that if you happen to be very fat and are a person who acts happy and cheerful all the time, you are probably pretending to be that way in order to make them forget how fat you are or cause them to forgive you for being so fat. They make this assumption, thinking you are so stupid that you imagine that you're getting away with this charade. From this assumption, they get confidence in the superiority of their intelligence over yours, and they get to pity you, too.

Those figments, those stepsisters, came to me and said, *Don't you know that we want to help you?* They came to me and said, *Can you tell us what your life is like?*

These moronic questions they asked over and over: *Are you all right? Is anything happening to you? Can you talk to us now, darling? Can you tell us about your life?*

I stared straight ahead, not looking at their pretty hair or pretty eyes or pretty mouths. I looked over their shoulders at the pattern on the wallpaper and tried not to blink until they stood up and went away.

What my *life* was like? What was *happening* to me?

Nothing was happening to me. I was *all right.*

They smiled briefly, like a twitch in their eyes and mouths, before they stood up and left me alone. I sat still on my chair and looked at the wallpaper while they talked to Zena.

The wallpaper was yellow, with white lines going up and down through it. The lines never touched—just when they were about to run into each other, they broke, and the fat thick yellow kept them apart.

I liked seeing the white lines hanging in the fat yellow, each one separate.

When the figments called me *darling*, ice and snow stormed into my mouth and went pushing down my throat into my stomach, freezing everything. They didn't know I was nothing, that I would never be like them, they didn't know that the only part of me that was not nothing was a small hard stone right at the center of me.

That stone has a name. MOTHER.

If you are a female kindergarten teacher in her fifties who happens to be very fat, people imagine that you must be truly dedicated to their children, because you cannot possibly have any sort of private life. If they are the parents of the children in your kindergarten class, they are almost grateful that you are so grotesque, because it means that you must really care about their children. After all, even though you couldn't possibly get any other sort of job, you can't be in it for the money, can you? Because what do people know about your salary? They know that garbage men make more money than kindergarten teachers. So at least you didn't decide to take care of their delightful, wonderful, lovable little children just because you thought you'd get rich, no no.

Therefore, even though they disbelieve all your smiles, all your pretty ways, even though they really do think of you with a mixture of pity and contempt, a little gratitude gets in there.

Sometimes when I meet with one of these parents, say a fluffy-haired young lawyer, say named Arnold Zoeller, Arnold and his wife, Kathi, Kathi with an i, mind you, sometimes when I sit behind my desk and watch these two slim handsome people struggle to keep the pity and contempt out of their well-cared-for faces, I catch that gratitude heating up behind their eyes.

Arnold and Kathi believe that a pathetic old lumpo like me must love their lovely little girl, a girl say named Tori, Tori with an i (for Victoria). And I think I do rather love little Tori Zoeller, yes I do think I love that little girl. My mother would have loved her, too. And that's the God's truth.

I can see myself in the world, in the middle of the world.

I see that I am the same as all nature.

In our minds exists an awareness of perfection, but nothing on earth, nothing in all of nature, is perfectly conceived. Every response comes straight out of the person who is responding.

I have no responsibility to stimulate or satisfy your needs. All that was taken care of a long time ago.

Even if you happen to be some kind of supposedly exalted person, like a lawyer. Even if your name is Arnold Zoeller, for example.

Once, briefly, there existed a golden time. In my mind existed an awareness of perfection, and all of nature echoed and repeated the awareness of perfection in my mind. My parents lived, and with them, I too was alive in the golden time. Our name was Asch, and in fact I am known now as Mrs. Asch, the Mrs. being entirely honorific, no husband having ever been in evidence, nor ever likely to be. (To some sixth-graders, those whom I did not beguile and enchant as kindergartners, those before whose parents I did not squeeze myself into my desk chair and pronounce their dull, their dreary treasures delightful, wonderful, lovable, above all *intelligent*, I am known as Mrs. Fat-Asch. Of this I pretend to be ignorant.) Mr. and Mrs. Asch did dwell together in the golden time, and both mightily did love their girl-child. And then, whoops, the girl-child's Mommy upped and died. The girl-child's Daddy buried her in the estate's church yard, with the minister and everything, in the coffin and everything, with hymns and talking and crying and the animals standing around, and Zena, I remember, Zena was already there, even then. So that was how things were, right from the start.

The figments came because of what I did later. They came from a long way away—the city, I think. We never saw city dresses like that, out where we lived. We never saw city hair like that, either. And one of those ladies had a veil!

One winter morning during my first year teaching kindergarten here, I got into my car—I *shoved myself* into my car, I should explain; this is different for me than for you, I *rammed myself* between the seat and the steering wheel, and I drove forty miles east, through three different suburbs, until I got to the city, and thereupon I drove through the city to the slummiest section, where dirty people sit in their cars and drink right in the middle of the day. I went to the department store nobody goes to unless they're on welfare and have five or six kids all with different last names. I just parked on the street and sailed in the door. People like that, they never hurt people like me.

Down in the basement was where they sold the wallpaper, so I huffed and puffed down the stairs, smiling cute as a button whenever anybody stopped to look at me, and shoved myself through the aisles until I got to the back wall, where the samples stood in big books like the fairy-tale book we used to have. I grabbed about four of those books off the wall and heaved them over onto a table there in that section and perched myself on a little tiny chair and started flipping the pages.

A scared-looking black kid in a cheap suit mumbled something about helping me, so I gave him my happiest, most pathetic smile and said, Well, I was here to get wallpaper, wasn't I? What color did I want, did I know? Well, I was thinking about yellow, I said. Uh-huh, he says, what kinda yellow you got in mind? Yellow with white lines in it. Uh-huh, says he, and starts helping me look through those books with all those samples in them. They have about the ugliest wallpaper in the world in this place, wallpaper like sores on the wall, wallpaper that looks like it got rained on before you get it home. Even the black kid knows this crap is ugly, but he's trying his damnedest not to show it.

I bestow smiles everywhere. I'm smiling like a queen riding through her kingdom in a carriage, like a little girl who just got a gold and silver dress from a turtledove up in a magic tree. I'm smiling as if Arnold Zoeller himself and of course his lovely wife are looking across my desk at me while I drown, suffocate, stifle, bury their *lovely, intelligent* little Tori in golden words.

I think we got some more yellow in this book here, he says, and fetches down another big fairy-tale book and plunks it between us on the table. His dirty-looking hands turn those big stiff pages. And just as I thought, just as I knew would happen, could happen, would probably happen, but only here in this filthy corner of a filthy department store, this ignorant but helpful lad opens the book to my mother's wallpaper pattern.

I see that fat yellow and those white lines that never touch anything, and I can't help myself, sweat breaks out all over my body, and I groan so horribly that the kid actually backs away from me, lucky for him, because in the next second I'm bending over and throwing up interesting-looking reddish goo all over the floor of the wallpaper department. Oh God, the kid says, oh lady. I groan, and all the rest of the goo comes jumping out of me and splatters down on the carpet. Some older black guy in a clip-on bow tie rushes up toward us but stops short with his mouth hanging open as soon as he sees the mess on the floor. I take my hankie out of my bag and wipe off my mouth. I try to smile at the kid, but my eyes are too blurry. No, I say, I'm fine, I want to buy this wallpaper for my kitchen, this one right here. I turn over the page to see the name of my mother's wallpaper—Zena's wallpaper, too—and discover that this kind of wallpaper is called "The Thinking Reed."

You don't have to be religious to have inspirations.

An adventurous state of mind is like a great dwelling place.

To be lived truly, life must be apprehended with an adventurous state of mind.

But no one on earth can explain the lure of adventure.

Zena's example gave me two tricks that work in my classroom, and the reason they work is that they are not actually tricks!

The first of these comes into play when a particular child is disobedient or inattentive, which, as you can imagine, often occurs in a room full of kindergarten-age children. I deal with these infractions in this fashion. I command the child to come to my desk. (Sometimes, I command two children to come to my desk.) I stare at the child until it begins to squirm. Sometimes it blushes or trembles. I await the physical signs of shame or discomfort. Then I pronounce the child's name. "Tori," I say, if the child is Tori. Its little eyes invariably fasten upon mine at this instant. "Tori," I say, "you know that what you did is wrong, don't you?" Ninety-nine times out of a hundred, the child nods its head. "And you will never do that wrong thing again, will you?" Most often the child can speak to say, *No.* "Well, you'd better not," I say, and then I lean forward until the little child can see nothing except my enormous, inflamed face. Then in a guttural, lethal, rumble-whisper, I utter, "OR ELSE." When I say, "OR ELSE," I am very emphatic. I am so very emphatic that I feel my eyes change shape. I am thinking of Zena and the time she told me that weeping on my mother's grave wouldn't make a glorious wonderful tree grow there, it would just drown my mother in mud.

The attractiveness of teaching is that it is adventurous, as adventurous as life.

My mother did not drown in mud. She died some other way. She fell down in the middle of the downstairs parlor, the parlor where Zena sat on her visits. Zena was just another lady then, and on her visits, her "social calls," she sat on the best antique chair and held her hands in her lap like the most modest, innocent little lady ever born. She was half Chinese, Zena, and I knew she was just like bright sharp metal inside of her, metal that could slice you but good. Zena was very adventurous, but not as adventurous as me. Zena never got out of that town. Of course, all that happened to Zena was that she got old, and everybody left her all alone because she wasn't pretty anymore, she was just an old yellow widow-lady, and then I heard that she died pulling up weeds in her garden. I heard this from two different people. You could say that Zena got drowned in mud, which proves that everything spoken on this earth contains a truth not always apparent at the time.

The other trick I learned from Zena that is not a trick is how to handle a whole class that has decided to act up. These children come from parents who, thinking they know everything, in fact know less than nothing. These children will never see a classical manner demonstrated at home. You must respond in a way that demonstrates your awareness of perfection. You must respond in a way that will bring this awareness to the unruly children, so that they too will possess it.

It can begin in a thousand different ways. Say I am in conference with a single student—say I am delivering the great OR ELSE. Say that my attention has wandered off for a moment, and that I am contemplating the myriad things I contemplate when my attention is wandering free. My mother's grave, watered by my tears. The women with city hair who desired to give me help, but could not, so left to be replaced by others, who in turn were replaced by yet others. How it felt to stand naked and besmeared with my own feces in the front yard, moveless as a statue, the same as all nature, classical. The gradual disappearance of my father, like that of a figure in a cartoon who grows increasingly transparent until total transparency is reached. Zena facedown in her garden, snuffling dirt up into her nostrils. The resemblance of the city women to certain wicked stepsisters in old tales. Also their resemblance to handsome princes in the same tales.

She who hears the tale makes the tale.

Say therefore that I am no longer quite anchored within the classroom, but that I float upward into one, several, or all of these realms. People get what they need from their own minds. Certain places, you can get in there and rest. The classical was a cool period. I am floating within my cool realms. At that moment, one child pulls another's hair. A third child hurls a spitball at the window. Another falls to the floor, emitting pathetic and mechanical cries. Instantly, what was order is misrule. Then I summon up the image of my ferocious female angels and am on my feet before the little beasts even notice that I have left my desk. In a flash, I am beside the light switch. The Toris and Tiffanys, the Joshuas and Jeremys, riot on. I slap down the switch, and the room goes dark.

Result? Silence. Inspired action is destiny.

The children freeze. Their pulses race—veins beat in not a few little blue temples. I say four words. I say, "Think what this means." They know what it means. I grow to twice my size with the meaning of these words. I loom over them, and darkness pours out of me. Then I switch the lights back on, and smile at them until they get what they need from my smiling face. These children will never call me Mrs. Fat-Asch; these children know that I am the same as all nature.

Once upon a time a dying queen sent for her daughter, and when her daughter came to her bedside the queen said, "I am leaving you, my darling. Say your prayers and be good to your father. Think of me always, and I will always be with you." Then she died. Every day the little girl watered her mother's grave with her tears. But her heart was dead. You cannot lie about a thing like this. Hatred is the inside part of love. And so her mother became a hard cold stone in her heart. And that was the meaning of the mother, for as long as the little girl lived.

Soon the king took another woman as his wife, and she was most beautiful, with skin the color of gold and eyes as black as jet. She was like a person pretending to be someone else inside another person pretending she couldn't pretend. She understood that reality was contextual. She understood about the condition of the observer.

One day when the king was going out to be among his people, he asked his wife, "What shall I bring you?"

"A diamond ring," said the queen. And the king could not tell who was speaking, the person inside pretending to be someone else, or the person outside who could not pretend.

"And you, my daughter," said the king, "what would you like?"

"A diamond ring," said the daughter.

The king smiled and shook his head.

"Then nothing," said the daughter. "Nothing at all."

When the king came home, he presented the queen with a diamond ring in a small blue box, and the queen opened the box and smiled at the ring and said, "It's a very small diamond, isn't it?" The king's daughter saw him stoop forward, his face whitening, as if he had just lost half his blood. "I like my small diamond," said the queen, and the king, straightened up, although he still looked white and shaken. He patted his daughter on the head on his way out of the room, but the girl merely looked forward and said nothing, in return for the nothing he had given her.

And that night, when the rest of the palace was asleep, the king's daughter crept to the kitchen and ate half of a loaf of bread and most of a quart of homemade peach ice cream. This was the most delicious food she had ever eaten in her whole entire life. The bread tasted like the sun on the wheat fields, and inside the taste of the sun was the taste of the bursting kernels of the wheat, even of the rich dark crumbly soil that surrounded the roots of the wheat, even of the lives of the bugs and animals that had scurried through the wheat, even of the droppings of those foxes, beetles, and mice. And the homemade peach ice cream tasted overwhelmingly of sugar, cream, and peaches, but also of the bark and meat of the peach tree and the pink feet of the birds that had landed on it, and the sharp, brittle voices of those birds, also of the effort of the hand crank, of the stained, whorly wood of its sides, and of the sweat of the man who had worked it so long. Every taste should be as complicated as possible, and every taste goes up and down at the same time: up past the turtledoves to the far reaches of the sky, so that one final taste in everything is *whiteness*, and down all the way to the mud at the bottom of graves, then to the mud beneath that mud, so that another final taste in everything, in even peach ice cream, is the taste of *blackness*.

From about this time, the king's daughter began to attract undue attention. From the night of the whiteness of turtledoves and the blackness of grave-mud to the final departure of the stepsisters was a period of something like six months.

I thought of myself as a work of art. I caused responses without being responsible for them. This is the great freedom of art.

They asked questions that enforced the terms of their own answers. *Don't you know we want to help you?* Such a question implies only two possible answers, 1: no, 2: yes. The stepsisters never understood the queen's daughter, therefore the turtledoves pecked out their eyes, first on the one side, then on the other. The correct answer—3: person to whom question is directed is not the one in need of help—cannot be given. Other correct answers, such as 4: help shall come from other sources, and 5: neither knowledge nor help mean what you imagine they mean, are also forbidden by the form of the question.

Assignment for tonight: make a list of proper but similarly forbidden answers to the question, *What is happening to you?* Note: be sure to consider conditions imposed by the use of the word *happening*.

The stepsisters arrived from the city in grand state. They resembled peacocks. The stepsisters accepted Zena's tea, they admired the house, the paintings, the furniture, just as if admiring these things, which everybody admired, meant that they, too, should be admired. The stepsisters wished to remove the king's daughter from this setting, but their power was not so great. Zena would not permit it, nor would the ailing king. (At night, Zena placed her subtle mouth over his sleeping mouth and drew breath straight out of his body.) Zena said that the condition of the king's daughter would prove to be temporary. The child was eating well. She was loved. In time, she would return to herself.

When the figments asked, *What is happening to you?* I could have answered, *Zena is happening to me.* This answer would not have been understood. Neither would the answer, *My mother is happening to me.*

Undue attention came about in the following fashion. Zena knew all about my midnight feasts, but was indifferent to them. Zena knew that each person must acquire what she needs. This is as true for a king's daughter as for any ordinary commoner. But she was ignorant of what I did in the name of art. Misery and anger made me a great artist, though now I am a much greater artist. I think I was twelve. (The age of an artist is of no importance.) Both my mother and Zena were happening to me, and I was happening to them, too. Such is the world of women. My mother, deep in her mud-grave, hated Zena. Zena, second in the king's affections, hated my mother. Speaking from the center of the stone at the center of me, my mother frequently advised me on how to deal with Zena. Silently, speaking with her eyes, Zena advised me on how to deal with my mother. I, who had to deal with both of them, hated them both.

And I possessed an adventurous mind.

The main feature of adventure is that it goes forward into unknown country.

Adventure is filled with a nameless joy.

Alone in my room in the middle of Saturday, on later occasions after my return from school, I removed my clothes and placed them neatly on my bed. (My canopied bed.) I had no feelings, apart from a sense of urgency, concerning the actions I was about to perform. Perhaps I experienced a nameless joy at this point. Later on, at the culmination of my self-display, I experienced a nameless joy. And later yet, I experienced the same nameless joy at the conclusions of my various adventures in art. In each of these adventures as in the first, I created responses not traceable within the artwork, but which derived from the conditions, etc., of the audience. Alone and unclothed now in my room, ready to create responses, I squatted on my heels and squeezed out onto the carpet a long cylinder of fecal matter, the residue of, dinner not included, an entire loaf of seven-grain bread, half a box of raisins, a can of peanuts, and a quarter pound of cervelat sausage, all consumed when everyone else was in bed and Zena was presumably leaning over the face of my sleeping father, greedily inhaling his life. I picked up the warm cylinder and felt it melt into my hands. I hastened this process by squeezing my palms together. Then I rubbed my hands over my body. What remained of the stinking cylinder I smeared along the walls of the bedroom. Then I wiped my hands on the carpet. (The white carpet.) My preparations concluded, I moved regally through the corridors until I reached the front door and let myself out.

I have worked as a certified grade-school teacher in three states. My record is spotless. I never left a school except by my own choice. When tragedies came to my charges or their parents, I invariably sent sympathetic notes, joined volunteer groups to search for bodies, attended funerals, etc., etc. Every teacher eventually becomes familiar with these unfortunate duties.

Outside, there was all the world, at least all of the estate, from which to choose. Two lines from Edna St. Vincent Millay best express my state of mind at this moment: The world stands out on either side / No wider than the heart is wide. I well remember the much-admired figure of Dave Garroway quoting these lovely words on his Sunday-afternoon television program, and I pass along this beautiful sentiment to each fresh class of kindergartners. They must start somewhere, and at other moments in their year with me they will have the opportunity to learn that nature never gives you a chance to rest. Every animal on earth is hungry.

Turning my back on the fields of grazing cows and sheep, ignoring the hills beyond, hills seething with coyotes, wildcats, and mountain lions, I moved with stately tread through the military rows of fruit trees and, with papery apple and peach blossoms adhering to my bare feet, passed into the expanse of the grass meadow where grew the great hazel tree. Had the meadow been recently mown, long green stalks the width of caterpillars leapt up from the ground to festoon my legs. (I often stretched out full-length and rolled in the freshly mown grass meadow.) And then, at the crest of the hill that marked the end of the meadow, I arrived at my destination. Below me lay the road to the unknown towns and cities in which I hoped one day to find my complicated destiny. Above me stood the hazel tree.

I have always known that I could save myself by looking into my own mind.

I stood above the road on the crest of the hill and raised my arms. When I looked into my mind I saw two distinct and necessary states, one that of the white line, the other that of the female angels, akin to the turtledoves.

The white line existed in a calm rapture of separation, touching neither sky nor meadow but suspended in the space between. The white line was silence, isolation, classicism. This state is one half of what is necessary in order to achieve the freedom of art, and it is called the Thinking Reed.

The angels and turtledoves existed in a rapture of power, activity, and rage. They were absolute whiteness and absolute blackness, gratification and gratification's handmaiden, revenge. The angels and turtledoves came streaming up out of my body and soared from the tips of my fingers into the sky, and when they returned they brought golden and silver dresses, diamond rings, and emerald tiaras.

I saw the figments slicing off their own toes, sawing off their heels, and stepping into shoes already slippery with blood. The figments were trying to smile, they were trying to stand up straight. They were like children before an angry teacher, a teacher transported by a righteous anger. Girls like the figments never did understand that what they needed, they must get from their own minds. Lacking this understanding, they tottered along, pretending that they were not mutilated, pretending that blood did not pour from their shoes, back to their pretend houses and pretend princes. The nameless joy distinguished every part of this process.

Lately, within the past twenty-four hours, a child has been lost.

A lost child lies deep within the ashes, her hands and feet mutilated, her face destroyed by fire. She has partaken of the great adventure, and now she is the same as all nature.

At night, I see the handsome, distracted, still hopeful parents on our local news programs. Arnold and Kathi, he as handsome as a prince, she as lovely as one of the figments, still have no idea of what has actually happened to them—they lived their whole lives in utter abyssal ignorance—they think of hope as an essential component of the universe. They think that other people, the people paid to perform this function, will conspire to satisfy their needs.

A child has been lost. Now her photograph appears each day on the front page of our sturdy little tabloid-style newspaper, beaming out with luminous ignorance beside the columns of print describing a sudden disappearance after the weekly Sunday school class at St.-Mary-in-the-Forest Episcopal church, the deepening fears of the concerned parents, the limitless charm of the girl herself, the searches of nearby video parlors and shopping malls, the draggings of two adjacent ponds, the slow, painstaking inspections of the neighboring woods, fields, farms, and outbuildings, the shock of the child's particularly well-off and socially prominent relatives, godparents included.

A particular child has been lost. A certain combination of variously shaded blonde hair and eyes the blue of early summer sky seen through a haze of cirrus clouds, of an endearingly puffy upper lip and a recurring smudge, like that left on Corrasable Bond typing paper by an unclean eraser, on the left side of the mouth, of an unaffected shyness and an occasional brittle arrogance destined soon to overshadow more attractive traits will never again be seen, not by parents, friends, teachers, or the passing strangers once given to spontaneous tributes to the child's beauty.

A child of her time has been lost. Of no interest to our local newspaper, unknown to the Sunday school classes at St.-Mary-in-the-Forest, were this moppet's obsession with the dolls Exercise Barbie and Malibu Barbie, her fanatical attachment to My Little Ponies Glory and Applejack, her insistence on introducing during class time observations upon the cartoon family named Simpson, and her precocious fascination with the music television channel, especially the "videos" featuring the groups Kris Kross and Boyz II Men. She was once observed holding hands with James Halliwell, a first-grade boy. Once, just before nap time, she turned upon a pudgy, unpopular girl of protosadistic tendencies named Deborah Monk and hissed, "Debbie, I hate to tell you this, but you *suck*."

A child of certain limitations has been lost. She could never learn to tie her cute but oddly blunt-looking size 1 running shoes and eventually had to become resigned to the sort fastened with Velcro straps. When combing her multishaded blonde hair with her fingers, she would invariably miss a cobwebby patch located two inches aft of her left ear. Her reading skills were somewhat, though not seriously, below average. She could recognize her name, when spelled out in separate capitals, with narcissistic glee; yet all other words, save *and* and *the*, turned beneath her impatient gaze into random, Sanskrit-like squiggles and uprights. (This would soon have corrected itself.) She could recite the alphabet all in a rush, by rote, but when questioned was incapable of remembering if *O* came before or after *S*. I doubt that she would have been capable of mastering long division during the appropriate academic term.

Across the wide, filmy screen of her eyes would now and then cross a haze of indefinable confusion. In a child of more finely tuned sensibilities, this momentary slippage might have suggested a sudden sense of loss, even perhaps a premonition of the loss to come. In her case, I imagine the expression was due to the transition from the world of complete unconsciousness (Barbie and My Little Ponies) to a more fully socialized state (Kris Kross). Introspection would have come only late in life, after long exposure to experiences of the kind from which her parents most wished to shelter her.

An irreplaceable child has been lost. What was once in the land of the Thinking Reed has been forever removed, like others before it, like all others in time, to turtledove territory. This fact is borne home on a daily basis. Should some informed anonymous observer report that the child is all right, that nothing is happening to her, the comforting message would be misunderstood as the prelude to a demand for ransom. The reason for this is that no human life can ever be truly substituted for another. The increasingly despairing parents cannot create or otherwise acquire a living replica, though they are certainly capable of reproducing again, should they stay married long enough to do so. The children in the lost one's class are reported to suffer nightmares and recurrent enuresis. In class, they exhibit lassitude, wariness, a new unwillingness to respond, like the unwillingness of the very old. At a school-wide assembly where the little ones sat right up in front, nearly everyone expressed the desire for the missing one to return. Letters and cards to the lost one now form two large, untidy stacks in the principal's office and, with parental appeals to the abductor or abductors broadcast every night, it is felt that the school will accumulate a third stack before these tributes are offered to the distraught parents.

Works of art generate responses not directly traceable to the work itself. Helplessness, grief, and sorrow may exist simultaneously alongside aggressiveness, hostility, anger, or even serenity and relief. The more profound and subtle the work, the more intense and long-lasting the responses it evokes.

Deep, deep in her muddy grave, the queen and mother felt the tears of her lost daughter. *All will pass.* In the form of a turtledove, she rose from grave darkness and ascended into the great arms of a hazel tree. *All will change.* From the topmost branch, the turtledove sang out her everlasting message. *All is hers, who will seek what is true.* "What is true?" cried the daughter, looking dazzled up. *All will pass, all will change, all is yours,* sang the turtledove.

In a recent private conference with the principal, I announced my decision to move to another section of the country after the semester's end.

The principal is a kindhearted, limited man still loyal, one might say rigidly loyal, to the values he absorbed from popular music at the end of the 1960s, and he has never quite been able to conceal the unease I arouse within him. Yet he is aware of the respect I command within every quarter of his school, and he has seen former kindergartners of mine, now freshmen in our tri-suburban high school, return to my classroom and inform the awed children seated before them that Mrs. Asch placed them on the right path, that Mrs. Asch's lessons would be responsible for seeing them successfully through high school and on to college.

Virtually unable to contain the conflict of feelings my announcement brought to birth within him, the principal assured me that he would that very night compose a letter of recommendation certain to gain me a post at any elementary school, public or private, of my choosing.

After thanking him, I replied, "I do not request this kindness of you, but neither will I refuse it."

The principal leaned back in his chair and gazed at me, not unkindly, through his granny glasses. His right hand rose like a turtledove to caress his graying beard, but ceased halfway in its flight, and returned to his lap. Then he lifted both hands to the surface of his desk and intertwined the fingers, still gazing quizzically at me.

"Are you all right?" he inquired.

"Define your terms," I said. "If you mean, am I in reasonable health, enjoying physical and mental stability, satisfied with my work, then the answer is yes, I am all right."

"You've done a wonderful job dealing with Tori's disappearance," he said. "But I can't help but wonder if all of that has played a part in your decision."

"My decisions make themselves," I said. "All will pass, all will change. I am a serene person."

He promised to get the letter of recommendation to me by lunchtime the next day, and as I knew he would, he kept his promise. Despite my serious reservations about his methods, attitude, and ideology—despite my virtual certainty that he will be unceremoniously forced from his job within the next year—I cannot refrain from wishing the poor fellow well.

Author's note: Certain phrases and sentences here have been adapted from similar phrases and sentences in the writings of the painter Agnes Martin. There is no similarity at all between Mrs. Asch and Agnes Martin.

Giants in the Earth

DALE BAILEY

Burns didn't imagine he could ever bring himself to really *like* Moore, but as he watched the man work the auger in the flickering shaft of his cap light, he had to admit a kind of grudging admiration for the fellow's grace. Down here in the mines, you noticed such things, for a clumsy man could kill you. It was just Moore's piety that bothered Burns; he had a way of preaching at a man.

Now, Moore swung back from the wall, nodding, a thin gaunt-featured man with lips pinched for want of living. The breast auger extended from his chest like a spear; it gleamed dully beyond a glittery haze of coal dust. Burns stepped forward, tamped a charge into the hole, plugged it with a dummy, and turned around to look for Moore, but the other man had already retreated through the blackness into the heading shaft. An empty cart stood on fresh-laid track, waiting to be filled, but otherwise the room was empty. Somewhere a miner hollered musically, and the sound chased itself through the darkness. There was a stink of metal and sweat, and the rattle of dust in his lungs. He could feel that old dread tighten through his chest.

Damn Blankenship for not wetting down the walls, he thought. Tight-fisted sonofabitch.

And then, with a guttural sigh for the way life had of creeping up on a man—first a wife, and then a baby, and then you were trapped, there was nothing to do but work the coal—Burns turned back to the wall. He struck a match and touched it to the fuse. The fuse sputtered uncertainly, and for a moment Burns thought it might be bad, and then it caught with a hiss that seemed thunderous. It flared a self-devouring cherry, and Burns spun away, squeezing the match between his fingers as he stumbled from the room and flattened himself against the wall in the main shaft.

The charge went up with a muffled thud, and he braced himself for a second, more-powerful explosion that did not come. The dust had not ignited. He heard the wall crumble, tumbling Blankenship's coal out of the seam, and a thick cloud mushroomed into the main shaft. Burns glanced over at Moore. In the glare of the cap light, the other man's face looked pale and washed out, his eyes like glinting sapphire chips set far back in bony hollows.

Moore smiled thinly and lifted the auger over his head. "The Lord's with us."

"Lucky, I reckon," Burns said. He hunkered down, dug through the tool poke, and hefted his shovel and axe. "Reckon we ought to get to it," he said.

Burns stood and ducked back into the room without waiting for Moore to follow. Coughing thick dust, he picked his way through the rubble to the chest-high hole the charge had gouged in the wall. He dropped the shovel and went to his knees to prop the axe against the sloping roof of the under-cut and that was when he saw it.

Or, rather, didn't see what he expected to see—what he had seen maybe a thousand times or more in the year since he and Rona had married, the baby had been born, and he had taken to working as a loader in Blankenship Coal's number-six hole. What he didn't see was the splash of his cap light against the wall, pitted by the charge he had rigged to loosen the seam. Instead, the beam probed out in a widening cone that dissipated into dust and swirling emptiness.

A black current of stale air swept out at him, and Burns quickly crab-walked backwards. He jarred the prop loose, and the heavy tongue of rock above him groaned deep within itself. Pebbles sifted down, rattling against his hardhat, and then the mountain lapsed into silence. When the callused hands closed about his upper arms, Burns nearly screamed.

"Goddammit," he snapped, "what the hell do you think you're doing?"

He spun around to face Moore, and the other man backed away, flattened palms extended before him. Moore looked like a vaudeville comic in blackface. Coal dust streaked his gaunt features, was tattooed into the very fabric of his flesh, and it would never wash away, not even with years of scrubbing. You could tell the old-timers by the dusky tone of their complexion. Burns knew that if Moore would strip away his shirt, the exposed flesh of his face and hands would meet the pale skin beyond in hard geometric planes.

He knew, too, that someday he also would look as if he wore perpetually a dusky mask and gloves, and he hated it. But there was Rona and the baby. Swirling in the veil of dust that hung between the two men, Burns could almost see them, their features etched with a beauty too real and fragile for life in these mountains. A year ago, he had not known that a man could feel this way, and sometimes still it crept up on him unawares, this love that had led him to this deep place far beneath the earth.

He glanced away before Moore saw his eyes throw back the dazzle of the cap light. "Get that light out of my eyes, you've about half-blinded me," he said, and he turned away to collect himself. The massive tongue of rock that projected over the hole seemed almost to mock him. So close, Burns thought, and then where would Rona and the baby have been?

"You okay?" Moore asked.

Burns looked up. "Hell," he said. "Sorry. I thought the rock was coming down on me."

Moore gave him a curt nod, bent to reset the fallen prop, and then wedged his own axe into the gap. "That ought to hold it," he said, extending a hand to Burns.

Burns took the hand, and lifted himself to his feet. He dusted off his clothes out of habit, not because it would do any good. "There's something else," he said.

"What's that?"

"Something ain't right. That hole don't stop. It just keeps on going."

Moore lifted an eyebrow and studied the undercut for a moment. "Well, let's have a look," he said. "I don't reckon there's anything to be afraid of." He hunkered down, slid into the gap, and vanished.

Examining these last words for some taint of suggested cowardice, Burns followed. The roof slanted down a bit and then disappeared entirely as he emerged into a larger darkness. Though he could not immediately see the space, some quality—the acoustics of a far-away water drip or perhaps the flat, dank taste of the air—told him that it was at least as large as the room he and Moore had been working, that it had been sealed beneath the mountain for long years.

Burns stood. His light stabbed into the dark. "Moore?" Abruptly, he became aware of a sound like muffled sobs. "Moore? What happened to your light?"

"I turned it off."

Burns turned to face the voice. Moore sat just beyond the darker mouth of the opening into the other room, his arms draped over drawn-up knees, his head slumped. When he looked up at Burns, the sapphire chips of his eyes were shiny with a kind of madness. Tears glittered like tiny diamonds on his dusky face, and Burns could see the clean tracks they had carved across his cheeks.

The room seemed to wheel about him for a moment, the gloom to press closer. Uneasiness knotted his guts.

"Why'd you turn off your light?"

"Giants in the earth," Moore whispered. "There were giants in the earth in those days."

"What are you talking about? Why did you turn off your light?"

Moore gestured with one hand toward the darkness farther into the room, and Burns felt ice creep out of his belly and begin the paralyzing ascent into his throat. Almost a year ago, just a month or so after Burns had started to work, a spark from somebody's axe had ignited the dust in the number-three hole. The men who survived the explosion came out of the mine with faces smoothed over by experience; the unique lines time and character had carved into their features had all at once been erased. They had no more individuality than babies, fresh from an earthen womb, and it occurred to Burns that Moore looked just that way now.

Burns did not want to look into the darkness at the center of the room. He liked his face. He did not want it to change. And yet he knew that if he did not move or speak, did not take action, the ice that was creeping slowly into his throat would fill up his mouth and paralyze him. He would be forever unable to move beyond this time and place, this moment.

He looked into the room.

In the flickering shaft of his cap light there lay a creature of such simple and inevitable beauty that Burns knew that for him the significance of that concept had been forever altered; it could never again be applied to mere human loveliness. Burns felt as if he had been swept up in a current of swift-running water, and in the grip of that current, he took a step forward, stunned by the apprehension of such beauty, unadulterated by any trace of pettiness, or ugliness, or mere humanity. He thought his heart might burst free of his chest. He had not known such creatures existed in the world.

And then, through that veil of terrible beauty, there penetrated to him the particular details of what he had seen; he came abruptly to a stop as that paralyzing ice of awe and fear at last rose into his mouth.

This is what he saw:

A being, like a man, but different, ten feet long, or twelve feet, curled naked in the heart of the mountain.

Wings, white rapturous wings, that swept up and around it like a cloak of molten feathers.

And in its breast, the rhythmic pulse of life.

Giants in the earth, he thought, and then—because he knew that if he did not look away, the lines of his face would be erased and he would lose forever some essential part of himself—Burns turned to look at Moore, who still sat against the wall. His gaunt face hung slack; tears glistened on his cheeks.

"I couldn't bear it," he said.

"We have to tell someone," Burns said.

"But who?"

"Someone who can do something."

"Who?"

Burns thought furiously. For a moment he thought he heard the rustle of feathers in the darkness behind him, and half-fearful, he turned to face the creature, but it had not moved. They could not be responsible for this,

Burns thought—and the word *responsible* was like a gift, for suddenly he knew.

He crossed the room, crouched by Moore, and peered into his face. The slap sounded like a pistol shot in the enclosed chamber. Burns drew back his stinging palm for another blow, but he saw it wasn't necessary, for the madness in Moore's eyes had retreated a little.

"Get the cashier," he said. "Get Holland." He reached out and snapped Moore's cap alight, saw the man's gaunt features tighten with wonder. "Go on, now," he said. "Not a word to anyone but Holland, hear?"

Moore stood without speaking and ducked through the undercut. Burns was alone. Once again, he remembered the miners, their faces smoothed by experience, as they emerged from the explosion-shattered heading of the number-three hole. And as he turned away from the undercut to look yet again at the awful beauty that lay slumberous in the center of the room, a terrible vision fractured his thought: his own face, smooth and featureless as a peeled egg.

In the wavering beam from his cap, Burns caught a single glimpse of the creature—

—the giant, the angel—

—and then he reached up with trembling fingers and shut off the light. In the succeeding blackness, sounds were magnified. The far-away drip of water became an intermittent clash of cymbals punctuated by measureless silences in which the creature's labored respiration sounded clamorous as a great bellows stoking the furnaces of the earth.

Finally, not because he dared to smoke but because he had to do something with his hands or go mad, Burns fumbled for tobacco and rolling papers and began to make a cigarette. Even in the darkness, his fingers fell without hesitation into the familiar rhythm of the process, and the prosaic nature of the task—here in the midst of wonders—enabled him to envision Moore as he made the long trek through the heading shaft to the surface. He imagined the annoyed glance Jeremiah Holland would direct at Moore when he stepped into the cashier's shack, could almost see the thoughtful look that would replace it when he heard what Moore had to say. Holland, Burns knew, was a thoughtful man, the kind of man who considered the angles of a thing, and could work them to his own advantage.

Burns licked the paper, twisted the cigarette into a cylinder, and slipped it into his mouth. The tobacco tasted sweet against his lips. Holland would be a good friend to have, he thought. Holland could help a man.

And yet....

He felt a flicker of doubt. Such beauty....

The sound of men crawling through the undercut came to him. A wavering light illuminated the chamber, and Burns's heart broke loose within him as he caught a glimpse of the creature, curled fetal on the stone floor. The light bobbed into the air, and he saw that it was Moore. A second ghostly shaft penetrated the darkness, and Burns heard a metallic rattle of tools. He stood, his fingers fumbling at his cap as he stepped forward to meet Holland.

The cashier emerged from the undercut and pushed himself erect, a thin, wiry man with a battered toolbox clutched in one hand. His lean face looked hollow, even skeletal, in the intersecting beams of the cap lights, and his dark eyes returned Burns's gaze from deeply recessed sockets.

"I hope you're not planning to light that thing," he said.

Burns plucked the cigarette from his mouth with shaking fingers. "I just had to do something with my hands. That thing—" Licking a moist fragment of tobacco from his lips, he slipped the cigarette into his shirt pocket.

Holland lowered the toolbox to the floor with a clatter. "Yes, that thing. Your friend wasn't very articulate about that...thing." He glanced ruefully at his clothing, store-bought linen several grades more expensive than the cheap flannel the miners wore, and Burns saw that the cloth was soiled with dark streaks of coal dust. "Where is it?"

Burns glanced at Moore, but the other man had retreated deep into himself.

"It's over there," Burns said. Almost unwillingly, he turned his head and impaled the creature on the flickering shaft of his cap light. Its breast kindled with life; wings stirred in the passing wind of a dream. Burns blinked back tears. It seemed as if each particle of the air had suddenly flared with radiance, and though in fact it did not diminish at all, Burns imagined that the darkness retreated a little.

Jeremiah Holland drew in his breath with a sharp hiss.

"I thought you ought to see it," Burns said. "I wanted to do the right thing. I got a wife and baby and I was hoping—" He stopped abruptly when he realized that Holland wasn't listening.

The cashier's face had gone very white, and as Burns looked on, the tip of his tongue crept out and eased over his lips. He turned to look at Burns through widened eyes. "Have either of you touched it?"

Burns shook his head.

The cashier crouched by the toolbox, threw back the latches with trembling fingers, and withdrew a tamping bar. He stood, clutching the bar in one white-knuckled hand, and looked from Burns to Moore, who stood a few feet away, his face looking new-minted. "Let's see if you can wake it up," he told Burns.

Burns hesitated, and Holland lifted the tamping bar a little. "Go on now."

His heart hammering, Burns began to creep across the room. That paralyzing ice once again edged into his throat. Blood pounded at his temples. He felt as if he had been wrapped in a thick suffocating layer of wool.

And then he was there, standing over the—

—*giant, the angel.*

The creature, he told himself.

"Careful," Holland whispered, and glancing over his shoulder, Burns saw the flesh beneath the cashier's right eye twitch. "Do you realize—" he said, "—have you any idea what we could *do* with this thing?" He laughed, a quick harsh detonation, abrasive as shattering glass, and brandished the tamping bar. "Go on now."

Burns felt breath catch in his throat. He tried to speak, to protest, but that paralyzing ice had frozen away his voice. Swallowing, he prodded the creature with his boot. Flesh gave, the thing shifted in its age-long sleep: a hush and sigh of wings in the enveloping dark, the rusty flex of ancient muscles, and all at once the creature lay prone, face turned away, arms outstretched, great wings flared across the dusty floor. Conflicting impressions of Promethean strength and gentleness swept through Burns, and—like nothing he had felt before—a swift and terrible hunger for such beauty, ethereal and mysterious.

Not until it passed did Burns realize he had been holding his breath. He released it and drew in a great draught of stale air. The ice had retreated a bit. Strangling a bout of hysterical laughter, he turned away.

"Maybe it's hibernating," he said, abruptly reminded of something he had heard at Rona's church—a story of an epoch impossibly distant, when graves would vomit forth the dead. Would angels ascend from the womb of the shattered planet?

Holland had returned to the toolbox. "We can't let it get away."

"Get away?"

Holland stood, his angular features ashen, and extended in his left hand the shining length of a hacksaw. The serrated blade threw off radiant sparks in the shifting luminescence of the cap lights. A sickening abyss opened inside of Burns.

"I don't think that's a good idea," Burns started to say, but he let the last word trail away, for he saw that a kind of lethargic energy had animated Moore's features. With the languor of drifting continents, half-formed expressions passed across the experience-scrubbed surface of his face.

"No," Moore whispered. "Please…please don't."

Holland spared him a single dismissive glance, and then he looked back to Burns and shook the hacksaw. The blade rattled against its casing.

Simultaneously, Moore also turned to face him. The twin glare of their cap lights nearly blinded him. He raised a hand to shield his eyes as the chasm that had opened within him yawned wider still. For a single uncertain moment, he felt as if he might plunge into the chaos that churned there.

As though from a great distance, he heard Moore's voice degenerate into sobs of desperation, saw Holland turn and strike him a single blow with the tamping bar. The glare diminished as Moore stumbled away.

Holland stepped up to meet him, the tamping bar up-raised, the hacksaw dangling in his left hand; there was no mistaking the threat implicit in his posture.

"Do it," he hissed.

Burns moved closer to the wiry cashier, suddenly aware that he could wrest the tamping bar from the smaller man in less than an instant; in a moment of sudden clarity, he saw that Holland knew this, too. Beyond the mask of his bravado there lay a core of desperate fear. Burns saw that Holland had not perceived the creature's beauty. He could not, for fear drove him; perhaps it always had.

Turning away, he began to move toward Moore, slumped by the dark mouth of the undercut. He hadn't gone more than two steps before Holland spoke. "Did you say you had a wife and child?"

Burns hunkered down by Moore, rested a callused hand against his shoulder. "That's what I said."

"Sauls Run," Holland said. "Not much work here, unless you're a miner."

"Please," Moore whispered. "Do you know what this means? It's true, all true...."

A fleeting image of that church story—the Rapture, Burns suddenly recalled—passed through his mind: angels, erupting by the thousands from beneath the mountains of the dying planet. True? *The Lord's with us*, Moore had said, and he had replied, *Lucky, I reckon.*

The hacksaw clattered to the floor behind him.

"Winter's coming," Holland said. "Hard season for a man without a job. Hard season for his family."

Burns emitted a strangled laugh, lifted his hand, and touched his fingers to Moore's stubbled face. Moore's lips trembled, and tears slid down his cheeks. Burns could smell the sour taint of his breath. "An angel," Moore whispered, and cursing, Burns stood and turned away.

That image—angels erupting from the subterranean dark—returned to haunt him as he stooped to pick up the hacksaw; he dismissed it with an almost physical effort. Not an angel, insisted some fragment of his mind. Some pagan god or demon; a monstrous creature out of myth; an evolutionary freak, caught in the midst of the transformation from beast to man—but not an angel.

A creature, nothing more.

He crossed the room without a word and knelt beside

—*the giant, the angel*—

—the creature. At the base of the thick-rooted wings, its flesh curled horny and tough, almost pebbled. Its back heaved with the regular cadence of its respiration. He could not bring himself to look it in the face.

Burns closed his eyes and drew in a long breath. He could hear the whispered litany of Moore's prayers, the faraway cymbal clash of the water drip. He thought of the coming winter, harsh in these mountains, and once again, that great love surprised him. For a moment, limned against the dark screens of his eyelids, he could almost see them, Rona and the baby, shining with an all-too-human beauty. Fragile and ephemeral, that beauty was, but a man could get his mind about it. A man could hold it.

He exhaled and opened his eyes.

Nothing had changed. Winged giants slept in the earth, but nothing had changed. The world was as it had been always.

"Do it, you son of a bitch," Holland said, and despite the fact that less than an hour ago Burns had not known that such creatures existed in the world, despite the fact that even now every molecule of air seemed to flare with a beauty so radiant that it was painful even to behold—despite all this, Burns began the terrible task.

The creature stirred when the hacksaw bit into the root of the near wing; its fingers drew into talons, its breath shuddered into a quicker rhythm, but it did not wake. Burns's muscles tightened into the work; sweat broke out along his hairline. The hide was tough as old hickory, but at last, with a noise like wind through dry leaves, the wing fell away. Burns kicked it aside. In the pale luminescence of his cap light, the wing stump glistened like a bloody mouth. Sighing, he stepped over the creature to start at the second wing. Once again, he leaned into the saw, once again dragged it back through the thick flesh, but this time—for no reason he would ever be able to discern—he looked up, looked directly into the creature's face.

And saw that it was awake.

The sounds of Moore's prayers and Holland's panicked respiration receded as Burns gazed into the creature's eye, so blue it might have been a scrap of April sky.

He felt as if he were falling, down and down into that endless blue, but he felt no fear. A wave of gratitude that he could not contain flooded through him—to have seen such beauty, to have touched it. Once again, the entire room seemed to flare with light, and for the space of a single instant, he perceived, beyond the shabby guise of reality, an inner radiance that permeated all things. Then, as suddenly as if he had shut off his cap light, the radiance was gone, overwhelmed by a tide of wretched exhilaration. No other man had ever mastered such a creature.

Burns flung away the hacksaw in disgust.

The creature's eye had closed. He could not tell that it had ever awakened.

A suffocating knot formed in his throat, and for the first time in the long year he had worked the mines, claustrophobia overcame him. The walls pressed inward. The entire weight of the mountain loomed over him.

Holland stepped up, his face blanched, his eyes reduced to glints far back in shadowy hollows. "Finish it," he said.

Burns wrested the tamping bar away from him and let it clatter to the floor. "Finish it yourself."

With a last glance at Moore, he pushed the cashier aside, ducked through the undercut and the empty room beyond, and emerged into the heading. From far down in the shaft, there echoed the din of a sledgehammer as a work crew snaked new track deeper into the planet.

He wondered what beauty they might eventually lay bare; he wondered what they would do with it.

Turning away, Burns began to walk slowly along the tracks that led to the surface. Men moved by him, nodding as they passed, and sometimes a loaded car muscled through the shaft; in the rooms that opened to either side, he heard the easy talk that came at shift's end. He had no part in that now. Deliberately, he turned his mind to other things, to the surface, where the sky would be fading toward night. He imagined the stench of burning slag riding the high currents; imagined the tin roofs of Sauls Run, faraway in the steep-walled valley, throwing off the last gleam of evening sun.

Presently, he emerged from the earth. He paused by the cashier's shack and fished the cigarette out of his breast pocket. His coal-smeared hands shook a little as he struck the match, and then harsh sweet smoke filled his lungs. He exhaled a gray plume and surveyed the valley below.

Everything—the sky, the smell, the flash of sunlight against the tin roofs of town—was just as he had imagined it. Nothing, nothing had changed. Drawing in another lungful of smoke, Burns started down the mountain to Sauls Run, to Rona and the baby. High above the painted ridges, the day began to blue into darkness, and a breath of autumn wind touched him, chill with the foreboding of winter.

The Beginning of the Year Without a Summer

CAITLÍN R. KIERNAN

This day and this night are a coin. Flip it, and in rapid succession first one thing and then the other, in constant, indecisive revolution. I am standing at the bottom of a steep paved road where the eastern edge of the cemetery meets the dirty slate-colored river, the Seekonk River, and it's a cold day in early May. As a lifelong Southerner, only recently transplanted to New England, that's a concept I'm still not comfortable with, cold days in early May. Standing here, looking out across the choppy waters of Bishop Cove, across almost four hundred yards to the opposite shore, the day seems even colder than it is, the wind sharp enough to peel back my skin and remind me how terrible was the winter. How terrible and how very recent and how soon it will return. The wind rattles the branches all around, and I reluctantly button my cardigan and hug myself. I look up into the stark face of the wide carnivorous sky, squinting at all that merciless blue, not a brushstroke of cloud anywhere at all. What sort of god permits a sky like that? It's a question I would ask in all seriousness, were I not an atheist. The trees sway and shudder in the wind like unmedicated epileptics. The new leaves are still bright, their greens not yet tempered by summer and inevitable age. This is the *face* of the coin, this afternoon at the edge of the cemetery. I'm not alone. There's a young woman sitting only a few feet away. She sits on the hood of her car and smokes cigarettes and talks as if we are old friends, when, in fact, we've only just met and only by the happenstance of our both having arrived at this spot at more or less the same time on the same cold, windy day in early May. She's at least twenty years my junior, dressed in a T-shirt and jeans, not even a sweater, as though this is a much warmer day than it is. There's a big padded camera bag on the hood beside her.

There are swans in the water.

"You teach?" she asks me, and I say that yes, I do.

"But I'm not a very good teacher," I add. "I didn't get into science to teach."

"You're at Brown?"

Around us, the trees sway and creak. The river laps against the shore. The swans, hardly even seeming to notice the wind, bob about on the waves and dip their heads beneath the water, foraging in the shallows. I notice that their long necks are dirty from all the sediment stirred up by the waves and the currents and by their hungry, probing bills. Their white feathers seem almost as if they've been stained with oil.

I point at the birds and ask the girl, "Is that why it's called Swan Point?"

She shrugs, stubs her cigarette out against the sole of her boot, then flicks the butt towards the river.

"You shouldn't do that," I tell her. "They're poisonous. Birds and fish eat them. Fish eat them, and then birds eat the fish. In experiments, the chemicals from a single filtered cigarette butt killed half the fish living in a one-liter container of water. Plus, they're made of nonbiodegradable acetate-cellulose. Every year, an estimated 1.6 billion pounds of—"

"Jesus, yeah, okay," she says and laughs. "This isn't a classroom. You're not on the clock, professor."

"Sorry," I say, not meaning it, not sorry at all, but I'm embarrassed, and so I apologize anyway.

This is the *face* of the coin.

The coin is in the air, turning and turning, ass over tit.

"I don't know why it's called Swan Point," the girl says, and she lights another cigarette. For only an instant, a caul of grey smoke hangs about her face before the wind takes it apart. "I never bothered to ask anyone. I just like coming here. I've been coming here since I was a teenager."

The wind, blowing up off Narragansett Bay, smells like low tide on mudflats, like sewage, like sex, primordial and faintly fishy. It roars across the water, ruffling the feathers of the swans, and it roars through the trees, giving them fits. I dislike the wind. Not as much as I dislike that blue sky hanging above me, and not as much as I dislike the cold, but enough that I wish I'd waited on a less blustery day to wander down to this spot I've glimpsed on other drives and walks through the cemetery. One of the swans turns its head towards me, seeming to glare with its tiny black eyes, such tiny eyes for so large a bird. It only watches me a few seconds before turning its attention back to feeding, and maybe it was only my imagination that it was ever watching me at all.

"They don't actually belong here," I say.

"What?" the girl asks. "What don't belong here?"

"Those swans. I mean, that particular species of swan. *Cygnus olor.* They're an invasive, introduced to North America from Europe back in the 1800s."

"Yeah," the girl says without looking at me. "Well, they don't hurt anyone, do they? And at least they're pretty to look at."

"They're that," I agree. "Pretty to look at, I mean."

"Someone murdered one last fall," she says. Not killed. She says *murdered.* "Broke its neck, then nailed it to a tree." And she points to a large red maple not far away. "That tree there. Drove a nail through the top of its skull, and one through each shoulder. Wait, do swans have shoulders?"

"Yeah," I tell her. "Swans have shoulders."

"Okay, well, that's what they did, whoever killed the swan. Almost like they were crucifying it, you know. There was a reward offered by the cops or the SPCA or someone like that. Two thousand dollars to help them catch the person who murdered the swan. The reward started off at fifteen hundred, but went up to two thousand. I gotta tell you, I could have used that money. But I don't think they ever caught the person responsible, the swan murderer. Who the fuck would do something like that? Who the fuck is sick enough to nail a swan to a tree?"

I didn't have an answer for her, and I didn't offer one. The sky had been bad enough without the mental image of a swan nailed to a tree.

"You know about birds," she says, then takes a long drag off her cigarette.

"It was just the one?" I ask her. "Only one swan was killed?"

"As far as I know," she replies. "Of course, who's to say the sick fuck didn't kill more of them, and all those others were just never found?"

"What an awful thing," I say. "What a terrible, awful thing." And I'm wishing that she hadn't told me, that she'd kept it to herself, wondering why she felt the need to tell a stranger about a *murdered* swan.

She shrugs again and exhales smoke. "I hope it was senseless," she says, "because I'd hate to know the logic that would lead a person to break a swan's neck and then nail its corpse to a tree. I'd prefer to believe there was no reasoning at all behind an act like that, that it was completely fucking thoughtless."

The coin that is on one side a day and on the other a night flips.

I close my eyes and rub at my eyelids, at the bridge of my nose, wanting to change the subject, but at a loss as to how I can do so.

And the tumbling coin turns its face away from me. Tails. So, I'm camped out on a settee upholstered with sky-blue velvet that, like everything else in this house, has been worn smooth and threadbare. The very floors beneath my feet are threadbare, having been so long trammeled by so many feet and with such force that the varnished pine boards seem to me exhausted and ready to shatter into splinters. The only light in the room, way up here on the third floor of the house, comes from tall cast-iron candelabras spaced out along the high walls, but it's plenty enough that I can see the dancer. The heavy drapes have been drawn against the July night, against the moon and the prying stars. In one corner of the room, there's a quartet: cellist, violist, the two violins. The air is thick with an incense formulated in accordance with Ayurvedic principles; in this instance, a hand-rolled tattva incense from some nook or cranny of the Himalayas, herbs, resins, gums brought together in the service of *air*, and my nose wrinkles at the almost overpowering reek of patchouli. I'm drinking beer. I don't even know what brand. It was placed in front of me, and I'm drinking it, and I'm watching the dancer as she whirls and swoops and bares herself for unseen Heaven beyond the ceiling of the room, beyond the attic, the roof of the house, the shingles. The beer is flat and going warm and tastes like fermented cornflakes. But that's okay. No one comes to this house to drink, this house hidden deep within the squalor of Federal Hill. My head hurts, and I pop two Vicodin, washing them down with the flat beer, and I wait for the tall, dark-complexioned man sitting beside me to say something. To say whatever it is he's going to say next.

That turns out to be, "So, does Providence agree with you? I trust you're settling in well?"

"I am," I reply. "As well as can be expected. I miss Birmingham."

The man sips his whiskey and bitters and nods his head. "I've never been so far south as that. Fact is, I've never been any farther south than Pittsburgh."

"You should remedy that," I tell him and smile. Despite my headache, I'm in good spirits, my mood buoyed by the dancer, by the musicians as they draw the strains of the second movement of Bedřich Smetana's "Z mého života" from their instruments, and by simply being here, in the house. The house itself is a tonic.

"You miss the heat?" he asks.

"I miss the heat," I reply, nodding my head, "and I miss the fieldwork, getting my hands dirty, the grit under my nails, the sweat, all that. But I have a good job here. I shouldn't complain so much."

The dancer comes very near the sky-blue settee then, and her white hair, plaited into a single braid that hangs down past her ass, swings like the tail of a beast. Her eyes meet mine, but only for an instant, half an instant. They are such a vivid, unreal shade of blue, lapis lazuli, ultramarine, that I know they must be contacts. Her bare, callused feet hammer the boards, and then she's gone again.

"She came to us all the way from Amsterdam," says the man, and he nods towards the dancer. I don't know the man's name, but I know better than to ask. "She's quite talented, yes?"

"Very much so," I say, knowing that the time for small talk is passing. The coin is turning, rotating as it's carried up and away from the surface of the world, vainly seeking escape velocity. We've sat here almost an hour now, me nursing my beer, him drinking scotch after scotch. For a time he talked about my work, in such a way that I could tell he wanted to impress me. He'd even read the papers in *Nature* and the *Journal of Vertebrate Paleontology*, and he asked specifically about the fauna from the Tuscaloosa Formation, about the basal hadrosauroids *Eolophorhothon progenitor* and *Tuscaloosaura psammophilum*, the tyrannosauroid *Phobocephalae australis*, and the little nodosaur, *Heliopelta belli*. However, he wasn't especially interested in what these discoveries from the Alabama Black Belt meant to paleontology and our understanding of the Late Cretaceous of the Appalachian subcontinent; he was, instead, fascinated by the nomenclature, the meanings of the binomina, the process of choosing and publishing names. Regardless, it was honest interest, and I appreciated that very much. There are few things I find more tiresome, more entirely exasperating, than politely feigned curiosity.

The book is resting on the settee between us, a small antique photo album that was already a century old when I was born. I gently touch the flaking red-leather cover with the fingers of my left hand.

The dancer passes very near again, naked except for her borrowed feathers.

The man glances at her, then me, then at the book.

"We all thought it was lost forever," he says. "We had every reason to believe exactly that after the fire, after the purge, what with all the years that came and went with no one having heard even a rumor the book might have survived the flames." He doesn't yet touch it. That'll come later, when it is finally no longer my burden.

"Your mother would be proud," the man says. "She was a strong, fine woman, a brilliant woman, and it is a crime she was denied her time as the book's keeper."

"When I was a kid," I say, not exactly changing the subject, "when I was very young, she would tell me stories of Providence. She'd tell me stories of this house and of the city, and she'd tell me stories of the swans and the river."

"I wish I could have met her," he says and smiles. I dislike his smile. His lips are pale and thin. One could look at his smile and be forgiven for thinking that he has too many teeth. "But, as I understand it, she never traveled, and, as I've said—"

"—you've never been farther south than Pittsburgh."

"Exactly," he says. "Now, please, tell me again of the day you found the book."

I'm wishing the Vicodin would kick in, impatiently waiting for the opioid rush to wash away my headache. I'm not exactly in the mood to repeat that story, how I found the photo album. I would far rather simply hand the book over to this man with too many teeth, this man who will be a proper guardian, and then watch the dancer and listen to the music. But I am a guest here, no matter my pedigree and no matter that I've come bearing so marvelous a gift. For now, I am a guest. And it would be a breach of etiquette to beg off. The observation of proper etiquette is very important here. It's only a story, even if it really happened, and it's a small thing to ask of me to tell it again. I have another sip of my flat beer, thinking back to how I told him the story before and trying to decide if I want to tell it the same way the second time around.

"It's not actually a random phenomenon," the man says.

"What isn't?" I ask him.

He leans over, depositing his empty glass on the floor at his feet. "A coin toss," he says as he sits up again. "So long as the initial conditions of the toss are known—velocity, angular momentum, position, etcetera—then it's a problem that can be modeled in Lagrangian mechanics. If you are intent on burying yourself so deeply in this metaphor, you ought to understand its limitations."

On the shore of the Seekonk River, a city of narrow houses at my back, I'm listening to a young woman who hasn't introduced herself talk about dead swans. In the house on Federal Hill, a man who can see my thoughts is asking me to tell him a story he's already heard from me twice.

"A practiced magician," he continues, "an accomplished illusionist, he can control a coin toss with a surprising degree of precision." And then the man laughs and taps the side of his nose. *A word to the wise. Just between you and me.*

The girl sitting on the hood of the car lights another cigarette.

The dancer spins.

"Please," says the man sitting beside me on the settee. "I'd love to hear it again."

I almost ask him for something stronger than the beer, but only almost.

"Well," I begin, "there was this one fellow kept stopping by the site. That pretty much always happens, the curious locals. If you're lucky, they just want to have a look at what you're up to, find out why someone would be rooting around in Farmer Joe's back forty or what have you. If you're lucky, they don't start in about Noah's Flood or the evils of the great lie of evolution. When they do, of course, you have to be polite and listen, nod your head, not get into arguments, because you never know who any given ignorant redneck might be related to. He could well be the first cousin of the guy who's given you permission to dig on his land. Anyway, this one guy, he wasn't like that. He'd studied some geology at Auburn, and he asked intelligent, thoughtful questions."

"And he told you about the train?" the man asks me, as though he doesn't already know the answer.

"He did," I reply. "He told me about the boxcars."

The dancer pirouettes, making three full turns on the ball of her left foot. The feathers along her arms and shoulders rustle like dead leaves, and I'm surprised that I can hear them over the music. I wonder if it's some trick of the room's acoustics, if it's a happy accident or by design. And, for the second time, I begin telling the man about the abandoned railroad cars and the dead crows. He seems to take great delight in the tale. I can't help but feel, now, that the coin has risen as high as it possibly can, and all of its momentum has been spent. At any second, I think, gravity will reclaim it, reasserting its primacy, and the coin will begin its rapid, inevitable descent.

Call it.

Kopf oder Zahl.

"Heads," says the girl at the eastern edge of Swan Point Cemetery. "I always hated the way that Granddad would cut off the heads of the ducks he killed and nail them to the boathouse wall. But it was how he kept up with what he'd shot over the season."

"I've never heard of anyone doing that," I say, and I check my watch. I have a four o'clock lecture, and it's already a quarter to three.

"Well, he'd do it every year," the girl says. "It's how me and my sister learned to tell mallards from mergansers, eiders from wood ducks, sitting out there with my grandfather's grisly little menagerie. Swans, they're not ducks, are they?"

"They're in the same family," I tell her, "but they're more closely related to geese than to ducks."

An especially strong gust of wind rolls off the river, and I turn my back to it. To the river and the wind. My ears are beginning to hurt from the cold. *How can this be May?* I think. *How can this possibly be May?* For a dizzying moment or so, I have trouble recalling the last time that I was truly warm.

"Can I tell you a story?" the girl asks. The wind doesn't seem to be bothering her the way it does me, or not bothering her as much, which, I admit, makes me angry.

"About your grandfather's boathouse?" I ask, turning up the collar of my cardigan and wishing I had a wool cap with me.

"No, no," she says. "I told you all there was to that. This is something else. But, I don't know, maybe they're connected somehow. At least, they seemed to be connected in my head." And, as she talks, she unzips her camera bag and takes out a Pentax K1000 35mm. It's refreshing to see someone as young as her using film instead of digital. She slips the strap around her neck, then checks the settings and peers through the viewfinder, aiming the camera nowhere in particular.

"Doesn't the wind bother you?" I ask her.

"I don't mind. It's not so bad today. It was worse yesterday."

"You were raised here?"

"No, I'm from Maine, not far from Portland."

I tell her that I've never been to Maine, and she tells me that I haven't really missed much.

"Anyway," she says, "the story, I won't get into it, not if you don't want to hear or don't have the time. I saw you check your watch." She lowers the camera and looks at me. "It's just, the thing with the murdered swan, and then Granddad's boathouse, you know the way shit reminds you of other shit, like dominoes getting knocked over. Free association. Whatever."

"Yeah," I say. "I know how that is. Sure, I've got time to hear a story."

"Okay, well, when I was eight, that summer, not long after my eighth birthday, there was a whole week in July when I kept finding feathers in my bed. Me and my mom both found them."

A few feet from shore, three of the swans, moving in what could pass for perfect unison, dip their heads and long necks beneath the dark river.

"Every night, I'd turn back the sheets, and the bed would be full of feathers."

"You didn't have a feather mattress, I assume."

"No, and besides, it wasn't like that. What do they stuff feather mattresses with? Chicken feathers? Duck feathers? No, these were all different sorts of feathers. Blue jays, cat birds, crows, mockingbirds, robins, even seagulls, and there were some sorts we never did figure out what they were. I'd turn back the covers, and there would be dozens of feathers in my bed. Jesus, it was weird. And it went on for a whole week, like I said. Dad was in Italy on business—"

"Italy? What does your dad do?"

"Did. He's retired."

"What did your dad do?"

"He was an engineer, but that doesn't have anything to do with the story, except that he was away when this happened. At first I thought it was my sister putting the feathers in my bed. She was a year older than me. We had a huge fight when I accused her of doing it, and Mom sent her to stay with my grandparents for a few days."

"Same grandparents had the boathouse?" I ask.

"No, that was my father's parents. These were my maternal grandparents. But it didn't matter. The feathers showed up, anyway, without her being there. Every night, a handful of them, all those different colors and shapes, and my mother kept having to change and wash the sheets, because she was paranoid about birds carrying diseases. My bed smelled like Lysol...."

The girl trails off for a moment, watching the swans bobbing on the rough, wind-tossed river. "What do you call a group of swans?" she asks.

"That depends. If they're flying, you call a group of swans a wedge, because of the formation they fly in, because it's wedge-shaped. If they're not flying, like these swans," and I motioned towards the river, "a group of swans is called a lamentation."

"That's sort of melodramatic, don't you think?" she says, then lifts her camera again and spends a few seconds watching the swans through the viewfinder.

"So, it wasn't your sister," I say, prompting her to continue.

She lowers the camera again and nods. "No, it wasn't my sister. It kept happening after she left, and never mind there was no way she'd ever have gathered up *that* many feathers. It really scared my mother. Me, I was mostly just annoyed and angry and wanted to know who was playing such a stupid trick on me. I even thought maybe my mom was doing it and just pretending it was upsetting her. That was even dumber than blaming my sister, of course, but at the time I either didn't realize it or, you know, just didn't care."

I look back up at that insatiable too-blue sky. "But then it just stopped, after a week?"

"No, something happened first, then it stopped after a week."

The dancer's bare and busy feet have made a percussive instrument of the floor, and I have the distinct impression that she's setting the tempo and the string quartet is having trouble keeping up. Her feet are dusted white with resin.

The coin is falling now.

"What was that?" I ask. "What happened?"

The girl takes a drag off her cigarette, then begins fussing about with the lens of her camera.

"I was sitting at the desk," she says, "the little desk in my room where I sat and did my homework and stuff. I was sitting there after breakfast one morning reading a book—I don't recall what the book was, I sort of wish that I did—and a raven flew into the window. It hit the glass so hard it was like a gun going off. *Bam!* Scared the shit out of me, and I screamed, and—"

"It killed the raven," I say, interrupting her.

The girl laughs. "Fuck yeah, it killed the raven. It even cracked the windowpane. Crushed the poor thing's skull, I guess. Broke its neck at the very least. Cracked the window and left a smear of blood on the glass, it hit so hard." And she laughs again. It's a nervous, uneasy sort of laugh. "How fast do ravens fly?"

"I don't know," I tell her. "But there were no more feathers in your bed after that? That's what made them stop appearing?"

She turns her head and stares at me. "Yeah, there were no more feathers in my bed after that, and at the *time*, that's how it seemed to me, that somehow the death of the raven had made whatever was happening stop. Like, I don't know, like a sacrifice?"

"But that's not what you think now?"

"I don't know. Questions of causation and correlation and what have you, right? But something else happened that same day, the same day the raven smacked into my bedroom window."

"And what was that?"

The wind blows, and I smell the salty, sour bay.

Drops of sweat fall from the dancer's naked body and speckle the dusty floor.

"I got my period. My first period. I was only eight, but...." And again she trails off and sits smoking and pretending to adjust the Pentax's aperture settings.

"You were young," I agree, "but it happens."

"Mom, she blamed hormones in milk and beef and stuff, but, like I said, causation and correlation. Who fucking knows? Point is, that day a raven went kamikaze on my bedroom window, *and* I got my period, *and* the creepy thing with the feathers in my bed stopped. And that was that. It's not a very satisfying ending to a story."

"Usually, the world doesn't come with satisfying endings attached," I tell her, and she shrugs and begins taking photographs of the feeding swans.

On the third floor of the house on Federal Hill, I sit with the smiling man on the blue settee, the antique photo album between us, and he listens to me tell my own story.

"I never did learn how or why or by whom all those railroad cars had been moved where they were, but there were about a dozen of them, half swallowed up by the kudzu vines, miles from the nearest tracks. They were all boxcars, except for that caboose."

"That's where you found the book?" he asks.

"Yeah."

"Is it true what they say about kudzu, how fast it grows?"

"Up to a foot a day, maybe more," I say. "It was introduced into the US in 1883, from Asia. Like those swans, it doesn't belong here. Anyway, I think we never would have gotten into the caboose if we hadn't had machetes."

"But you did have machetes, and you did get in," says the man.

"Yes, on both counts."

...and in rapid succession first one thing and then the other, in constant, indecisive revolution...

The man lays his hand on the cover of the book, so that I can no longer see it, which, I discover, makes it easier for me to tell him about the caboose. I dream about it most nights and suspect that I always will. Knowledge comes at a price, my mother would have said, and often that price is our sense of well-being. Or our innocence. Or our ability to sleep without nightmares.

"I was surprised that the kudzu hadn't gotten inside," I say.

"Maybe something kept it out," replies the man, and he leans forward a bit, watching the dancer intently now.

"The windows weren't broken out, which is nothing short of a miracle. No telling how long it had been sitting there. Decades. But the windows weren't broken out, and the rear door opened as easily as if the hinges had just recently been oiled. There was a pot-bellied stove, bunks, a desk. The walls were painted a muddy sort of mint green and photographs of naked women had been cut out and tacked and pasted all over them."

"Kids," the man whispers, the smile returning to his thin lips.

"And there were the birds," I say.

"'When you have shot one bird flying,'" says the smiling man, "'you have shot all birds flying.' That's Ernest Hemingway. You dislike talking about the birds. I can tell. I'd not thought you'd be squeamish about a thing like that."

I didn't reply right away. I wanted to deny the charge, his casual accusation that I didn't have the stomach for the life that had been passed down to me. But I let the charge stand. He would know my denial was a lie, and, more importantly, I would know it was a lie.

"We counted the bodies of seventy-five crows," I say, instead. "Some were hardly more than skeletons, sort of mummified, skin and feathers stretched over bone. Others couldn't have been dead more than a few hours. Each one had been nailed to the mint-green walls with three two-penny nails. One nail through the back of the skull, and—"

"It must have been very hot," the man whispers. "It must have been very hot inside the caboose."

"It was late summer. August. Dog days. Yes, it was very hot."

"But you're used that that," says the man.

"The book, it was lying on a shelf above the brakeman's desk. There was nothing else on the shelf, just the one book. It was dusty, but it wasn't moldy, which is at least as unlikely as none of the windows being broken out."

"Maybe it hadn't been there very long."

"Maybe not. There's no way to know, and I don't suppose it matters."

"Not in the least."

I take a small sip of my flat beer, because my mouth has gone very dry. I can taste the incense now, hot and cloying, as much as I can smell it. The music and the rhythmic tattoo of the dancer's feet on the floor have grown inexplicably, uncomfortably loud. I glance towards the book, mostly hidden from view by the man's hand, but I don't have to *see* the book to see it. The image of it is worked into my mind, tooled there as surely as the grotesque patterns worked into its tooled leather cover, that album with its gilded fore edge and the cracked leather binding stained red and black like dried blood on the feathers of dead crows. There is a single word blind stamped into the spine, and there's a brass hasp and a staple, but no lock to keep it shut. Anyone can open the book and see what's inside.

Anyone can turn a page.

Or flip a coin.

"Well, you've brought it home," says the man, "which is really all that matters."

By the polluted river, at the eastern edge of Swan Point Cemetery, the girl smokes cigarettes and sits on the hood of her car, snapping pictures.

I say that I should be going, and she nods and takes another photograph.

"Do you believe in evil?" she asks me.

72

"I do," I reply, without giving the matter a second thought. "I haven't been left with much choice in the matter."

"Well, I believe in evil," she says. "Murdering a swan, nailing it to a tree, that's evil, pure and fucking simple."

Before the music began, and before I took the book from my satchel and presented it to the man who seems to have too many teeth when he smiles, before *that*, the dancer knelt on the floor, and she bowed her head, and everyone assembled in the room watched as the alabaster feathers were inserted beneath her skin. The hollow quill tips of primary and secondary flight feathers, the feathers of swans, had been fitted into seventy-four 22-gauge hypodermic needles, and then the needles were artfully arranged in rows along her shoulders and forearms. I was surprised that the piercing had taken only half an hour. She had not been given wings, but only the suggestion of wings, a shaman's trick that she could fly and yet still be bound by the same cruel gravity that pulls a coin toss back towards earth.

And now the fourth movement has ended, and the musicians are waiting patiently for what comes next. The dancer has stopped dancing. She stands perfectly still at the center of the room, her counterfeit wings folded modestly across her breasts, the candlelight painting her with flickering shades of yellow and white and orange. And the woman who gave her those wings reappears from the shadows; she carries a ballpeen hammer and three heavy forty-penny nails. She whispers something to the dancer, kisses her on the cheek, and then they walk together to the north end of the room, where a sturdy cross carved of red maple has been erected.

"A shame your mother can't see this," says the man, and he picks the book up off the sky-blue settee and sets it in his lap. He has taken the weight of it from me and made it his own, and for that I might almost be moved to worship him as an atheist's god. "A crying shame," he says.

The dancer, the evening's surrogate, never utters a sound. Her whole life has prepared her for this moment and led her here, and she faces her fate with the dignity and poise of a swan.

"You're an ornithologist?" asks the girl as she stubs out another cigarette on the sole of her boot. This time, she doesn't flick the butt towards the river, but places it into an empty film canister.

"No," I say. "I'm a paleontologist. That's what I teach."

"But you know a lot about birds."

"I suppose I do," I reply.

"Well, maybe we'll run into each other again," she says. "I come here a lot."

We exchange good-byes, and then I turn and walk to my own car, parked farther from the water, and she goes back to taking pictures of the swans. The insistent wind is behind me, pushing me along, urging me forward.

The man with the book in his lap looks away from the spectacle just long enough to offer me a wink and to tap the side of his nose again.

A word to the wise.

He has the black eyes of a crow.

"She was a fine woman, your mother," he says.

And the world spins, like a tossed coin, moving in constant, indecisive, predictable revolutions, and I hold it in the palm of my hand.

A Wish from a Bone

GEMMA FILES

War zone archaeology is the best kind, Hynde liked to say, when drunk—
and Goss couldn't disagree, at least in terms of ratings. The danger,
the constant threat, was a clarifying influence, lending everything
they did an extra meaty heft. Better yet, it was the world's best excuse
for having to wrap real quick and pull out ahead of the tanks, regardless of
whether or not they'd actually found anything.

The site for their latest TV special was miles out from anywhere else,
far enough from the border between Eritrea and the Sudan that the first
surveys missed it—first, second, third, fifteenth—until updated satellite
surveillance finally revealed minute differences between what local experts
could only assume was some sort of temple and all the similarly coloured
detritus surrounding it. It didn't help that it was only a few clicks (compara-
tively) away from the Meroitic pyramid find in Gebel Barkal, which had
naturally kept most "real" archaeologists too busy to check out what the
fuck that low-lying, hill-like building lurking in the middle distance might
or might not be.

Yet on closer examination, of course, it turned out somebody already
had stumbled over it, a couple of different times; the soldiers who'd set
up initial camp inside in order to avoid a dust storm had found two separate batches of bodies, fresh-ish enough that their shreds of clothing and
artefacts could be dated back to the 1930s on the one hand, the 1890s on

the other. Gentlemen explorers, native guides, mercenaries. Same as today, pretty much, without the "gentlemen" part.

Partially ruined, and rudimentary, to say the least. It was laid out somewhat like El-Marraqua, or the temples of Lake Nasser: a roughly half-circular building with the rectangular section facing outwards like a big, blank wall centred by a single, permanently open doorway, twelve feet high by five feet wide. No windows, though the roof remained surprisingly intact.

"This whole area was underwater, a million years ago," Hynde told Goss. "See these rocks? All sedimentary. Chalk, fossils, bone-bed silica and radiolarite—amazing any of it's still here, given the wind. Must've formed in a channel or a basin…but no, that doesn't make sense either, because the *inside* of the place is stable, no matter how much the outside erodes."

"So they quarried stone from somewhere else, brought it here, shored it up."

"Do you know how long that would've taken? Nearest hard-rock deposits are like—five hundred miles thataway. Besides, that's not even vaguely how it looks. It's more…unformed, like somebody set up channels while a lava flow was going on and shepherded it into a hexagonal pattern, then waited for it to cool enough that the up-thrust slabs fit together like walls, blending at the seams."

"What's the roof made of?"

"Interlocking bricks of mud, weed, and gravel fix-baked in the sun, then fitted together and fired afterwards, from the outside in; must've piled flammable stuff on top of it, set it alight, let it cook. The glue for the gravel was bone dust and chunks, marinated in vinegar."

"*Seriously*," Goss said, perking up. "Human? This a necropolis, or what?"

"We don't know, to either."

Outside, that new chick—Camberwell? The one who'd replaced that massive Eurasian guy they'd all just called "Gojira," rumoured to have finally screwed himself to death between projects—was wrangling their trucks into camp formation, angled to provide a combination of lookout, cover, and windbreak. Moving inside, meanwhile, Goss began taking light-meter readings and setting up his initial shots, while Hynde showed him around this particular iteration of the Oh God Can Such Things Be travelling road show.

"Watch your step," Hynde told him, all but leading him by the sleeve. "The floor slopes down, a series of shallow shelves.... It's an old trick, designed to force perspective, move you further in. To develop a sense of awe."

Goss nodded, allowing Hynde to draw him towards what at first looked like one back wall, but quickly proved to be a clever illusion—two slightly overlapping partial walls, slim as theatrical flats, set up to hide a sharply zig-zagging passage beyond. This, in turn, gave access to a tunnel curling downwards into a sort of cavern underneath the temple floor, through which Hynde was all too happy to conduct Goss, filming as they went.

"Take a gander at all the mosaics," Hynde told him. "Get in close. See those hieroglyphics?"

"Is that what those are? They look sort of...organic, almost."

"They should; they were, once. Fossils."

Goss focused his lens closer, and grinned so wide his cheeks hurt. Because yes yes fucking YES, they were: rows on rows of skeletal little pressed-flat, stonified shrimp, fish, sea ferns, and other assorted what-the-fuck-evers, painstakingly selected, sorted, and slotted into patterns that started at calf-level and rose almost to the equally creepy baked-bone brick roof, blending into darkness.

"Jesus," he said, out loud. "This is *gold*, man, even if it turns out you can't read 'em. This is an Emmy, right here."

Hynde nodded, grinning too now, though maybe not as wide. And told him: "Wait 'til you see the well."

The cistern in question, hand-dug down through rock and paved inside with slimy sandstone, had a roughly twenty-foot diameter and a depth that proved unsoundable even with the party's longest reel of rope, which put it at something over sixty-one metres. Whatever had once been inside it appeared to have dried up long since, though a certain liquid quality to the echoes it produced gave indications that there might still be the remains of a water table—poisoned or pure, no way to tell—lingering at its bottom. There was a weird saline quality to the crust inside its lip, a sort of whitish, gypsum-esque candle-wax-dripping formation that looked as though it was just on the verge of blooming into stalactites.

Far more interesting, however, was the design scheme its excavators had chosen to decorate the well's exterior with—a mosaic, also assembled from fossils, though in this case the rocks themselves had been pulverized before use, reduced to fragments so that they could be recombined into surreally alien patterns: fish-eyed, weed-legged, shell-winged monstrosities, cut here and there with what might be fins or wings or insect torsos halved, quartered, chimerically repurposed and slapped together to form even larger, more complex figures of which these initial grotesques were only the pointillist building blocks. Step back far enough, and they coalesced into seven figures looking off into almost every possible direction save for where the southeast compass point should go. That spot was completely blank.

"I'm thinking the well chamber was constructed first," Hynde explained, "here, under the ground—possibly around an already-existing cave, hollowed out by water that no longer exists, through limestone that *shouldn't* exist. After which the entire temple would've been built overtop, to hide and protect it...protect *them*."

"The statues." Hynde nodded. "Are those angels?" Goss asked, knowing they couldn't be.

"Do they *look* like angels?"

"Hey, there are some pretty fucked-up-looking angels, is what I hear. Like—rings of eyes covered in wings, or those four-headed ones from *The X-Files*."

"Or the ones that look like Christopher Walken."

"Gabriel, in *The Prophecy*. Viggo Mortensen played Satan." Goss squinted. "But these sort of look like...Pazuzu."

Hynde nodded, pleased. "Good call: four wings, like a moth—definitely Sumerian. This one has clawed feet; this one's head is turned backwards, or maybe upside-down. *This* one looks like it's got no lower jaw. This one has a tail and no legs at all, like a snake...."

"Dude, do you actually know what they are, or are you just fucking with me?"

"How much do you know about the Terrible Seven?"

"Nothing."

"Excellent. That means our viewers won't, either."

They set up in front of the door, before they lost the sun. A tight shot on Hynde, hands thrown out in what Goss had come to call his classic Profsplaining pose; Goss shot from below, framing him in the temple's gaping maw, while 'Lij the sound guy checked his levels and everybody else shut the fuck up. From the corner of one eye, Goss could just glimpse Camberwell leaning back against the point truck's wheel with her distractingly curvy legs crossed, arms braced like she was about to start doing reverse triceps push-ups. Though it was hard to tell from behind those massive sun-goggles, she didn't seem too impressed.

"The Terrible Seven were mankind's first boogeymen," Hynde told whoever would eventually be up at three in the morning, or whenever the History Channel chose to run this. "To call them demons would be too... Christian. To the people who feared them most, the Sumerians, they were simply a group of incredibly powerful creatures responsible for every sort of human misery, invisible and unutterably malign—literally unnamable, since to name them was, inevitably, to invite their attention. According to experts, the only way to fend them off was with the so-called 'Maskim Chant,' a prayer for protection collected by E. Campbell Thompson in his book *The Devils and Evil Spirits Of Babylonia, Vols. 1–2*...and even that was no sure guarantee of safety, depending just how annoyed one—or all—of the Seven might be feeling, any given day of the week...."

Straightening slightly, he raised one hand in mock supplication, reciting:

"They are Seven! They are Seven!

"Seven in the depths of the ocean, Seven in the Heavens above.

"Those who are neither male nor female, those who stretch themselves out like chains...

"Terrible beyond description.

"Those who are Nameless. Those who must not be named.

"The enemies! The enemies! Bitter poison sent by the Gods.

"Seven are they! Seven!"

Nice, Goss thought, and went to cut Hynde off. But there was more, apparently—a lot of it, and Hynde seemed intent on getting it all out. Good for inserts, Goss guessed, 'specially when cut together with the spooky shit from inside....

"In heaven they are unknown. On earth they are not understood.

"They neither stand nor sit, nor eat nor drink.

"Spirits that minish the earth, that minish the land, of giant strength and giant tread—"

("Minish"?)

"Demons like raging bulls, great ghosts,

"Ghosts that break through all the houses, demons that have no shame, seven are they!

"Knowing no care, they grind the land like corn.

"Knowing no mercy, they rage against mankind.

"They are demons full of violence, ceaselessly devouring blood.

"Seven are they! Seven are they! Seven!

"They are Seven! They are Seven! They are twice Seven! They are Seven times seven!"

Camberwell was sitting up now, almost standing, while the rest of the crew made faces at each other. Goss had been sawing a finger across his throat since *knowing no care*, but Hynde just kept on going, hair crested, complexion purpling; he looked unhealthily sweat-shiny, spraying spit. Was that froth on his lower lip?

"The wicked *Arralu* and *Allatu*, who wander alone in the wilderness, covering man like a garment,

"The wicked *Namtaru*, who seizes by the throat.

"The wicked *Asakku*, who envelops the skull like a fever.

"The wicked *Utukku*, who slays man alive on the plain.

"The wicked *Lammyatu*, who causes disease in every portion.

"The wicked *Ekimmu*, who draws out the bowels.

"The wicked *Gallu* and *Alu*, who bind the hands and body...."

By this point even 'Lij was looking up, visibly worried. Hynde began to shake, eyes stutter-lidded, and fell sidelong even as Goss moved to catch him, only to find himself blocked—Camberwell was there already, folding Hynde into a brisk paramedic's hold. "A rag, *something*," she ordered 'Lij, who whipped his shirt off so fast his 'phones went bouncing, rolling it flat enough it'd fit between Hynde's teeth; Goss didn't feel like being in the way, so he drew back, kept rolling. As they laid Hynde back, limbs flailing hard enough to make dust-angels, Goss could just make out more words seeping out half through the cloth stopper and half through Hynde's bleeding nose, quick and dry: rhythmic, nasal, ancient. Another chant he could only assume, this time left entirely untranslated, though words here and there popped as familiar from the preceding bunch of rabid mystic bullshit—

Arralu-Allatu Namtaru Maskim
Asakku Utukku Lammyatu Maskim
Ekimmu Gallu-Alu Maskim
Maskim Maskim Maskim

Voices to his right, his left, while his lens-sight steadily narrowed and dimmed: *Go get Doc Journee, man! The fuck's head office pay her for, exactly?* 'Lij and Camberwell kneeling in the dirt, holding Hynde down, trying their best to make sure he didn't hurt himself 'til the only person on site with an actual medical license got there. And all the while that same babble rising, louder and ever more throb-buzz deformed, like the guy had a swarm of bees stuck in his clogged and swelling throat....

ArralAllatNamtarAssakUtukkLammyatEkimmGalluAluMaskim-MaskimMaskim

(Maskim)

The dust storm kicked up while Journee was still attending to Hynde, getting him safely laid down in a corner of the temple's outer chamber and doing her best to stabilize him even as he resolved down into some shallow-breathing species of coma. "Any one of these fuckers flips, they'll take out a fuckin' wall!" Camberwell yelled, as the other two drivers scrambled to get the trucks as stable as possible, digging out 'round the wheels and anchoring them with rocks, applying locks to axles and steering wheels. Goss, for his own part, was already busy helping hustle the supplies inside, stacking ration packs around Hynde like sandbags; a crash from the door made his head jerk up, just in time to see that chick Lao and her friend-who-was-a-boy Katz (both from craft services) staring at each other over a mess of broken plastic, floor between them suddenly half-turned to mud.

Katz: "What the *shit*, man!"

Lao: "I don't know, Christ! Those bottles aren't s'posed to *break*—"

The well, something dry and small "said" at the back of Goss's head, barely a voice at all—more a touch, in passing, in the dark. And: "There's a well," he heard himself say, before he could think better of it. "Down through there, behind the walls."

Katz looked at Lao, shrugged. "Better check it out, then," he suggested—started to, anyhow. Until Camberwell somehow turned up between them, half stepping sidelong and half like she'd just materialized, the rotating storm her personal wormhole.

"I'll do that," she said, firmly. "Still two gallon cans in the back of Truck Two, for weight; cut a path, make sure we can get to 'em. I'll tell you if what's down there's viable."

"Deal," Lao agreed, visibly grateful—and Camberwell was gone a second later, down into the passage, a shadow into shadow. While at almost the same time, from Goss's elbow, 'Lij suddenly asked (of no one in particular, given *he* was the resident expert): "Sat-phones aren't supposed to just stop working, right?"

Katz: "Nope."

"Could be we're in a dead zone, I guess…or the storm…."

"Yeah, good luck on that, buddy."

Across the room, the rest of the party were congregating in a clot, huddled 'round a cracked packet of glow sticks because nobody wanted to break out the lanterns, not in this weather. Journee had opened Hynde's shirt to give him CPR, but left off when he stopped seizing. Now she sat crouched above him, peering down at his chest like she was trying to play connect-the-dots with moles, hair, and nipples.

"Got a weird rash forming here," she told Goss, when he squatted down beside her. "Allergy? Or photosensitive, maybe, if he's prone to that, 'cause… it really does seem to turn darker the closer you move the flashlight."

"He uses a lot of sunscreen."

"Don't we all. Seriously, look for yourself."

He did. Thinking: *optical illusion, has to be*…but wondering, all the same. Because—it was just so clear, so defined, rucking Hynde's skin as though something were raising it up from inside. Like a letter from some completely alien alphabet; a symbol, unrecognizable, unreadable.

(*A sigil*, the same tiny voice corrected. And Goss felt the hairs on his back ruffle, sudden-slick with cold, foul sweat.)

It took a few minutes more for 'Lij to give up on the sat-phone, tossing it aside so hard it bounced. "Try the radio mikes," Goss heard him tell himself, "see what kind'a bandwidth we can...back to Gebel, might be somebody listening. But not the border, nope, gotta keep off *that* squawk-channel, for sure. Don't want the military gettin' wind, on either side...."

By then, Camberwell had been gone for almost ten minutes, so Goss felt free to leave Hynde in Journee's care and follow, at his own pace—through the passage and into the tunnel, feeling along the wall, trying to be quiet. But two painful stumbles later, halfway down the tunnel's curve, he had to flip open his phone just to see; the stone-bone walls gave off a faint, ill light, vaguely slick, a dead jellyfish luminescence.

He drew within just enough range to hear Camberwell's boots rasp on the downward slope, then pause—saw her glance over one shoulder, eyes weirdly bright through a dim fall of hair gust-popped from her severe, sweat-soaked working gal's braid.

Asking, as she did: "Want me to wait while you catch up?"

Boss, other people might've appended, almost automatically, but never her. Then again, Goss had to admit, he wouldn't have really believed that shit coming from Camberwell, even if she had.

He straightened up, sighing, and joined her—standing pretty much exactly where he thought she'd've ended up, right next to the well, though keeping a careful distance between herself and its creepy-coated sides. "Try sending down a cup yet, or what?"

"Why? Oh, right...no, no point; that's why I volunteered, so those dumbasses *wouldn't* try. Don't want to be drinking *any* of the shit comes out of there, believe you me."

"Oh, I do, and that's—kinda interesting, given. Rings a bit like you obviously know more about this than you're letting on."

She arched a brow, denial reflex-quick, though not particularly convincing. "Hey, who was it sent Lao and what's-his-name down here in the first place? I'm motor pool, man. Cryptoarchaeology is you and coma-boy's gig."

"Says the chick who knows the correct terminology."

"Look who I work for."

Goss sighed. "Okay, I'll bite. What's in the well?"

"What's *on* the well? Should give you some idea. Or, better yet—"

She held out her hand for his phone, the little glowing screen, with its pathetic rectangular light. After a moment, he gave it over and watched her cast it 'round, outlining the chamber's canted, circular floor: seen face on, those ridges he'd felt under his feet when Hynde first brought him in here and dismissed without a first glance, let alone a second, proved to be in-spiralling channels stained black from centuries of use: run-off ditches once used for drainage, aimed at drawing some sort of liquid—layered and faded now into muck and dust, a resinous stew clogged with dead insects—away from (what else) seven separate niches set into the surrounding walls, inset so sharply they only became apparent when you observed them at an angle.

In front of each niche, one of the mosaicked figures, with a funnelling spout set at ditch-level under the creature in question's feet, or lack thereof. Inside each niche, meanwhile, a quartet of hooked spikes set vertically, may-be five feet apart: two up top, possibly for hands or wrists, depending if you were doing things Roman- or Renaissance-style; two down below, suitable for lashing somebody's ankles to. And now Goss looked closer, something else as well, in each of those upright stone coffins...

(Ivory scraps, shattered yellow-brown shards, broken down by time and gravity alike, and painted to match their surroundings by lack of light. Bones, piled where they fell.)

"What the fuck *was* this place?" Goss asked, out loud. But mainly be-cause he wanted confirmation, more than anything else.

Camberwell shrugged, yet again—her default setting, he guessed. "A trap," she answered. "And you fell in it, but don't feel bad—you weren't to know, right?"

"We found it, though. Hynde and me...."

"If not you, somebody else. Some places are already empty, already ruined—they just wait, long as it takes. They don't ever go away. 'Cause they *want* to be found."

Goss felt his stomach roil, fresh sweat springing up even colder, so rank he could smell it. "A trap," he repeated, biting down, as Camberwell nodded. Then: "For us?"

But here she shook her head, pointing back at the well, with its seven watchful guardians. Saying, as she did—

"Naw, man. For *them*."

She laid her hand on his, half its size but twice as strong, and walked him through it—puppeted his numb and clumsy finger-pads bodily over the clumps of fossil chunks in turn, allowing him time to recognize what was hidden inside the mosaic's design more by touch than by sight: a symbol (*sigil*) for every figure, tumour-blooming and weirdly organic, each one just ever-so-slightly different from the next. He found the thing Hynde's rash most reminded him of on number four, and stopped dead; Camberwell's gaze flicked down to confirm, her mouth moving slightly, shaping words. *Ah*, one looked like—*ah, I see.* Or maybe *I see you.*

"What?" he demanded, for what seemed like the tenth time in quick succession. Thinking: *I sound like a damn parrot.*

Camberwell didn't seem to mind, though. "Ashreel," she replied, not looking up. "That's what I said. The Terrible Ashreel, who wears us like clothing."

"Allatu, you mean. The wicked, who covers man like a garment—"

"Whatever, Mister G. If you prefer."

"It's just—I mean, that's nothing like what Hynde said, up there—"

"Yeah sure, 'cause that shit was what the Sumerians and Babylonians called 'em, from that book Hynde was quoting." She knocked knuckles against Hynde's brand, then the ones on either side—three sharp little raps, invisible cross-nails. "*These* are their actual *names*. Like...what they call *themselves*."

"How the fuck would you know that? Camberwell, what the hell."

Straightening, shrugging yet again, like she was throwing off flies. "There's a book, okay? The *Liber Carne*—'Book of Meat.' And all's it has is just a list of names with these symbols carved alongside, so you'll know which one you're looking at, when they're—embodied. In the flesh."

"In the—you mean *bodies*, like possession? Like that's what's happening to Hynde?" At her nod: "Well…makes sense, I guess, in context; he already said they were demons."

"Oh, that's a misnomer, actually. 'Terrible' used to mean 'awe-inspiring,' 'more whatever than any other whatever,' like Tsar Ivan of all the Russias. So the Seven, the *Terrible* Seven, what they really are is angels, just like you thought."

"Fallen angels."

"Nope, those are Goetim, like you call the ones who stayed up top Elohim—*these* are Maskim, same as the Chant. Arralu-Allatu, Namtaru, Asakku, Utukku, Gallu-Alu, Ekimmu, Lammyatu; Ashreel, Yphemaal, Zemyel, Eshphoriel, Immoel, Coiab, Ushephekad. Angel of Confusion, the Mender Angel, Angel of Severance, Angel of Whispers, Angel of Translation, Angel of Ripening, Angel of the Empty…."

All these half-foreign words spilling from her mouth, impossibly glib, ringing in Goss's head like popped blood vessels. But: "Wait," he threw back, struggling. "A 'trap'…I thought this place was supposed to be a temple. Like the people who built it worshipped these things."

"Okay, then play that out. Given how Hynde described 'em, what sort of people would *worship* the Seven, you think?"

"… terrible people?"

"You got it. Sad people, weird people, crazy people. People who get off on power, good, bad, or indifferent. People who hate the world they got so damn bad they don't really care what they swap it for, as long as it's *something else*."

"And they expect—the Seven—to do that for them."

"It's what they were made for."

Straight through cryptoarchaeology and out the other side, into a version of the Creation so literally Apocryphal it would've gotten them both burnt at the stake just a few hundred years earlier. Because to hear Camberwell tell it, sometimes, when a Creator got very, verrry lonely, It decided to make Itself some friends—after which, needing someplace to put them,

It contracted the making of such a place out to creatures themselves made to order: fragments of Its own reflected glory haphazardly hammered into vaguely human-esque form, perfectly suited to this one colossal task, and almost nothing else.

"They made the world, in other words," Goss said. "All seven of them."

"Yeah. 'Cept back then they were still one angel in seven parts—the Voltron angel, I call it. Splitting apart came later on, after the schism."

"Lucifer, war in heaven, cast down into hell and yadda yadda. All that. So this is all, what…some sort of metaphysical labour dispute?"

"They wouldn't think of it that way."

"How *do* they think of it?"

"*Differently*, like every other thing. Look, once the shit hit the cosmic fan, the Seven didn't stay with God, but they didn't go with the devil, either—they just went, forced themselves from outside space and time into the universe they'd made, and never looked back. And that was because they wanted something angels are uniquely unqualified for: free will. They wanted to be us."

Back to the fast-forward, then, the bend and the warp, 'til her ridiculously plausible-seeming exposition dump seemed to come at him from everywhere at once, a perfect storm. Because: *misery's their meat, see—the honey that draws flies, by-product of every worst moment of all our brief lives, when people will cry out for anything who'll listen. That's when one of the Seven usually shows up, offering help—except the kind of help they come up with's usually nothing very helpful at all, considering how they just don't really get the way things work for us, even now. And it's always just one of them at first, 'cause they each blame the other for having made the decision to run, stranding themselves in the here and now, so they don't want to be anywhere near each other…but if you can get 'em all in one place—someplace like here, say, with seven bleeding, suffering vessels left all ready and waiting for 'em—then they'll be automatically drawn back together, like gravity, a black-hole event horizon. They'll form a vector, and at the middle of that cyclone they'll become a single angel once again, ready to tear everything they built up right the fuck on back down.*

Words words words, every one more painful than the last. Goss looked at Camberwell as she spoke, straight on, the way he didn't think he'd ever actually done, previously. She was short and stacked, skin tanned and plentiful, eyes darkish brown shot with a sort of creamier shade, like petrified wood. A barely visible scar quirked through one eyebrow, threading down over the cheekbone beneath to intersect with another at the corner of her mouth, keloid raised in their wake like a negative-image beauty mark, a reversed dimple.

Examined this way, at close quarters, he found he liked the look of her, suddenly and sharply—and for some reason, that mainly made him angry.

"This is a fairy tale," he heard himself tell her, with what seemed like over-the-top emphasis. "I'm sitting here in the dark, letting you spout some…Catholic campfire story about angel traps, free will, fuckin' misery vectors…." A quick headshake, firm enough to hurt. "None of it's true."

"Yeah, okay, you want to play it that way."

"If I *want*—?"

Here she turned on *him*, abruptly equal-fierce, clearing her throat to hork a contemptuous wad out on the ground between them, like she was making a point. "Look, you think I give a runny jack-shit if you believe me or not? *I know what I know.* It's just that things are gonna start to move fast from now on, so you need to know that; *somebody* in this crap pit does, aside from me. And I guess—" Stopping and hissing, annoyed with herself, before adding, quieter: "I guess I wanted to just say it, too—out loud, for once. For all the good it'll probably do either of us."

They stood there a second, listening, Goss didn't know for what—nothing but muffled wind, people murmuring scared out beyond the passage, a general scrape and drip. 'Til he asked: "What about Hynde? Can we, like, *do* anything?"

"Not much. Why? You guys friends?"

Yes, damnit, Goss wanted to snap, but he was pretty sure she had lie-dar to go with her Seven-dar. "There's…not really a show, without him," was all he said, finally.

"All right, well—he's pretty good and got, at this point, so. I'd keep him sedated, restrained if I could, and wait, see who else shows up: there's six more to go, after all."

"What happens if they all show up?"

"All Seven? Then we're fucked, basically, as a species. Stuck back to-gether, the Maskim are a load-bearing boss the likes of which this world was not designed to contain, and the vector they form in proximity, well—it's like putting too much weight on a sheet of…something. Do it long enough, it rips wide open."

"*What* rips?"

"The crap you think? Everything."

There was a sort of a jump cut, and Goss found himself tagging along beside her as Camberwell strode back up the passageway, listening to her tell him: "Important point about Hynde, as of right now, is to make sure he doesn't start doin' stuff to himself."

"… like?"

"Well—"

As she said it, though, there came a scream-led general uproar up in front, making them both break into a run. They tumbled back into the light sticks' circular glow to find Journee contorted on the ground with her heels drumming, chewing at her own lips—everybody else had already shrunk back, eyes and mouths covered like it was catching, save for big, stupid 'Lij, who was trying his level best to pry her jaws apart and thrust his folding pocket spork in between. Goss darted forward to grab one arm, Camberwell the other, but Journee used the leverage to flip back up onto her feet, throwing them both off against the walls. She looked straight at Camberwell, spit blood and grinned wide, as though she recognized her: *Oh, it's you. How do, buddy? Welcome to the main event.*

Then reached back into her own sides, fingers plunging straight down through flesh to grip bone—ripped her red ribs wide, whole back opening up like that meat book Camberwell'd mentioned and both lungs flopping out, way too large for comfort: two dirty grey-pink balloons breathing and growing, already disgustingly over-swollen yet inflating even further, like mammoth water wings.

The pain of it made her roar and jackknife, vomiting on her own feet. And when Journee looked up once more, horrid grin trailing yellow sick-strings, Goss saw she now had a sigil of her own embossed on her forehead, fresh as some stomped-in bone bruise.

"Asakku, the Terrible Zemyel," Camberwell said, to no one in particular. "Who desecrates the faithful."

And: "God!" Somebody else—Lao?—could be heard to sob, behind them. But: "Fuck Him," Journee rasped back, throwing the tarp pinned 'cross the permanently open doorway wide and taking impossibly off up into the storm with a single flap, blood splattering everywhere, a foul red spindrift.

'Lij slapped both hands up to seal his mouth, retching loudly; Katz fell on his ass, hind-skull colliding with the wall's sharp surface, so hard he knocked himself out. Lao continued to sob-pray on, mindless, while everybody else just stared. And Goss found himself looking over at Camberwell, automatically, only to catch her nodding—just once, like she'd seen it coming.

"—like *that*, basically," she concluded, without a shred of surprise.

Five minutes at most, but it felt like an hour: things narrowed, got treacly, in that accident-in-progress way. Outside, the dust had thickened into its own artificial night; they could hear the thing inside Journee swooping high above it, laughing like a loon, yelling raucous insults at the sky. The other two drivers had never come back inside, lost in the storm; Katz crawled away and tore at the floor with his hands, badger-style, like he wanted to bury himself alive headfirst. Lao wept and wept. 'Lij came feeling towards Camberwell and Goss as the glow sticks dimmed, almost clambering over Hynde, whose breathing had sunk so low his chest barely seemed to move. "Gotta *do* something, man," he told them, like he was the first one ever to have that particular thought. "*Something.* Y'know? Before it's too late."

"It was too late when we got here," Goss heard himself reply—again, not what he'd thought he was going to say, when he'd opened his mouth. His tongue felt suddenly hot, inside of his mouth gone all itchy, swollen tight; strep? Tonsillitis? Jesus, if he could only reach back in there and *scratch*....

And Camberwell was looking at him sidelong now, with interest, though 'Lij just continued on blissfully unaware of anything, aside from his own worries. "Look, fuck *that* shit," he said, before asking her: "Can we get to the trucks?"

She shook her head. "No driving in this weather, even if we did. You ever raise anybody, or did the mikes crap out too?"

"Uh, I don't think so; caught somebody talkin' in Arabic one time, close-ish, but it sounded military, so I rung off real quick. Something about containment protocol."

Goss: *"What?"*

"Well, I thought maybe that was 'cause they were doing minefield sweeps, or whatever—"

"When *was* this?"

"… fifteen minutes ago, when you guys were still down there, 'bout the time the storm went mega. Why?"

Goss opened his mouth again, but Camberwell was already bolting up, grabbing both Katz and Hynde at once by their shirt collars, ready to heave and drag. The wind's whistle had taken on a weird, sharp edge, an atonal descending keen, so loud Goss could barely hear her—though he sure as hell saw her lips move, *read* them with widening, horrified eyes, at almost the same split-second he found himself turning, already in mid-leap towards the descending passage—

"—INCOMING, get the shit downstairs, before those sons of bitches bring this whole fuckin' place down around our goddamn—"

(ears)

Three hits, Goss thought, or maybe two-and-a-half; it was hard to tell, when your head wouldn't stop ringing. What he could only assume was at least two of the trucks had gone up right as the walls came down, or perhaps a shade before. Now the top half of the temple was flattened, once more indistinguishable from the mountainside above and around it, a deadfall of shattered lava-rock, bone bricks, and fossils. No more missiles fell, which was good, yet—so far as they could tell, pinned beneath slabs and sediment—the storm above still raged on. And now they were all down in the well room, trapped, with only a flickering congregation of phones to raise against the dark.

"Did you have any kind of *plan* when you came here, exactly?" Goss asked Camberwell, hoarsely. "I mean, aside from 'find Seven congregation site—question mark—profit'?" To which she simply sighed, and replied—

"Yeah, sort of. But you're not gonna like it."

"Try me."

Reluctantly: "The last couple times I did this, there was a physical copy of the *Liber Carne* in play, so getting rid of that helped—but there's no copy here, which makes *us* the *Liber Carne*, the human pages being Inscribed." He could hear the big I on that last word, and it scared him. "And when people are being Inscribed, well...the *best* plan is usually to just start killing those who aren't possessed until you've got less than seven left, because then why bother?"

"Uh-huh...."

"Getting to know you people well enough to *like* you, that was my mistake, obviously," she continued, partly under her breath, like she was talking to herself. Then added, louder: "Anyhow. What we're dealing with right now is two people definitely Inscribed and possessed, four potential Inscriptions, and one halfway gone...."

"Halfway? Who?"

She shot him that look, yet one more time—softer, almost sympathetic. "Open your mouth, Goss."

"Why? What f—Oh, you gotta be kidding."

No change, just a slightly raised eyebrow, as if to say: *Do I look it, motherfucker?* Which, he was forced to admit, she very much did not.

Nothing to do but obey, then. Or scream, and keep on screaming.

Goss felt his jaw slacken, pop out and down like an unhinged jewel box, revealing all its secrets. His tongue's itch was approaching some sort of critical mass. And then, right then, was when he felt it—fully and completely, without even trying. Some kind of raised area on his own soft palate, yearning down as sharply as the rest of his mouth's sensitive insides yearned up, straining to map its impossibly angled curves. His eyes skittered to the well's rim, where he knew he would find its twin, if he only searched long enough.

"Uck ee," he got out, consonants drowned away in a mixture of hot spit and cold sweat. "Oh it, uck *ee*."

A small, sad nod. "The Terrible Eshphoriel," Camberwell confirmed. "Who whispers in the empty places."

Goss closed his mouth, then spat like he was trying to clear it, for all he knew that wouldn't work. Then asked, hoarsely, stumbling slightly over the words he found increasingly difficult to form: "How mush…time I got?"

"Not much, probably."

"'S what I fought." He looked down, then back up at her, eyes sharpening. "How you geh those scars uh yers, Cammerwell?"

"Knowing's not gonna help you, Goss." But since he didn't look away, she sighed, and replied. "Hunting accident. Okay?"

"Hmh, 'kay. Then…thing we need uh…new plan, mebbe. You 'gree?"

She nodded, twisting her lips; he could see her thinking, literally, cross-referencing what had to be a thousand scribbled notes from the margins of her mental grand grimoire. Time slowed to an excruciating crawl, within which Goss began to hear that still, small voice begin to mount up again, no doubt aware it no longer had to be particularly subtle about things anymore: *Eshphoriel Maskim, sometimes called Utukku, Angel of Whispers…and yes, I can hear you, little fleshbag, as you hear me; feel you, in all your incipient flowering and decay, your time-anchored freedom. We are all the same in this way, and yes, we mostly hate you for it, which only makes your pain all the sweeter, in context—though not quite so much, at this point, as we imitation-of-passionately strive to hate each other.*

You guys stand outside space and time, though, right? he longed to demand, as he felt the constant background chatter of what he'd always thought of as "him" start to dim. *Laid the foundations of the Earth—you're megaton bombs, and we're like…viruses. So why the hell would you want to be* anything *like us? To lower yourselves that way?*

A small pause came in this last idea's wake, not quite present, yet too much there to be absent, somehow: a breath, perhaps, or the concept of one, drawn from the non-throat of something far infinitely larger. The feather's shadow, floating above the Word of God.

It does make you wonder, does it not? the small voice "said." *I know I do, and have, since before your first cells split.*

But: *Because they want to defile the creation they set in place, yet have no real part in,* Goss's mind—*his* mind, yes, he was *almost* sure—chimed in. *Because they long to insert themselves where they have no cause to be and let it shiver apart all around them, to run counter to everything, a curse on heaven. To make themselves the worm in the cosmic apple, rotting everything they touch....*

The breath returned, drawn harder this time in a semi-insulted way, a universal "tch!" But at the same time, something else presented itself—just as likely, or un-valid as anything else, in a world touched by the Seven.

(Or because...maybe, this is all there is. Maybe, this is as good as it gets.)
That's all.

"I have an idea," Camberwell said, at last, from somewhere nearby. And Goss opened his mouth to answer only to hear the angel's still, small voice issue from between his teeth, replying, mildly—

"Do you, huntress? Then please, say on."

This, then, was how they all finally came to be arrayed 'round the well's rim, the seven of them who were left, standing—or propped up/lying, in Hynde's and Katz's cases—in front of those awful wall orifices, staring into the multifaceted mosaic eyes of God's former *Flip My Universe* crew. 'Lij stood at the empty southeastern point, looking nervous, for which neither Goss nor the creature inhabiting his brain pan could possibly blame him, while Camberwell busied herself moving from person to person, sketching quick and dirty versions of the sigils on them with the point of a flick knife she'd produced from one of her boots. Lao opened her mouth like she was gonna start crying even harder when she first saw it, but Camberwell just shot her the fearsomest glare yet—Medusa-grade, for sure—and watched her shut the fuck up, with a hitchy little gasp.

"This will bring us together sooner rather than later, you must realize," Eshphoriel told Camberwell, who nodded. Replying: "That's the idea."

"Ah. That seems somewhat...antithetical, knowing our works, as you claim to."

"Maybe so. But you tell me—what's better? Stay down here in the dark waiting for the air to run out only to have you celestial tapeworms soul-rape us all at the last minute anyways, when we're too weak to put up a fight? Or force an end now, while we're all semi-fresh, and see what happens?"

"Fine tactics, yes—very born-again barbarian. Your own pocket Ragnarok, with all that the term implies."

"Yeah, yeah: clam up, Legion, if you don't have anything useful to con-tribute." To 'Lij: "You ready, sound boy?"

"Uhhhh...."

"I'll take that as a 'yes.'"

Done with Katz, she swapped places with 'Lij, handing him the knife as she went, and tapping the relevant sigil. "Like that," she said. "Try to do it all in one motion, if you can—it'll hurt less."

'Lij looked dubious. **"One can't fail to notice *you* aren't volunteering for im-promptu body modification,"** Eshphoriel noted, through Goss's lips, while Camberwell met the comment with a tiny, bitter smile. Replying, as she hiked her shirt up to demonstrate—

"That'd be 'cause I've already got one."

Cocking a hip to display the thing in question where it nestled in the hollow at the base of her spine, more a scab than a scar, edges blurred like some infinitely fucked-up tramp stamp. And as she did, Goss saw *something* come fluttering up behind her skin, a parallel-dimension full-body ripple, the barest glowing shadow of a disproportionately huge tentacle tip still up-thrust through Camberwell's whole being, as though everything she was, had been, and would ever come to be was nothing more than some indis-tinct non-creature's fleshy finger puppet.

One cream-brown eye flushed with livid colour, green on yellow, while the other stayed exactly the same—human, weary, bitter to its soul's bones. And Camberwell opened her mouth to let her tongue protrude, pink and healthy except for an odd whitish strip that ran ragged down its centre from tip to—not exactly *tail*, Goss assumed, since the tongue was fairly huge, or so he seemed to recall. But definitely almost to the uvula, and: oh God, oh shit, was it actually splitting as he watched, bisecting itself not-so-neatly into two separate semi-points, like a child's snakey scribble?

Camberwell gave it a flourish, swallowed the resultant spit-mouthful, then said, without much affect: "Yeah, that's right—'Gallu-Alu, the Terrible Immoel, who speaks with a dead tongue....'" Camberwell fluttered the or-gan in question at what had taken control of Goss, showing its central scars long-healed, extending the smile into a wide, entirely unamused grin. "So say hey, assfuck. Remember me now?"

"You were its vessel, then, once before," Goss heard his lips reply. "And...yes, yes, I do recall it. Apologies, huntress; I cannot say, with the best will in all this world, that any of you look so very different, to me."

Camberwell snapped her fingers. "Aw, gee." To 'Lij, sharper: "I tell you to stop cutting?"

Goss felt "his" eyes slide to poor 'Lij, caught and wavering (his face a sickly grey-green, chest heaving slightly, like he didn't know whether to run or puke), then watched him shake his head, and bow back down to it. The knife went in shallow, blunter than the job called for—he had to drag it, hooking up underneath his own hide, to make the meat part as cleanly as the job required, while Camberwell kept a sure and steady watch on the other well-riders, all of whom were beginning to look equally disturbed, even those who were supposedly unconscious. Goss felt his own lips curve, far more genuinely amused, even as an alien emotion-tangle wound itself invasively throughout his chest: half proprietorially expectant, half vaguely annoyed. And—

"We are coming," he heard himself say. "All of us. Meaning you may have miscalculated, somewhat...what a sad state of affairs indeed, when the prospective welfare of your entire species depends on you not doing so."

That same interior ripple ran 'round the well's perimeter as 'Lij pulled the knife past "his" sigil's final slashing loop and yanked it free, splattering the frieze in front of him; in response, the very stones seemed to arch hungrily, that composite mouth gaping, eager for blood. Above, even through the heavy-pressing rubble mound which must be all that was left of the temple proper, Goss could hear Journee-Zemyel swooping and cawing in the updraft, swirled on endless waves of storm; from his eye's corner he saw Hynde-whoever (*Arralu-Allatu, the Terrible Ashreel,* Eshphoriel supplied, helpfully) open one similarly particoloured eye and lever himself up, clumsy-clambering to his feet. Katz's head fell back, spine suddenly hooping so heels struck shoulder blades with a wetly awful crack, and began to lift off, levitating gently, turning in the air like some horrible ornament. Meanwhile, Lao continued to grind her fisted knuckles into both eyes at once, bruising lids but hopefully held back from pulping the balls themselves, at least so long as her sockets held fast....

(Ekimmu, the Terrible Coaib, who seeds without regard. Lamyatu, the Terrible Ushephekad, who opens the ground beneath us.)

From the well, dusty mortar popped forth between every suture, and the thing as a whole gave one great shrug, shivering itself apart—began caving in and expanding at the same time, becoming a nothing-column for its parts to revolve around, an incipient reality fabric tear. And in turn, the urge to rotate likewise—just let go of gravity's pull, throw physical law to the winds, and see where that might lead—cored through Goss ass to cranium, Vlad Tepes–style, a phantom impalement pole spearing every neural pathway. Simultaneously gone limp *and* stiff, he didn't have to look down to know his crotch must be darkening, or over to 'Lij to confirm how the same invisible angel-driven marionette hooks were now pulling at *his* muscles, making his knife-hand grip and flex, sharp enough the handle almost broke free of his sweaty palm entirely—

(Namtaru, the Terrible Yphemaal, who stitches what was rent asunder.)

"**And now we *are* Seven, without a doubt,**" Goss heard that voice in his throat note, its disappointment audible. "**For all your bravado, perhaps you are not as well-educated as you believe.**"

Camberwell shrugged yet one more time, slow but distinct; her possessed eye widened slightly, as though in surprise. And in that instant, it occurred to Goss how much of herself she still retained, even in the Immoel-thing's grip, which seemed far—slipperier, in her case, than with everybody else. Because maybe coming pre-Inscribed built up a certain pad of scar tissue in the soul, in situations like these; maybe that's what she'd been gambling on, amongst other things. Having just enough slack on her lead to allow her to do stuff like (for example) reach down into her other boot, the way she was even as they "spoke," and—

Holy crap, just how many knives does this chick walk around with, exactly?

—bring up the second of a matched pair, trigger already thumbed, blade halfway from its socket. Tucking it beneath her jaw, point tapping at her jugular, and saying, as she did—

"Never claimed to be, but I do know *this* much: Sam Raimi got it wrong. You guys don't like wearing nothin' *dead*."

And: *That's your plan?* Goss wanted to yell, right in the face of her martyr-stupid, *fuck all y'all* snarl. Except that that was when the thing inside 'Lij (Yphemaal, its name is Yphemaal) turned him, bodily—two great twitches, a child "walking" a doll. Its purple eyes fell on Camberwell in mid-move, and narrowed; Goss heard something rush up and out in every direction, rustle-ruffling as it went: some massive and indistinct pair of wings, mostly elsewhere, only a few pinions intruding to lash the blade from Camberwell's throat before the cut could complete itself, leaving a shallow red trail in its wake....

(Another "hunting" trophy, Goss guessed, eventually. Not that she'd probably notice.)

"**No**," 'Lij-Yphemaal told the room at large, all its hovering sibling-selves, in a voice colder than orbit-bound satellite skin. "**Enough**."

"**We are Seven**," Eshphoriel Maskim replied, with Goss's flayed mouth. "**The huntress has the right of it: remove one vessel, break the quorum, before we reassemble. If she wants to sacrifice herself, who are we to interfere?**"

"**Who *were* we to, ever, every time we have? But there is another way.**"

The sigils flowed each to each, Goss recalled having noticed at this freak show's outset, albeit only subconsciously—one basic design exponentially added upon, a fresh new (literal) twist summoning Two out of One, Three out of Two, Four out of Three, etcetera. Which left Immoel and Yphemaal separated by both a pair of places and a triad of contortionate squiggle-slashes; far more work to imitate than 'Lij could possibly do under pressure with his semi-blunt knife, his wholly inadequate human hands and brain....

But Yphemaal wasn't 'Lij. Hell, this very second, *'Lij* wasn't even 'Lij.

The Mender-angel was at least merciful enough to let him scream as it remade its sigil into Immoel's with three quick cuts, then slipped forth, blowing away up through the well's centre spoke like a backwards lightning rod. Two niches on, Katz lit back to earth with a cartilaginous creak, while Lao let go just in time to avoid tearing her own corneas; Hynde's head whipped up, face gone trauma-slack but finally recognizable, abruptly vacated. And Immoel Maskim spurted forth from Camberwell in a gross black cloud from mouth, nose, the corner of the eyes, its passage dimming her yellow-green eye back to brown, then buzzed angrily back and forth between two equally useless prospective vessels until seeming to give up in disgust.

Seemed even angels couldn't be in two places at once. Who knew?

Not inside time and space, no. And unfortunately—

That's where we *live*, Goss realized.

Yes.

Goss saw the bulk of the Immoel-stuff blend into the well room's wall, sucked away like blotted ink. Then fell to his knees, as though prompted, only to see the well collapse in upon its own shaft, ruined forever—its final cosmic strut removed, solved away like some video game's culminative challenge.

Beneath, the ground shook, like jelly. Above, a thunderclap whoosh sucked all the dust away, darkness boiling up, peeling itself away like an onion 'til only the sun remained, pale and high and bright. And straight through the hole in the "roof" dropped all that was left of Journee-turned-Zemyel—facedown, from a twenty-plus-foot height, horrible thunk of impact driving her features right back into her skull, leaving nothing behind but a smashed-flat, raw meat mask.

Goss watched those wing-lungs of hers deflate, thinking: *She couldn't've survived.* And felt Eshphoriel, still lingering clawed to his brain's pathways even in the face of utter defeat, interiorly agree that: *It does seem unlikely. But then, my sister loves to leave no toy unbroken, if only to spit in your—and our—Maker's absent eye.*

Uh-huh, Goss thought back, suddenly far too tired for fear, or even sorrow. *So maybe it's time to get the fuck out too, huh, while the going's good? "Minish" yourself, like the old chant goes....*

Perhaps, yes. For now.

He looked to Camberwell, who stood there shaking slightly, caught off guard for once—amazed to be alive, it was fairly obvious, part-cut throat and all. Asking 'Lij, as she dabbed at the blood: "What did you *do*, dude?"

To which 'Lij only shook his head, equally freaked. "I...yeah, dunno, really. I don't—even think that was *me*."

"No, 'course not: Yphemaal, right? Who sews crooked seams straight...." She shook her head, cracked her neck back and forth. "Only one of 'em still *building* stuff, these days, instead of tearing down or undermining, so maybe it's the only one of 'em who really *doesn't* want to go back, 'cause it knows what'll happen next."

"Maaaaybe," 'Lij said, dubious—then grabbed his wound, like something'd just reminded him it was there. "Oh, *shit*, that hurts!"

"You'll be fine, ya big baby—magic shit heals fast, like you wouldn't believe. Makes for a great conversation piece, too."

"Okay, sure. Hey…I saved your life."

Camberwell snorted. "Yeah, well—I would've saved yours, you hadn't beat me to it. Which makes us even."

'Lij opened his mouth at that, perhaps to object, but was interrupted by Hynde, his voice creaky with disuse. Demanding, of Goss directly—

"Hey, Arthur, what…the hell *happened* here? Last thing I remember was doing pick-ups, outside, and then—" His eyes fell on Journee, widening. "—*then* I, oh Christ, is that—who *is* that?"

Goss sighed, equally hoarse. "Long story."

By the time he was done, they were all outside—even poor Journee, who 'Lij had badgered Katz and Lao into helping roll up in a tarp, stowing her for transport in the back of the one blessedly still-operative truck Camberwell'd managed to excavate from the missile strike's wreckage. Better yet, it ensued that 'Lij's back-up sat-phone was now once again functional; once contacted, the production office informed them that border skirmishes had definitely spilled over into undeclared war, thus necessitating a quick retreat to the airstrip they'd rented near Karima town. Camberwell reckoned they could make it if they started now, though the last mile or so might be mainly on fumes.

"Better saddle up," she told Goss, briskly, as she brushed past, headed for the truck's cab. Adding, to a visibly gobsmacked Hynde: "Yo, Professor: you gonna be okay? 'Cause the fact is, we kinda can't stop to let you process."

Hynde shook his head, wincing; one hand went to his chest, probably just as raw as Goss's mouth-roof. "No, I'll…be okay. Eventually."

"Mmm. Won't we all."

Lao opened the truck's back door and beckoned, face wan—all cried out, at least for the nonce. Prayed too, probably.

Goss clambered in first, offering his hand. "Did we at least get enough footage to make a show?" Hynde had the insufferable balls to ask him, taking it.

"Just get in the fucking truck, Lyman."

Weeks after, Goss came awake with a full-body slam, tangled in his sleeping bag and coated with cold sweat, as though having just been ejected from his dreams like a cannonball. They were in the Falklands by then, investigating a weird earthwork discovered in and amongst the 1982 war's detritus—it wound like a harrow, a potential subterranean grinding room for squishy human corn, but thankfully, nothing they'd discovered inside seemed (thus far) to indicate any sort of connection to the Seven, either directly or metaphorically.

In the interim since the Sudan, Katz had quit, for which Goss could hardly blame him—but Camberwell was still with them, which didn't make either Goss or Hynde exactly comfortable, though neither felt like calling her on it. When pressed, she'd admitted to 'Lij that her hunting "methods" involved a fair deal of intuition-surfing, moving hither and yon at the call of her own angel voice–tainted subconscious, letting her post-Immoelization hangover do the psychic driving. Which did all seem to imply they were stuck with her, at least until the tides told her to move elsewhere....

She is a woman of fate, your huntress, the still, small voice of Eshphoriel Maskim told him, in the darkness of his tent. *Thus, where we go, she follows—and vice versa.*

Goss took a breath, tasting his own fear-stink. *Are you here for me?* he made himself wonder, though the possible answer terrified him even more.

Oh, I am not here at all, meat-sack. I suppose I am...bored, you might say, and find you a welcome distraction. For there is so much misery everywhere here, in this world of yours, and so very little I am allowed to do with it.

Having frankly no idea what to say to that, Goss simply hugged his knees and struggled to keep his breathing regular, his pulse calm and steady. His mouth prickled with gooseflesh, as though something were feeling its way around his tongue: the Whisper-angel, exploring his soul's ill-kept boundaries with unsympathetic care, from somewhere entirely Other.

I thought you were—done, is all. With me.

Did you? Yet the universe is far too complicated a place for that. And so it is that you are none of you ever so alone as you fear, nor as you hope. A pause. *Nonetheless, I am...glad to see you well, I find, or as much as I can be. Her too, for all her inconvenience.*

Here, however, Goss felt fear give way to anger, a welcome palate cleanser. Because it seemed like maybe he'd finally developed an allergy to bullshit, at least when it came to the Maskim—or this Maskim, to be exact—and their fucked-up version of what passed for a celestial-to-human pep talk.

Would've been perfectly content to let Camberwell cut her own throat, though, wouldn't you? he pointed out, shoulders rucking, hair rising like quills. *If that—brother-sister-whatever of yours hadn't made 'Lij interfere...*

Indubitably, yes. Did you expect anything else?

Yes! What kind of angels are *you, goddamnit?*

The God-damned kind, Eshphoriel Maskim replied, without a shred of irony.

You damned yourselves, is what I hear, Goss snapped back—then froze, appalled by his own hubris. But no bolt of lightning fell; the ground stayed firm, the night around him quiet, aside from lapping waves. Outside, someone turned in their sleep, moaning. And beyond it all, the earthwork's narrow descending groove stood open to the stars, ready to receive whatever might arrive, as Heaven dictated.

...there is that, too, the still, small voice admitted, so low Goss could feel more than hear it, tolling like a dim bone bell.

(But then again—what is free will for, in the end, except to let us make our own mistakes?)

Even quieter still, that last part. So much so that, in the end—no matter how long, or hard, he considered it—Goss eventually realized it was impossible to tell if it had been meant to be the angel's thought or his own.

Doesn't matter, he thought, closing his eyes. And went back to sleep.

The Last, Clean, Bright Summer

LIVIA LLEWELLYN

THIS JOURNAL BELONGS TO:

Hailie

TACOMA, JUNE 15TH

'm writing this in the car. Mom cried again this morning when we left the house. Everything was spotless and put away just like we were going on a vacation for a little while, even though we're not coming back until late fall. She'd been cleaning like crazy since last year, like literally starting on my fourteenth birthday. Dad says she's nesting, because when we come back home, it'll be with a new baby brother, and maybe a sister too. Which totally shocked me, because I didn't even know she was pregnant. There were so many things she wanted to take, but Dad wouldn't rent one of those big RVs, and everything had to fit in our crappy old VW camper instead. So she just made everything look super neat and nice. I swear, I did more laundry and dishes in the last month than in the last five years! Anyway, so we packed two suitcases and one large backpack each, and got rid of most of the food that might spoil, except for what we're taking (which is currently sitting in paper bags and boxes next to me on the back-seat, and all around my feet), and that's it. We pulled out of the driveway early this morning, before it was really light, and I turned around and watched my little yellow house disappear. Last night Dad went out into

107

the backyard with Abby, our dog, to the spot in the back where Alex was. That was the only time I cried.

And now we're on our way down the freeway to Olympia. Dad isn't taking the longer scenic way around the peninsula, but it'll still be a couple of days before we get to the town (which has almost NO Internet access, of course), so I brought this journal (even though I'm totally lazy about writing in it) and a couple books. We're going to Oceanside for a humungous family reunion—I was born there, and so was my mom. My parents moved away when I was born, but we used to go back every summer until five years ago, when my younger brother died and my mom said she couldn't do it anymore, at least for a while. I remember we stayed at a really cute cottage inland from Oceanside, a kind of suburban area called the Dunes, where my mother's aunt used to live. She would babysit us while my parents went to the parties—we were always too young to go. I remember it was all shiny wood, and Great Auntie had two huge trunks, one filled with puzzles and one filled with the most beautiful dolls. And if you stood in the road outside her driveway, you could see past the houses and scrubby trees all the way to the ocean, even though it was almost a mile away. That's how flat it is. That's why the reunion is held there, Dad says, because of the strong tides and the flat beach. Mom doesn't like to talk very much about it. I know she's never liked the reunions, but I'm kind of looking forward to it. I just hope there'll be some interesting boys in town.

ABERDEEN, JUNE 16TH

This town is super creepy, but kind of cool in that weird way. Mom says all the geometry of the architecture here is wrong, and it makes everyone depressed. I have no idea what that means. We stayed the night in a motel just off the highway, and I kept waking up to all the traffic sounds. So, after Mom and Dad were asleep for a while, I got dressed and snuck outside. We were the only ones checked in, and all the other windows were dark. I could see the highway from the balcony, all the lights of the trucks and cars. I just stood there in the dark for a while, listening to the sound of all those cars, watching the red lights stream constantly away.

And then I saw them. I don't know where they came from, but it was like all of a sudden they were just there, standing under the bright yellow parking lot lights. It was two faceless men, although I could barely tell. They were naked except for very tall black top hats, with very shimmery pale skin, all scales, I think, or maybe skin like an alligator. I was so shocked I almost peed my pants! I just stood there frozen, and my skin got all hot and cold like it does when you're so frightened you can't move. They stood there too, looking up at me. I thought about running, but Dad had said that they weren't dangerous. Just be respectful, and think of them as our summer observers, he had said. Just let them watch us, and we'll all get along just fine. And then they started walking very slowly and gracefully across the parking lot, and I don't know why I did this, but I waved, in a very slow and dignified arc. And they both waved back! I was so happy. And then they disappeared, and I stood there a while longer, watching the cars' lights twinkling and all the stars rush past me overhead. It was a pretty good night.

This morning before we left Aberdeen, we had breakfast at the restaurant downtown that we used to go to all the time when we came down here, in the old brick building near the factories Dad would visit as part of his job. We all had that awesome French toast, just like we used to, and Mom asked the cook for his secret recipe, and he said no, just like he used to. And then they got in a fight, and Mom was all like, I don't know why you won't give it to me since we're probably the last customers you'll have all summer, and he was all like, well, summer's not over yet and besides, in the fall I'm heading down to South America and taking my recipe with me, and then she was all, it's not South America anymore, you idiot, who do you think is left down there who eats French toast, and then she ran off to the bathroom. The cook grew super angry and quiet, and then my dad took him aside, probably to apologize and tell him Mom's all hormonal and everyone down in Obsidia will totally love his secret french toast.

Mom needs to chill out. She explained what's going to happen at the reunion, that we have to dance around some big-ass dying sea creature in some ancient tribal ceremony to honor our ancestors, and throw some spears into it to "defeat" it, and it's totally not going to be hard at all. It sounds stupid and completely lame.

THE DUNES, OCEANSIDE, JUNE 23RD

We're at the cottage now. It's been kind of a strange couple of days. I'm kind of bored and anxious and I don't know. I guess just it's weird to feel like you're on summer vacation when something so incredible and important is going to happen and you finally get to take part. Mom and Dad are in the town on a dinner date, and this is the first chance I've really had to myself. We got to Oceanside on the 16th. It's straight up the coast from Ocean Shores, but it's a long drive, and the highway gives out to dirt roads and logging roads after a while, and those are a bit hard to find. There were less cars, though. People up here are like us, they're relatives, part of the family, or they're company people like Dad who are cool about everything and stay out of our way. We didn't stop at Ocean Shores, even though I wanted to, but Dad said it was off limits because they'd already done their ceremony and totally fucked it up (his swear word, not mine!) and the town was a total mess. We did stop at this really awesome beach farther up the coast, just outside this huge area of abandoned quarry pits. It's hard to describe how the ocean was there. I mean, there were these waves that were so high and grey and hard, you could feel the beach quake when they crashed down, and they sounded like thunder. They would rise up in the air, and just hang there like they were alive, like they were waiting. For what, I don't know. All the sand was pure black, just like in parts of Hawaii, and we found a skeleton of some huge whale thing that was about as long as our old neighborhood road. Dad kept calling it a kraken, which was hilarious. Mom got pretty excited when she saw it, and took all kinds of pictures, and had us all pose next to the skull. I sat in the eye socket. Yeah, it was kind of neat! I was just happy to see Mom so happy. It was sunny and warm out, and there were gulls everywhere and the funniest-looking crabs.

Anyway, so we got to Oceanside in the late afternoon, when the sun was setting over the Pacific and the sky was pink and orange and red, and the air smelled all sandy and salty like brine. Dad drove down the main street and parked next to the chowder house where we'd have dinner, and we got out and stood in the middle of the road. Just like near the cottage, you'd usually be able to see all the way to the ocean—it would look like the road just kept going on through the beach and then under the waves. Except, not anymore, because of the wall. Dad's a really important architect and he helped design this, for Oceanside and for other towns all up and down the coast that are having family reunions, for whenever it's their time. Except Ocean Shores, of course, and a couple other places that didn't build a wall and got destroyed. Mom took more pictures, and then we went inside.

We got to the cottage after dark. It was exactly like I remembered it, all the nautical stuff everywhere and the flowered couch that turns into a bed. Mom got teary-eyed when she saw the trunks of toys, but she covered it up and fussed around in the kitchen with the food while Dad and I pretended not to notice. I'll admit, I got a bit sad when I saw the puzzles too. I remember Alex and me putting them together on the rickety cardboard table Great Auntie set up for us. That was the last summer before he started getting sick. It was the inoculations. All the men in our family start taking it when they're about nine, to fight some infection they're not immune to when they grow up, but sometimes they'd have allergic reactions to it, and it would do terrible things to their bodies, like it did to Alex. Dad felt so guilty, but how could he have known?

Anyway, it's been quiet. There aren't any interesting boys here at all, they're all at the wall, I guess, along with the men. I've been spending the days with my mom, and some of the other relatives and their daughters, who I guess are my cousins, reading and getting a tan in their yards. No one cool is around here. None of my cousins are interesting. One girl didn't even know who Beyoncé was! I brought my good bikini for nothing.

THE WALL, OCEANSIDE, JULY 5TH

Yesterday was the 4th, of course, and all over the Dunes there were lots of backyard parties and barbeques. I finally met a few cute boys, but they were all my cousins, of course, and they wouldn't even talk to me and were pretty rude. Of course, we all ate dinner in the afternoon, because when it got dark, everyone in the town and from the Dunes met at the wall. It was insane. We all walked down the long main road, no one was in their car, and none of us were allowed to bring our cameras or phones. Most of the lights were off except for some crazy lamps in a few store and restaurant fronts, these large circles of glass that glowed a deep green. They were so pretty and strange. I kept looking down at my skin—it looked like it was being lit from inside. All the women and the girls looked like that. All the boys and men were dressed in black suits, even though it was really hot. I mean, this is the middle of summer, after all. A lot of them didn't look very happy about it. But it's tradition, Dad says. It's part of the reunion. And another tradition is that this was the one night all the men escorted the women to the top of the wall, the only time we were allowed to be up there. Well, I'm sure the tradition started out as another night, but having it on the Fourth of July probably gave them an excuse for all the fireworks and beer.

When we got to the wall, the men escorted us single file inside, up these long narrow corridors of stairs that go to the top. It was kind of like a school fire drill in reverse. There were no lights in the stairs, and I pretty much had to climb them with my hands and feet like a dog. I have no idea who was behind me, but I'm glad they couldn't see my butt in their face. When we got to the top, there were about ten observers waiting for us like the ones I saw in the parking lot, naked and faceless with high top hats. I couldn't tell if some of them were the same ones from the parking lot. They didn't look so friendly close up. Everyone grew really quiet and still. We all stood in line around the curved edge, all the women in front so they could see over the metal railing, and the men behind them. I wanted to see the town because we were so high up, but the guy behind me grabbed me and forced me to turn back around. What an asshole.

Anyway. We all stood there for a few minutes, in the dark. If we were supposed to be looking at something, no one said. No one spoke. The beach was black, with that same sand Dad and Mom and I had found by the quarry site, but here it was smooth and completely bare. I didn't realize how high the wall was, but it's enormous, so wide that all of us—maybe close to a thousand people—can stand on it, and the beach that it circles around is huge. The waves were farther back than I remember, or at least farther back than they are by the Dunes, and they were massive. I was shocked. If they'd been any closer, they would have come right over the wall. They would rush in toward the wall like a herd of gigantic animals, like serpents made out of water and foam, and I felt everyone sort of gasp and shrink back all at once, me included, and then they'd come crashing down, dragging the sand away and leaving the beach smooth and clean.

So we watched for a few more minutes, and then the fireworks started over the town, and everyone turned to the other side of the wall and oohed and awed. It was a pretty good show. I kept turning back to the beach, though. Having my back to those waves made me a bit nervous. I bent over the railing slightly to get a better view of the beach and the bottom of the wall. I don't know how we're expected to get down there for the ceremony—I couldn't see any stairway openings, and the wall goes right into the ocean, for a really long way. Maybe we take boats around the edges? I don't know. And then the fireworks were over and everyone went back down the steps. There were some parties in town, at the bars and restaurants, but Mom and Dad went home with me instead. The neighbors down the road were having a big pool party, which seems really redundant (having a pool, that is) when you live next to the ocean, but whatever, so I knew they'd go there. Mom asked me if I had any questions about the beach, and I said no, but I was lying. I don't know, I didn't want to talk about it. Mom put her arm around me and said everything would be fine. Funny, when just three weeks ago she was the one having complete kittens about the reunion.

When we got to the edge of the Dunes, Dad tapped my shoulder and told me to look around. All along the wall, those green globe lamps had been placed. You could see this huge curve of weird green lights hovering in the air between the town and the beach, all of them flashing like little lighthouse beacons or the lights along a runway. He asked me if I thought that was cool and I said yeah, awesome, or something like that. And that's when I really started to bug out about this whole reunion thing, and felt my skin grow all hot and cold and shivery again, although I acted like I was totally chilled out and fine.

Here's the thing. When I was staring out at the ocean, when everyone else was looking at the fireworks, I saw something. I swear I saw something. Way far off in the ocean, past all the waves, it was in the moonlight, just for a second, and then it was gone. It wasn't an orca or a blue whale, I've seen those tons of times before. I swear to god I saw a gigantic hand.

THE DUNES, JULY 11TH

Nothing has been happening. I guess it'd be a great vacation, if it were a vacation, if I didn't have this constant ball of anxiety inside that makes me double over in pain every once in a while. It's really hot now, almost 85 every day. I go to the neighbor's house most days, and lay on a blanket by the pool listening to my iPod or reading. I've got a great tan. Mom goes with me and gossips with the other women, or sometimes we'll go into Oceanside and just walk around, shopping for trinkets or clothes at the little stores, buying magazines, eating lunch at the one café. When we're outside, walking down the narrow sidewalks, I'll try so hard not to, but I always look up at the wall. I can't help it. The lights are still flashing, day and night, and sometimes there's a huge booming sound and the ground shakes a little, like the waves are reaching the wall and trying to knock it down. Most of the men from the town and the Dunes are up there, and a lot of observers, too. Dad spends every day there. He doesn't talk about it, and I am so relieved that he doesn't. We'll have dinner—Mom's teaching me how to cook, I made spaghetti last night!—and then we'll watch TV if the reception is good, or play board games, or go over to a relative's house and hang out. No one talks about the wall. Sometimes I'll look up and catch a bunch of Mom and Dad's friends or relatives looking at me, and they'll stop talking and look away. They do this with all the girls. Super creepy.

Last night I snuck outside and tried to take a picture of the lights, but something's wrong with my phone, it doesn't work at all. I think it's broken. This summer blows.

THE DUNES, JULY 23RD

I'm so tired, but I can't get to sleep. Dad just left. It's about midnight, and maybe about an hour ago, some men knocked on the door, and Dad spoke with them for a few minutes, and then he changed into his black suit and left. He told us it's almost time, and to get a good night's sleep, and early tomorrow morning the men would come for us and the ceremony would begin. I kind of freaked out a little, but Mom calmed me down, then she poured us both a small glass of wine—my first ever!—and she got all teary-eyed again and gave a little speech about how everything was going to change and tomorrow I was going to become a woman (GOD! so embarrassing) and how she was so proud of me and that she knew that no matter what happened, someday I'd be a wonderful mom. The wine tasted terrible, I thought wine was supposed to taste like fruit, but she made me drink the whole glass. I feel a little gross now, kind of floppy and fuzzy. I keep thinking about Alex. I think about his skeleton, under our backyard, all twisted and spiraled and decayed. And Abby, my big-eyed pug, her little skull filled with worms and dirt.

Why do all the men wear top hats?

Why do I hear horns?

The Dunes, August 29th

Wow. I lost a month.

The cast has been off my arm for a couple of days now, and even though the fingers are a bit stiff, I can finally write again without bursting into tears. When I say that, I mean I can write without my fingers hurting, and I can write about what happened without tears rolling down my face, without dropping my pen to the floor, staring off into space, at the wall, through the window, staring anywhere except my journal, where I have to remember what happened and put it into words. Which I guess we're not supposed to do—that is, the women aren't supposed to do this, make records of anything. But I think I should, for reasons I won't go into just right now. I just think it's important to remember, to have a record of my own. Mom and Dad have gone into town for the afternoon to check on my new sisters, so I'm all alone.

So this is what happened.

THE BEACH, July 24th

I don't remember falling asleep. It was the wine, Mom explained later. The men put a little something in it to help us sleep. It just makes it easier for everyone.

I woke up in a cage, naked. My head was against Mom's thigh, and she was stroking my hair like she used to when I was a little girl. The cage was iron or steel, and it was covered with thick canvas and fastened underneath the bottom, so you couldn't lift it or see outside no matter which way you looked. I could smell the salt of the ocean, and hear the rumble of waves. I knew we were outside, right on the beach, but it sounded far away, like at low tide in the morning. I felt really disoriented, I sat up and tried to ask Mom what was happening, but she shushed me. She was naked, too. I was so embarrassed, I wanted to die. Then she whispered to keep quiet, and just do everything she and the other women did. She said if we got separated and I got confused or afraid, my instincts would tell me what to do.

The canvas rose up—and the smell hit us, not just of the ocean but the low-tide stench of something leviathan and dying. I heard a couple girls vomit. The wall was on one side of our cages, and the beach on the other. It was early morning, so early that the sand and water and sky looked all the same color, sort of a flat dark blue. Something was on the beach, white and malformed. I guess I thought it was a whale at first—what else could be that big? And then I realized it was an ocean liner—no whale could be that huge. Mom pushed at the cage, and one side swung open. All around us, against the curve of the wall, cages were opening, and women and their daughters were stepping out onto the sands, maybe five hundred of us in all. We were all barefoot, and all naked and shivering in the cool air. I squinted and turned my head, and that's when I realized. It was so large, I hadn't recognized it at first. But then, yes. I'd seen it before.

It was a woman. A woman so massive I couldn't see the ends of her legs. They were still in the water, the waves lapping at her knees. Her arm was stretched out, fingertips almost touching the row of cages. That was the hand I knew I'd seen at the ocean's edge that night, pale and grasping in the distant moonlight. We started to walk down the beach toward her face, some of us running. Long blue-green hair like seaweed, spread across the black beach. She lay on her back, face to the side, saucer-wide eyes open. She didn't look like some hideous fish creature. She looked like any of us. She looked like me. I could feel the heat of her breath. She was beached but alive, barely. And her stomach! It rose up like Mount Rainier, white and round and full.

She's pregnant, I whispered to Mom, and she nodded. *Are we supposed to dance around her?* I asked.

Not quite. We have to help her give birth, she replied. *But before that, we need to be brave. There's something very difficult we need to do.*

An object slid off the woman's belly and dropped onto the sands. I almost didn't see it at first, it was the same color as her mottled flesh. It rose up from the sand, and everyone jumped back a bit. Another object slid down her belly, and one more slithered out from under her breast. All across her body, I could see movement, hundreds of ripples breaking free. Mom grabbed my arm, hard, so I couldn't run. All around me, the women were whispering to the girls, holding their arms.

Don't fight them, Mom whispered. *And don't run. Just let them do what they need to do.*

What are they? I asked.

I don't know. Maybe the men know. They ride her body up to the surface of the ocean, and now they're waiting for her babies to be born.

Babies? I asked.

She has eggs, hundreds of female eggs, and when they hatch, they'll be waiting for the girls.

To eat them? I said.

No, Mom said. *To spawn.*

From beside me, a high-pitched scream. I saw a girl break free and start to run, and then we all screamed, the thin sounds bouncing back and forth across the wall. I punched my mother in the stomach and pushed her away. We all ran, we ran as fast as we could across the soft slow sands back to the cages and it didn't make any difference, none of us were fast enough and none of us were strong and something grabbed my hair and flipped me up high in the air like one of my auntie's dolls. I came down flat on my back, and it was on me in a flash, soft squishy skin and sucking mouth and the smell. And it was hammering into me, with its huge hard lumpy thing that hurt so much I cried and threw up, and it licked my face and stuck its flappy tongue in my mouth and I threw up some more and choked and it just wouldn't stop pounding against me and I felt my right wrist snap under its grip, and the sudden pain made everything bright and calm and clear. I lay still, and the creature fucked me over and over and I looked up at the iron sky and waited for the sun to break over the wall.

And after a while it stopped, and rolled off me, shuddering and flopping like a giant fish. I lay on the sands with my legs open, mouth open, watching it die. All around me, girls and women were fighting and screaming, the grunts and groans filling the air, the smell of rancid water and vomit and semen and chum. Everyone sobbed. I sat up, slowly. Every muscle in my body hurt, every bone felt broken or bruised. Already half of the creatures were dying or dead. Some were fighting viciously over girls, tearing off each other's limbs with thick claws and lantern-jawed teeth. I didn't know where my mother was, but I didn't want to look. Next to me, a girl lay half buried in the sand. I recognized her from the Dunes. Her head was caved in, the dead creature's thing still resting in the broken nest of teeth spilling out of her mouth.

I would have thrown up again, but I was completely empty inside.

Behind me, the cages started to clatter. I turned around, keeping my head low. Large knives were falling onto the tops of the cages, some of them bouncing onto the sands. Long sharp butcher knives and machetes. Nets followed, huge fishing nets slithering down like punctured balloons. I stared up at the wall. In the growing light, I could see some of the men hurling the knives down the long curve of stone. The rest of them stood at the railing, writing notes in books, talking to the observers, staring down at us through telescopes and binoculars. And then I saw. Most of the men had their penises out. They were masturbating. They were watching us, watching their wives and their daughters scream and break apart and die on the beach just like that giantess, and they were masturbating through the metal rails as if it were the most exciting thing in the world.

I felt a hand on my foot, and I whipped my leg back, swallowing my scream. My mother, crawling past me. *Grab a knife and a net*, she said. *We have to harvest the eggs.* I watched her move past me, blood on her broken nose, blood trickling between her legs. *My arm is broken*, I said. *Then use your other arm.* She threw a machete at me, and it landed against my legs, slicing open my skin. I glared at her, but she just walked past. I followed her, limping, tears running down my face. *That's for the punch in the stomach*, she finally said.

When does the dancing start? I said.

Don't start that shit with me, she replied. She didn't look back, only kept walking toward the giantess. The other older women were limping and crawling to the cages, grabbing knives, helping the younger girls get up, heading down to the large stomach. Some of them were walking around, sticking their knives into the creatures that weren't quite dead. Some of them stuck them into the girls.

My mother walked down to the woman's neck. Her breath was so shallow now, she was almost gone. She wasn't moving at all. I stopped in front of her eyes. I'd never seen such large eyes in my life, and the colors—I can't describe them. Like no colors on earth, and the colors moved and shifted like strands of jewels dancing in starry waters. I think she saw me. I'll never know. She gave a shudder, and one long sigh, and then I could tell she wasn't staring at me or anything else on the beach anymore.

Come on. My mother, standing in a river of blood, her machete and half her body red and wet. *You killed her*, I said.

She was dying anyway. She comes here to give birth on the beach and die, that's what her kind does.

And she gives birth to us? That's how we were born?

Mom nodded. *That's right. We don't give birth to girls. We're not allowed. And this thing*, she pointed to the body, *only gives birth to females. So, I got you here, and my mother got me here, when we came out of the ocean in someone like this, many years ago.*

But Dad said we'd be coming back with a boy, remember? That you were going to have a boy.

Mom pointed to one of the creatures. *That's what he does. That's what he's good for, every time. Next year, we're both giving birth, and we can keep them if they're boys.*

In the distance, the women let out a shout. They had split open the stomach with their machetes, and masses of blood and placenta were spilling across the beach. Inside the thick gore, round objects, no larger than beach balls, rolled and spun.

But Mommy. I was starting to cry. I didn't understand what she was saying, what she meant. I placed my broken hand against my stomach. *I'm pregnant? What happens if I'm pregnant with a girl? What happens to the girl babies if we're only allowed to have boys?* And Mom let out this long sigh like I was just SO stupid, and gave me a funny, tight grin, and said, *What makes you think your brother and your dog are the only bodies buried in the backyard?* And she walked away from me toward the eggs, dragging her empty net.

I walked back up to the woman's outstretched hand, and stood there for the longest time, my five small fingertips against the massive whorls of her rough skin, thinking about all the smooth flat rocks I sat on and skipped across in our backyard, and all the times when I was really little and Mom wore those pretty loose-fitting dresses and how instead of hugging her, she would only let me hold her hand. And then the sun broke through the grey clouds, and it was really low in the sky, and everything just lit up so lovely and bright, all the black sand and the steaming red mounds of organs and the white hills of flesh everywhere and the woman's beautiful dimming eyes. Wide rivers of shit and afterbirth and viscera, blossoming into dark clouds as they slid under the waters. And those eggs being packed into the nets and dragged up to the empty cages, those gross pink sacs that we, that I, were stealing out of the dead giantess, that a bunch of strangers would be mothers to for the rest of their lives. Just like all the women on the beach. Just like me. And all the seawater and semen running down my purpling legs, and now the walls opened up and men in hazmat suits came out with giant axes and bone saws and ran toward the body, and wet shards of the dead giantess spurted into the bright morning sky and the seagulls went joyfully insane.

And I looked up at the sunlit wall, all those black-suited men and boys staring and talking about the other women and me, still making their little observations and notes, still with their cocks in their hands, laughing and staring down. And this was the beach I was born on, the beautiful beach of my childhood, and everywhere I looked, there was nothing but grime and foam and ugliness and death.

And that was the end of summer.

THE DUNES, AUGUST 29TH

Anyway. Yeah, so. Family reunion.

I don't know what happened to all the parts of the giantess's body. More men came, and carted everything away, and then they worked nonstop on dismantling the wall. It'll be shipped off to some other town that needs it next. We'll be driving back to Tacoma in a couple of days. And then school starts, which is just so weird to think about that I can't even. Funny, though, how all the boys I could never find all summer long or who were never interested have suddenly shown up, hanging around the cottages of me and the other girls, totally paying attention, totally competing for us, making sure we don't forget them when we're gone. Even the man who pretends to be my father looks at me strange when the woman who calls herself my mother isn't around, although I stare him down so hard he knows he'd never fucking dare. I don't know, now that everyone knows I'm pregnant, maybe they think I'll be a good wife, a good mom to what they hope will be their son. Yeah, everyone wants a good catch. Or maybe they're just pretending. Maybe they're keeping track of me like they were on the wall. Maybe they're afraid of what I'll do to them if their backs are turned, what I'll do to them like the wave of a hard ocean storm.

Someday.

The Totals

ADAM-TROY CASTRO

Clutch has killed somebody recently.

This goes without saying.

For as long as Clutch can remember, he has always killed somebody "recently." If not within the last few hours, then certainly within the last few days. He may have gone as long as a couple of weeks without, from time to time, when circumstances conspired against him. But never as long as a month, no, not for living memory.

Of course, Clutch has never had much of a memory. All the events of his violent life pass before him like dream images, fading into the past almost as soon as the screams people make at the sight of him are reduced by his misshapen hands to gurgled death rattles, fading to silence. He has never had any real sense of time, and almost no understanding beyond the direction of his next step, the scent of the next living thing he must throttle. But in that part of his mind that works, he still knows that his last kill was not long ago. His hands are still sticky with blood and his nostrils still tangy with the smell of voiding bowels and his general simmering rage is mostly sated, so it just stands to reason, that's all.

He has no immediate needs of that sort to satisfy.

Life, or whatever it is he has, is good.

But he is hungry.

It is a cold night beneath pinprick stars and he has emerged from a cross-country hike through a stand of pines to a two-lane road that looks like every other strip of featureless blacktop he has ever wandered.

The unusual sense that he has been here before leaves him unsurprised when he recognizes the sight up ahead, a low silver building hemorrhaging electric light into the surrounding darkness; he feels that he has returned to some place he knows. When he steps off the road and onto gravel, his disfigured expression resolves into something that could almost be called a smile.

Clutch lurches through the double doors, and into the vestibule with the gumball dispensers and the cardboard display with slots where quarters can be inserted for a charity benefiting a sad-eyed child on crutches. It seems strange but right for the door on the other side of the vestibule, leading to the diner interior, to be scaled to his dimensions: a novelty, he's always possessed an awkward shape and monstrous bulk that makes breaking down doors somewhat more natural than opening them. He's also oddly gratified that the dining room he finds past that inner door is also scaled for him, with booths he could actually fit into if he wanted, and stools that seem just the right size to sit on, and not crush.

It's not a busy night. Two of the booths and one of the stools are occupied by creatures that make no sense to him, things that are as alien to him as he has long been to the world. One is mostly scales and teeth; the other is mostly slime and structures that would remind a human being of hypodermic needles. They pay him no mind and Clutch grants them the same courtesy.

The man behind the counter is just as odd, in that he does seem to be a man but unlike most men is tall enough to look Clutch in the eye. That is unheard of in a world where the tallest men only stand as tall as Clutch's ribs, but this place's defiance of the way things usually are seems universal, and so it is no surprise when the steaming mug that man sets on the counter before him is also sized for him, complete with a handle capable of accommodating his massive fingers.

Clutch takes a sip. It is not coffee. He has never had coffee, as far as he remembers, but he knows this is not coffee. It is not blood, either—that, he has had—but it is alive, not just the product of life. It swirls of its own volition, and seems to protest being consumed. It is good.

The counter man says, "Want the usual?"

Clutch has no idea what his usual is but decides it's good to have one.

He sips some more, feeling a rare peace coming over him, the peace that comes with belonging, even if only for the duration of a rare meal consumed in a welcoming place. To be sure, the stool proves awkward. He has never been quite symmetrical, and even when he adjusts himself his left arm rests easily on the counter while the right dangles almost all the way to the checkerboard-pattern floor. He is aware of how unclean he is, how stained he has become with blood and other things. When he shifts his left arm away from his cup, the countertop is left covered with a viscous rainbow sheen. The counter man, fussing with other things, does not seem to mind, and that, too, brings a sense of unfamiliar peace.

The vestibule door opens, admitting a new patron with a gray profile and grayer suit, who would be easy to mistake for what the world sees as normal until after he hangs up his coat, revealing that at least half of him is a jagged landscape of ribs that protrude from his flesh like daggers. Impaled on a number of those ribs like pinned butterflies, the severed heads of recently murdered human beings dangle ribbons of ragged flesh still fresh enough to drip. Though their skulls are pierced in places that compromise whatever gray matter still exists inside, their eyes still roll, their lips still grimace, and their mouths still struggle to scream.

Clutch, who for as long as he can remember has never understood the concept of names and came up with his own only because it's what he remembers doing most, stirs as he realizes that he knows what this newcomer calls himself: a name that is also a reflection of his favorite activity.

Pierce takes the next stool over and accepts a mug from the proprietor. "Man. I've been looking forward to this."

Clutch moans incoherently.

"Yeah, I know what you mean. It's good work, but there's a sameness to it after a while. I keep wishing I could take a break from it, get away from the grind, see a place for longer than it takes to do a proper cull. Not that I'd want to be on the other side, but you know how it is."

Clutch, who doesn't know how anything is, *raaars*, trailing off into a whine when he recognizes that rarest of all sensations for him: empathy.

Pierce sips from his mug, then lights a cig and blows out smoke, though the smoke emerges from his lips before he puts the filter to his mouth. "Hey, Mack!"

The counter man returns from the grill, slinging a rag over his shoulder. "What?"

"Wanna hear a great one I heard on the road?"

The counter man winces. "Not if it's bad as the last one."

"No, no, this one's good. I need you, anyway, because my pal here's never been all that talented at jokes that required audience participation."

"Okay," the counter man says. "Shoot."

"Knock, Knock."

The counter man replies in a cynical monotone. "Who's th—ohmigod ohmigod no no no, what is that thing, somebody help me, help!!!!!"

"Damn," Pierce says. "You know it already."

"Known it forever," the counter man says, without heat. "That chestnut's older than Cthulhu's childhood nanny. Want me to heat that up for you?"

"Not necessary," says Pierce, dipping an index finger into his mug, bringing it to a boil.

The counter man returns with Clutch's usual. It's alive, though terrible things have been done to it to make that a very unhappy and unfortunate condition. The gaze the meal directs at the being about to dine is not afraid, but eager—finding the only form of hope available to it in the promise of its own imminent extinction. Clutch snarls at it and rips off a chunk of meat, the wrong chunk to give the meal what it wants.

Its cries are too faint to inhibit conversation, which allows Pierce, stirring his beverage, to move on: "Anyway, it just gets to be a bit much, that's all. I did a school bus, a few days ago. Not kids. You know that's where I draw the line. I never do kids. I don't judge the guys who do, but hell, we all have our preferences. The bus is carrying twenty-three septuagenarian church ladies on their way back from some outing or another, singing hymns as they head home in the dark. I get them broken down on some old country road, and circle them for eight hours, tearing down trees and sticking to the shadows, so they only get fleeting glimpses of what's come for them. I kept chanting that they'd be dead by dawn. They were, of course, but you wouldn't believe how much of that I had to go through before one of them finally came out and waved her Bible in my face, which was of course the dramatic first kill I wanted. *Hours*, man. Just to get corpse one. *Hours*." He shakes his head, and sips from his cup, washing down the burning cigarette. "In my day, people used to have the courage of their convictions."

One of the creatures in the booths, the one Clutch noticed before, whose maw is studded with shapes like hypodermic needles, feels encouraged to speak up. "Oi know what you mean. Oi went after this one nutter living in a garret, should have been a straight go from me going *ooga-booga* to his mind shattering like a dropped glass. It looked real promising at first; he had the walls covered wif newspaper clippings, and old books wif sketches that didn't even come close to capturing what Oi really look like. You know what the mugger did when Oi came in through the crack in the wall? Took out his bloody iPhone, he did, to get a picture of me for his Facebook friends. Oi was gobsmacked. 'Course, Oi ate his brains anyway, but it wasn't exactly the most filling meal Oi ever had."

Pierce commiserates. "It's like you can't take two steps anymore without tripping over an asshole."

The door opens again, admitting more patrons. One is a transparent, man-sized pillar of smoke, churning like an oncoming storm. The other is a creature made out of shiny black tar, who appears to have made a hobby of rolling about in broken glass. More follow. There are beings with flesh that flows like filthy water, beings who appear to be two mismatched halves sewn together by untalented craftsmen, beings who reek of ruptured bowel, and beings who could almost be men, but for the obsidian jewels that shine from the places where men would have eyes. They laugh and say hello to one another and swap tales of children they snatched into the empty dark spaces beneath beds, of the unlucky wanderers they found venturing down the wrong alleys, of reaching up through shifting sands to pull uncomprehending men into the earth.

Clutch, who does not seem to possess the same gift of speech that these others trade with such casual abandon, understands only that these beings are old acquaintances, who remember him even if his memory of them is an elusive presence just beyond his grasp. He feels warm among them, happy in a way he has never been happy unless something alive was turning to something dead in his hands.

It is only when the diner is full and every seat is taken and every obscene thing has been served its favorite obscene food that the door opens again and a diminutive man walks in. Clutch, who's been playing with his food for a while—much to his food's intense displeasure—believes at first that this must be just some unlucky traveler, drawn by more conventional hungers to wander unaware into this place populated by creatures designed to make him scream his last breaths. But instead of pouncing on him from all sides and ripping his limbs off, the diners just murmur and wait.

The little man says, "Good evening, all."

The creatures at their tables all chime out a cordial good evening, Clutch speaking up half a beat after the others, because he's late in realizing that this is what he is supposed to do.

This is actually a man of average size, who is merely dwarfed by the fittings of this particular diner; if he stayed to eat, he would likely need a child's booster seat. But even adjusted for scale, he gives the impression of insignificance. He has a fussy pencil-thin mustache and wears big round glasses that magnify his eyes into moist blobs. Every occupant of the diner is focused on the object he holds, a clipboard.

"As always," he says, "I don't want to cut into your down time, so I'll cover the bullet points quickly. First, the quarterly figures. We've have a slight dip over our last period, and that's unfortunate, but the head office says we can mostly attribute that to the cold weather. Frankly, I think that's bullshit. I think those of you assigned to the warmer states should be doing a little more to carry the slack, and those of you in the less temperate areas really need to start exploiting ski resorts, ice skating rinks, and the like for the special opportunities they provide. I mean, it's not like these people *never* go outside. Their roads get plowed, their jobs still expect them behind their desks on time. There's any number of things you could be doing, if you put a little more thought into it. Otherwise, it's impossible to look at the figures and not know that some of you must be slacking."

He adjusts his Coke-bottle eyeglasses.

"That said, a number of you remain solid producers and have banged out truly superlative totals."

A quick look at his clipboard.

"The winners of our mortality contest for the months of December, January, and February are as follows. Third-highest victim count goes to... ah, forgive me, this is always so hard to pronounce...N'loghthl Impo'teb... Teb?"

"Tep," says an unhappy creature whose facial tentacles dangle into his soup.

"Yes, you. N'loghthl. Pretty good figures for a guy with the Vermont territory. As promised, you win a framed certificate of excellence from the head office and five thousand points toward our incentive program. Congratulations, N'loghthl."

The polite scattered applause does not touch the creature with the damp tentacles, who instead seethes and mutters, "Whatever."

"Come on, Loggy: you know it's an achievement just to come so close. You just need a little more edge, that's all. Second place, and I've got to stress that this was very, very close—less than five removed from the rep who won the top slot, so close that we were tempted to declare it a tie, but you just don't go changing your rules at the last minute, do you? Winner of our second prize, the set of steak knives, the rep *who's won second prize four quarters in a row*—"

"Dammit!" cries a gravelly voice from the back.

"—and really is closing on that top slot so quickly that our number-one guy is really gonna have to watch out, let's hear it for Mister Thumbs!"

This time the applause surrounds a figure with a head that narrows to a pin and a pair of arms that, displayed for all to see when he waves them all to silence, end in serrated bony spurs. He is the one who cried out, and he isn't happy with his position on the winner's roster, either. Even as the ovation starts to die down, he cries an aghast, "What use do I have for another set of steak knives?" that leaves his peers roaring and pounding their tables in hilarious appreciation.

"Don't worry about it," says the man with the clipboard. "You can trade them in for their equivalent value in incentive points. Just come to me after the dinner, and I'll take care of it." He flips the top sheet of paper. "Anyway, so that brings us to our number-one producer, and I've really got to say here, fellas, that the rest of you can honestly do worse than taking a close look at this guy and learning how he does it. He doesn't complain about his territory. He doesn't make excuses about management playing favorites. He doesn't ask for special favors or try to wangle any special treatment from the main office. He just puts his nose to the grindstone and, well, *does it*, plugging away like the professional he is.

"Winner of the big prize everyone here wants, the master of disaster, the lean green killing machine, the big kahuna himself, our perennial hero—"

And everybody chants the name at once, at a volume that rattles the metal walls, that shakes the Formica tables, that makes the dishes in their racks crack from the violence of the sympathetic vibration:

"Clutch! Clutch! Clutch! CLUTCH!"

Clutch needs several seconds to remember that this is his name, and to realize this means that they must be cheering him. The epiphany un-mans—or un-whatever-he-isses—him. He bows his craggy knob of a head and lets the adulation wash over him like heavy surf. Then a little tickle builds inside his chest, and he feels it move up his windpipe to his throat and then to the lumpy thing he has for a tongue, and he discovers for the first time that it is actually a question, the first sentence he has uttered in a full night of listening to his peers speak. In a voice like a rusty hinge, producing words that escape one at a time with long pauses between them, he begs, "What...do...I...win?"

"What you always win," the man with the clipboard says. "What everybody here wants: Oblivion."

For a moment Clutch has absolutely no idea what the man with the clipboard is talking about. But as he gropes for an explanation, other things come to him: the particular look on the face of innocents, in the seconds before he rends and tears; the families who have screamed, watching loved ones torn from them; the special feeling of revulsion that has always wanted to come over him whenever he caught his own reflection in a storefront window, or in some full-length mirror passed in the many houses he's broken into, or in the reflective surface of some mirrored lake. He remembers waking to every fresh dawn, not just acting according to his nature, but understanding it. It is, he realizes for the first time since the last time, not anything he particularly enjoys being, and behind that terrible epiphany—racing into his suddenly waking consciousness like the nightmare it is—comes a horror equal to that which he has always so excelled at bringing to others.

He almost screams.

But then comes the sharp jab of pain, a lot like dying, and all of that disappears, contracting into a single bright point before being subsumed by darkness. He knows nothing, only that it has been some time since he last killed. Dully, he is aware that as soon as they free him from this place he will have to do something about that. It is not like he has anything else to occupy his time. Or any thoughts to occupy his head.

Pierce pulls his burning fingertips from the crater he has gouged in Clutch's skull, pulling with them the few gobbets of bloody gray matter that have managed to heal and resume thinking since the last time.

Clutch has no opinion. Literally, no opinion. He has no thoughts, no soul, no regrets, no hunger, no understanding of what he is or what has always been expected of him; just a dull, burning resentment of anything that lives and breathes and moves. Sometime soon, he will be trucked to a fine killing ground and set free, to wander. And when he does, he will not overthink, or for that matter consider at all, any of the impulses driving him to do what comes next.

Somebody mutters, "Lucky bastard."

There is a general murmuring of consensus over this, until the man with the clipboard adjusts his glasses and says, "Yes, well…remember that it's something you can all earn, at any time."

A scaled half-man, half-fish mutters, "Yeah. In Minnesota. Right. How the hell am I ever gonna get into the top three, frozen under ice half the year?"

The dispatcher adjusts his horn-rimmed glasses.

"You know the way it is, Gil. The top territories go to closers."

The Chill Clutch of the Unseen

KIM NEWMAN

t was autumn, kissing close to winter; late November, early December; the daytime a few dim drab moments between elongated hours of heavy, cold dark. The last of the unswept leaves were dull orange, frost-crispy under his boots. He could not feel his toes. But the other aches were all there, in his leg-bones, his knuckles, his *face*. Your pains calling in, all present and correct, Chief Stockton, sir. Hell, any day without blood in the toilet bowl was a good one. He was so old that the boy who'd taken over his job was retired (and buried). Someone he didn't know had sat in his old seat down at the police station for as long as most folks could remember. Someone with his name was on the highway patrol, so he supposed that the family tradition was being carried on. Stocktons had helped police this stretch of Connecticut since witch-hanging times. The family had been there for all the things worse than witches that came down the pike or stepped off the train.

Usually, it was the train.

That was why he kept his routine, trudging early to the railroad station and taking his chair—out on the platform in the balmy days of spring and summer, in the waiting room close to the black iron stove as winter's shroud descended—so he could keep to his watch. He knew most folks saw him as an old-timer who liked to get out of his empty house and be among people coming and going. Plenty were willing to stop and pass the time with him, talking about TV shows he'd never watch—*Ex-Flies* or some such. The town had long-time residents he thought of as incomers, whose names he needn't learn. Always, he kept a lazy eye out for movements. Most of the town had forgotten. Things that couldn't be explained by light of day, it was most comfortable to tidy up and dismiss as imaginings of the night. It had been a long time since the worst of it. But he knew it wasn't over. The things he watched out for were like him and took the long view. They could afford to wait it out. In the end, they'd be drawn to this place, to this station, to him.

And then…?

"Mornin'?" said the station-master's daughter Irene, who turned everything into a question. Or was it "Mournin'?"

"Ayup," he responded.

It was and he was. No further editorial needed.

Irene rattled the scuttle into the stove. The embers of yesterday's fuel were buried under fresh black coal. Smoke soon curled and she dropped the lid. The fire in the station waiting room stove had been burning since before she was born, never dying overnight even when snow lay three or four feet deep and tears turned to frost on your face. It was a phenomenon, he supposed. One of the many tiny things about the place no one even questioned.

Irene wore heavy boots, work-jeans and a check shirt. Her hair was done in two thick rope-braids like a storybook child. She might be pretty, and he hoped someone would find out. Then again, the joke was that when she got married she'd even make "I do" into a question. "I do?"

He settled in his seat.

The next stopping train was due at 7.12. A commuter crawl, picking up fellows (and ladies, these days) in suits, snaking them off to work in the city. He needn't pay it much attention. That train started up North and collected people as it wound through the state; the rare people who ever got off were day visitors from one or two towns up the line. It was the 7.32 he needed to pay mind to, the empty train coming the other way, from the city—the last train of yesterday, sent back to the terminus so it could return mid-morning and scoop up those who didn't need to be in the city until after the working day started, the shoppers-and-lunchers and the work-at-homes with meetings to make.

Almost no one came in on the 7.32. But it was a bad one. It came from New York, and the city was a stage most things passed through on their way here. He wondered sometimes why they didn't stop there, where they could hide among—how had folks once put it?—the "teeming millions." Up here, no matter how subtle their ways, they'd eventually be noticed. But a giant octopus could get lost in the concrete canyons. Let alone a shroud-thin tatter which could as easily have been a tangle of discarded newspapers as what it was.

Today, there'd be something.

Stockton *knew* this, the way some old folks knew the weather. The quality of his pain changed. He'd learned to read the signs.

Others had known, but they were gone. Their kids had never believed the yarns or had closed their minds firmly. There weren't such things. Not any more. And especially not here. Think of what it'd mean for property values. And we've got too much else on our plates. There are enough real dangers to worry about, in these times of terror and disgrace, without being troubled by yesterday's phantasms, by the outgrown nightmares of generations past.

They weren't fools. They were just children.

Kids.

"Coffee?"

That genuinely was a question.

"Thank you, Irene, yes."

She kept a percolator in the office. Her father had maintained a coffee-pot in the same manner as he kept the stove burning, continually topping up sludge built up over decades. Irene had put an end to that, carefully losing the pot and buying a new, complicated machine with her own money.

Stockton took a gulp. He was expecting the coffee taste, but something else swarmed into his mouth.

"Hazelnut and rum?" Irene question-explained.

To which he would have said, "no, thank you," but it was too late.

Some commuting fellow brought back these mutant concoctions from a place in the city. Coffee polluted with *flavors*. Stockton believed potato chips should taste of salt and nothing else. He had little time for any product described as "French" or with an acute accent in the brand name.

Still, the warmth in his throat was welcome.

And the coffee taste was still there, underneath.

Irene left him and busied herself in the office. Stockton didn't see her father around much any more. It occurred to him that she might have inherited the job of station-master—station-mistress?—while he was paying attention to what might be coming into town as opposed to what was happening right here. The last-but-one police chief had been a woman, and nobody seemed to mind. She'd looked like a little girl dressed up for trick-or-treat in the bulky padded jacket and baseball cap that passed for a uniform these days, but her watch had been quiet. He'd have liked to see how she'd have handled the run of things he and his family had coped with.

The memories—the *stories*—crept unbidden into his mind.

Late, late show names. Totemic words and symbols.

Beast. Bat. Bandage.

Moon. Dead. Grave.

They didn't even have a late, late show anymore. Turn on the TV after midnight and it was all infomercials for exercise equipment.

Twenty years back, when a bulky crate had been unloaded from the train, he had thought it was the last of them. He'd been waiting for the fourth asphalt-spreader's boot to drop. He had known what lay inside.

A monster. The Monster.

The crate was delivered to Doc Stone's place. Doc, whose medical records were hard to track down and who went by an Ellis Island name. His well-equipped basement workroom drained a power surge and put the lights out all over the county just as the thing in his crate broke loose. Doc had tried to get between the party of Stockton's men and the thing he said was his child. Now, he lay at the bottom of the river in the embrace of a skeleton with yard-long arm-bones.

That had been the Big One. After that, the others who knew how things were around here thought it was over and drifted away or died. Only he knew it wasn't over.

Would never be over.

On the late, late show, there was always next week and a sequel.

Tune in again to *Shock Theater*.

Bodies were rarely found. Fur, dust, bones. That meant nothing. There were always ways. Curses could be passed on with a bite or a legacy. Another electrical storm, a parchment translated aloud, a scientific breakthrough with unexpected consequences.

They would be back.

Something would be here. Soon.

Beast. Bat. Bandage. Body.

The casually interested thought that was the Full House. Those four were all there was, all there would be. The famous names, the face cards.

Stockton thought of the others, the ones who had passed through or ended up. The ones who weren't headliners.

The Amazon Manfish, broken out of a research institute in '56, gulping air through gills unequipped to process anything but warm water, shocked dead or comatose by a plunge through ice into Williamson's Kill. The madman's brain, disembodied in its jar, bubbling and flashing party lights as its mentacles kept the hump-backed surgeon in thrall, using his rheumy eyes to see and his warty hands to throttle. The roadhouse singer who exactly resembled a great-grandmother whose picture lay forgotten in the *Herald* archives, and whose bell-clear high notes stayed in the minds of men who found themselves ageing decades overnight. The long-nailed Chinaman with his platoon of silent servants, hatchets inside their sleeves, and his hot-house menagerie of exotic and deadly fauna. The slithering stretch of rancid greenery which sometimes took the form of a man of muck and root and opened huge, lucid eyes in its face of filth. The quiet, violet-eyed Christian family who spoke in even monotones and kept to themselves until someone noticed that if you told one of the children something then its parents—all the way across town—suddenly knew it too. The travelling freak show and its too-tall, too-clever ringmaster. The lights in the sky and mysterious live-stock fatalities. The experiments gone wrong in neglected houses outside the town limits. The gray-faced motorcycle gang whose fingers clicked to a rockin' beat as they tore apart the succession of ugly fast-food outlets thrown up on the site of the diner where they were ambushed and apparently wiped out in 1965, whose arrival was always prefaced by teenage death songs of the '60s coming unbidden from every radio and jukebox in town. The gentle murderer whose skull was swollen with acromegaly and whose heart pulsed only for the beautiful blind piano virtuoso whose short-tempered teachers tended to show up with their spines snapped. The extreme aesthete who could only paint masterworks if his subjects were beautiful and bloodless. The sheeted ghosts who were really scheming heirs, or vice versa. The neon-eyed swami who was always in plain view of a dozen witnesses, performing his mind-reading act, as the professors who once profaned a temple in a far-off land were struck down one by one with distinctive wavy daggers in their chests. The clever ape.

Most of them were buried out of the way and hushed up. The bound back-numbers of the *Herald* in the town library were full of neatly clipped holes, sometimes extending to entire editions but for the weather reports. For one month in 1908, *only* the weather reports were clipped—which often made Stockton ponder what had passed through back then, making itself known only through climatic influence.

A clatter, and he was out of his reverie.

A train, pulling out. The 7.12, leaving for the city.

He hadn't noticed who got on, hadn't cared, but it disturbed him that his vigilance had clouded even for a minute. The past, the old stories, had swarmed in on him, settling on his brain. He had been running through a medley of monsters.

He focused.

On the 7.32.

It would be a bad one.

And then everyone would remember. The yarns their parents and grandparents had told him. They were *true*! Eventually, they'd remember him, thank him for standing watch, need his advice. His hands couldn't wrap 'round a shotgun and his legs weren't up to a hike through the woods holding up a flaming torch, but his mind was still sharp. He still had the expertise.

There'd be bodies, of course.

He regretted that, but knew it was a stage. Before he'd be believed, before people paid attention, someone had to die. And die ugly, die strange. Two ragged holes in the throat of a woman bled whiter than virgin snow. A child torn to pieces as if by a wild animal but with clearly scratched gypsy signs in his tattered skin. A succession of elderly academics alone in locked libraries with their hearts stopped as if by an icy fist squeezing them dry. Men turned inside-out. Glowing green alien matter in wounds. Sea-widows drowned miles from water. Eyes or whole heads missing.

He couldn't think of the people who would become these bodies.

They were a necessary stage. Material he needed to work with.

Irene looked in on him.

"Looks like a chiller?"

She was commenting on the weather. But she spoke a deeper truth, asked a more pertinent question.

"Ayup."

He got up out of his chair, a process that became more difficult every single time. He saw Irene thinking about helping him and knew that eventually she'd give in and step forward, reaching for his arm. He kept his grunt to himself, felt the ache wriggle up and down his back.

A bad one.

His intention was to stroll casually out onto the platform, but he creaked as he walked, every step as clumsy as Doc Stone's "child." Irene did open the door for him, the courtesy he should be showing her. He nodded a thanks.

The cold outside was good for the pain, froze it away.

The 7.32 was coming. He felt the vibration in his gums, rattling his partial plates, before he even heard the train.

Before he saw the sleek, dull metal tube of the commuter train, he held in his head the picture of a real locomotive. Pistons and a funnel, clouds of steam, a shrill whistle. When those clanking things were phased out, the bullet-headed electrical creatures that replaced them seemed like things off the cover of *Amazing Science Fiction*. Streamlined, beautiful *Flash Gordon* props. When did they become just a part of the furniture?

The train came in and stopped.

He looked for a door opening. Not all the town's visitors needed to open doors, but most did. He supposed it was fair, that even the unnatural needed to grip a handle and turn.

A door did open.

Another person might have thought no one got off, but Stockton saw clearer.

A man-shaped bubble, shot through with black filaments, moving slowly. The prints of bare feet among the wet leaves left on the platform. A chattering of unseen teeth.

He congratulated himself on having worked it out ahead of time.

This was the only one left. The Man.

"You," he called, "I've been waiting."

The bubble froze, turned sideways, disappeared into stillness.

There was a coughing and racking. Somehow with a British accent.

Stockton stepped towards the noise. He saw small movements in the air. Up close, the Man was discernible by dozens of tiny tell-tales. Feet naturally picked up dirt, and so outlines that looked like grubby ankle-socks stamped up and down against the cold. Ten black crescents—dirt under fingernails. A shell-like spiral of clotted blood lining an infected invisible ear. A wrinkled, mottled sleeve of gray, dead skin. Irregular black discs that floated—breaks in bones set but not healed, suggesting a body bent and crooked by age and abuse. A squeezed tube of digested food, palely transparent in the twisted bulb of the stomach, blackening in the wrap of the lower bowel to form what looked like a nasty obstruction. And the dark tendrils winding around bone and through the meat, making unhealthy balloons of the weakly pulsing lung-sacs. He'd seen enough friends pass to recognise the symptoms. The crab. He knew the Man was a heavy smoker, liked to take the smoke in and fill out the shape of his gullet and lungs as a party piece. Now he was paying for it.

"Aren't you in bad shape, though," he declared.

The cough became a cackle. A cracked cackle. Never forget that the Man was mad. Even before disappearing, he'd been odd. Now, uniquely apart from mankind, he'd be completely crazy.

Before—on the late, late show—when a man like this died, he faded into view. He could only be invisible when alive; in death, he appeared. Obviously, from what Stockton could see, he was a quarter-dead already.

"Welcome, stranger," he said. "Welcome to the Elephants' Graveyard."

This was where the monsters came to die. It was in the natural supernatural order of things that there be a place like this. And a man like Stockton.

"You're the last of them, as far as I can tell."

"Once, I—or someone like me—called himself Invisible Man the First," said a voice from nowhere. No, not from nowhere.

Stockton saw a faint funnel in the air, smelled bad breath, could even make out a brown tooth. The voice came through pain. It was cultured and croaky at the same time, speaking with the clipped, artificial tones he associated with knighted theatrical actors slumming as Nazi war criminals in very poor films. The Brits you heard on TV these days—prime ministers and pop stars—didn't sound like this any more, if any real folks ever had.

The Man wouldn't take much killing.

No struggle to shove a stake in its heart, or a dozen men tossed about like straw dummies as they tried to wrestle it down, no bell-book-and-candle recitals, no calling-out-the-national-guard.

He could just reach out and break it, then watch it turn into an old, naked, dead man.

The Man *wanted* him to do it.

That was what he had come to understand. These things came to town to make a last stand, to do their shtick one final time for an appreciative audience and then fade away completely. Or, in this case, shade in completely.

The clutch came, at his throat, surprisingly fierce, cold and dry as black ice.

That rotten tooth came closer. The sick breath stench was stronger.

Stockton cursed himself for thinking too much, drifting off. He had made the mistake too many folks made. He had momentarily been taken with the wonder of the creature before him, had felt not only an empathy with the Man's plight, a kinship with its all-too-familiar pains, but even a fondness for its uncomplicated madness, a *nostalgia* for the world it had terrorized and which was as long-gone as steam trains and old-time radio serials.

For a moment, he had forgotten what it was to be a *monster*.

A thumb was under his ear, pressing on the rope of vein, long-nailed fingers were in his neck, ragged edges cutting the skin.

"You all right, Mr. Stockton?"

Irene was looking at him. From twenty feet away.

He was being held upright by the grip on his throat. His arms and legs dangled. He couldn't speak, but he tried to gurgle.

"If you let her get suspicious," whispered words directly in his ear, "I will kill her."

He raised a hand and waved, tried to construct a reassuring smile.

Irene shrugged and went inside again.

His arm dropped. It hurt a great deal.

"Very sensible," said the voice, more conversational now, more upper-hand.

Stockton looked down, trying to swivel his eyeballs to the grip. He saw a seam in the air, an old scar.

The Man changed hands, letting him go with his right and taking up the grip almost as severely with his left. Bloody fingerprints floated in the air and rubbed together.

"I'm most fearfully sorry, old son," said the voice, tittering on the edge of hilarity. "One of my great practical problems is trimming my nails. I imagine they're horny talons."

Stockton tried to get hold of the arm that must stretch out beyond the grip. His fingers scrabbled on greasy, cold skin.

"That tickles."

He was punched in the stomach. A solid drive, dimpling his padded hunter's jacket. The pain roiled in his belly, shook his bowels.

He did not intend to have an "accident."

"Elephants' Graveyard?" mused the monster. "I like that."

"You're all here," Stockton snarled, with difficulty. "All dead and gone. Dust and bone."

"You miss the point, chief."

The voice seemed genuinely friendly, amused, superior.

"Now, let us go for a little walk."

He was jerked along the platform, taking more puppet-steps. His left ankle turned and he yelped, then dragged his foot.

"Easy now, old-timer. Don't go on and on and on."

"Where are we going?"

"Why, to your house, of course. I could do with some breakfast, and you're having a trying day."

An old suit of clothes sat in his favorite armchair, casually comfortable, trouser-legs crossed, empty space between the cuff and a dangling slipper that pointed up or down as an unseen foot stretched.

Though they were indoors, the Man had decided to wear a hat, a hunter's cap with flap-downs over the ears and the back of the head. Stockton found it impossible not to look at the hole where the face should be and focus on the ragged fleece lining of the back-flap. The offer of a pair of sunglasses had been rejected with a tart "indoors and in Autumn, I don't think so."

Stockton couldn't help noticing the Man seemed healthier, as if exerting his power over someone else assuaged his own hurts. He was bundled up and wrapped away now, but it seemed the black filaments he had noticed earlier were far less apparent.

His guest was disgusted that Stockton didn't have any cigarettes. He'd given up, on doctor's orders, years ago. The doctor who'd ordered him was dead. Emphysema, so he'd known what he was talking about.

"This is a very decent cup of tea," said the voice.

The cup tipped in the air. Liquid slithered around the shape of a tongue and mouth, then squirted down past the collar of Stockton's old wedding-and-funeral shirt.

"Far better than one would expect to find in heathen Yankeeland."

Stockton's throat still hurt. He had examined the scratches in the mirror and saw rimmed white pressure-spots that would last for days.

"So you think we're the last?" asked the Man.

"You're the last."

"Invisible Man the Last?" Shoulders lifted in a shrug. "Perhaps. Though that's been said before, too many times. And I deliberately used the first person plural. We. You're a part of this too. You're as much a coelacanth as I am."

"Coelacanth?"

"Living fossil. Prehistoric fish. Thought extinct for millennia, until one showed up in some African peasant fisherman's net back in the '20s."

"I've heard of that story."

"Good. It's the duty of a lively mind to take an interest in sports and freaks, don't you think. You might aver that it was your specialist subject."

Stockton nodded.

"How many of us have you killed, Chief Stockton?"

The question was a surprise, a slap.

"Come on, don't be modest. I'll admit to all my murders. Little men and big, women and children. Dogs. I've happily killed dogs. It used to be that not a day went past that I didn't murder something. Now, as time creeps on, why...it's been months, maybe years. And the last time was a farce. Took forever to throttle and stifle some twig-like spinster I'd have done for in a trice on my best day. We're both professionals. We have licenses. I have my...condition," a handless sleeve up before an absence of face suggesting a gesture, "and you had a badge and gun. I imagine you've still got your old trusty service special around. You Yanks and your blessed firearms. Makes everything too easy. You're not a proper killer unless you get up close, feel the flesh part, the warmth dissipate, the heart stop. It's a good thing you can't see my face, because I know it's arranged into an expression you would find even more horrifying than my words. And you know why my words horrify you? Of course you do, Chief. It's because you *understand*."

Stockton remembered a scatter of dust on a red-lined cloak, a spike stuck into its folds; the pie-sized scarlet holes in hairy black hide made by a scattergun packed with shot mixed in with ground-up sterling silver dollars; various steaming piles of loathsome putrescence. Monsters dying. That he had seen a deal of.

"For you this isn't a graveyard, it's Death Row. And you pull the switch."

"You're all monsters."

"And monsters can't live? We kill people. No argument here, old thing. It's just that...well, chief, how can I put this without seeming ungracious about your hospitality, but perhaps you shouldn't enjoy *destroying* us quite so much. Your kind always hates and fears the extraordinary."

"Uh-uh," Stockton said, bristling, "you don't get me like that, Mr. Clever Man. I didn't start this. We—regular folks—we didn't set out to hunt you all down and see you dead just because you were different. Nothing wrong with being different. We took objection to the murders. And the other things, the worse crimes."

A sleeve hung in the air, invisible finger tapping invisible chin.

"Of course you did."

They were argued into a corner.

"I put rat poison in your tea," Stockton said.

"I know. I drank it."

White lines were winding up around inside his head, outlining a skull. Red wires crept over it. A face was forming.

"Soon you'll be face to face with the Visible Man."

An old face, of course. Weatherbeaten. Eyes mushroomed in sockets, watery blue, lids forming around them.

"Then it'll be over," muscle flaps in the shape of lips formed the words. "You'll have killed the last but one coelacanth, and it'll be down to you. My guess is you won't see out the winter. Spring will come and you'll be gone. Without us, what's the point of you?"

"That doesn't bother me. I've lived my life justified."

"I suppose you have. I say, this poison is rather painful. Stomach feels as if it's been through a mangle. You could have just shot me, you know."

"Then we wouldn't be having this…little chat."

He tried to mimic the Man's clipped tones.

The Man laughed. "What do you think you sound like?"

Skin was forming—pale from years out of the sun, withered over bone, white beard thick on the cheeks but scraggy under the chin. Of course, he couldn't have done much of a job of shaving.

"It'll start again, chief. It always does. It's what makes monsters monstrous, in a way. We can be killed, but we come back. When I'm fully opaque, some other idealist or madman will start to disappear. Knowledge is out in the world and can't be taken back. This town isn't just a graveyard, it's a spawning ground. Sure, we come here to die, but we also come to be reborn. And many of us are *from* here. Just like you."

The voice stilled. There was a dead old man in Stockton's favourite armchair.

For a while, the air was clear and the pain was gone. There were no monsters in the world, in this town.

Then, a black little bulb under a field somewhere nearby began to sprout.

Stockton saw it in his mind and knew he was seeing a truth. It was part of his legacy, his gift. He also recognised that somewhere this morning he had suffered another stroke. He couldn't feel his left arm, and a cord in his neck was spasming beyond his control.

Damn monsters.

He needed to do something about the body. This was a particularly inconvenient one. Some dead things resolved to bone and ash or were such obvious inexplicable departures from the norm that cops and coroners quietly absolved their destroyers from legal blame. This one lost its defining feature in death and looked uncomfortably like a poor old vagrant poisoned by a mad old cop. There were precedents, and he hoped his name still had enough pull—but it didn't matter. The way justice ground on these days, this wouldn't come to trial before spring and his visitor had been right in estimating that Stockton wasn't liable to be around when the leaves greened.

He picked up the phone, ready to dial—no, the rotary phone was long gone, to punch out—the familiar number. He would talk to the new chief. No, he realized, he had to talk to someone else first. That black bulb had spider-limbs now, reaching above ground.

If the pests came back, so must the pest-controllers.

He stabbed buttons.

This would take some convincing talk, but there was evidence enough. A duty could be passed on, as it had been passed on to him.

At the end of the line, the phone rang once.

"Highway Patrol," responded a voice.

"Get me Stockton," he said.

"Is this police business? I can take your call. Stockton's out on the road and won't be back 'til later."

"It's police business," he said. "And family business. Get her to call her father's uncle. There are things she needs to know."

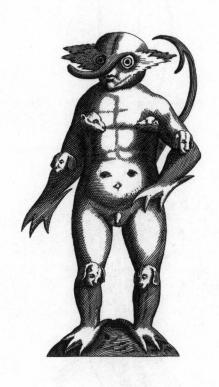

Down Among the Dead Men

JACK DANN & GARDNER DOZOIS

ruckman first discovered that Wernecke was a vampire when they went to the quarry that morning.

He was bending down to pick up a large rock when he thought he heard something in the gully nearby. He looked around and saw Wernecke huddled over a *Musselmänn*, one of the walking dead, a new man who had not been able to wake up to the terrible reality of the camp.

"Do you need any help?" Bruckman asked Wernecke in a low voice.

Wernecke looked up, startled, and covered his mouth with his hand, as if he were signing to Bruckman to be quiet.

But Bruckman was certain that he had glimpsed blood smeared on Wernecke's mouth. "The Musselmänn, is he alive?" Wernecke had often risked his own life to save one or another of the men in his barracks. But to risk one's life for a Musselmänn? "What's wrong?"

"Get away."

All right, Bruckman thought. Best to leave him alone. He looked pale, perhaps it was typhus. The guards were working him hard enough, and Wernecke was older than the rest of the men in the work gang. Let him sit for a moment and rest. But what about that blood…?

"Hey, you, what are you doing?" one of the young SS guards shouted to Bruckman.

Bruckman picked up the rock and, as if he had not heard the guard, began to walk away from the gully, toward the rusty brown cart on the tracks that led back to the barbed-wire fence of the camp. He would try to draw the guard's attention away from Wernecke.

But the guard shouted at him to halt. "Were you taking a little rest, is that it?" he asked, and Bruckman tensed, ready for a beating. This guard was new, neatly and cleanly dressed—and an unknown quantity. He walked over to the gully and, seeing Wernecke and the Musselmänn, said, "Aha, so your friend is taking care of the sick." He motioned Bruckman to follow him into the gully.

Bruckman had done the unpardonable—he had brought it on Wernecke. He swore at himself. He had been in this camp long enough to know to keep his mouth shut.

The guard kicked Wernecke sharply in the ribs. "I want you to put the Musselmänn in the cart. Now!" He kicked Wernecke again, as if as an afterthought. Wernecke groaned, but got to his feet. "Help him put the Musselmänn in the cart," the guard said to Bruckman; then he smiled and drew a circle in the air—the sign of smoke, the smoke that rose from the tall, gray chimneys behind them. This Musselmänn would be in the oven within an hour, his ashes soon to be floating in the hot, stale air, as if they were the very particles of his soul.

Wernecke kicked the Musselmänn, and the guard chuckled, waved to another guard who had been watching, and stepped back a few feet. He stood with his hands on his hips. "Come on, dead man, get up or you're going to die in the oven," Wernecke whispered as he tried to pull the man to his feet. Bruckman supported the unsteady Musselmänn, who began to wail softly. Wernecke slapped him hard. "Do you want to live, Musselmänn? Do you want to see your family again, feel the touch of a woman, smell grass after it's been mowed? Then move." The Musselmänn shambled forward between Wernecke and Bruckman. "You're dead, aren't you Musselmänn," goaded Wernecke. "As dead as your father and mother, as dead as your sweet wife, if you ever had one, aren't you? Dead!"

The Musselmänn groaned, shook his head, and whispered, "Not dead, my wife...."

"Ah, it talks," Wernecke said, loud enough so the guard walking a step behind them could hear. "Do you have a name, corpse?"

"Josef, and I'm not a Musselmänn."

"The corpse says he's alive," Wernecke said, again loud enough for the SS guard to hear. Then in a whisper, he said, "Josef, if you're not a Musselmänn, then you must work now, do you understand?" Josef tripped, and Bruckman caught him. "Let him be," said Wernecke. "Let him walk to the cart himself."

"Not the cart," Josef mumbled. "Not to die, not—"

"Then get down and pick up stones, show the fart-eating guard you can work."

"Can't. I'm sick, I'm...."

"Musselmänn!"

Josef bent down, fell to his knees, but took hold of a stone and stood up.

"You see," Wernecke said to the guard, "it's not dead yet. It can still work."

"I told you to carry him to the cart, didn't I," the guard said petulantly.

"Show him you can work," Wernecke said to Josef, "or you'll surely be smoke."

And Josef stumbled away from Wernecke and Bruckman, leaning forward, as if following the rock he was carrying.

"Bring him back!" shouted the guard, but his attention was distracted from Josef by some other prisoners, who, sensing the trouble, began to mill about. One of the other guards began to shout and kick at the men on the periphery, and the new guard joined him. For the moment, he had forgotten about Josef.

"Let's get to work, lest they notice us again," Wernecke said.

"I'm sorry that I—"

Wernecke laughed and made a fluttering gesture with his hand—smoke rising. "It's all hazard, my friend. All luck." Again the laugh. "It was a venial sin," and his face seemed to darken. "Never do it again, though, lest I think of you as bad luck."

"Eduard, are you all right?" Bruckman asked. "I noticed some blood when—"

"Do the sores on your feet bleed in the morning?" Wernecke countered angrily. Bruckman nodded, feeling foolish and embarrassed. "And so it is with my gums. Now go away, unlucky one, and let me live."

At dusk, the guards broke the hypnosis of lifting and grunting and sweating and formed the prisoners into ranks. They marched back to the camp through the fields, beside the railroad tracks, the electrified wire, conical towers, and into the main gate of the camp.

Josef walked beside them, but he kept stumbling, as he was once again slipping back into death, becoming a Musselmänn. Wernecke helped him walk, pushed him along. "We should let this man become dead," Wernecke said to Bruckman.

Bruckman only nodded, but he felt a chill sweep over his sweating back. He was seeing Wernecke's face again as it was for that instant in the morning. Smeared with blood.

Yes, Bruckman thought, we should let the Musselmänn become dead. We should all be dead....

Wernecke served up the lukewarm water with bits of spoiled turnip floating on the top, what passed as soup for the prisoners. Everyone sat or kneeled on the rough-planked floor, as there were no chairs.

Bruckman ate his portion, counting the sips and bites, forcing himself to take his time. Later, he would take a very small bite of the bread he had in his pocket. He always saved a small morsel of food for later—in the endless world of the camp, he had learned to give himself things to look forward to. Better to dream of bread than to get lost in the present. That was the fate of the Musselmänner.

But he always dreamed of food. Hunger was with him every moment of the day and night. Those times when he actually ate were in a way the most difficult, for there was never enough to satisfy him. There was the taste of softness in his mouth, and then in an instant it was gone. The emptiness took the form of pain—it hurt to eat. For bread, he thought, he would have killed his father, or his wife. God forgive me, and he watched Wernecke— Wernecke, who had shared his bread with him, who had died a little so he could live. He's a better man than I, Bruckman thought.

It was dim inside the barracks. A bare light bulb hung from the ceiling and cast sharp shadows across the cavernous room. Two tiers of five-foot-deep shelves ran around the room on three sides, bare, wooden shelves where the men slept without blankets or mattresses. Set high in the northern wall was a slatted window, which let in the stark, white light of the kliegs. Outside, the lights turned the grounds into a deathly imitation of day; only inside the barracks was it night.

"Do you know what tonight is, my friends?" Wernecke asked. He sat in the far corner of the room with Josef, who, hour by hour, was reverting back into a Musselmänn. Wernecke's face looked hollow and drawn in the light from the window and the light bulb; his eyes were deep-set and his face was long with deep creases running from his nose to the corners of his thin mouth. His hair was black, and even since Bruckman had known him, quite a bit of it had fallen out. He was a very tall man, almost six feet four, and that made him stand out in a crowd, which was dangerous in a death camp. But Wernecke had his own secret ways of blending with the crowd, of making himself invisible.

"No, tell us what tonight is," crazy old Bohme said. That men such as Bohme could survive was a miracle—or, as Bruckman thought—a testament to men such as Wernecke, who somehow found the strength to help the others live.

"It's Passover," Wernecke said.

"How does he know that?" someone mumbled, but it didn't matter how Wernecke knew because he knew—even if it really wasn't Passover by the calendar. In this dimly lit barrack, it was Passover, the feast of freedom, the time of thanksgiving.

"But how can we have Passover without a *seder*?" asked Bohme. "We don't even have any *matzoh*," he whined.

"Nor do we have candles, or a silver cup for Elijah, or the shank bone, or *haroset*—nor would I make a seder over the *treif* the Nazis are so generous in giving us," replied Wernecke with a smile. "But we can pray, can't we? And when we all get out of here, when we're in our own homes in the coming year with God's help, then we'll have twice as much food—two *afikomens*, a bottle of wine for Elijah, and the *haggadahs* that our fathers and our fathers' fathers used."

It *was* Passover.

"Isadore, do you remember the four questions?" Wernecke asked Bruckman.

And Bruckman heard himself speaking. He was twelve years old again at the long table beside his father, who sat in the seat of honor. To sit next to him was itself an honor. "How does this night differ from all other nights? On all other nights we eat bread and matzoh; why on this night do we eat only matzoh?

"Mah nishtanah ha-laylah ha-zeh...."

Sleep would not come to Bruckman that night, although he was so tired that he felt as if the marrow of his bones had been sucked away and replaced with lead.

He lay there in the semidarkness, feeling his muscles ache, feeling the acid biting of his hunger. Usually he was numb enough with exhaustion that he could empty his mind, close himself down, and fall rapidly into oblivion, but not tonight. Tonight he was noticing things again, his surroundings were getting through to him again, in a way that they had not since he had been new in camp. It was smotheringly hot, and the air was filled with the stinks of death and sweat and fever, of stale urine and drying blood. The sleepers thrashed and turned, as though they fought with sleep, and as they slept, many of them talked or muttered or screamed aloud; they lived other lives in their dreams, intensely compressed lives dreamed quickly, for soon it would be dawn, and once more they would be thrust into hell. Cramped in the midst of them, sleepers squeezed in all around him, it suddenly seemed to Bruckman that these pallid, white bodies were already dead, that he was sleeping in a graveyard. Suddenly it was the boxcar again. And his wife Miriam was dead again, dead and rotting unburied....

Resolutely, Bruckman emptied his mind. He felt feverish and shaky, and wondered if the typhus was coming back, but he couldn't afford to worry about it. Those who couldn't sleep couldn't survive. Regulate your breathing, force your muscles to relax, don't think. Don't think.

For some reason, after he had managed to banish even the memory of his dead wife, he couldn't shake the image of the blood on Wernecke's mouth.

There were other images mixed in with it: Wernecke's uplifted arms and upturned face as he led them in prayer; the pale, strained face of the stumbling Musselmänn; Wernecke looking up, startled, as he crouched over Josef...but it was the blood to which Bruckman's feverish thoughts returned, and he pictured it again and again as he lay in the rustling, fart-smelling darkness, the watery sheen of blood over Wernecke's lips, the tarry trickle of blood in the corner of his mouth, like a tiny, scarlet worm....

Just then a shadow crossed in front of the window, silhouetted blackly for an instant against the harsh, white glare, and Bruckman knew from the shadow's height and its curious forward stoop that it was Wernecke.

Where could he be going? Sometimes a prisoner would be unable to wait until morning, when the Germans would let them out to visit the slit-trench latrine again, and would slink shamefacedly into a far corner to piss against a wall, but surely Wernecke was too much of an old hand for that.... Most of the prisoners slept on the sleeping platforms, especially during the cold nights when they would huddle together for warmth, but sometimes during the hot weather, people would drift away and sleep on the floor instead; Bruckman had been thinking of doing that, as the jostling bodies of the sleepers around him helped to keep him from sleep. Perhaps Wernecke, who always had trouble fitting into the cramped sleeping niches, was merely looking for a place where he could lie down and stretch his legs....

Then Bruckman remembered that Josef had fallen asleep in the corner of the room where Wernecke had sat and prayed, and that they had left him there alone.

Without knowing why, Bruckman found himself on his feet. As silently as the ghost he sometimes felt he was becoming, he walked across the room in the direction Wernecke had gone, not understanding what he was doing or why he was doing it. The face of the Musselmänn, Josef, seemed to float behind his eyes. Bruckman's feet hurt, and he knew, without looking, that they were bleeding, leaving faint tracks behind him. It was dimmer here in the far corner, away from the window, but Bruckman knew that he must be near the wall by now, and he stopped to let his eyes readjust.

When his eyes had adapted to the dimmer light, he saw Josef sitting on the floor, propped up against the wall. Wernecke was hunched over the

Musselmänn. Kissing him. One of Josef's hands was tangled in Wernecke's thinning hair.

Before Bruckman could react—such things had been known to happen once or twice before, although it shocked him deeply that Wernecke would be involved in such filth—Josef released his grip on Wernecke's hair. Josef's upraised arm fell limply to the side, his hand hitting the floor with a muffled but solid impact that should have been painful—but Josef made no sound.

Wernecke straightened up and turned around. Stronger light from the high window caught him as he straightened to his full height, momentarily illuminating his face.

Wernecke's mouth was smeared with blood.

"My God," Bruckman cried.

Startled, Wernecke flinched, then took two quick steps forward and seized Bruckman by the arm. "Quiet!" Wernecke hissed. His fingers were cold and hard.

At that moment, as though Wernecke's sudden movement were a cue, Josef began to slip down sideways along the wall. As Wernecke and Bruckman watched, both momentarily riveted by the sight, Josef toppled over to the floor, his head striking against the floorboards with a sound such as a dropped melon might make. He had made no attempt to break his fall or cushion his head, and lay now unmoving.

"My *God*," Bruckman said again.

"Quiet, I'll explain," Wernecke said, his lips still glazed with the Musselmänn blood. "Do you want to ruin us all? For the love of God, be *quiet*."

But Bruckman had shaken free of Wernecke's grip and crossed to kneel by Josef, leaning over him as Wernecke had done, placing a hand flat on Josef's chest for a moment, then touching the side of Josef's neck. Bruckman looked slowly up at Wernecke. "He's dead," Bruckman said, more quietly.

Wernecke squatted on the other side of Josef's body, and the rest of their conversation was carried out in whispers over Josef's chest, like friends conversing at the sickbed of another friend who has finally fallen into a fitful doze.

"Yes, he's dead," Wernecke said. "He was dead yesterday, wasn't he? To-day he had just stopped walking." His eyes were hidden here, in the deeper shadow nearer to the floor, but there was still enough light for Bruckman to see that Wernecke had wiped his lips clean. Or licked them clean, Bruckman thought, and felt a spasm of nausea go through him.

"But you," Bruckman said, haltingly. "You were...."

"Drinking his blood?" Wernecke said. "Yes, I was drinking his blood."

Bruckman's mind was numb. He couldn't deal with this, he couldn't understand it at all. "But *why*, Eduard? Why?"

"To live, of course. Why do any of us do anything here? If I am to live, I must have blood. Without it, I'd face a death even more certain than that doled out by the Nazis."

Bruckman opened and closed his mouth, but no sound came out, as if the words he wished to speak were too jagged to fit through his throat. At last he managed to croak, "A vampire? You're a vampire? Like in the old stories?"

Wernecke said calmly, "Men would call me that." He paused, then nodded. "Yes, that's what men would call me.... As though they can understand something simply by giving it a name."

"But Eduard," Bruckman said weakly, almost petulantly. "The Musselmänn...."

"Remember that he was a Musselmänn," Wernecke said, leaning forward and speaking more fiercely. "His strength was going, he was sinking. He would have been dead by morning anyway. I took from him something that he no longer needed, but that I needed in order to live. Does it matter? Starving men in lifeboats have eaten the bodies of their dead companions in order to live. Is what I've done any worse than that?"

"But he didn't just die. You *killed* him...."

Wernecke was silent for a moment, and then said, quietly, "What better thing could I have done for him? I won't apologize for what I do, Isadore; I do what I have to do to live. Usually I take only a little blood from a number of men, just enough to survive. And that's fair, isn't it? Haven't I given food to others, to help them survive? To you, Isadore? Only very rarely do I take more than a minimum from any one man, although I'm weak and hungry all the time, believe me. And never have I drained the life from someone who wished to live. Instead I've helped them fight for survival in every way I can, you know that."

He reached out as though to touch Bruckman, then thought better of it and put his hand back on his own knee. He shook his head. "But these Musselmänner, the ones who have given up on life, the walking dead—it is a favor to them to take them, to give them the solace of death. Can you honestly say it is not, here? That it is better for them to walk around while they are dead, being beaten and abused by the Nazis until their bodies cannot go on, and then to be thrown into the ovens and burned like trash? Can you say that? Would they say that, if they knew what was going on? Or would they thank me?"

Wernecke suddenly stood up, and Bruckman stood up with him. As Wernecke's face came again into the stronger light, Bruckman could see that his eyes had filled with tears. "You have lived under the Nazis," Wernecke said. "Can you really call me a monster? Aren't I still a Jew, whatever else I might be? Aren't I here, in a death camp? Aren't I being persecuted, too, as much as any other? Aren't I in as much danger as anyone else? If I'm not a Jew, then tell the Nazis—they seem to think so." He paused for a moment, and then smiled wryly. "And forget your superstitious boogey tales. I'm no night spirit. If I could turn myself into a bat and fly away from here, I would have done it long before now, believe me."

Bruckman smiled reflectively, then grimaced. The two men avoided each other's eyes, Bruckman looking at the floor, and there was an uneasy silence, punctured only by the sighing and moaning of the sleepers on the other side of the cabin. Then, without looking up, in tacit surrender, Bruckman said, "What about him? The Nazis will find the body and cause trouble...."

"Don't worry," Wernecke said. "There are no obvious marks. And nobody performs autopsies in a death camp. To the Nazis, he'll be just another Jew who had died of the heat, or from starvation or sickness, or from a broken heart."

Bruckman raised his head then and they stared eye to eye for a moment. Even knowing what he knew, Bruckman found it hard to see Wernecke as anything other than what he appeared to be: an aging, balding Jew, stooping and thin, with sad eyes and a tired, compassionate face.

"Well, then, Isadore," Wernecke said at last, matter-of-factly. "My life is in your hands. I will not be indelicate enough to remind you of how many times your life has been in mine."

Then he was gone, walking back toward the sleeping platforms, a shadow soon lost among other shadows.

Bruckman stood by himself in the gloom for a long time, and then followed him. It took all of his will not to look back over his shoulder at the corner where Josef lay, and even so Bruckman imagined that he could feel Josef's dead eyes watching him, watching reproachfully as he walked away abandoning Josef to the cold and isolated company of the dead.

Bruckman got no more sleep that night, and in the morning, when the Nazis shattered the gray, predawn stillness by bursting into the shack with shouts and shrill whistles and barking police dogs, he felt as if he were a thousand years old.

They were formed into two lines, shivering in the raw morning air, and marched off to the quarry. The clammy dawn mist had yet to burn off, and marching through it, through a white, shadowless void, with only the back of the man in front of him dimly visible, Bruckman felt more than ever like a ghost, suspended bodiless in some limbo between Heaven and Earth. Only the bite of pebbles and cinders into his raw, bleeding feet kept him anchored to the world, and he clung to the pain as a lifeline, fighting to shake off a feeling of numbness and unreality. However strange, however outré, the events of the previous night had *happened*. To doubt it, to wonder now if it had all been a feverish dream brought on by starvation and exhaustion, was to take the first step on the road to becoming a Musselmänn.

Wernecke is a vampire, he told himself. That was the harsh, unyielding reality that, like the reality of the camp itself, must be faced. Was it any more surreal, any more impossible than the nightmare around them? He must forget the tales that his grandmother had told him as a boy, "boogey tales" as Wernecke himself had called them, half-remembered tales that turned his knees to water whenever he thought of the blood smeared on Wernecke's mouth, whenever he thought of Wernecke's eyes watching him in the dark....

"Wake up, Jew!" the guard alongside him snarled, whacking him lightly on the arm with his rifle butt. Bruckman stumbled, managed to stay upright and keep going. Yes, he thought, wake up. Wake up to the reality of this, just as you once had to wake up to the reality of the camp. It was just one more unpleasant fact he would have to adapt to, learn to deal with....

Deal with how? he thought, and shivered.

By the time they reached the quarry, the mist had burned off, swirling past them in rags and tatters, and it was already beginning to get hot. There was Wernecke, his balding head gleaming dully in the harsh morning light. He didn't dissolve in the sunlight—there was one boogey tale disproved....

They set to work, like golems, like ragtag, clockwork automatons.

Lack of sleep had drained what small reserves of strength Bruckman had, and the work was very hard for him that day. He had learned long ago all the tricks of timing and misdirection, the safe way to snatch short moments of rest, the ways to do a minimum of work with the maximum display of effort, the ways to keep the guards from noticing you, to fade into the faceless crowd of prisoners and not be singled out, but today his head was muzzy and slow, and none of the tricks seemed to work.

His body felt like a sheet of glass, fragile, ready to shatter into dust, and the painful, arthritic slowness of his movements got him first shouted at, and then knocked down. The guard kicked him twice for good measure before he could get up.

When Bruckman had climbed back to his feet again, he saw that Wernecke was watching him, face blank, eyes expressionless, a look that could have meant anything at all.

Bruckman felt the blood trickling from the corner of his mouth and thought, *the blood...he's watching the blood...*and once again he shivered.

Somehow, Bruckman forced himself to work faster, and although his muscles blazed with pain, he wasn't hit again, and the day passed.

When they formed up to go back to camp, Bruckman, almost unconsciously, made sure that he was in a different line than Wernecke.

That night in the cabin, Bruckman watched as Wernecke talked with the other men, here trying to help a new man named Melnick—no more than a boy—adjust to the dreadful reality of the camp, there exhorting someone who was slipping into despair to live and spite his tormentors, joking with old hands in the flat, black, bitter way that passed for humor among them, eliciting a wan smile or occasionally even a laugh from them, finally leading them all in prayer again, his strong, calm voice raised in the ancient words, giving meaning to those words again....

He keeps us together, Bruckman thought, he keeps us going. Without him, we wouldn't last a week. Surely that's worth a little blood, a bit from each man, not even enough to hurt.... Surely they wouldn't even begrudge him it, if they knew and really understood.... No, he is a good man, better than the rest of us, in spite of his terrible affliction.

Bruckman had been avoiding Wernecke's eyes, hadn't spoken to him at all that day, and suddenly felt a wave of shame go through him at the thought of how shabbily he had been treating his friend. Yes, his friend, regardless, the man who had saved his life.... Deliberately, he caught Wernecke's eyes, and nodded, and then somewhat sheepishly, smiled. After a moment, Wernecke smiled back, and Bruckman felt a spreading warmth and relief uncoil his guts. Everything was going to be all right, as all right as it could be, here....

Nevertheless, as soon as the inside lights clicked off that night, and Bruckman found himself lying alone in the darkness, his flesh began to crawl.

He had been unable to keep his eyes open a moment before, but now, in the sudden darkness, he found himself tensely and tickingly awake. Where was Wernecke? What was he doing, whom was he visiting tonight? Was he out there in the darkness even now, creeping closer, creeping nearer...? Stop it, Bruckman told himself uneasily, forget the boogey tales. This is your friend, a good man, not a monster.... But he couldn't control the fear that made the small hairs on his arms stand bristlingly erect, couldn't stop the grisly images from coming....

Wernecke's eyes, gleaming in the darkness...was the blood already glistening on Wernecke's lips, as he drank...? The thought of the blood staining Wernecke's yellowing teeth made Bruckman cold and nauseous, but the image that he couldn't get out of his mind tonight was an image of Josef toppling over in that sinister, boneless way, striking his head against the floor.... Bruckman had seen people die in many more gruesome ways during his time at the camp, seen people shot, beaten to death, seen them die in convulsions from high fevers or cough their lungs up in bloody tatters from pneumonia, seen them hanging like charred-black scarecrows from the electrified fences, seen them torn apart by dogs...but somehow it was Josef's soft, passive, almost restful slumping into death that bothered him. That, and the obscene limpness of Josef's limbs as he sprawled there like a discarded rag doll, his pale and haggard face gleaming reproachfully in the dark....

When Bruckman could stand it no longer, he got shakily to his feet and moved off through the shadows, once again not knowing where he was going or what he was going to do, but drawn forward by some obscure instinct he himself did not understand. This time he went cautiously, feeling his way and trying to be silent, expecting every second to see Wernecke's coal-black shadow rise up before him.

He paused, a faint noise scratching at his ears, then went on again, even more cautiously, crouching low, almost crawling across the grimy floor.

Whatever instinct had guided him—sounds heard and interpreted subliminally, perhaps?—it had timed his arrival well. Wernecke had someone down on the floor there, perhaps someone he seized and dragged away from the huddled mass of sleepers on one of the sleeping platforms, someone from the outer edge of bodies whose presence would not be missed, or perhaps someone who had gone to sleep on the floor, seeking solitude or greater comfort.

Whoever he was, he struggled in Wernecke's grip, but Wernecke handled him easily, almost negligently, in a manner that spoke of great physical power. Bruckman could hear the man trying to scream, but Wernecke had one hand on his throat, half-throttling him, and all that would come out was a sort of whistling gasp. The man thrashed in Wernecke's hands like a kite in a child's hands flapping in the wind, and, moving deliberately, Wernecke smoothed him out like a kite, pressing him slowly flat on the floor.

Then Wernecke bent over him, and lowered his mouth to his throat.

Bruckman watched in horror, knowing that he should shout, scream, try to rouse the other prisoners, but somehow unable to move, unable to make his mouth open, his lungs pump. He was paralyzed by fear, like a rabbit in the presence of a predator, a terror sharper and more intense than any he'd ever known.

The man's struggles were growing weaker, and Wernecke must have eased up some on the throttling pressure of his hand, because the man moaned "Don't...please don't..." in a weaker, slurred voice. The man had been drumming his fists against Wernecke's back and sides, but now the tempo of the drumming slowed, slowed, and then stopped, the man's arms falling laxly to the floor. "Don't..." the man whispered; he groaned and muttered incomprehensibly for a moment or two longer, then became silent. The silence stretched out for a minute, two, three, and Wernecke still crouched over his victim, who was now not moving at all....

Wernecke stirred, a kind of shudder going through him, like a cat stretching. He stood up. His face became visible as he straightened up into the full light from the window, and there was blood on it, glistening black under the harsh glare of the kliegs. As Bruckman watched, Wernecke began to lick his lips clean, his tongue, also black in this light, sliding like some sort of sinuous, ebony snake around the rim of his mouth, darting and probing for the last lingering drops....

How smug he looks, Bruckman thought, like a cat who has found the cream, and the anger that flashed through him at the thought enabled him to move and speak again. "Wernecke," he said harshly.

Wernecke glanced casually in his direction. "You again, Isadore?" Wernecke said. "Don't you ever sleep?" Wernecke spoke lazily, quizzically, without surprise, and Bruckman wondered if Wernecke had known all along that he was there. "Or do you just enjoy watching me?"

"Lies," Bruckman said. "You told me nothing but lies. Why did you bother?"

"You were excited," Wernecke said. "You had surprised me. It seemed best to tell you what you wanted to hear. If it satisfied you, then that was an easy solution to the problem."

"Never have I drained the life from someone who wanted to live," Bruckman said bitterly, mimicking Wernecke. "Only a little from each man! My God—and I believed you! I even felt sorry for you!"

Wernecke shrugged. "Most of it was true. Usually I only take a little from each man, softly and carefully, so that they never know, so that in the morning they are only a little weaker than they would have been anyway...."

"Like Josef?" Bruckman said angrily. "Like the poor devil you killed tonight?"

Wernecke shrugged again. "I have been careless the last few nights, I admit. But I need to build up my strength again." His eyes gleamed in the darkness. "Events are coming to a head here. Can't you feel it, Isadore, can't you sense it? Soon the war will be over, everyone knows that. Before then, this camp will be shut down, and the Nazis will move us back into the interior—either that, or kill us. I have grown weak here, and I will soon need all my strength to survive, to take whatever opportunity presents itself to escape. I *must* be ready. And so I have let myself drink deeply again, drink my fill for the first time in months...." Wernecke licked his lips again, perhaps unconsciously, then smiled bleakly at Bruckman. "You don't appreciate my restraint, Isadore. You don't understand how hard it has been for me to hold back, to take only a little each night. You don't understand how much that restraint has cost me...."

"You are gracious," Bruckman sneered.

Wernecke laughed. "No, but I am a rational man; I pride myself on that. You other prisoners were my only source of food, and I have had to be very careful to make sure that you would last. I have no access to the Nazis, after all. I am trapped here, a prisoner just like you, whatever else you may believe—and I have not only had to find ways to survive here in the camp, I have had to procure my own food as well! No shepherd has ever watched over his flock more tenderly than I."

"Is that all we are to you—sheep? Animals to be slaughtered?"

Wernecke smiled. "Precisely."

When he could control his voice enough to speak, Bruckman said, "You're worse than the Nazis."

"I hardly think so," Wernecke said quietly, and for a moment he looked tired, as though something unimaginably old and unutterably weary had looked out through his eyes. "This camp was built by the Nazis—it wasn't my doing. The Nazis sent you here—not I. The Nazis have tried to kill you every day since, in one way or another—and I have tried to keep you alive, even at some risk to myself. No one has more of a vested interest in the survival of his livestock than the farmer, after all, even if he does occasionally slaughter an inferior animal. I have given you food—"

"Food you had no use for yourself! You sacrificed nothing!"

"That's true, of course. But you needed it, remember that. Whatever my motives, I have helped you to survive here—you and many others. By doing so I also acted in my own self-interest, of course, but can you have experienced this camp and still believe in things like altruism? What difference does it make what my reason for helping was—I still helped you, didn't I?"

"Sophistries!" Bruckman said. "Rationalizations! You twist words to justify yourself, but you can't disguise what you really are—a monster!"

Wernecke smiled gently, as though Bruckman's words amused him, and made as if to pass by, but Bruckman raised an arm to bar his way. They did not touch each other, but Wernecke stopped short, and a new quivering kind of tension sprung into existence in the air between them.

"I'll stop you," Bruckman said. "Somehow I'll stop you, I'll keep you from doing this terrible thing—"

"You'll do nothing," Wernecke said. His voice was hard and cold and flat, like a rock speaking. "What can you do? Tell the other prisoners? Who would believe you? They'd think you'd gone insane. Tell the Nazis, then?" Wernecke laughed harshly. "They'd think you'd gone crazy, too, and they'd take you to the hospital—and I don't have to tell you what your chances of getting out of there alive are, do I? No, you'll do nothing."

Wernecke took a step forward; his eyes were shiny and black and hard, like ice, like the pitiless eyes of a predatory bird, and Bruckman felt a sick rush of fear cut through his anger. Bruckman gave way, stepping backward involuntarily, and Wernecke pushed past him, seeming to brush him aside without touching him.

Once past, Wernecke turned to stare at Bruckman, and Bruckman had to summon up all the defiance that remained in him not to look uneasily away from Wernecke's agate-hard eyes. "You are the strongest and cleverest of all the other animals, Isadore," Wernecke said in a calm, conversational voice. "You have been useful to me. Every shepherd needs a good sheep dog.

I still need you, to help me manage the others, and to help me keep them going long enough to serve my needs. This is the reason why I have taken so much time with you, instead of just killing you outright." He shrugged. "So let us both be rational about this—you leave me alone, Isadore, and I will leave you alone also. We will stay away from each other and look after our own affairs. Yes?"

"The others..." Bruckman said weakly.

"They must look after themselves," Wernecke said. He smiled, a thin and almost invisible motion of his lips. "What did I teach you, Isadore? Here everyone must look after themselves. What difference does it make what happens to the others? In a few weeks almost all of them will be dead anyway."

"You *are* a monster," Bruckman said.

"I'm not much different from you, Isadore. The strong survive, whatever the cost."

"I am *nothing* like you," Bruckman said, with loathing.

"No?" Wernecke asked, ironically, and moved away; within a few paces he was hobbling and stooping, vanishing into the shadows, once more the harmless, old Jew.

Bruckman stood motionless for a moment, and then, moving slowly and reluctantly, he stepped across to where Wernecke's victim lay.

It was one of the new men Wernecke had been talking to earlier in the evening, and, of course, he was quite dead.

Shame and guilt took Bruckman then, emotions he thought he had forgotten—black and strong and bitter, they shook him by the throat the way Wernecke had shaken the new man.

Bruckman couldn't remember returning across the room to his sleeping platform, but suddenly he was there, lying on his back and staring into the stifling darkness, surrounded by the moaning, thrashing, stinking mass of sleepers. His hands were clasped protectively over his throat, although he couldn't remember putting them there, and he was shivering convulsively. How many mornings had he awoken with a dull ache in his neck, thinking it was no more than the habitual body aches and strained muscles they had all learned to take for granted? How many nights had Wernecke fed on him?

Every time Bruckman closed his eyes he would see Wernecke's face floating there in the luminous darkness behind his eyelids...Wernecke with his
eyes half-closed, his face vulpine and cruel and satiated...Wernecke's face
moving closer and closer to him, his eyes opening like black pits, his lips smiling back from his teeth...Wernecke's lips, sticky and red with blood...and
then Bruckman would seem to feel the wet touch of Wernecke's lips on *his*
throat, feel Wernecke's teeth biting into *his* flesh, and Bruckman's eyes would
fly open again. Staring into the darkness. Nothing there. Nothing there *yet*....

Dawn was a dirty gray imminence against the cabin window before
Bruckman could force himself to lower his shielding arms from his throat,
and once again he had not slept at all.

That day's work was a nightmare of pain and exhaustion for Bruckman,
harder than anything he had known since his first few days at the camp.
Somehow he forced himself to get up, somehow he stumbled outside and up
the path to the quarry, seeming to float along high off the ground, his head
a bloated balloon, his feet a thousand miles away at the end of boneless,
beanstalk legs he could barely control at all. Twice he fell, and was kicked
several times before he could drag himself back to his feet and lurch forward
again. The sun was coming up in front of them, a hard, red disk in a sickly
yellow sky, and to Bruckman it seemed to be a glazed and lidless eye staring
dispassionately into the world to watch them flail and struggle and die, like
the eye of a scientist peering into a laboratory maze.

He watched the disk of the sun as he stumbled toward it; it seemed to
bob and shimmer with every painful step, expanding, swelling, and bloat-
ing until it swallowed the sky....

Then he was picking up a rock, moaning with the effort, feeling the
rough stone tear his hands....

Reality began to slide away from Bruckman. There were long periods
when the world was blank, and he would come slowly back to himself as if
from a great distance, and hear his own voice speaking words that he could
not understand, or keening mindlessly, or grunting in a hoarse, animalistic
way, and he would find that his body was working mechanically, stooping
and lifting and carrying, all without volition....

A Musselmänn, Bruckman thought, I'm becoming a Musselmänn… and felt a chill of fear sweep through him. He fought to hold onto the world, afraid that the next time he slipped away from himself he would not come back, deliberately banging his hands into the rocks, cutting himself, clearing his head with pain.

The world steadied around him. A guard shouted a hoarse admonishment at him and slapped his rifle butt, and Bruckman forced himself to work faster, although he could not keep himself from weeping silently with the pain his movements cost him.

He discovered that Wernecke was watching him, and stared back defiantly, the bitter tears still runneling his dirty cheeks, thinking, *I won't become a* Musselmänn *for you, I won't make it easy for you, I won't provide another helpless victim for you.…* Wernecke met Bruckman's gaze for a moment, and then shrugged and turned away.

Bruckman bent for another stone, feeling the muscles in his back crack and the pain drive in like knives. What had Wernecke been thinking behind the blankness of his expressionless face? Had Wernecke, sensing weakness, marked Bruckman for his next victim? Had Wernecke been disappointed or dismayed by the strength of Bruckman's will to survive? Would Wernecke now settle upon someone else?

The morning passed, and Bruckman grew feverish again. He could feel the fever in his face, making his eyes feel sandy and hot, pulling the skin taut over his cheekbones, and he wondered how long he could manage to stay on his feet. To falter, to grow weak and insensible, was certain death; if the Nazis didn't kill him, Wernecke would.… Wernecke was out of sight now, on the other side of the quarry, but it seemed to Bruckman that Wernecke's hard and flinty eyes were everywhere, floating in the air around him, looking out momentarily from the back of a Nazi soldier's head, watching him from the dulled iron side of a quarry cart, peering at him from a dozen different angles. He bent ponderously for another rock, and when he had pried it up from the earth he found Wernecke's eyes beneath it, staring unblinkingly up at him from the damp and pallid soil.…

That afternoon there were great flashes of light on the eastern horizon out across the endless, flat expanse of the steppe, flares in rapid sequence that lit up the sullen, gray sky, all without sound. The Nazi guards had gathered in a group, looking to the east and talking in subdued voices, ignoring the prisoners for the moment. For the first time Bruckman noticed how disheveled and unshaven the guards had become in the last few days, as though they had given up, as though they no longer cared. Their faces were strained and tight, and more than one of them seemed to be fascinated by the leaping fires on the distant edge of the world.

Melnick said that it was only a thunderstorm, but old Bohme said that it was an artillery battle being fought, and that that meant the Russians were coming, that soon they would all be liberated.

Bohme grew so excited at the thought that he began shouting, "The Russians! It's the Russians! The Russians are coming to free us!" Dichstein, another one of the new prisoners, and Melnick tried to hush him, but Bohme continued to caper and shout—doing a grotesque kind of jig while he yelled and flapped his arms—until he had attracted the attention of the guards. Infuriated, two of the guards fell upon Bohme and beat him severely, striking him with their rifle butts with more than usual force, knocking him to the ground, continuing to flail at him and kick him while he was down, Bohme writhing like an injured worm under their stamping boots. They probably would have beaten Bohme to death on the spot, but Wernecke organized a distraction among some of the other prisoners, and when the guards moved away to deal with it, Wernecke helped Bohme to stand up and hobble away to the other side of the quarry, where the rest of the prisoners shielded him from sight with their bodies as best they could for the rest of the afternoon.

Something about the way Wernecke urged Bohme to his feet and helped him to limp and lurch away, something about the protective, possessive curve of Wernecke's arm around Bohme's shoulders, told Bruckman that Wernecke had selected his next victim.

That night Bruckman vomited up the meager and rancid meal that they were allowed, his stomach convulsing uncontrollably after the first few bites. Trembling with hunger and exhaustion and fever, he leaned against the wall and watched as Wernecke fussed over Bohme, nursing him as a man might nurse a sick child, talking gently to him, wiping away some of the blood that still oozed from the corner of Bohme's mouth, coaxing Bohme to drink a few sips of soup, finally arranging that Bohme should stretch out on the floor away from the sleeping platforms, where he would not be jostled by the others....

As soon as the interior lights went out that night, Bruckman got up, crossed the floor quickly and unhesitantly, and lay down in the shadows near the spot where Bohme muttered and twitched and groaned.

Shivering, Bruckman lay in the darkness, the strong smell of the earth in his nostrils, waiting for Wernecke to come....

In Bruckman's hand, held close to his chest, was a spoon that had been sharpened to a jagged needle point, a spoon he had stolen and begun to sharpen while he was still in a civilian prison in Cologne, so long ago that he almost couldn't remember, scraping it back and forth against the stone wall of his cell every night for hours, managing to keep it hidden on his person during the nightmarish ride in the sweltering boxcar, the first few terrible days at the camp, telling no one about it, not even Wernecke during the months when he'd thought of Wernecke as a kind of saint, keeping it hidden long after the possibility of escape had become too remote even to fantasize about, retaining it then more as a tangible link with the day-dream country of his past than as a tool he ever actually hoped to employ, cherishing it almost as a holy relic, as a remnant of a vanished world that he otherwise might almost believe had never existed at all....

And now that it was time to use it at last, he was almost reluctant to do so, to soil it with another man's blood....

He fingered the spoon compulsively, turning it over and over; it was hard and smooth and cold, and he clenched it as tightly as he could, trying to ignore the fine tremoring of his hands.

He had to kill Wernecke....

Nausea and an odd feeling of panic flashed through Bruckman at the thought, but there was no other choice, there was no other way.... He couldn't go on like this, his strength was failing; Wernecke was killing him, as surely as he had killed the others, just by keeping him from sleeping.... And as long as Wernecke lived, he would never be safe: always there would be the chance that Wernecke would come for him, that Wernecke would strike as soon as his guard was down.... Would Wernecke scruple for a second to kill him, after all, if he thought that he could do it safely...? No, of course not.... Given the chance, Wernecke would kill him without a moment's further thought.... No, he must strike *first*....

Bruckman licked his lips uneasily. Tonight. He had to kill Wernecke *tonight*....

There was a stirring, a rustling: Someone was getting up, working his way free from the mass of sleepers on one of the platforms. A shadowy figure crossed the room toward Bruckman, and Bruckman tensed, reflexively running his thumb along the jagged end of the spoon, readying himself to rise, to strike—but at the last second, the figure veered aside and stumbled toward another corner. There was a sound like rain drumming on cloth; the man swayed there for a moment, mumbling, and then slowly returned to his pallet, dragging his feet, as if he had pissed his very life away against the wall. It was not Wernecke.

Bruckman eased himself back down to the floor, his heart seeming to shake his wasted body back and forth with the force of its beating. His hand was damp with sweat. He wiped it against his tattered pants, and then clutched the spoon again....

Time seemed to stop. Bruckman waited, stretched out along the hard floorboards, the raw wood rasping his skin, dust clogging his mouth and nose, feeling as though he were already dead, a corpse laid out in the rough pine coffin, feeling eternity pile up on his chest like heavy clots of wet, black earth.... Outside the hut, the kliegs blazed, banishing night, abolishing it, but here inside the hut it was night, here night survived, perhaps the only pocket of night remaining on a klieg-lit planet, the shafts of light that came in through the slatted windows only serving to accentuate the surrounding darkness, to make it greater and more puissant by comparison.... Here in the darkness, nothing ever changed...there was only the smothering heat, and the weight of eternal darkness, and the changeless moments that could not pass because there was nothing to differentiate them one from the other....

Many times as he waited Bruckman's eyes would grow heavy and slowly close, but each time his eyes would spring open again at once, and he would find himself staring into the shadows for Wernecke. Sleep would no longer have him, it was a kingdom closed to him now; it spat him out each time he tried to enter it, just as his stomach now spat out the food he placed in it....

The thought of food brought Bruckman to a sharper awareness, and there in the darkness he huddled around his hunger, momentarily forgetting everything else. Never had he been so hungry.... He thought of the food he had wasted earlier in the evening, and only the last few shreds of his self-control kept him from moaning aloud.

Bohme did moan aloud then, as though unease were contagious. As Bruckman glanced at him, Bohme said, "Anya," in a clear, calm voice; he mumbled a little, and then, a bit more loudly, said, "Tseitel, have you set the table yet?" and Bruckman realized that Bohme was no longer in the camp, that Bohme was back in Düsseldorf in the tiny apartment with his fat wife and his four healthy children, and Bruckman felt a pang of envy go through him, for Bohme, who had escaped.

It was at that moment that Bruckman realized that Wernecke was standing there, just beyond Bohme.

There had been no movement that Bruckman had seen. Wernecke had seemed to slowly materialize from the darkness, atom by atom, bit by incremental bit, until at some point he had been solid enough for his presence to register on Bruckman's consciousness, so that what had been only a shadow a moment before was now unmistakably Wernecke as well, however much a shadow it remained.

Bruckman's mouth went dry with terror, and it almost seemed that he could hear the voice of his dead grandmother whispering in his ears. Boogey tales...Wernecke had said *I'm no night spirit.* Remember that he had said that....

Wernecke was almost close enough to touch. He was staring down at Bohme; his face, lit by a dusty shaft of light from the window, was cold and remote, only the total lack of expression hinting at the passion that strained and quivered behind the mask. Slowly, lingeringly, Wernecke stooped over Bohme. "Anya," Bohme said again, caressingly, and then Wernecke's mouth was on his throat.

Let him feed, said a cold, remorseless voice in Bruckman's mind. It will be easier to take him when he's nearly sated, when he's fully preoccupied and growing lethargic and logy…growing full….

Slowly, with infinite caution, Bruckman gathered himself to spring, watching in horror and fascination as Wernecke fed. He could hear Wernecke sucking the juice out of Bohme, as if there were not enough blood in the foolish old man to satiate him, as if there were not enough blood in the whole camp…or perhaps, the whole world…. And now Bohme was ceasing his feeble struggling, was becoming still….

Bruckman flung himself upon Wernecke, stabbing him twice in the back before his weight bowled them both over. There was a moment of confusion as they rolled and struggled together, all without sound, and then Bruckman found himself sitting atop Wernecke, Wernecke's white face turned up to him. Bruckman drove his weapon into Wernecke again, the shock of the blow jarring Bruckman's arm to the shoulder. Wernecke made no outcry; his eyes were already glazing, but they looked at Bruckman with recognition, with cold anger, with bitter irony and, oddly, with what might have been resignation or relief, with what might almost have been pity….

Bruckman stabbed again and again, driving the blows home with hysterical strength, panting, rocking atop his victim, feeling Wernecke's blood spatter against his face, wrapped in the heat and steam that rose from Wernecke's torn-open body like a smothering black cloud, coughing and choking on it for a moment, feeling the steam seep in through his pores and sink deep into the marrow of his bones, feeling the world seem to pulse and shimmer and change around him, as though he were suddenly seeing through new eyes, as though something had been born anew inside him, and then abruptly he was *smelling* Wernecke's blood, the hot, organic reek of it, leaning closer to drink in that sudden overpowering smell, better than the smell of freshly baked bread, better than anything he could remember, rich and heady and strong beyond imagining.

There was a moment of revulsion and horror, and he tried to wonder how long the ancient contamination had been passing from man to man to man, how far into the past the chain of lives stretched, how Wernecke himself had been trapped, and then his parched lips touched wetness, and he was drinking, drinking deeply and greedily, and his mouth was filled with the strong, clean taste of copper.

The following night, after Bruckman led the memorial prayers for Wernecke and Bohme, Melnick came to him. Melnick's eyes were bright with tears. "How can we go on without Eduard? He was everything to us. What will we do now…?"

"It will be all right, Moishe," Bruckman said. "I promise you, everything will be all right." He put his arm around Melnick for a moment to comfort him, and at the touch sensed the hot blood that pumped through the intricate network of the boy's veins, just under the skin, rich and warm and nourishing, waiting there inviolate for him to set it free.

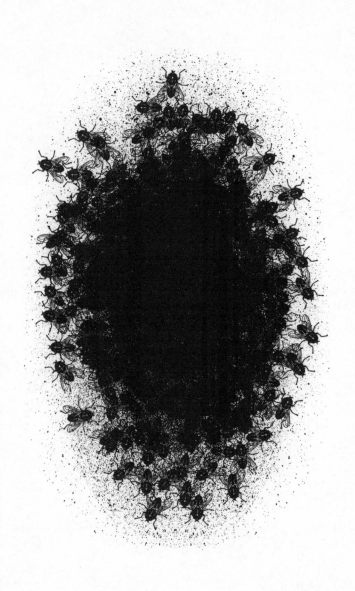

Catching Flies

CAROLE JOHNSTONE

ometimes I pretend I'm a Roman lady in my Roman villa in a countryside which has got long pointy trees and marching soldiers and wide tinkly rivers with ducks and swans. I used to spy on mum watching a TV show called *Rome* and that's where I got the idea. There was lots of blood and guts and sex in it and mum's face went pink when she found my hiding place behind dad's armchair and she told me to close my mouth and sent me to my room and told me never to spy on her watching it again.

But sometimes when mum's busy with Wobs I sneak into the kitchen and pour some of her baking raisins into the bowl that she grinds stuff up in and then some Ribena into the chipped wine glass next to the sink 'cause I can't reach the good ones. I get the old dust sheet from under the stairs and wrap it round me as many times as I can and still breathe and sometimes I try to pile my hair up on top of my head using string or elastic bands but it doesn't usually work.

There's an old shezlong in the living room that came in a van after granny M died. It's just a couch really—with a low back and only one side—but after I asked mum if granny M died on it and she said no it became the thing that I sit on all the time. Especially when I'm being a Roman lady.

That was what I was doing when mum shouted on me. When she screamed.

Now I'm scared. I'm *more* scared. I'm in a strange room in a strange place and there's people outside it but I don't know who they are. I think they might be policemen and policewomen but they don't have uniforms on.

I don't know where mum is. I don't know where Wobs is. But all the people outside want to know is where dad is and I don't know that either. On Fridays after school he and Sadie-who-tries-to-make-me-call-her-mummy wait outside our house in their car to pick me up. Mum doesn't come out and she thinks I don't know it's 'cause she hates them and then they take me to their house and it takes a while to get there. Their house is much bigger than ours is but I don't like it as much. But I like my room okay. It's painted with big yellow daisies.

I don't like this room. It's wee and white and it smells like the stuff mum puts on my cuts. In it is a bed and a table and a chair and a window that doesn't open 'cause I've tried. I don't like the bed. It's metal and cold. Even the bit where my head goes when I'm sitting up. My bedroom at home is yellow and green and the window opens and has Angelina Ballerina curtains (I've told mum I'm a bit old for them now). My bed is soft and squishy all over and I've got a really cool Lord of the Rings light that stays on all night 'cause I still don't like the dark. There's only one light in here and it's just a bulb hanging from the middle of the ceiling.

I hear the door creak and I open my eyes and swing my legs 'round so I can get up off the bed. My knees are shaking but I pretend they're not. I close my mouth and make sure with my fingers. A man comes in. He's fat and hairy and he's wearing a stripy jumper that's too small. He's got a white something over his arm. He says, "hello, Joanne" and then, "can I sit down, Joanne?" and then he does it anyway when I don't say yes.

"Where's my mum?"

"I'm not here to talk about your mum just yet, Joanne."

"Where's my mum? Where's Wobs?" I put my hands on my hips and pretend to be mad. Mum says I'm a stroppy little madam but she smiles when she says it so I think it's a good thing. And sometimes it gets me what I want.

The man tries to smile but his lips won't stretch right. I think there's something wrong with his nose 'cause he sounds coldy and I can hear his breath. I can see his teeth. I can see his *tongue*. It's got white bits on it.

"Let's get you sorted out first, Joanne. I've got you some new clothes to get changed into." He shows me the white things: a T-shirt and joggy bottoms.

"Where's my mum? Where's Wobs?" I'm starting to get scared again. I keep checking my mouth in between speaking 'cause I have to open it to do that.

The man makes a big rattly sigh that makes me feel a bit sick. His eyes look red like dad's used to when he came home late from work. "Wobs is Colin, yes?" He doesn't wait for me to say yes. "He's okay, Joanne. He's in the room right next to you, snug as a bug. He got changed into his new clothes without any fuss at all."

I roll my eyes and forget to be scared. "He's a baby."

The man blinks and tries to smile again. I can't stop hearing his horrible breath. I think I can hear a buzzing noise too and my heart gets jumpy. "Nevertheless—"

"Where's my mum?"

"Joanne." He screws up his fat hairy face. Now he looks the same as dad did when he lied and said he had to go away for a bit. He uses the same kind of voice too. "You *know* what happened to your mum, sweetie."

I shriek when he gets up off the chair and starts coming towards me and then remember to clap my hands over my face. I step backwards and the bed bangs cold at the back of my legs. I think the buzzing is getting louder. Nearer. I look at his horrible tongue and his horrible teeth.

"You should shut your mouth," I say through my fingers.

"We'll talk about your mum soon, I promise, sweetie." His fat face looks worried like he's done something wrong. "Just not yet."

"Shut your mouth!"

"Joanne—"

I'm angry and hot and scared and the backs of my legs are cold *cold* against the bed. "You'll catch flies," I whisper.

He doesn't listen. He keeps on breathing his horrible breath through his horrible mouth and I can tell that he's getting angry now too. He throws the white clothes on the white bed. "You need to get changed, Joanne. You don't have to do it now while I'm here, but you—"

"I've got clothes on!" I shout and one of my fingers slides over my teeth.

He steps back away from me and folds his arms. "But they're dirty, aren't they, Joanne?" he says in dad's voice again. "Look at them. They're dirty."

I look at them. I have to take my hands away from my mouth or else I can't see. I've got on a pair of jeans and my favourite yellow jumper. It's got daisies on it. And blood. Lots of blood. Even though it's dried and even though it's nearly brown. I still remember that it's blood.

I didn't cry when granny M died even though I think I was supposed to. Granny M was mum's mum but she was very strict and very cross and very ugly. When she came 'round to visit she sat at the table in the kitchen with her cross face and a china cup of tea. She had no lips and lots of wrinkles so her mouth looked all sewed up like a scary puppet.

When she saw me or heard me she'd say to mum, "you let that child get away with far too much, Mary." To me she always said, "you'll catch flies, girlie!"

Mum said that to me too—all the time in fact, ever since I could talk I bet—but she didn't *just* say that and nothing else. She was fun so it was okay. She let me paint flowers on the walls in our garden and we had Mad Hatter tea parties and when I helped her with dee-I-why and other boring stuff she said things like "hi-ho, hi-ho, it's off to work we go" and "triumph begins with try and ends with umpf!" just to make me giggle I think. Sometimes we danced around the living room to loud music with the curtains shut and she laughed and went pink and forgot to look scared. Sometimes when she tucked me into bed and switched on my Lord of the Rings light and stroked my hair and whispered, "I love you, Jojo" I wanted to cry. But it was a nice kind of wanting to cry.

When she shouted for me—when she screamed for me—I got off the shezlong and ran to the stairs. My heart was beating very fast but I still stopped at the bottom to unwind the dust sheet before going up. I wondered if I was in trouble—if she'd heard me saying things like "bastards of Dis!" and "you piss-drinking sons of circus whores!" while I'd been pretending to be a Roman lady. I knew it wasn't that though. I was just trying not to be scared.

Mum had stopped screaming when I got to the landing. I went into Wobs's room on tiptoe though 'cause I was still scared. She was standing next to his cot and her hands were over her mouth. I started to do the same but then she took hers away.

"It's okay now, I think. I'm sorry, Jojo, I didn't mean to frighten you again."

The sun was going down to sleep and the room was full of yellow. It made mum look like an angel. Her face was bright and her hair was glowy like my nightlight. Wobs was still sleeping in the cot like always. His fuzzy hair was sticking up and his dummy tit was taped to his big pink cheeks so I couldn't see the rubber sucky bit inside his mouth.

Colin is a really stupid name for a baby. Before dad left to make new babies with Sadie-who-tries-to-make-me-call-her-mummy he'd give me piggybacks around the landing and dangle me upside down till I screamed, "uncle!" and then he'd laugh and say, "Joanne has got the Collywobbles! Wobbles have her Colly got!" I didn't know what it meant but he laughed even more when I started to call Colin Wobs. Mum didn't like it at first but now she calls him it too.

"Is Wobs okay?" I whispered.

"Yes, sweetie, he's okay." Mum looked like she was going to cry again and I didn't like that. I hate it when she cries. Me and Wobs are the ones who are supposed to cry. After dad left she was sad a lot. We didn't have many Mad Hatter tea parties anymore and she got scary letters that she tried to hide and she thought I didn't know what all the brown boxes full of our stuff in the hall meant but I thought I did. "Thank you for coming when I called you, Jojo."

"That's okay," I said. "Can I go away now?"

Mum smiled but I saw her closed lips wobble. "Can you stay here for a wee while maybe?"

I wanted to ask why but I didn't 'cause I thought I knew anyway. I was thinking about the last big time she cried—more than when granny M died or dad went away—the day when the Really Bad Thing happened to mister and missus S next door. Their house is all boarded up now and the FOR SALE sign has fallen over but lots of people still come and point and stare. "Okay."

She left Wobs to come over and cuddle me. My nose went funny when I smelled her—it was like the smell in dad's tool shed: like the big metal vice on the wooden bench. The big metal vice with its wide wide teeth. Mum usually smelled like the flowers in our garden.

"What would you have done if it wasn't okay, sweetie?"

"Mum—"

She pinched my arms till it hurt a bit.

"I know it!" I said. "I know what to do!" 'Cause then I knew for sure she was talking about mister and missus S and I didn't want to talk about it back. It made me think about all the screams and then the quiet and the policemen and the black trolleys on wheels that dripped black stuff down the path like the slime behind a slug.

"I know you do, Jojo," she said and she let me go and went down on her knees to give me a proper cuddle. "I'm sorry, sweetie, I'm sorry."

I cuddled back but I could still smell that nasty smell and she felt funny too. Cold but wet. And I knew what both those things meant. It meant mum was still scared.

"It's just that's it's getting worse, sweetie. It just keeps on getting worse." Her breath tickled my ear but I didn't want to laugh. She'd said that a lot since granny M died. She'd said it nearly every day and every night.

I wake up and it's night time again. The horrible hard bed creaks as I sit up and then stand up. The floor is cold. The stupid white clothes don't fit me. The T-shirt is too tight and the joggy bottoms are too long—they swish on the floor as I creep to the door.

There's a funny feeling in my tummy. Mum said I would feel it one day and now I do. It's not horrible like I thought but fluttery like there's birds inside me. Which there isn't.

The fat hairy man said dad's coming tomorrow. He'll take me and Wobs to his and Sadie-who-tries-to-make-me-call-her-mummy's big house and I won't be able to dance around the living room with the curtains shut or have Mad Hatter tea parties or pretend to be a Roman lady in her Roman villa anymore.

Mum always says that I'm older than my age but I don't think anyone else thinks so. Whenever something went wrong (usually during dee-I-why 'cause I'm clumsy mum says) I'd shout, "fils de pute!" or "me cago en todo lo que se menea!" and mum would laugh and choke and tell me never to say things like that in front of any other grownups or else they'd take me away. And now they have.

I push down the handle and pull open the door. It creaks again but not too much. When I'm in the corridor I let the door go slowly till it stops moving and then I roll up my joggy bottoms to my ankles. The corridor is cold and shiny. I know Wobs is in the room next to mine but I don't know which one. I tiptoe left and my tummy is flapping and flapping inside. Before I can try the black door next to mine I hear voices and freeze.

"It's a crying shame," a lady says. "An absolute crying shame."

I can hear other people muttering and yes-ing but they don't get closer. I hear the roll of a chair on wheels and look at my room door and pretend I can't feel the birds inside me.

"We think there's abuse." It's the fat hairy man—I can tell by his wheezy nose. "I phoned the school, spoke to the girl's teacher. It runs in the family. Apparently she refused to speak at all for the first three years."

"A crying shame," the lady mutters again like it's the only thing she can say.

They're talking about me and mum and Wobs and maybe even granny M. Bastards, cunts, and short-arsed shits. I think it inside my head just like mum told me to. The fat hairy man is the son of a Narbo scrotum. My tummy jumps and flutters and then I remember that I'm trying to find Wobs.

I turn 'round and go back past my horrible room. The door on the other side of mine has a little window in it. I try to look inside it but it's dark. I try the handle and the door opens with no creak. I put my hand over my mouth and I go inside but it still stays dark. I don't like the dark. I wait till the door shuts again and then whisper, "Wobs?"

I don't hear anything back. It's stupid that I wanted to—he's just a baby. But that fluttery funny feeling in my tummy is getting worse and I know it's 'cause he's in here. I know it's 'cause he's in here and the flies are coming and there's no mum to look after us anymore. No mum to feel a fluttery funny feeling in her tummy and know what to do about it. Or to tell me what to do about it.

"Wobs?" I slap the hand that's not on my mouth against the wall 'cause there must be a bulb hanging from the middle of the ceiling and so there must be a light switch.

And then I find it. The light is very bright. I move my hand from my mouth to my eyes till I can see right. Wobs is lying in a cot just like the one in his room at home. He's wearing white pyjamas and lying on his back with his legs and arms out but he doesn't have a dummy in and his mouth's wide open.

That fluttery feeling in my tummy gets worse and now I can hear the buzzy sound again too. The buzzy sound that keeps on getting louder and louder even though the other window in Wobs's room is just like mine: mean and wee and locked. There's a funny mini room in the other corner—it's made of glass and has a little door in the side. Someone's left a cup of coffee on a table inside it but there's no one there to drink it.

My legs get shaky when the buzzy sound gets even louder and my knees smack against the cold floor before I know I've fallen down. I keep whispering for Wobs even though he's a baby—a baby who slept all the way through his mummy dying and me and him getting taken away to here.

They're coming. *They're coming.* I'm older than my age. I'm clever. I'm nearly a grownup really. I keep thinking these things as the fluttering gets harder and the buzzy sound gets louder. But I don't believe them. I'm just really *really* scared. And I want my mum.

And then the light buzzes too and then it goes out. The dark is darker. The buzzy sound is so loud I can't hear anything else. I think of mum saying, "I love you, Jojo." I think of her pinching my arms till it hurt and asking, "what would you have done if it wasn't okay, sweetie?" And I think of all our practicing after mister and missus S and the screaming and then the quiet and all the policemen in uniforms who came to ask us questions 'cause mum said she'd been too scared to stop the Really Bad Thing. And then dad lying to me like mum lied to them when he took me to see the monkeys in the zoo and said he had to go away for a bit.

I march into the middle of the room and I reach out into the dark till I feel the bars of Wobs's cot. And then I think of mum smiling in the living room with the curtains shut and the stereo on and whispering in my ear, "come on, Inch-high Private Eye, what's your plan?"

Keep your mouth shut, I think. Or you'll catch flies.

I thought everything was okay again till I was halfways down the stairs looking at the messy sheet on the floor. This time mum didn't scream my name—she just screamed and screamed. And then she stopped. I turned 'round and ran back up but I didn't want to. Wobs's room was dark 'cause the sun had gone away behind the wall at the end of our garden.

Mum stood in the middle of the room. Her face looked strange. Fat and black and full. When she saw me she shook her head from side to side and her eyes were wide. She closed them once and then waved a hand over her face.

"Mum!" I shouted and I didn't care that my mouth was open 'cause I knew that they'd come back and I was scared. They'd come back 'cause of granny M and dad and Sadie-who-tries-to-make-me-call-her-mummy and their new baby and the scary letters and the brown boxes. And I was scared the most 'cause mum had done the thing she'd always told me not to—the thing she'd been too scared to do too.

She put out her hands to stop me running to her and then covered her mouth with her fingers till I remembered I was supposed to do that too. I could hear Wobs trying to cry but he couldn't 'cause of the taped up dummy.

Mum ran out the door and onto the landing. I saw her eyes fill up black when she turned round to check I was coming and then she stopped and pulled open the cupboard door next to the stairs and ran inside.

When I got there she'd shut the door already but she'd pulled the string that lit the bulb so I could see her through the little slats. Her face was still fat and black and full and her eyes were still wide and her fingers were still over her mouth. She banged at the door till the key fell out onto the floor and I remembered what I was supposed to do and picked it up and put it in the lock and turned it till I heard the click just like we'd practiced.

I saw mum fall a bit when she heard the click too and then she couldn't hold her breath in anymore. She let a bit of it out and some of the flies came out too. They buzzed black at the slats. I heard her scream a bit and then she waved her hands about trying to make them go back into her mouth. She was crying but I could only tell 'cause her face was all wet when she looked at me through the slats.

"Mummy, make it stop! Make them go away! Make them go away, please!" I wanted her to stop crying and holding her breath too. I wanted that the most.

She stared at me till her eyes went as black as her face and I couldn't see them anymore. And then she smiled. I think she smiled 'cause I saw the white flash of her teeth before I heard her twist the stick that closed the slats and then I couldn't see anything anymore.

The light on the landing got dim but it didn't go out. I heard the buzzy sound get louder and louder and I heard mummy scream and scream and kick and punch and rattle the door and I ran back into Wobs's room and sat on the floor and cried and cried and held his pudgy hands till it all stopped.

The fluttery feeling in my tummy and chest is starting to hurt now. I don't like it. I didn't like it anyway but now I really don't. The buzzy sound is so loud it's like it's *inside* my ears and I've got one hand over my shut mouth but I don't think they're here yet. Wobs's cot isn't just like the one at home 'cause I can't fit my arm through the slats to cover his mouth too and when I stand up I'm too short to reach over the top.

They're coming. They're coming. My heart is banging really hard and really fast in the wrong place—I don't like that either. I try not to cry 'cause mum says that doesn't ever help but I'm scared. And I need to look after Wobs but I can't 'cause he doesn't have a dummy and the cot is different and I can't fit my arm through.

The flappy feeling in my chest is in my throat and it and the buzzy sound nearly makes me scream till I remember to keep my mouth shut. Something fizzes the back of my tongue like sherbet and then I start to gag like when I have a tummy bug and then it all comes up out of me in a big chokey rush.

And then the light comes on again. It buzzes buzzes buzzes and then goes on completely and it makes me blink.

The room is full of black. It's filled up with it. Black that came from *me*. I put my hand over my mouth again and I want to scream and cry but then I remember Wobs. He's still lying on his back with his legs and arms out and his mouth wide open.

"Mummy, make it stop. Make them go away, please!" I whisper into my sweaty and wet hand.

But mum is dead.

After the screaming and punching and rattling and buzzing stopped I went back out onto the landing and stood at the cupboard door and stared at the key. After nothing happened I turned it till it clicked again and pulled it slowly open.

Mum was curled up on the floor like we used to do in the garden when it was too sunny for dancing. There was no buzzy sound and her face wasn't black anymore but she was covered in blood like a dead gladiator in an amp theatre and most of it was coming from her mouth and nose and ears. Her eyes were staring up at the ceiling and her tears were red too. Her hands were like claws and some of her nails were gone I think.

I went down the stairs really slowly 'cause my knees felt funny and then I picked up the dust sheet and then I climbed back up. At the top I listened again but I couldn't hear Wobs and I couldn't hear the buzzy sound so I went back in the cupboard and lay down next to mum and pulled the dust sheet over us both and waited for dad.

He didn't come but other people did. And they took me and Wobs away and left mum behind.

I'm older than my age. I'm clever. I'm nearly a grownup really. And I have to be brave. Mum always said that I have to be brave. No matter what.

I look down at Wobs. The buzzy sound is making him twitch and breathe faster. I think he's about to wake up.

The room is still black and buzzy and full of flies. Our bit of room is the only bit left.

I take my hand away from my mouth but it's very shaky and my mouth is shaky too. I Have To Be Brave. I look down at Wobs again and hope his eyes won't open. I try to reach him over the top of the cot but I still can't do it.

"I'm sorry, Wobs," I whisper. "I've got to go away." I look at his pudgy fingers and red cheeks and silly fuzzy hair. "I've got to catch them so you don't."

And then I leave our bit of the room and run into the black buzzy noise. I put my hands over my mouth again and hold my breath and close my eyes and pretend I'm not crying. I pretend I'm not scared and my heart isn't banging really hard and really fast in the wrong place.

And then when I think I'm far enough away and when it feels right—which means when it feels really really *wrong*—I take my hands away and I open my mouth. Wide. Wider than a tinkly river with ducks and swans. Wider than the throwing net of a fisherman gladiator. Wider than the teeth in the big metal vice on the wooden bench in dad's tool shed. And then I breathe in.

It hurts. The things I breathe in hurt. Much more than when they came out. Much more than I thought they would and I'd thought they would. I nearly scream as they rattle and buzz in my ears in my nose in my mouth in my throat in my tummy. They scrape and scratch and flap and buzz 'cause now they're angry. I keep breathing in and in and in till the room stops being black and I've got no breath left and then I clap my hands over my mouth and stop breathing anything at all.

I run to the little door in the glass room and when I let one of my hands go to try the handle it opens. I run inside and turn around and shut it again. I can see Wobs's cot through the fuzzy glass but I don't think I'm far enough away yet for him to be safe.

It's hard to hold your breath. It's even harder when you're scared and your mum's dead and you're trying to be brave but you don't know what to do. And when angry things are scraping and scratching and buzzing and trying to get out again. I hit my leg against the table with the coffee cup and it topples over spilling everywhere. My spare hand hits the window and bounces back to hit my face. Letting some flies out before I manage to breathe them back in.

I'll be able to get back out too. When my eyes go black and I start to scream and punch and kick and rattle like mum did I'll still be able to escape. I'll be able to run to Wobs's cot and let all the black out. I'm scared and I'm sore and my heart's still wrong and I'm full of flies but I'm still Brave like a Gladiator. I still remember what mum said. I've got to have a plan. After mister and missus S we always *always* had A Plan.

I look back at the door and there's a card sticking out of a slot like a key. I don't know if it's the same thing but while I can still hold my breath I pull it out and drop to my knees and push it as far under the door as I can till it's gone and I can't see it.

And then I have to breathe out. I can't hold it anymore. I feel sick and scared and hot and sore and all I can see now are black spots. The flies buzz and buzz and fill the mini room black but I can breathe again and when they push me into the door it doesn't open.

I think of Wobs's room when it was full of yellow. I think of mum when she looked like an angel. Her face bright and her hair glowy like my nightlight. I cough and choke and breathe.

I look at Wobs through the fuzzy glass. I can see his pudgy arms waving through the bars of the cot as he starts to cry. I can see the fat hairy man and maybe the lady who kept saying, "it's a crying shame" barging through the door with the window in. But I keep looking at Wobs.

"I love you," I think inside my head 'cause I think that's what mum was thinking inside hers when she looked at me before her eyes went black and she twisted the stick that closed the slats in the cupboard door. And I hope it won't ever be the same for him. The same as for granny M and mum and me. I don't think it will be.

I try to smile again before I forget how to. Wobs *will* call Sadie mummy. But I don't mind. And I don't think mum will either.

The fat hairy man and the crying shame lady run out into the corridor with a screaming Wobs between them. The flies turn back from the fuzzy glass and the locked door. They fill me with black and angry. They choke till I can't remember being scared or sore or me.

And the flies. Filled with fury and stymied grief. Anomalies. The divine and diabolical; the magical and humoural. The obtuse, the diseased, the misunderstood. Never any of it more than flies.

And now, an opportunity too many lost. Finally, an end. We know it's over. And so we stop flying.

Our Turn Too Will One Day Come

BRIAN HODGE

They're the phone calls we hate most. That unnerving 2 a.m. jangle that drills your gut the way a dentist drills a tooth. If you've been out of college for much longer than a year, nobody has anything to tell you after midnight that you want to hear.

And could you bring a shovel? I can't find ours.

Things like that least of all.

Yes, I went to college. Took a year or two longer than it should have. I had a habit of arguing with professors. Except for the extended trip back to the auld ancestral homeland—a given, in our family, a rite of passage that somewhere along the way seems to have lost most of its original significance—college was the farthest away from home I'd ever gotten for any length of time.

Otherwise, thirty-eight miles—that's it. I rolled down the mountains, bounced across the foothills of the Rockies, and had just enough momentum to make it as far as Boulder. Not a bad place to land, really. It put a little distance between me and where I grew up, but not so much that I didn't have a ready sanctuary close by in case I ever needed it. In case I had another of those phases in which I couldn't quite trust my eyes and ears.

The drive back up, I've never minded it in the day. At night, that's something else. Get past a town called Lyons and the spine of the North American continent starts to wrap around you. The road winds. A lot. Cliffs tower on one side while gorges yawn on the other. Narrow, as gorges go, and not terribly deep, but enough to swallow your car and leave you broken on a rocky streambed below.

When the settlers of the New World left their homes in the Old, it was only natural that they look for things that would be a reminder of what they would never see again. The Dutch who founded New Amsterdam, later to become New York, were drawn to Manhattan because the encircling river there reminded them of the lowland waters back home. Germans who made it past the Mississippi found, another hundred or so miles west, a region around the Missouri River that seemed very much like the Rhineland.

And the Scots from whom my sister and I descended? They had to go farther before they were satisfied. Occasionally I've wondered whether it was blind chance or ordained fate that drew them up into the Rocky Mountains until, at the site of what would one day become Estes Park, they looked around at the peaks and crags, and knew that here was as passable a substitute for the Highlands as they were ever likely to find.

While staking their claims in a world that could be as hostile as it was unfamiliar, these immigrants couldn't have helped but take comfort in whatever semblances of home they could find. I've always understood that.

What I never really thought about was what they might have brought with them.

She was waiting for me outside the front door, Noelle sitting on the ground with a candle. I didn't know if the candle was for her benefit, to keep her occupied, or for mine, so I wouldn't trip over her in the dark. This house sits on the edge of town, up against the old scar where pines were cleared to make room for cattle, so you can't see much here at night. There are no streetlights here. There never have been. There probably never will be.

Not much of a street, either. More like a neglected road and a pervading sense that what happens around these old pines and aspens stays within them.

Noelle's candle was a big, fat pillar brimming over with melted wax. My sister took hold of it and tipped it, poured the molten wax over her hand, over the crust already there. Turning her hand as it ran, cooled, hardened. She must have done that when we were kids, although now wasn't the moment to ask. There were times when we were growing up that I wondered how her hand got so chapped looking, but only ever the left one, and just as often in the middle of summer as the dead of winter.

"Brandt," she said. The name of her ex-husband came out of her as if it had been lodged deep, had to be yanked out skewered on the barbs of a fish-hook. "He killed her. He's killed my baby."

It cut the legs right out from under me. Down on the ground, hugging my sister, feeling that if I didn't have her to hold onto, I'd just keep falling, up to my clawing fingertips in clotted earth.

Should I lie, to pound home the sense of tragedy? Prattle on about what a little beauty queen my niece was, radiant and full of poise and charm beyond her years? That's what sells the grief: the image of a potential that people can recognize at once, without having to look deeper or think; someone they want to wrap their arms around and protect from every bad thing until she's old enough to fuck.

Except she wasn't a cute child. Not on the outside. It was like she'd taken the least appealing attributes from both parents, then made the worst of them. Maybe she would have grown out of it, duckling into swan, but prob-ably not. So this is what she would've grown into: a homely young woman ignored by the world, except for the parts that she touched directly because she loved the world anyway. Six years old and already, on some level, she knew what lay ahead, so she'd begun to prepare. Bugs and plants and mam-mals, Joy just couldn't get enough of them...especially the herds of elk that ambled through Estes Park every autumn rutting season. I adored her all the more for it—that hopeful, melancholy spark of awareness.

So did her father. That's what I want to think: that he loved her more than he simply hated losing. Loved her enough to break into his one-time home and try to take her away into his new world. Except he didn't love her enough to do it competently. In the middle of the night, the haste with which he was trying to get the job done...maybe she didn't realize who it was, just that she was draped over some man's shoulder and that was how you made the news, as long as you were cute enough. No wonder she fought. Six years old and groggy and still she sent a grown man down a flight of 125-year-old stairs.

In a just world, Joy would've landed on her father, not the other way around. He would have broken her fall instead of her neck.

Noelle's hand was starting to look truly deformed. I should've blown out the candle, except that would've left us in the dark, and just hearing her cry would've been worse somehow than seeing her.

"A shovel—did you bring one? I looked and looked for ours, but...."

No one could blame her for not thinking straight. What jury would fault her for finishing the job on her ex-husband that the stairs had started? What cop wouldn't have coached her, however subtly, to spin her story to eliminate her culpability? Okay, she took the big iron fireplace tongs to the back of his skull—so?

"You didn't do anything wrong," I told her. "There's nothing to bury here."

I'm more familiar than I would like to be with how, even in the most crushing moments of her life, a woman can look at you as though you're the biggest fool she's ever seen.

Noelle peeled the wax from her hand and snuffed the candle, then stood, and like a wraith, turned and walked toward the front door.

This house. We've always lived in this house.

It was built by ancestors who died when my grandparents were young, by that first generation of immigrants who came and saw and set down roots, sinking them deep in the cool, mist-dampened earth.

This house. Sprawling and dark, its timbers hug the land as if it had come to a respectful truce with the hills and trees rather than trying to defy them. When it was new, could anyone have looked at this house and not seen that it was built by people who were determined to dig in, hunker down, and stay? Could anyone have failed to recognize that these were people who would love the land and bring down a terrible wrath on neighbors who might oppose or try to cheat them?

It's their blood that flows through my veins, even if these people couldn't be much more remote if they were characters from myth. Their names were spoken with reverence even in my own lifetime, during my first few years, with my grandparents living in their own wing of the house.

We've always lived in this house. But there was never the remotest chance that it could one day be mine. It's always been passed down to the daughters.

Tradition like that, you change it at your peril.

As for the boys, I suppose we learned to never ask why.

Inside the house, Brandt lay where he'd died. He had managed to get up and stagger away from where he'd landed at the foot of the stairs, but appeared not to have made it far before Noelle brained him.

"I hit him once to keep him still right after it happened. So he wouldn't get in the way while I was taking care of Joy," Noelle told me. "Then…when I knew…I must have come back and hit him some more."

The back of his head was buckled and broken, mostly intact but smashed in like the shell of a hard-boiled egg. His face seemed to have shifted, displaced from the inside, his eyes protruding and his jaw jutting crooked. Everything a head could leak had oozed out of one orifice or crack or other.

The fireplace tongs lay nearby, a huge iron scissors-like utensil ending in curved pincers big enough to grapple onto burning logs. This contraption had fascinated me as a boy, one of those things that you instinctively know has a history, has been gripped by generations of hands, as much a part of the fireplace as the flat blackened stones of its hearth. I would imagine our great-great-grandfather pausing in negotiations with someone who had come to buy cattle, or sell him horses, stooping before a blazing fire and using the tongs to wrestle the biggest log into place. I imagined him standing up straight again without setting the tongs aside, instead flexing their heavy, hinged handles and clanging the pincers together to knock loose the ash—once, twice, three times—but eyeing his guest in such a way as to tell him that this display was really to demonstrate that my family had a long reach.

I can only think that this forefather would've been fiercely proud of Noelle.

What about Joy, though—would he have thought much of her? Her ungainly little body, her inquisitive scrunched-up monkey face? He probably would have, for her love of animals, but even if not, one thing mattered much more: She was one of ours, and she'd been taken from us by a thief in the night.

I'd always sensed that, both here and in Scotland, our family was no stranger to feuds and blood.

Joy lay on the sofa where Noelle had put her, still wearing her pajamas, pale blue and full of Dalmatians. My sister had straightened her head so she would look like she was only sleeping, but then, there was that awful bruise down the side of her neck.

I knelt to hold her, and remembered so much, and never until this moment knew which of my feelings for her had outweighed the other: love, or pity.

Noelle leaned against my back, her freshest tears on my shoulder.

"You should start digging," she said, finally. "One for each of them. Near the treeline. Anywhere along there should be good. And not too deep."

"Wouldn't *in* the trees be better?" I still wasn't sure why we were going through with this. Maybe I would strain and sweat awhile before she came to her senses and realized, no, that's not the way we handle things in this day and age. "Not so...in the open?"

"It needs to be away from too many roots," she said. "So you really never knew? You never actually saw anything before, or figured anything out on your own?"

Whatever that implied, I had to tell her no, I must not have.

"I want to stay in here with Joy as long as I can. But not with *him* around." She pointed at Brandt. "Can you get him out back on your own?"

I found an old blanket that would do for dragging him. Didn't much want to touch him to get him onto it, though.

But the fireplace tongs fit his neck just fine.

It wasn't until I was old enough to not much care that I realized our family was different in some ways. Like my grandparents, and the flashes of memory that I swear I have of my great-grandmother, although everyone says I was too little when she died to have remembered anything.

In virtually all the families I've known, or heard friends reminisce about, it's the grandfathers who like to scare you—all in fun—while the grandmothers sit back and shake their heads and tut-tut and warn the grinning old men that they're going to give the children nightmares.

In our family it was the other way around. Which isn't to say that our grandfather couldn't play the game, it's just that our grandmother was the one to send us off to sleep burrowing under our blankets and watching for shadows.

Bedtime stories—if Noelle and I heard this one once, we must've heard some variation of it two dozen times:

My grandparents—your great-greats—they wasn't poor when they come over. Not like so many of 'em back then, especially them filthy Irish. No, they had a nice tidy sum that had come down through the family. Always been wealth in cattle. And there always will be.

But back then, there wasn't no planes to fly in, the way there is today. Back then, if you had a long trip you needed to take, you had to do it slow, no matter how fast you wanted to put some distance between you and wherever you was coming from. So to cross that wide old ocean, they had to get on a big ship. That was the only way in them days. It was one of them big pretty ships like the Titanic, *except older and not as fancy, plus this was one of the ones that didn't sink.*

So it was big and pretty enough, all right, but it was slow. Some of 'em took over a week to cross the ocean, but that's if you got a captain on board that knew his business. Not all of them captains did, you know. Some of them captains were just as dumb as rocks and didn't even have the good sense to realize it, so they'd get lost and the trip might take a little longer. And some of 'em took a lot longer. They might be out there a month or two. And some of 'em never did find their way into port, so they must still be out there today, sailing 'round and 'round and not even knowing it, maybe not even knowing they've been dead most of this time, too. Terrible, just terrible.

But the voyage our family come over on was one of the regular length ones, or near to it. Except it was long enough for what usually couldn't be avoided on trips like that. People died during the middle of it. Nothing sinister about that, just tragic, from natural causes. It's bound to happen. You get that many people together on one boat, especially when they're packed together the way them Irish traveled, and some of 'em are bound to turn toes up. They show up sick and near to dead already, and the strain of the trip finishes 'em off. Or they show up not too bad off and might've survived the crossing, except for breathing somebody else's sick air, and the combination takes its toll.

Now, they couldn't just give them poor folks a burial at sea. It wasn't like the Navy. Their families was right there, and if the sailors had've dumped them bodies over the sides and let the waves take 'em, the families would've raised holy hell. Maybe there would've even been a mutiny, and throats would've got cut, and that wouldn't've been good for anybody. So what they done was wrap them bodies up decent and respectful, and box 'em up in crates, and put 'em way down in the hold, in the bottom of the ship, where it was nice and cool and they might keep a little fresher.

Except what do you think they found after they got to port and it was time to give them families back their dead?

It was only a surprise the first time. All the other times I knew what was coming. I kept hoping that somehow the story would turn out differently for a change, and this part never did.

That's right—there wasn't any bodies left. Just the biggest of the bones and some old dried stains, and the tore-up shrouds, and the holes in the crates where they'd been pried into.

But our family was lucky. They was healthy and strong when they stepped on the ship, and they stepped off the same way. And down that gangplank they walked, your two great-great-grandparents, and my own momma, just a girl then, and my two uncles, and the two babes in arms that my grandma and momma held close and wouldn't ever let another soul see, and nobody kept asking once it was explained how sickly the pair was.

And that's how we come from Scotland to America, so you could grow up in this big house and lay there in that nice bed.

Then she would kiss us goodnight and turn out the light.

There were many other stories that she told my sister and wouldn't tell me, and worse, had instructed Noelle that she was to *never* share them with me, under penalty of…well, I never knew what that would've been, either.

At first I believed Noelle, that for some reason I'd been excluded. Then I refused to believe her at all, figured she was just being malicious, only trying to make me *think* I'd been excluded—looking for that wounding edge the way siblings do. Because she never once cracked and uttered a word of what those other stories were about. That isn't natural. If she'd had anything, wouldn't she have let it slip? Teased me with a few hints?

I'm not sure when I reverted and started believing her all over again.

Maybe soon after our grandmother was dead, and our mother had indisputably assumed the mantle of matriarch, with Noelle grown old enough to feel weighed down by secrets and obligations, and her hand looking chapped sometimes, but only ever the left one, and just as often in the middle of summer as the dead of winter.

Like the opposite of a grave robber working by moonlight, I put shovel to earth and broke the soil.

A few yards in front of me, the pines and aspens rose in a dense, murmuring thicket, poured full of night. Their tops were black cones against the sky, sometimes swaying as if to swat down the stars, blind the only witnesses. Behind me was the house where we've always lived, vast and dark, lights showing in only a couple of windows. Such a big house for so few people these days, with both our parents gone.

And in between, closer to the house than to the treeline, stood the stout wooden post that supported the iron bell. Just as we've always lived in the house, the post has always stood there—replaced each time it grew weathered and weak—and the bell has always hung from it, as much a part of each generation as the fireplace tongs.

I'd never dug a grave before, let alone two. Noelle had stressed that she wanted plenty of space between them. To dig them side by side would have been an insult to Joy and the way she'd died. It would have given Brandt more consideration than he was due, either on the earth or under it.

No doubt there are men for whom gravedigging feels like honest work, or the last kindness they can show the dead. There was none of that for me and my shovel. We were accomplices, guilty of something I couldn't specify, although it mattered less here than it might have elsewhere. It may have been wrong, but down deep I knew that the greater right was to stand with family.

One adult, one child....

The thing about graves, I learned, is knowing when to stop. Six feet under is the rule of thumb, and even though I wouldn't be digging that far—not too deep, Noelle had said—I knew even that wouldn't feel far down enough. Things like this, they feel as though they should be buried deeper.

Behind me, nearer to the house than to the graves, the bell seemed to watch, to make sure it was all done properly.

At just past three feet, the shovel blade scraped something hard and unyielding, although it didn't feel big. Easy to pry out of the hole, caked with earth like a flattened dirt clod, and wash off with the bottled water I'd brought from the kitchen.

Even in the moonlight I could tell what it was. It was corroded by perhaps decades underground, but so thick and sturdy it was still mostly intact: a gigantic belt buckle of brass or iron. Just the kind of thing a man might wear if he had a lot of cattle and not much taste.

It should've been a bigger surprise to think, finally, that I hadn't really known my family at all. But it wasn't.

During the years I spent growing up, I couldn't think of a single occasion, with absolute certainty, that I'd heard the bell ring. A time or two, maybe, or three or four, late at night, the sort of event you can't be sure whether it really happened or whether you'd dreamed it. The sort of thing you might ask about over breakfast, like any boy trying to satisfy his curiosity without going too far, making someone angry. And of course they never got angry, my parents. They would just look at each other, blank and quizzical, as if to silently inquire of each other how I could ever have gotten such an idea. Then they would tell me no, no, the bell hadn't rung. How could it? The bell was just for show, remember. The bell wasn't for ringing.

And it wasn't, so far as I knew. It was the only bell I'd ever seen that spent its life with a sleeve secured over its clapper. A thick old leather sheath with an intricate weave of ancient rawhide that laced up one side, and whose tip, like some kind of strange condom, was stuffed with fresh-shorn wool.

I would've only been a toddler the afternoon my great-grandmother caught me staring up at the bell with helpless longing. The time they later told me I would've been too young to remember, so I must've been making it up.

"Don't you ever ring that bell there just to be ringing it," she warned me, as if I were tall enough to even try. "Do that, and you just might look down to find your toes gone."

The holes were dug, the bodies placed inside—Joy's lowered with tender care, Brandt's rolled in the way you'd kick a can to the gutter. All that was left was to replace the upturned earth. Because Noelle never had come to her senses. She was adamant: *This had to be done.*

So I did it, and night was kind, keeping me from seeing the soil in much detail. I imagined that mingled within the two mounds, in each shovelful, there must have been other trinkets: buttons and rings and boot nails and scraps of rotted leather. But as long as I didn't notice bones or teeth, I could tell myself that those pale glints were bits of milk glass, chips of ceramic.

"Thank you. So much," Noelle told me after it was done. "You should go now."

"That's it? Just *go*—like that?"

"It would be better if you did."

"I'm not some hired hand," I said, and thought of my niece in the ground. "Family, *that's* who comes out in the middle of the night, no questions asked." Thought of the little girl to whom, last Christmas, I had given a telescope, and how much she'd loved it, even though she quickly grew bored with looking at the sky and instead wanted to turn it on the earth, the woods. Looking for her cherished elk and whatever else that roamed. "Is there something that makes you more family than I am?"

"So what if there is? That doesn't have to mean it's a *good* thing." She wiped dirt from my cheek. "So please...just leave now and be glad you grew up sheltered."

"I didn't grow up sheltered, Noelle. I grew up being lied to. Sheltered is when you're blissfully ignorant. Lied to, that's when you know there's something not right but everyone you trust tells you you're imagining things. Tells you that so often that one day you're just not sure when you can believe your eyes and ears, and when you can't. Was that somebody's idea of doing me a favor? Because there were some years there that I was pretty well unemployable."

"There was always money. You never had to worry about that."

"Aren't you even listening? Isn't that kind of beside the point?"

That was the remark that made me decide to shut up, no matter what.

For a woman who's just buried her only child, the point is whatever she says it is.

Noelle draped both hands onto my shoulders, on the verge of…something. Tears, yes, always those, but now more, as if she wanted to tell me something but didn't yet dare to. She had looked this way so many times while we were growing up that I was used to it. Or just decided that I was imagining it.

Gran's not here anymore to punish you if you tell me anything, I almost said, and any other night, would have. It wasn't that I knew for sure Gran used to do anything. It's just that I started to wonder where Noelle had picked up the bit with the hot wax.

"Okay. Stay," she said. "You can't say you weren't warned."

She went for the bell, hanging from the post with its clapper sheathed, and in the near-dark Noelle untied the complex knotwork of the rawhide lacing as though her fingers had always known how.

She struck the bell then, a short but consistent pattern rung three times, and left to hang in the pre-dawn chill like so many recollections from dreams that they'd never entirely managed to convince me weren't real.

Here's another one that never happened:

There was this boy, see, who grew up in a mountain valley on the edge of a one-time resort town whose main streets had gradually become clogged with touristy kitsch. But the past was never entirely out of reach there. On a prominent hill, presiding over Estes Park like a dignified old mayor, stood the rambling Stanley Hotel and the ghosts that called it home. Below, sometimes all but forgotten, were even older pockets of time, bygone traces of the trappers and hunters and prospectors and ranchers who settled the valley first, fighting—sometimes to the death—for their rights to take and make, as settlers always do.

The boy's roots went deep here, even if he was too young to know it at the time.

He must have been four, maybe closer to five, because his sister was still in the crib that summer. Even today he remembers that part quite clearly, and how attentively their grandmother used to watch over her as she slept. There were times the old woman seemed to see everything, but not while she was tending the baby. This, and their father and grandfather's habit of retreating to the den after dinner, was what finally gave him the courage to slip outside one evening. Because lately he'd been wondering where their mother disappeared to this time of evening.

At first he looked for her up and down the empty road, trying to push back the gnawing sense of dread he got whenever he wondered what would happen if one evening she never came back.

He tried behind the house next, past the muffled bell hanging like a poison fruit he was already too intimidated to touch, and following his instincts into the pines and aspens. They were as good a place to walk alone as any. There seemed to be no end to them, their depth unknowable, and you might walk and walk for days, yet never come close to emerging on the other side.

Her back was to him when he first spotted her in a cluster of trees going dark with pooled shadows, as she sat upon a sun-bleached fallen log. Before her, obscured by the log, he could see the upper curve of a dark bulky stone. Her hair was long then, halfway down her spine. For a moment he stood and watched. Her elbows were thrust out behind her, as if she were holding something close to her body. Whatever it was, it seemed to be squirming.

Pretty soon, he started forward again, to close the gap between them.

It was inevitable that she would hear him eventually. Even a woodland filled mostly with evergreens can be a noisy place to walk. She whirled, her hair like a lashing whip, her eyes fixing on him first with fright and then with fury and, if his memory could be trusted, something he later identified as guilt.

His gaze lowered to the bundle in her arms—the wrinkled pink-gray skin that seemed to bristle with coarse dark hairs, and the conical face whose spade-like snout was clamped over her exposed breast. Surely he hadn't imagined the little peg teeth; why else would he have wondered if they hurt? Surely he hadn't imagined the way it seemed to sense his mother's abrupt distress, and pulled away to open its mouth—inside, the roof was ridged and spotted—with a squall like that of a bear cub.

When the stone sitting before his mother rose with a shudder and a thick wet snort, he turned and ran.

She was all smiles the next morning. Made him his favorite breakfast—waffles and bacon. Told him what an imagination he had, that she'd only been out there with Noelle, in a small threadbare blanket, the same blanket she used to carry him out as a baby too, to nurse him within the trees so that he would learn to love nature and its bounty. Like everyone in the family.

The boy ate his waffles. He let her stroke his hair. He decided to try harder to believe.

"I guess if you take most any family that has old money coming down through the generations," Noelle said, "the farther back you go, the more likely you are to find that so much of what they have is built on the bodies of people who got in their way."

We were sitting on the wide, open porch along the back of the house, where we used to play as children and dream of the adventures the world held for us. It had been a long night, and the sky was beginning to lighten with pink and blue and orange, just enough dawn to make out the pair of dark rounded mounds near the treeline.

"We were never the Hearsts or the Rockefellers, not even close," she said. "But there still were bodies."

The last echoes of the bell had faded minutes ago, but I thought I could still hear them, pealing across the open ground and ricocheting among tree trunks.

"It started in Scotland, but not even Gran was sure how far back it actually went, or who was the first. I mean, Gran used to tell me stories about those parts, too. But not long before she died she told me that she'd made up parts of them herself, because she had to tell me something. It was easier than admitting she didn't know. You can't tell little kids stories without personalities in them."

If the look on Noelle's face some mornings had been anything to go by, there were stories you shouldn't tell kids at all.

"So let's call her Jenny, okay? Our great-great-great-whatever grandmother. And even though she was a good woman, she always turned a blind eye to what her father and grandfather and brothers and uncles and husband did: stealing cattle—those big shaggy Scottish cattle that look like walking carpets—and sometimes killing the rightful owners and *their* men when they came to get them back. Or killing other thieves who tried to take what they'd stolen first."

Stolen fair and square, I imagined our grandmother saying. I could hear none of her voice in Noelle's hollow recitation, my sister murmuring her way through this as if she'd waited so long it finally seemed to involve some other family. Except I still couldn't help but think of the words that Gran might use instead, the old woman forcing herself between us even though she'd been dead for years.

"So Jenny had seen enough men in her life get hanged for murder by sheriffs, and wanted to do something about it before it reached her own sons. Only she was enough of a pragmatist to realize that she couldn't stop them from following the same path if that's what they meant to do. So instead of trying prevention, Jenny turned to the cleanup."

By now, long minutes after the bell had rung its last, I could hear something heavy crashing through the still-darkened woods.

"God knows how she did it. How she managed to find them. And then how she managed to communicate with them. It's not like they speak, you know. But when you're looking in their eyes...you see something there that gives you the impression that some part of them is listening." Noelle kept watch, her eyes as dead now as the daughter we'd buried. "I don't know, maybe I'm giving them too much credit. Gran never said so, but more than once I've wondered if we weren't only descended from cattle thieves and killers, but a witch, too."

From out of the trees, where the dawn had not yet reached, they came: six dark shapes, thick and low to the ground, like boars, their round muscled shoulders and backs bouncing along with eager purpose.

"They're called yird swine," Noelle said. "They like to dig into graves for food. And these are ours. They've always been ours."

They attacked the fresh shallow graves with snorts and squeals, sounding not quite like any hogs I'd ever heard—like if you listened closely enough to the grunting, you could make out the rudiments of voices. And they were ravenous, burrowing into the mounds and churning through earth with forelimbs that I was too far away to see, with too little light yet, but their snouts, their claws…the soil flew as though they'd been made for this and nothing else.

You can watch things that hold you rapt with fascination even as they sicken you. And so it was, here and now. Because I began to understand. They weren't merely ours; we were theirs, too. Just as the murderous blood of our fathers ran through our veins, the milk of our mothers ran through theirs. They would demand it as part of their bargain.

"So Jenny, whatever her name really was, she went out in secret to these *things*, that her neighbors felt nothing but dread for. However she managed it—and I don't think I ever want to know—she turned them into allies. Then she came home and demanded of the men left in her family that if they took another's life, she had to know about it immediately… and that she would take care of it. At least that's the way Gran told it. More or less."

Over at the mounds, they were shoulders deep and going strong.

"Why wasn't I supposed to know any of this?" I asked her.

"That's just how it all came about. Having a way to get rid of the bodies…quickly, completely…it only made things worse, in a way."

Yes. I imagined that it did. It gave our forefathers a license to kill. Made them arrogant, maybe even prolific. I could imagine sons, brothers, uncles, cousins, drunk on ale and their own impunity, battering on Jenny's door in the middle of the night, their saddles draped with the corpses of those they'd killed on the road after some trivial insult in the taverns.

"So you—all the men in the family, I mean—weren't supposed to know until there wasn't any way to avoid it," Noelle said. "Gran loved men, I know. But she didn't have a very high opinion of your self-control."

Over at the graves, they'd reached the bodies. Noelle snapped out of her muted trance and buried her face in her hands.

"I can't watch it. Not this time," she said, and the slammed door off the end of the porch was the last I would hear of her for hours.

So I stayed to do my family duty, because while Noelle hadn't said so, I suspected that this was a vital part of the process; that *they* expected one of us to remain and bear witness, remembering the covenant between our species, our clans.

So I stayed, and watched as they ferociously tugged the bodies halfway from their graves, to feed on what lay helpless and exposed, then tug a little more to expose that too. I listened as their tusks ripped through skin and muscle, to the bursting of tender organs, to the grinding of their teeth on bones.

It was clear to me now, finally, Gran's old story about our family coming over on that ship: what was really swaddled in the blankets and what they'd grown into, what they'd bred. I'd always thought we'd come because this was the land of opportunity, and maybe that's really how my ancestors saw it...but only after they'd done things so terrible they could no longer remain on the far side of the ocean.

So because of their sins, I watched, listened, as their youngest descendant was ground into gristle.

We, too, were a part of the old bargain. Noelle hadn't said this either, but didn't have to. She'd been raised to believe, obviously, that there was no other way. Why else would she turn her daughter over to *this*? I could imagine the things our grandmother must have told her, things that Gran maybe even believed herself: *You've seen them things dig, so don't think you could ever get away. They got the smell of you in their noses, you know, and they was fed on the same milk that you suckled from your momma, so there's no place you could go that they couldn't sniff you out and dig their way to, some day.*

And still, I loved her.

It all explained some things—why I had never once visited the graves of my grandparents—but called so many others into question: If my mother, after the cancer took her, had really donated her remains to science. If my father, the day he left, had truly left for the reasons he'd said, and why he hadn't tried harder to take me with him.

And because I knew so much more now about where and what I came from, I thought about families, and the roles everyone seems to fall into: givers and takers, the feeders and the fed upon.

Turns out we were a lot more normal than I ever gave us credit for.

Grindstone

STEPHEN GRAHAM JONES

TINCHERA PASS, COLORADO, 1885

Derle had fourteen slugs in him by the time he made it into the trees. Six of them had splintered bone. His chest whistled when he breathed. They couldn't stop him from smiling, though.

He pulled himself past one tree, reached ahead for another, and felt the heat of a slug as it passed by his face, leaving a suck in the air that pulled him over just enough that, for an instant, before the splinters exploded, he could see a perfect hole punched in the tree he was reaching for.

Ten paces past that tree, the slug was sizzling into the wet undergrowth, writhing like the air hurt it.

Derle picked it up, turned, threw it as hard he could down his back path, his fingers smoldering, numb.

He was dying. No two ways about it.

His left hand was the only thing holding his intestines in. They looked just like sheep guts. When they'd spread out into Derle's lap, that was the first thing he'd thought—sheep—and then from there had stepped back into his childhood, the smells, the sounds. The way a lamb can scream, if you want it to. If you know what you're doing.

Derle fell forward, caught himself on his right hand, stumbled forward.

It wasn't what he'd been trying to do to the girl named Suzanne that had got everybody on the wagon train reaching for their long rifles. It was what he'd been doing to their livestock for the last two months.

Last week, the heifer had given birth to something the preacher they had along had to turn his face from.

Derle had smiled then too, but covered it with his hand.

That night, as if in answer to the birth, an angel had screamed across the sky, on fire.

Or that's what the preacher said it was.

Derle didn't know, had been hiding with a stray, trusting dog, sure that if that light threw his shadow on the ground, it would split him in half.

In trade for getting to live, he'd let that dog go.

It never came back.

In the trees now, bleeding out, Derle wondered what strange litter that bitch was going to throw here in a couple of months. Whether she'd know to bite through their thin skulls or not. If they'd be satisfied with just milk.

Derle didn't think so. Not if they took after their old man.

Behind him now, the shots were farther and farther apart from each other, just so he could hear them, he knew. Just so he would know not to come back.

Derle laughed and dark, rich blood welled up, seeped down his chin. He burbled his lips in it like a child, caught himself on a tree. Shook his head at how stupid this all was.

They were just animals, right?

Taking everything into account though, it was probably best they'd caught him before he had a chance to take Suzanne any farther than he already had. The designs he had on her involved acts he hadn't even been able to subject the sheep of his childhood to, just because they weren't built right. If they'd caught him in the middle of that—of her—then....

Derle collected the blood from his chin, flung it down to the ground. If they'd caught him with Suzanne, it wouldn't have been enough just to put him down. Instead, they'd have got the preacher man involved, probably. The end result would have been the same, probably—Derle, dead—but it would have taken a sight longer. They'd have stretched him first. Maybe taken the skin off in strips. Done stuff to his eyes.

No, this was better.

This way, he could die without anybody watching.

All he had to do now was find a good place, wait it out.

Derle shook his head again, rubbed his eye with his bloody hand—a mistake—and turned his head as much as he still could, spying for a place to rot, a place to get his bones good and bleached. Because that was what really mattered. He'd thought about it a lot already, going up and down Goodnight's trail these last four years. He needed some place in the sun, so he'd dry out, and so the birds could find him, deliver him to the sky mouthful by mouthful.

He got hard, thinking about that—the birds, sitting on him with their sharp feet, digging into his chest cavity with their perfect beaks, the muscles on the backs of their necks bunching—but then, when he lowered his hand, there was just blood in his pants, and he didn't know what he was feeling.

He stumbled on, feeling his way, finally fell out into the clearing he'd always known was waiting for him.

It was the creek bed of the creek everybody'd been counting on two days back, the creek whose absence they were probably blaming Derle for now as well.

This one wasn't on him, though.

He shook his head no, that this wasn't on him at all.

This was God's fault.

Dead center in the creek, buried deep in what had been mud, was the angel. It wasn't on fire anymore, was the color of ash now. Just a shoulder-high knob of speckled grey rock. The water had cooled it, Derle knew, but had steamed off doing it. He could tell because there were fish and turtles rotting all over the place. Fish and turtles the raccoons hadn't touched.

It made the rock interesting.

Maybe it *was* an angel, he told himself, or a demon, just tucked into a ball, its chin between its knees, wings folded all around it.

Derle nodded to himself, licked his lip again—more blood—and took a step towards it, fell face first into the rocky creek bed. What teeth he still had in front cracked off at the gumline, then night sifted down all around him and he dreamed, and in his dream he was risen, standing where he'd just fallen, and, instead of running back the way he'd come, he was watching the rock, unable to look away.

It was trying to catch fire again. There was no water to douse it anymore. Except—it was like at the blacksmith's shop, if he had the big grindwheel spinning. Sparks. They were popping off the surface of the rock in…in regular patterns. Like writing.

Derle looked all around to be sure nobody was around to see that he couldn't make these words out. If these marks were even letters.

Soon enough the sparks were gone, and the whole rock was smoking, smoldering, popping, baking the creek bed's fine silt of sand into a shell.

Derle cocked his head over.

It was an egg, he figured. Had to be. Because this was how it worked after you died, or when you were dying: something had to come collect you, pull you to where you belonged. Like he'd wanted with the birds. Only—he knew this now, should have known all along—Derle was a special case, was the one who'd figured out how to leave his seed inside an animal so that it took.

The preacher man had been right: for him, they'd sent an angel. All it had to do was shake off the rock it had traveled in and stand to its full height, the ram's horns on its head curving back along its skull, its cloven hooves shiny and hard. It would be the child Derle could have fathered, given enough time, and enough sheep.

It was all a man could hope for, really. To leave a legacy.

Derle spit a long string of blood, and looked past the rock, into a pair of green eyes. It was a doe, watching him.

"Mama," Derle said to it, blacking out a little on his feet, and thought he was getting hard again but knew too he could never catch this doe, or talk her in. Not smelling of blood like he did. The next time he blinked, she disappeared, then, a moment later, there were twelve eyes, sixteen.

They'd all come to watch.

Derle lowered his head, understood.

It's not every day a man like him passes over.

Nine lunging steps later, he was at the rock, falling into it. The letters were still hot; one of them burned into his cheek. Derle offered his palms as well, and then his other cheek. It kept him awake, made him breathe faster.

He wasn't dreaming, he knew that now. Dying maybe, but not dead yet. The slugs from the rifle had just taken his body.

There was more to him than that, though. There always had been. It was why his grandmother had had to lock him in the basement all those years. Why he could never stay in one place for more than a week or two. Why cats stared at him.

Derle narrowed his eyes, breathed two times, then nodded, reached as high up onto the rock as he could, fixing his fingers into one of the letter marks. His fingertip smoked and sizzled but he held on, started climbing, and then, unable to stand anymore once he was on top, he just held himself up with his palms, started shivering, heard more than felt one of the lead slugs plunk from his chest, clatter onto the rock. It didn't roll away like it should have but clung at an impossible angle, standing up on its mushroom nose. And then another, and another, until all eight of the slugs still in Derle had been pulled out, some completing the line they'd been trying to push through him, some coming back out the same hole, trailing muscle.

None of them rolled off.

Derle focused on them as best he could, even touched one with the pad of his thumb. It was tacky, the lead giving under his thumb then seeping bit by bit into the pores of the rock.

Derle laughed, fell hard on his stomach, and spit out another part of a tooth. Because it wasn't metal, it clattered away, rolled into the creek bed. With his tongue he could feel the stumps in his gums, and then the warmth from the rock started blistering its way up through his body, and all at once he knew what he was doing here: instead of being on top of a sheep or a heifer or a stray dog, he was astride an angel, his fluids coating her, seeping into the pores after the lead, so that they were one, him and the angel. They were joined.

This wasn't his child, but his lover.

Not that it would have mattered, he smiled to himself, and the effort it took to part his lips was the final thing that killed him, and it wasn't like when he'd fallen at the edge of the clearing and blacked out. Real death was like suffocation; he could hear insects scrabbling after each other in the recesses of his mind, then massing in his throat, welling into his mouth, choking him, so that all he could see anymore was light, light everywhere, so cold.

Derle relaxed into it, gave up finally, ready to surrender himself to whatever was out there.

Except the rock was holding onto him, wasn't ready to give him up.

Minutes later—hours, maybe—Derle opened his eyes again, was on his back now, as if his front had already cooked enough.

Against the backdrop of stars, he held his hand up, the one he'd fingered the hot slug up with.

It wasn't burned anymore. The skin was new, sensitive.

Derle smiled, his eyes filling with water, and was able to sit up, *breathe*, cough out the bit of shiny whiteness that had been lodged in his throat, rub the pad of his thumb over the two flat nobs on either side of his forehead, like someone had set the feet of a draft horse's shoe against his head and hit the butt of it with a hammer.

The rock below him was cool now, sated. No blood dried on it at all.

Derle nodded to himself, breathed some more just to be sure he could, then turned his head to a sound in the creek bed behind him.

It was Suzanne, in her gingham dress, the one she wore on Sundays.

Derle nodded once to her in acknowledgment, around the rifle she had leveled on him, and then she fired. The slug went in through his right eye, misted the back of his skull out behind him, one long strand of red looping out then coiling back in. The second shot took him in the chest, severing his spine, the third knocked most of his right arm off, and then, when he tried to hold his hands out in front of him, only one of his arms complying, she shot through his left palm as well, the slug burrowing up the hollow bone of his forearm, exploding through his shoulder blade, and by then she had the breech of the rifle pressed right up against her cheekbone and she was screaming and pulling the trigger, and levering another round in, and pushing it into him too, until the rifle exploded in her face.

It threw her back into the grass, her right eye a mess, her right cheekbone showing white, the ragged skin there smoking, bloodied, gone.

Like Derle, she died smiling, all her accounts settled.

The next morning the green-backed flies found the two of them, coated the parts of them that had been open to the night, and, though the birds settled down around the rock, they never drew any closer to the body of the man on it, and the coyotes kept their distance as well, and so the flies ate their fill and deposited their eggs and the blind white maggots swelled up from the corpse on the rock by the thousands, and then the sun drank all the fluids up like Derle had wanted, and the rains came, and the dry creek bed ran enough water to float a small child, and the next summer, two miles downstream, where the creek crossed the twin ruts in the grass, there was a bleached white skull grinning up, half buried in the dirt until the spoked front wheel of a wooden wagon rolled across it, then the back wheel, and it would have ended there, except a boy hanging his bare feet over the back of the wagon dropped down from the gate, collected the thing he thought was going to be a rock, at first, or an Indian grindstone.

Because his family's wagon was moving, he didn't have time to look at what he'd found until he'd caught back up, let his sisters pull him in.

They crowded around him, blocking the find from their mother.

"What is it?" the eldest sister said, taking the skull into her lap, her eyes glittering. "Look at his teeth…," she said, running her finger along the line of top ones. "He must have been rich, a prince or some—"

The boy pulled it back from her, brushed the rest of the dirt from it, and there, unmistakable above the eyes, at what would have been the hairline, were the bony nubs of two horns, too dull to have even pushed through the skin of the scalp, probably.

The boy dropped the skull, and it broke the rest of the way open.

Inside, nested up against the sun, were maggots that shouldn't have been there, some of them already crawling into green-backed flies, rising sluggishly into the air of the wagon.

Later that night, all twenty-two wagons of the train would burn. This is a recorded thing. What wouldn't be recorded was the boy, running for the woods, his sister chasing him, running on all fours. What wouldn't be recorded was that she was growling.

Doll Hands

ADAM L. G. NEVILL

I am the one with the big white head and the doll hands. I work behind the desk in the West block of Gruut Huis. When I'm not taking delivered medicines upstairs to the residents who slowly die in their beds, I watch the greenish screens of the security monitors that cover every inch of Gruut Huis's big red brick walls and its empty tarmac forecourt.

I watch out for deliveries and for intruders. Deliveries come every day. Intruders not so much anymore. They have mostly died out there in the draughty buildings of the dead city, or are lying still on the dark stones before the Church of Our Lady. In Brugge the dying shuffle and crawl to the church. It's like they have lost everything but a memory of where to go.

Last Christmas I was sent out with two porters to find the baboon child of Mr. Hussain who lives in the east wing. The baboon boy escaped from his cage and blinded his carer. And as I searched for the boy in Guido Gezelleplein, I saw all of the wet stiff bodies beneath the tower, lying down in the mist.

One of the day porters, Vinegar Irish, beat the baboon boy when we found him feeding amongst the bodies. Like the residents, the baboon boy had grown tired of the yeast from the tanks in the basement. He wanted meat.

At ten in the morning, there is movement on the monitor screens. Someone has arrived at the GOODS AND SERVICES entrance of Gruut

Huis. Out of the mist the squarish front of a white truck appears and waits by the roller gate. It's the caterers. Inside my stomach I feel a sickish skitter.

With my teeny fingers I press the buttons on the security console and open Door Eight. On the screen I watch the metal grill rise. The truck passes into the central court of Gruut Huis and parks the rear doors by the utility door of the service area. Behind this utility door are the storage cages for the residents' old possessions, as well as the porter's dormitory, the staff room, the stock cupboards, the boiler room, the workshop, the staff wash-room, and the yeast tanks that feed us with their yellow softness. Today, the caterers will need to use the staff washroom for their work.

Yesterday, we were told a delivery of food was arriving for the Head Residents' Annual Banquet. Mrs. Van den Broeck, the Head Resident of the building, also informed us that our showers were to be cancelled and that we were not allowed into the staff room all day because the caterers needed to use these areas to prepare the banquet. But none of the staff ever want to go into the washroom anyway if the caterers are on site. Despite the sleepiness of the white ape, who is night watchman, and the drunkenness of Vinegar Irish, and the slow movements of Les Spider, handyman, and the merry giggles of the two cleaning girls, we can all remember the other times when the little white truck came to Gruut Huis for the banquets. None of the staff talk about the days of the General Meetings and Annual Banquets. We all pretend they're normal days, but Vinegar Irish drinks more cleaning fluid than usual.

Using the desk phone I call Vinegar Irish, who is the porter on duty in the east wing. He takes a long time to answer the phone. On the security console, I switch to the camera above his reception desk to see what he is doing. Slowly, like his pants are full of shit and he can't walk straight, I see him stumble into the green underwater world of the monitor screen. Even on camera I can see the bulgy veins under his strawberry face. He's been in the key cupboard drinking fluids and not beside his monitors like he is supposed to be at all times. If he was behind his desk he would have heard the alarm sound when I opened the outer gate, and he would have known a delivery had arrived. His barking voice is slurred. "What you want?"

"Delivery," I say. "Watch my side. I'm going down."

"Aye. Aye. Truck's come. What you need to do—" I put the phone down while he is speaking. It will make him go shaky with rage in the east wing. He'll call me a bastard and swear to punch his trembly hands at my big head, while spit flies out of his vinegar mouth. But he won't remember the altercation tonight when we finish the day shift, and I have no time right now for a slurred lecture about all the things I already know about our duties that he cannot manage to do.

As I walk across the lobby to the porter's door, with my sack-cloth mask in my doll hands, the phone rings behind my desk. I know it is Vinegar Irish in a spitting rage. All the residents are still asleep. Those that can still walk never come down before noon.

Smiling to myself, at this little way I get revenge on Vinegar Irish, I stretch the brownish mask over my head. Then I open the airlock and duck through the escape hatch to the metal staircase outside. As I trot down the stairs, the mist rushes in to cover my little shiny shoes. Even with the mask pulled over my fat octopus head, I can smell the sulphur-rust of the chemical air.

At the bottom of the staircase, I enter the courtyard. The courtyard is right in the middle of all four blocks of flats. The residents can look down and into the courtyard from their kitchen windows. I bet their mouths fill with water when they see the white van parked by the utility door. What the Head Residents don't eat, we porters deliver up to their flats in white plastic bags.

Seeing the caterer's truck makes my stomach turn over with a wallop. The two caterers who came in the white truck are standing by the driver's door, talking, and waiting for me to open the utility area. Both of them are wearing rubber hoods shaped into pig faces. The pig faces are supposed to be smiling, but they look like the faces in dreams that wake you up with a scream.

The caterers are wearing rubber boots to their knees too, and stripy trousers tucked into the tops of their boots. Over their stripy trousers and white smocks they wear long black rubber aprons. They are both putting on gloves made from wire mesh.

"Christ. Would you look at the cunt's head," the older caterer says. His son giggles inside his rubber pig mask.

I clench my tiny hands into marble hammers.

"Awright?" the father says to me. Under the mask I know he is laughing at my big white head and stick body. The father gives me a clipboard. There is a plastic pen under the metal clasp that holds the pink delivery note to the clipboard. With my doll hands I take the pen and sign and print my name, then date the slip: 10/04/2152. They watch my hands in silence. The world goes quiet when my hands go to work, like no one can believe they have any use.

On the *Grote and Sons Fine Foods and Gourmet Catering* sales slip, I see I am signing for: *2 livestock. Extra lean, premium fresh. 120 kilos.*

The caterers go into the cabin of their truck and drag their equipment out. "Let's get set up. Give us hand," the father says to me.

From behind the two seats in the dirty cabin that smells of metal and floor bleach, they pass two big grey sacks to me. They are heavy with dark stains at the bottom and around the top are little brass holes for chains to pass through. Touching the sacks makes my legs shake. I tuck them under my arm. In my other hand I am given a metal box to carry. It has little red numbers by the lock. The box is cold to touch and is patterned with black and yellow stripes.

"Careful with that," the fat father says as I take the cold box in my small hand. "Is for the hearts and livers. We sell them, see. They is worth more than you are."

The son hangs heavy chains over one arm and grabs a black cloth bag. As he walks, the black cloth sack makes a hollow knocking sound as the wooden clubs inside bang together. The father carries two small steel cases the size of small suitcases in one hand, and two big white plastic buckets in the other that are reddish-grubby inside. "Same place as before?" he asks me.

"Follow me," I say, and walk to the utility door of the basement. We go inside and pass the iron storage cages and are watched by the rocking horse with the big blue eyes and lady lashes. We go through the white door with the STAFF ONLY sign on it, and the floor changes from cement to tiles. In the white tiled corridor I take them to the washroom where they will work. In here it always smells of the bleach used by the whispering cleaners. The cleaners sleep in the cupboard with all the bottles, mops, and cloths and are not allowed to use the staff room. When the white ape catches them in there smiling at the television, he roars.

I take the caterers into the big washroom that is tiled to the ceiling and divided in two by a metal rail and shower curtain. There is a sink and toilet on one side and the other half has a floor that slopes to the plug grate under the big round shower head. Against the wall in the shower section is a wooden bench, bolted to the wall. The father drops his cases and mask on to the bench. His head is round and pink as the flavoured yeast the residents eat from square ration tins.

The son coils his chains on the bench and removes his hood too. He has a weasel face with many pimples among the scruffy whiskers on his chin. His tiny black eyes flit about and his thin lips curl away from long gums and two sharp teeth like he is about to laugh.

"Luvverly," the father says, looking around the washroom. I notice the father has no neck.

"Perfek," the weasel son adds, grinning and sniffing.

"Your night boy asleep?" the father asks. His fat body sweats under his smock and apron. His sweat smells of beef powder. Small and yellow and sharp, his two snaggle teeth are the same as the son's. When he squints, his tiny red eyes sink into his face.

I nod.

"Not for long," the weasel says, and then shuffles about, giggling. They both smell of sweat and old blood.

I shuffle towards the door.

"Hang on. Hang on," the father says. "We need you to open that friggin' door when we bring the meat in."

"Yeah," Weasel agrees, while he threads the chains through the brass eyes in the top of the sacks.

The father opens the cases on the bench. Stainless steel gleams under the yellow lights. His tools are carefully fitted into little trays. In his world of dirty trucks, old sacks, rusty chains, and snaggle teeth, it surprises me to see his fat fingers become gentle on the steel of his tools.

With eyes full of glee, the weasel son watches his father remove the two biggest knives from a metal case. Weasel then unties the ribbon of the last sack with the hollow wooden sounds inside, and pulls out two thick clubs. He stands with a club in each hand, staring at me. He is pleased to see the horror on my little face. At the bottom of the clubs the wood is stained a dark colour and some bits have chipped off.

"Go fetch 'em in," the father says, while he lays two cleavers with black handles on an oily cloth.

"Right," the weasel son says.

We go back down the tiled corridor. I walk slowly because I am in no hurry to see the livestock. When Mrs. Van den Broeck, the Head Resident, announced the banquet, I decided I would show the livestock a friendly face before they were taken into the washroom; otherwise, the fat father and the weasel son would be the last people they would see in this world, before they were stuffed inside the sacks and chained up.

When we reach the courtyard, I remember what the fat father told me last time, about how the meat tastes better with bruises under the skin. That's why they use the clubs. To tenderise the meat and get blood into the flesh. When he told me that, I wanted to escape from Gruut Huis and keep running into the poisonous mist until I fell down, until no one in the building could ever find me again. The residents don't need to eat the fresh meats. Like the staff they can eat the soft yellow yeast from the tanks, but the residents are rich and can afford variety.

We go back into the courtyard. Above us some lights have come on in the flats. I can see the dark lumps of the residents' heads watching from kitchen windows. And suddenly, from the east wing, the baboon child of Mr. Hussain screams. It rips the smoky air apart. Weasel Boy flinches. You never get used to the sound of the baboon child in the cage.

The weasel son rattles keys in his chainmail hand. "We done a wedding last week. St. Jan in de Meers."

I can't speak with all the churning in my tummy.

"We done eight livestock for the barbecue. Da girl's farver was loaded. Had a tent built and everything. Ya know, a marquee. All in this garden, under a glass roof. Me and dad was up at five. They had fifty guests, like. We filled four ice-chests with fillets. Done the sausages the day before. For the kids, like."

He finds the correct key and unlocks the back doors of the truck. Under his pig mask I know he is smiling. "We made a few shillings. There's a few shillings to be made at weddings in this part of town."

When Weasel opens the back doors, I feel the hot air puff out of the truck. With it comes the smell of pee and sweat to mix with the chemical stink of the swirly air. Two small shapes are huddled at the far end of the truck, near the engine where it is warmer.

I walk away from the open doors of the truck and look up at the vapours. They drift and show little pieces of grey sky. There is a smudgy yellow stain where the sun must be. But you can never tell with the cloud so low. I wish I was in heaven.

"C'mon ya shit-brains," Weasel shouts from inside the truck. He's climbed in to get the livestock out. They never want to come out.

I cringe as if he is about to pull a lion out of the back. Through the white sides of the truck comes a bumping of bare feet on metal and then the *chinka, chinka, chinka* of a chain.

Weasel Boy jumps out of the truck, holding a rope in both hands. "They as dumb as shit, but it's like they know when this day is coming. Get outta there. Git! Git!"

Out of the back of the truck two pale yellowish figures stumble and then drop onto the misty slabs of the courtyard. They fall down and are yanked back to their feet by the weasel.

The livestock is skinny and completely shaven. Their elbows are tied together and their hands are tucked under their chins. They are young males with big eyes. They look like each other. Like angels with pretty faces and slender bodies. They start to cough in the acid-stinging air.

Shivering against each other, the smaller one starts to cry and hides behind the taller one, who is too frightened to cry, but pees instead, down the inside of his thighs. It steams in the cold air.

"Dirty bastards. They'll piss anywhere. Trucks full of it. Yous'll have to wash that corridor down after we're gone." Weasel Boy pulls the rope taut. Each male wears a thick iron collar that looks loose on his yellowish neck. A rope is attached to the short chains welded to the collars. In his metal hands Weasel Boy holds the slack rope.

As Weasel Boy pulls them across the courtyard, the livestock jogs and jostles together for warmth in the cold air. I run ahead to open the utility door, but can't feel my legs properly, even when my knees bang together.

Inside the corridor I take off my mask and walk behind the livestock. Weasel Boy leads the way to the washroom. The livestock peer about at the storage cages. The small one stops crying, distracted by the paintings and furniture and boxes inside the cages. The taller one looks over his shoulder at me. He smiles. His eyes are full of water. I try to smile back at him, but my jaw is numb. So I just stare at him. His face is scared, but trusting and wanting a friend who smiles on this day when he is frightened.

I think what I think every time the caterers come to Gruut Huis, that there must be some kind of mistake. Livestock is supposed to be dumb. It has no feelings we're told. But in these eyes I can see a frightened boy.

"No," I say, before I even know I am speaking.

Weasel Boy turns around and stares at me. "You what?"

"This can't be right."

Weasel Boy laughs under his pig mask. "Don't you believe it. They got human faces, but they is shit-brains. Pretty as pitchers, but dead in the head. They ain't like us."

There is so much I want to say, but all the words vanish off my tongue and my head is filled with wind. A big lump chokes my sparrow throat shut.

"Git! Git!" Weasel snarls at the livestock, who cringe at the sound of his voice. On the back of each livestock-boy I see the scars. Long pinkish scars with little holes around the slits, where the stitches once were, after things had been taken out of their thin bodies for the sick. "Best meat in town," Weasel says to me, grinning. "They cook up lovely like. Thousand euro a kilo, they cost. More than fruit in them tins, like. Think of that. *More than fruit in tins.*"

Weasel Boy is pleased I am feeling dizzy and sick. And, like most people in this building, he likes to tell me things I don't want to hear. "These two, we been feeding for months. Shut it!" He straps the smaller one, who has started to cry again, on the backside with the end of the rope. The little one suddenly stops crying when the rope makes a wet sound on his yellow buttock. The mark goes white. Then back to yellow again. The force of the blow makes him trip over the feet of the taller boy, who is still looking at me with watery eyes, wanting a smile from me. They have long toenails.

"Where…?"

Weasel Boy stops dragging the livestock and looks at me. "Aye?"

I clear my throat. "Where they from?"

"Nuns."

"What?"

"Nuns. Them old nuns up in Brussels all died of the milk-leg. So all their shit-brains went to auction. These two were like strips of piss when me and me dad looked at them. No meat on them. All they got fed from them nuns was yeast and water. No good for the meat, see. So we been feeding them for months. Who's they for, like?"

"Head Residents." My voice is a whisper.

"Aye?"

"The Head Residents of the building. For the Annual Banquet."

"They gonna love them." Weasel Boy rips his mask off and points his septic muzzle at the livestock in a grimace to frighten them. They both try and hide behind each other, but get tangled.

The weasel's bristle hair is wet with sweat. I wondered if the salt stings his pimples. They go down his neck and on to his back. I can smell the sickish vinegar of his boils.

"Are…Are…Are you sure it's OK?" I know the answers to all of my stupid questions, asked in my stupid voice, but I have to keep speaking to hold my panic back. The livestock starts to giggle.

"Like I said, don't be fooled. They's useless. Was nothing but pets to them nuns. Only me and me dad make them worth anything. They is worth more than the organs in you and me put together." He tugs the rope hard so the livestock make chokey noises and their naked bodies slap against his rubber apron. Their eyes are watering. The little one looks up into the Weasel Boy's rat eyes and tries to hug him.

But the livestock go quiet when the washroom door is opened. Weasel Boy shoves them inside. Through the gap in the door, I can see his fat dad holding a sack open. "Get in here," he growls at the big one. Both livestocks start to cry.

"I have to get back to my desk," I say, even though I can't feel my jaw.

"Fair enough," Weasel says, with a smirk. "We need you to open the doors when we finish the first one. Me mam is coming at three. She's the cook. Me dad'll bring her later. We'll *do* the second one in the morning."

He closes the door. Behind me the livestock is crying in the washroom. The Fat Dad is shouting and the Weasel Son is laughing. I can hear it all through the white tiled walls. I put my fingers inside my ears as I run away.

Follow me through the dark house. Watch me kill the old lady. It won't take long.

My little brass clock says it's three in the morning, so I'll go and put a pillow over Mrs. Van den Broeck's bird mouth until she stops breathing. It'll be all right as long as I pretend it's just an ordinary thing that I'm doing. I know because I've done this before.

Above my bunk, Vinegar Irish is asleep and snoring in his bed. He won't see me leave the dormitory room. After drinking so much this evening—the cleaning liquid with the wet paint smell that I stole from the stores for him—he climbed into bed on his hands and knees with eyes looking at nothing in particular. Most mornings it takes me over twenty minutes to wake him for our work upstairs behind the reception desks. He drinks all day, can remember nothing, and needs his sleep. His face is purple with veins and his lumpy nose smells of bad yeast.

I go out of the dormitory with the bunk beds and I follow the cement path through the big storeroom. There are no lights on in the store because we are forbidden to come here at night, but I know my way around in the dark. Sometimes at night I go into the cages with a torch and the master keys to poke around the boxes, trunks, and cases full of things that used to matter in the world. But nothing you can eat or sell for food so it has no value now. Sometimes, as I walk through the store, I feel I'm being watched from inside the cages.

Slowly, I unlock the air-tight door that opens into the courtyard. Already, since I have worked here, five residents have jumped from the sixth floor and smashed themselves on the tarmac below. They had the lunger disease and were choking on red brine. At night you could hear their voices in the cold courtyard, drifting out of windows and spanking off all the brick walls as they drowned in bed. *Whuff, whuff, whuff* they went.

I go out from the store and step into the mist. The door shuts behind me with a wheeze. Cold out here and the rain sizzles through the fog to sting the thin skin over my skull. Then the air gets inside my nose and mouth too and it feels like I am sucking a battery. No one is permitted to go outdoors without a mask because of the poison in the air, but the porters' masks are only sacks with plastic cups sewn over the mouth-part. My face stings just as much with a mask on and I sweat too much inside the linen, so when no one is watching I go out without a mask over my big white head. I'm not too worried about dying. At the boys' home I came from, the nurses told me, "People in your condition never see their teens." I'm eighteen so I should be dead soon. Inside my see-through chest one of the little grey pumps or blackish lumps will just stop working. Maybe I'll go greyish first like most of the residents dying upstairs inside the flats.

Crouching down, my shoulder in the nightgown slides against the red brick walls. A special coating to stop the air dissolving the whole place has made the bricks smooth. Taking shallow stinging breaths, I look up. Most of the apartments are dark, but a few yellowy kitchens shine like little boxes, high up in the vapours that fill the world outside our airlocks and sealed doors.

I go up the giant black metal fire escape to the airlock that will get me into the west wing reception. If there was a fire here, and the thought of it makes me grin, where could the residents be evacuated to? They would stand in the courtyard and watch the building blaze around them until the air in their masks ran out. This is the last place they can retreat to in the city. There's nowhere left to hide from the mist in the world. At night, when I stand on the roof by the big satellite dishes, I see fewer lights out there in the city. Like the people, the lights are all being turned off one by one.

Outside the little back door of the west wing, I wait for the dizzies in my head to stop. I'm so scared now my dolly hands and puppet legs have gone all shaky. Closing my eyes, I tell myself this is going to be easy, it's just an ordinary thing that I'm about to do.

I think of the two little boys who came here inside the white truck. I will always see their frightened faces as they are pulled by the caterer's ropes. Mrs. Van den Broeck wanted them. She brought them here. So now I am going to her.

Feeling stronger after the attack of the dizzies passes, I tap the code into the steel number pad on the wall beside the little back door: 1, 2, 3, 4. An easy sequence to remember so Vinegar Irish can always get inside. The door unlocks with a click and hiss. I push it open.

Yellow corridor light, the smell of cleaned carpets, and polished wood comes out the door to die in the mist. Ducking my head, I climb through quickly. If any of the doors of the building are open for longer than five seconds a buzzer will go off behind the reception desk and wake the night porter.

Blinking my black button eyes I get rid of the outside mist in my tears. The corridor becomes clear. It's empty. Only thing I can hear is the sound of the ceiling lights as they buzz inside their glass shades. My thin feet go warm on the red carpet. This corridor will take me down to reception.

Creeping and sneaking, I go grinning down the passage and stop at the end where it opens into the reception. Listening hard with my eyes closed I try to hear the squeak of the porter's chair. But there is only silence down there behind the reception desk. Good.

Going down to my hands and knees I peek the top half of my head around the corner. I smile. Leaning back in his chair with his red face pointed at the ceiling, the white ape sleeps tonight. Big purple tongue and one brown tooth, hot with shit-breath, swallowing the clean air. He is supposed to be watching the monitor screens on his desk. But he has even taken his glasses and shoes off. I can see his black socks full of white hair and yellow claws on top of the desk.

I go into reception on my dolly hands and bony knees and I crawl to the staircase that will take me up to *her*. Even if the white ape's eyes open now, he won't see me because of the desk's high front. He would have to stand up and put his glasses on to catch sight of my thin bones in the nightgown and my swollen skull going up the stairs like a spider.

I go up the stairs to the second floor and stand outside the door marked number five. Her smell is strong up here, perfume and medicine.

When I think of Mrs. Van den Broeck's grey bird head on a fat silk pillow, sleeping somewhere on the other side of this wooden door, my slit-mouth trembles.

All day long I run up and down these stairs on errands for the residents, they who cannot be argued with at any time. But now I am up here in a flappy nightshirt with a stolen key because I mean to drown one of them in pillow softness. A big part of me wants to run back down the stairs, go through the building and across the courtyard to my little warm bunk in the dormitory where Vinegar Irish snores and wheezes above me.

Resting on my ankles, I put my head between my knees and screw my eyes shut. All of this—the building of old brick, the shiny wooden doors, the marble skirting boards, the wall mirrors and brass lights, the rich people and Mrs. Van den Broeck with her white gloves and pecking face—are so much bigger than me. I am a grain of seed that cannot escape her yellow teeth. In my left doll hand I squeeze the key until it hurts.

Today, two pale boys with pee on their hairless legs stepped about on cold toes in the back of the caterer's truck. They held each other with small hands, crying and smiling, and making throaty sounds to each other. They were marched by the caterers to the washroom with the white tiles and the big plug in the middle. And then the smaller one had to watch his brother being put inside a sack....

Inside my slit-mouth my squarish milk teeth grind together. Inside my fists my long nails make red half-moons on my palms. She brought them here. Mrs. Van den Broeck called for the white truck that had the bumping sounds of boys inside. My stomach makes squally sounds as the rage makes me shake and go the pink colour of the blind things that no chemicals can kill, who flit deep in the hot oceans, so far down they cannot be caught and eaten.

With a snarl, I stand up. Into the brass lock of her front door goes the key. The thunk of the lock opening feels good within the china bones of my dollish hand. My fingers look so small against the brown wood. I push the heavy door. A sigh of air escapes. The whisper of her apartment's air runs over my face: medicine, dusty silk, old lady sour smell.

Inside it is dark. The door closes behind me with a tired sound.

Waiting for my eyes to get used to the place, the outlines of vases, dry flowers, picture frames, a hat stand and mirror appear out of the gloom. Then I notice a faint bluish light spilling from the kitchen. It comes from the electric panel with the warning lights about leaks and gases and fires; all the flats have them. In the kitchen is where I usually take yeast tins and put them on the blue table for the maid Gemima to unpack. Gemima is the tiny woman who wears rubber sandals and who never speaks. But after tonight, Gemima will also be free of Mrs. Van den Broeck, and there will be no more journeys up here for me with the wet meats inside the plastic bags. No more feeling like my body is made of glass that will shatter when she shouts. No more poking from her bird claws. No more squinting from her tiny pink eyes when she teeters out of the elevator in the afternoon and sees my big head behind the reception desk.

I look down the hallway and see her bedroom door at the end. I pass the living room where she sits in the long silk gown and scolds us porters down the house phone. Then I tippy-toe past the bathroom where Gemima scrubs Mrs. Van den Broeck's spiny back and rinses her shrunken chest.

I stand outside the two bedrooms. Gemima sleeps in the left one. Now she will be resting for a few hours until her mistress's sharp voice begins another day for her. But part of Gemima never sleeps. The part of Gemima that must listen for the sound of Mrs. Van den Broeck's bird feet on the marble tiles and the scratch of her voice, calling out for attention from among the crystals and china cups and photos of smiling men with big teeth and thick hair in her room. This part of Gemima I must be careful of.

Mrs. Van den Broeck sleeps behind the right door in a big bed. I go in on legs I cannot feel. In here there is no light, the curtains are thick and fall to the floor. There is complete darkness…and a voice. It crackles in my ears. "Who's there?"

I stop moving and feel like I am underwater and trying to gulp a breath that will never come. Taking a step back, I want to run from here. Then I am about to say my own name, like I do on the house phone when the residents call down from upstairs. *Hello, Bobby speaking. How may I help?* I stop myself before my lips form the shape of the first word.

"Is that you, Gemima?"

Has my heart stopped beating inside its cage of thin bone and see-through skin?

"What's the time? Where are my glasses?"

I listen out for Gemima and imagine her rising without thought or choice from her cot next door. The other room stays silent, but it won't for long if Mrs. Van den Broeck keeps talking. Somewhere in front of me I hear a rustling. Out there in the dark I know a birdie claw is reaching for the switch of a table lamp. If the light comes on there might be a scream.

I cannot move.

"Who is there?" she says, her voice deeper. I can imagine the squinty eyes and pointy mouth with no lips. Again, I hear her long claws rake across the wooden surface of the side table by the bed. The light cannot come on or I am finished. I race to the sound of her voice.

Something hard and cold hits my shin bones and blue streaks of pain enter my head. It is the end of her metal bed-frame that I have run into, so I am not in the part of the room I thought I was.

Greenish light explodes through the glass shade of the table lamp and makes me flinch. Propped up among fat pillows with shiny cases is Mrs. Van den Broeck. I can see her pointy shoulders and satin nightgown where the bedclothes have slipped down. Collarbones stick through skin. She must sleep with her head raised and ready to snap at Gemima when she comes in with the breakfast.

Small red eyes watch me. Her face is surprised, but not afraid. For a while she cannot speak and I stand dizzy before her with pinpricks of sweat growing out of my whole head.

"What are you doing in my room?" There is no sleepiness in her voice, she has been awake for a long time. Not even her hair is mussed up or flat at the back. Her voice gets sharper. It fills the room. "I knew it was you. I always knew you were not to be trusted. You've been taking things. Jewellery. I suspected you from the start."

"No. It wasn't me." I feel like I'm five again, before the desk of the director at the boys' home.

"I'll have you executed in the morning. You disgust me." Her face has begun to shake and she pulls her bedsheets up to her chin, as if to stop me looking at her bird body in the shiny nighty. "People will thank me for having you put down. You should have been smothered in the cradle. Why do they let things like you live?" All this I have heard before when she is in a spiteful mood. But the thing that makes me so angry is her suspicion that I want to look at her skeleton body in the silk gown.

At any moment I expect Gemima to come in and start wailing. Then the white ape will be up here too and I will have a few hours to live. I stare at the bird-face with the plume of grey hair. Never have I hated anything so much. A little gargle comes out of my throat and I am at her bedside before she can say another word.

She looks up at me with surprise in her eyes. Neither of us can believe we are facing each other like this in her bedroom. This is not how I imagined it would be: the light on, me in my nightgown, and Mrs. Van den Broeck's dry-stick body sitting upright and supported by pillows.

She opens her mouth to speak, but no spiky words come out to hurt my ears. It is my time to speak. "You," I say. "The boys. The boys in the truck. You brought them here."

"What are you talking about? Have you lost your mind?"

I take one of the pillows from behind her back. Mrs. Van den Broeck never liked to see my china-doll hands poking from the sleeves of my uniform, so it is only right they are the last things she sees before I put the pillow over her face.

"Oh," she says in a little girl voice. Her frown is still asking me a question when I put her in the dark and take away the thin streams of air that must whistle through her beak holes. I grin the wild grin I cannot control that makes my whole face shake. This bully-bird can't peck me now.

Her pigeon skull fidgets under the pressing pillow. Twiggish legs with brown spots on the skin kick out inside the sheets, but only make whispers like mice behind the skirting boards. Claws open, claws close, claws open, claws stop moving.

I put my big onion skull against the pillow to add weight to my late-night pressings. Now our faces are closer together than they have ever been before, but we can't see each other. A few feathers and some silk are the only things between us. The pillow smells of perfume and old lady.

Squirts of excitement start in my belly. Triumph makes me want to take a shit.

I whisper words through the veil between us. I send her on her way with mutterings. "The little boys from the truck were crying when they were taken into the tiled room"—flicker of talon on the mattress—"They were scared, but didn't know why they were going to be hurt. They didn't understand"—stretching of a single bony leg under the sheets—"What do they look like on your plate?"—final kick of twisted foot, and a yellow nail snags on silk—"There was laughter in the boardroom during dinner. I heard you. I was outside and I heard you all"—all the thin bones relax and go soft under me—"Then you made me bring the leftovers up here in white bags. They banged against my legs on the stairs. They felt heavy. The bags were wet inside."

Now she's still. Nothing under me but bird bones, fossils wrapped in silk, and some hair, but not much else.

I stay on top of her for a while. Now it's done I feel warm inside. Milky sweat cools on the skin under my nightgown. I take the pillow off Mrs. Van den Broeck's face and step back from the bed. I pad out the part that was over her beak. Leaning across her I put the pillow back behind her warm body.

Underneath my body one of her chicken-bone arms suddenly moves, quicker than I thought something old and skinny could move. Yellow claws curl around my elbow. I look down. An eggshell brow wrinkles. Pink eyes open and make me gasp. I try to pull away.

Bird snarl.

Pinched mouth opens wide. Two rows of tiny yellow teeth sink into my wrist.

Now I'm drowning. Pain and panic fills my balloon skull like hot water. I pull and tug and yanky-shake at her biting beak that wants to saw off my dolly hand. Grunting, she holds on. How can an old thing like Mrs. Van den Broeck, made from such tiny bones and paper skin, make so deep a noise?

Digging my heels into the rug, I push backwards with all my strength, but her body comes forward in a tangle of sheets, pulled across the mattress by her mouth. Snarly and spitting, she shakes her head from side to side and

I think my wrist is broken. I should have guessed 170 years of her evil life could not be stopped by a soft pillow in the night.

Mad from the pain, I swat my free hand around in the air and it hits something solid. Now there are stabbing pains in the knuckles of that hand too from where it struck the heavy lamp. Strength leaks out of my feet and into the rug. Black dots float in front of my eyes. I might faint. It feels like her serrated beak has gone through a nerve.

I fall backwards and pull her whole body off the bed. Her stick-body hits the floor but makes no sound. I stand up and try to shake her off like I'm trying to pull off a tight shirt that has gone inside-out over my face. Tears blur my eyes.

I reach for the lamp on the bedside table. My little hand circles the hot smooth neck below the bulb. Pulling it off the table, I watch the thick green marble-base drop to the biting head on the rug. There is a *thock* sound as the sharp stone corner strikes the side of her head by the small ear. She stops biting.

I twist my wrist free of the loose beak and step away. I look down and can't believe so much liquid could spill from the broken head of a very old bird. The liquid is black. It's been going through her thin pipes and tubes for 170 years, and now it is soaking into a rug.

Working fast I wrap the white cord of the lamp around her claw and make it go tight. Maybe they will think she fell from her pillows and pulled the lamp down on top of her bird head. With the tail of my nightshirt I then wipe at all the things my dollish fingers have touched around the bed.

I flit from her room like a ghost. Go down the long hall and close the front door behind me. In the light of the landing I inspect the circle of bruises and cuts her beak has made on my stiff wrist. Not as bad as it felt.

I find it hard to believe Gemima is not screaming and that doors are not opening and that phones are not ringing and that residents are not shuffling down the stairs in dressing gowns. But there is only silence in the west wing.

Then the shaking starts.

Down the stairs I go on my hands and knees like a spider with four legs torn off. Back to my bunk.

Curled up in the warm place I have made in the middle of my bed, with the thin sheet and itchy grey blanket pulled over my head, I try and stop the shakes and try and wipe away all the pictures that swirl around my pumpkin skull. There is so much room inside the big space, so I guess it can hold more memories than a smaller head. Over and over I see the chewing bird that was Mrs. Van den Broeck, her beak fastened on my wrist, and then I see the heavy lamp land with a *thock...thock...thock....* It's all I can hear: the sharp marble corner breaking the wafer of her veiny temple.

What have I done in this giant house? What will become of me? They will know that my dolly hands got busy with a pillow and bedside lamp to crush that flightless vulture in its own nest. I wonder if turning back the hands on my little brass clock will take me back to the time before I went sneaking and creeping into her room.

An impulse makes my face scrunch up to cry and my body shivers under the blankets. Then I stand up beside the bunk and peer into the top bed where Vinegar Irish snores. I wish I was him. With no killing pictures inside his head, only thoughts of clear liquid to sup from plastic containers, flowing through his twitchy sleep.

The cold in the porters' dormitory makes my shaking worse. My wrist throbs. I want to get back into my bed and curl into a ball. Like the baby in the tummy before I was cut out and made my momma die.

I leave the dormitory and look down to the washroom door.

No one is shouting, there are no alarms or lights being turned on. All is quiet in the building. No one knows Mrs. Van den Broeck is dead. No one knows it was me, yet.

Inside I feel better. No one saw me. No one heard me. Gemima was asleep the whole time, dreaming of the hot green place across the oceans where she was born. I just have to stay calm. Maybe no one will suspect me, the big-headed boy with the doll hands. What can he do with those puppet legs and pencil arms? That big bulb head with the baby face stuck on the front is not capable of thinking of such things, maybe that's what they will think. That's what they thought at the orphanage too. That's how I got away with it before. They never even thought of me at the same time as they thought about the nasty smacking carers all found dead in their beds. I did three of them carers with these small china hands.

I grin with joy. My little grey heart slows down its pumping. All the pebbles of sweat dry across my skin. Warmth spreads through every teeny toe and twig finger, up through my see-through body to my roundish head, until I am glowing with the happiness of escaping and of tricking them. All of them who don't know about the power in my tiny hands.

And in my head now, I see the little boy who came in the white truck. The one they ate yesterday. He is dancing in heaven. Up there, the sky is totally blue. He likes the long grass that is soft between his toes and he likes the way the yellow sun warms his jumping running body. It was for him and his brother that I dropped the heavy lamp. *Thock.* What happened to him must always be remembered. I see it again now. I see it all behind my squeezed-shut, black-button eyes.

But what of the other one?

And then I go down to the washroom and I unlock the door. Behind the wood of the door before it is even open, I hear the skitter of dry feet retreat into a corner. A whimper.

No, they shall not have you too.

I open the door and walk past the dark wet bench beside the white wall. And I go to the huddled yellowish boy in the corner. I smile. He takes my small outstretched hand. Blinks wet eyes.

I think of the Cathedral of Our Lady and of the mist. We'll need a blanket.

"Your brother's waiting for us," I say, and he stands up.

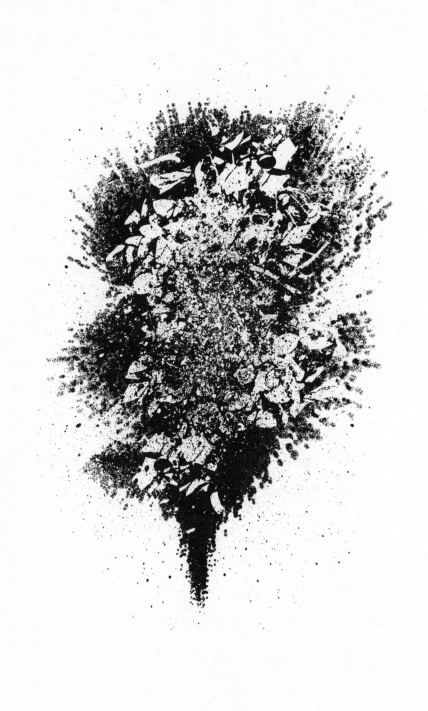

How I Met the Ghoul

SOFIA SAMATAR

The poet Ta'abbata Sharran met the ghoul in the fifth century and composed a poem about it known as "The Short Poem Rhyming in Nūn." He says he struck the ghoul with his sword, and she told him to strike again, but he refused, by which we are to understand that the man was no fool, because of course if you strike a ghoul twice it won't die until you strike a thousand more blows: you have to kill it with one blow or one thousand and two. So instead of striking again Ta'abbata Sharran lay on the ghoul all night. He doesn't say exactly what was going on with that. In the morning he looked at her and saw *"two eyes in a hideous head, like the head of a split-tongued cat / legs of a misshapen fetus, back of a dog, clothes of striped cloth or skin."*

I met the ghoul in 2008. She agreed to give me half an hour in the airport. We sat at the back of a restaurant where we could watch the planes take off. I was too wound up to feel like eating, but I ordered some onion rings for show. The ghoul had the Hungry Highflyer Special with curly fries and cream of mushroom soup.

She also ordered a Coke, and I guess I gave her a look because she said: "What?"

"Nothing," I said. She had eyes like illustrated pages, one larger than the other. There was a mark on her temple, probably made by one of God's meteors, but she'd done a good job covering it with makeup.

I asked her if it was easy for her to travel, if she ever got held up at customs or anything. She asked if I was a real reporter or just some small-time blogger. One of her ears was like a dead mine-shaft, the other like a window in some desolate bed-and-breakfast of the plains.

"Look," she said, "I go everywhere. You could say it's in my blood."

I asked if she really had blood, and she picked up her fork like she was going to jam it into her arm.

"Don't!" I yelped.

People looked at us then, and she put the fork down and laughed. She had a nice laugh, like an electric mixer making cake in a distant apartment.

Our food came. I asked if she missed the desert. She said: "Where do you think you are?" She seemed to be having trouble fitting into her T-shirt. My guess is that this was a deliberate effect, like the whirl of her postage-stamp eyes. The T-shirt was red; I think it said something about Cancún.

"What is your favorite book?" I asked.

"Al-Maarri's *Epistle of Forgiveness*."

"Favorite film?"

"*Titanic*."

"Favorite food?"

"Reporters. Kidding! I don't know, maybe duck?"

"Have you given many interviews?"

"No. This is my very first. I chose you because you're special, and I will never forget you."

She drank the last of her Coke and belched. Her hair grew all over the wall. She said she liked planes, she didn't make many of them go down. Mostly she liked to look out the window. When everyone was asleep, she'd put her eye to the window and grow her eyeball until it covered the glass.

"What are you looking for?"

"Other planes to wink at. Lightning. Lightning is useful, like string. And I look for things to remember later. Burnt cities. Ruins."

She admitted she also looked for her brother the Qutrub, a demon in the shape of a cat. She didn't think she'd ever find him. For this reason, cats made her sad.

To take her mind off it, and to make sure I got the question in before the end of the interview, I asked about Ta'abbata Sharran.

"Sixty hells, not him again."

"My readers are interested."

She rolled her eyes. One escaped across her forehead, but she caught it.

"What do you want to know? What exactly he meant by 'lay upon her'?"

"No," I lied. "But can you tell me anything about his name?"

Ta'abbata Sharran is a nickname; it means "He Carried Evil Under His Arm." There are several stories explaining how he got the name, but no one knows for sure. The ghoul said it wasn't her fault if I wanted to ask questions a ten-year-old could answer. "He stank, all right?"

"The poet stank?"

"To the moon and back."

She took out a pack of cigarettes, and I reminded her there was no smoking. I asked if her body functioned like that of a human being.

"No," she said. She ate one of her cigarettes.

I asked if it was true that she existed mainly to cause harm to travelers.

"Define 'mainly.'"

Afterward people asked me what she was like. When I said, "I can't say," they called it a cop-out. So now I try to break her down and describe her in pieces. Her upper lip was like a broken roof, her lower lip like a beached canoe. It made me feel good when she took my onion rings.

I asked her if modern development had made things harder for ghouls. She said there were more waste places in the world than ever before. I asked her if she was worried about climate change, and she said it was basically a ghoul's dream. She was optimistic about the future.

After a while her hair came down and curled up on her shoulder, and she picked up her bag and slid out of her seat while I paid for lunch. She wouldn't let me walk her to her gate. I asked for her autograph and she said um no, she wasn't born yesterday, but in a nice way.

"Do you think you'd let me interview you again?"

She wavered in the air, and nausea filled me up like breathing. *They are known by name,* I thought in a daze, *but not by shape.* I tried to focus on her: it was like staring into an April dust storm, electric blackness blotting out the sky. Buried cities whirled in the chaos, broken dishes, bones, syringes, words without meaning, fingernails, so much hair. More paper than you could cover in your life. All of it pulled in, animated, fierce and beating like a heart.

I closed my eyes. *Nothing is wasted.*

The ghoul heard my thought, and snorted. "Everything is wasted." I opened my eyes, and she was stable again, her arms crossed. Her smile was vast and white and kind and a little bit detached, like the ceiling of a room where you have woken up with head trauma.

"So I guess that's a 'no,'" I said. "About the interview."

She laughed her electric-mixer laugh. We didn't shake hands. I watched her until she disappeared in the crowd. It didn't take long: as she turned away, she was already changing shape, on her way to the next brief shelter, the next campsite, the next ruin.

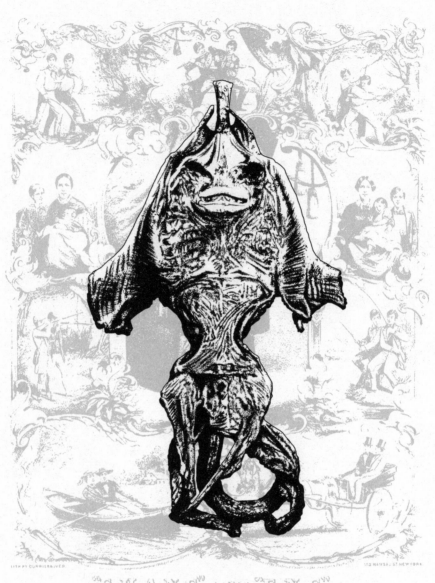

"CHANG" AND "ENG"
THE WORLD RENOWNED UNITED
SIAMESE TWINS.

Jenny Come to Play

TERRY DOWLING

When Dan Truswell learned from the activities coordinator soon after 2 p.m. that Wednesday afternoon that Julie Haniver was sitting catatonic in the hospital library, he took it as a routine shutdown by the slim, nervous, young woman, paged Hans and Carla, and left them to deal with it.

It was when Peter Rait knocked at his door less than two minutes later and said Dan had to come see Julie, talk to Julie, that Dan decided to check on her himself. Peter was one of Blackwater's star "attractions," an amiable, likeable schizophrenic who had an uncanny knack for reading his fellow inmates. When Peter showed worry, it was usually worth worrying about.

Dan locked his office and accompanied Peter around to the library in the Prior Wing.

"What does Phil say?" Dan asked his frowning companion, knowing how Peter and his schizoid friend, Phillip Crow, made a fascinating double-act.

Peter shrugged, which was more exasperating than it ought to have been. Phil hadn't expressed an opinion this time. That meant Peter had reacted on his own, which was even more amazing. Then again, he'd shown Julie a lot of attention in the four months she'd been at Blackwater.

Dan trusted Peter's insights enough to let him be there when they entered the library. Hans and Carla were already with Denise, the activities coordinator, but hadn't yet approached the girl sitting by the corner window, looking out at the fine spring afternoon. When Dan indicated Peter, they nodded and stayed at the desk. They knew Peter was good at getting through to Julie.

Dan crossed the room, sat near the petite, olive-skinned young woman with the short black hair and very pretty elfin features. Peter stood to one side.

"Julie?" Dan said gently. "Can you hear me, Julie?"

The young woman showed no sign of having heard. She sat absolutely still, gazing out the window, her eyes unfocused, watching yet watching nothing.

"Ask her who she's looking out for," Peter said, with uncommon directness.

"Peter, let me handle this."

But it was as if Peter hadn't heard. "Ask her, Doctor Dan. Ask who she's watching for!"

"Peter! That's enough!"

His tone at least made Julie blink.

"Ask her about Jackie!" Peter said, his parting shot because Carla was there then to lead him away.

But it was Peter suggesting it, and it was Julie—this withdrawn, shy, young woman who'd turned up one day back in June and signed herself in, without any identity but her name, no next of kin she could give, no family, no memories (she claimed) to help them build a past, the backgrounds of heredity and environment that had produced her.

"Julie, are you waiting for someone?"

Still the eyes gazed out at the grounds, broke into the emptiness and infinities of reverie before ever reaching the sunny lawns and trees.

"Julie, who is Jackie?"

Julie blinked once, twice. The eyes grabbed, locked into focus. She turned to face him, gave a nervous, embarrassed smile.

"Are you okay now?" Dan asked.

She nodded, ventured another tentative smile, noticed Peter and the others over by the desk.

Normally Dan would've left it to Carla at this point, but Peter going solo over this kept him there.

"Julie, who is Jackie?"

Julie frowned, sighed and looked directly at him.

"Jackie's my sister."

"Really? You never said you had a sister." Dan held back the rush of questions that were immediately there. There might be no sister at all, just an imaginary one, a convenient fiction. It hadn't surfaced during the hypnotherapy sessions. Nor did he want to move over to the armchairs or to an interview room. The view out the library window was probably part of it. She'd been watching for this "sister" most likely.

"Tell me about Jackie."

"It's why I'm here."

"Jackie wanted you here?" Dan truly expected her to have forgotten how she came to be at Blackwater, to say that this sister had been the one who'd committed her, part of a familiar-enough persecution and betrayal scenario. Julie's answer surprised him only by its opposite tack, not its content.

"No. I came here to escape Jackie. I thought she wouldn't be able to find me here."

"Ah, I see," Dan said, kindly. He'd heard this sequence of events many times too. Only the look of intense concern on Peter's face when Dan glanced round at the others kept him with her. "And have you seen her out there, Julie?"

"She's coming today. I thought it'd be last night but it will be today."

"How do you know?"

"Jackie always leaves things."

"Oh, like what? What sort of things?"

"Just things. Signs."

"You've seen these signs? What are they?"

When Julie didn't answer, Dan tried again. "But she wouldn't come from out there, would she, Julie? She'd come in by the front gate."

The young woman frowned, studied the grounds with renewed concentration. The emotion in her eyes could have been terror, panic, utter dread. (Phobos and Deimos, the twin moons of insanity—one of Peter's lines.)

Not for a moment did Dan see it as guile, the sort of cunning so many para-noid schizophrenics affected. This woman seemed truly terrified.

"Julie?" he said, both to keep her with him and to comfort her.

"She won't give up. She'll keep looking."

"Yes, well, we'll keep an eye out for her too."

Dan almost fell off his chair when she turned and grabbed his arms.

"Don't tell her I'm here!" She spat the words at him, eyes wide, face twisted by fear.

"You're safe here, Julie," Dan managed, and by then Carla was there, soothing her, urging her up, Hans assisting, leading her off to her room, leaving Denise by the desk and Peter desperately wanting to follow, to do something. He came over to Dan.

"She's really scared of her sister," Peter said, as if it hadn't been obvious. "We have to protect her. Keep her hidden."

"There may not be a sister," Dan said, wondering as always why he both-ered to tell Peter Rait these things.

"There is and there isn't," Peter said, frowning with what seemed to be both puzzlement and concern. "But Julie's right. Jackie does leave things."

This was where Peter Rait was his brilliant, entertainment-value best. It was just that Phillip Crow wasn't with him, making it unprecedented, almost as disturbing in a way as Julie's outburst.

"Oh, what sort of things?"

"Last week a piece of cloth tied to that pine over there." He pointed out the window. "Last night she would've put something closer to let Julie know she's coming."

"What sort of thing?"

Peter shrugged. "Something closer. Maybe not visible from the library window, but sharing a connection, yeah. Can I go sit with her?"

"She's resting now. You can see her later. Go wait for her in the Games Room."

Peter nodded, then smiled as if grasping some secret strategy Dan had suggested. "Right. The play's the thing, isn't it?"

Dan said nothing. From long experience he knew enough just to watch him go.

What Dan did do when he reached his office again was go over Julie Haniver's file, reacquainting himself with what little they had. She'd admitted herself on June 4, uncertain of her age but probably around 22 to 24, had been diagnosed as stressed and exhausted, subject to unspecified feelings of persecution, anxiety attacks, even catatonic withdrawal, real or feigned.

Though testing initially as a disorganised personality, she'd responded well to treatment and was usually calm and controlled. She could have been a case of nervous exhaustion following prolonged drug abuse, but her initial physical showed none of the attendant signs of that, no signs of harm at all apart from a nasty childhood or early adolescent scar above the hip on her right side. The distinctive double hand-sized patch of keloid ridges and welts may have been from an accident involving fire or acid, possibly was the result of extreme parental or sibling abuse. That might explain the disordered, dissociated behaviour—the anxiety of residual trauma. Someone named Jackie may have been responsible. Friend, relative, or carer, who could say?

But nothing else in the file. Just ID shots and dated close-ups of the wound for the usual information, legal and insurance reasons. If it hadn't been for the scar and the memory loss (alleged, never proven), with its significant implications, Julie Haniver could have been discharged.

The more Dan considered it, the more she did seem like someone who might feign a mental disorder to be in a safe place. It certainly happened from time to time.

But the scar. Raw and brutal-looking. An acid burn? The result of a very clumsy, even amateur, medical procedure?

It was the photographs of the scar (and remembering Peter Rait's concern) that made Dan go out onto the terrace and walk round the outside of the building to the library windows in the Prior Wing. There was nothing tied to the low bushes or the pilasters of the terrace balustrade, but just below the window near where Julie had been sitting, there was a small stack of stones—maybe ten in all, just piled atop one another and collapsed in against the wall.

Dan immediately thought of Peter, yet knew that he would never knowingly interfere with a fellow inmate's treatment. There seemed to be only three explanations: it was coincidence—someone had just happened to leave a construct in that spot, or Peter had done it to confirm Jackie's existence for this newfound friend who desperately needed to believe she did exist, or that Jackie was indeed out there.

Dan left the stones where they were and returned to his office. No sooner had he put Julie's file away, then, like Fate on his heels, Angela phoned to say a Ms. Jackie Haniver was waiting in Reception to see him about her sister.

Though Dan would have preferred to collect his thoughts, take time to consider the rush of events, he felt a real curiosity, even a sense of urgency about the whole business. He told Angela to have one of the staff bring Ms. Haniver through at once. There were often days when Blackwater's well-established routines came undone in spectacular, sometimes alarming, usually comical ways, but this time Dan felt an uncommon pressure, as if the "briars of unreason" (as Peter Rait and Phillip Crow put it) were indeed taking over the garden.

Less than ten minutes after discovering the pile of stones, he was sitting in his office across from what seemed to be Julie's identical twin. The young woman wore a smart blue suit, was well groomed and carefully made up, and appeared very composed about the whole matter, radiating a charm and poise well beyond her years.

"You understand, Dr. Truswell, that I've been looking for Julie for quite some time. I can't make her come back with me, I know, even were you to allow it, but naturally I do feel responsible for her care and safety."

"And we're naturally very glad to see you, Ms. Haniver. We've had so little to go on where Julie's concerned."

"Please. Call me Jackie. And it's Perfini, not Haniver. That's a name Julie's been using. I used it at Reception because I knew it would identify me to you. I have certified copies of Julie's birth documentation here. You can keep the photocopies." Dan scanned them when she passed them over, passed back the originals. "'Haniver' was a family *nom de guerre* or *nom de théâtre*. Can I see my sister?"

"I'd like you to," Dan said, making notes on the writing pad in front of him. "But not right away. We have to deal with your appearance in terms of

Julie's needs. She said she didn't *want* you to know she was here, and seems highly agitated at the thought of you finding her. Letting you see her could well seem like a betrayal. Forgive how this sounds but Julie's well-being must come first. You can help us prepare her for meeting you. Help us to get her to ask for you."

"I have to take your word for all this, don't I? That she's agitated? That she doesn't want to see me?"

"I'm afraid so. If you have doubts, there are legal procedures we can suggest. You can bring legal representation to our next meeting. Outside experts can verify admission and diagnostic protocols."

Jackie Perfini smiled and raised a hand. "Unnecessary, Doctor. I accept what you're telling me. I'm just surprised and hurt about this. Of course I accept your professional judgement. But what are the chances of her being released into my care? The legalities?"

"Again that will depend on her recovery. You're probably aware that once someone is committed, or commits themselves as Julie has, they can only be discharged when a qualified person deems their condition satisfactory."

"Julie must be that, surely. She's dreamy and distracted and withdrawn, but hardly crazy. I'm surprised she's so upset and amazed to think she might have committed herself just to be away from us."

"Who is us, Jackie?"

"Our father died last year. I meant our sister, Jenny, and me."

"Your mother?"

"Died soon after Julie and Jenny were born."

"You and Julie look identical."

Jackie smiled. "Dr Truswell, I think you're interrogating me. In a moment you'll be asking if I have a scar of my left side just above the hip."

"Do you?"

"I'm afraid not. I'm eighteen months older than Julie and Jenny. We do look alike, I know, but Julie and Jenny were born conjoined. Congenitally united, as they say."

"Jackie, Siamese twins not sharing vital organs or major skeletal features are usually separated as soon after birth as safely possible. That's a nasty scar. A bad separation procedure."

"Bad 'procedure'! God, I love these terms! It was butchery! It's a wonder they survived. Dr. Truswell, my family emigrated from Sicily. Lots of faith in the old ways. Lots of family honour. Lots of shame in having deformed children. Julie and Jenny were born there."

"It wasn't a hospital birth."

"Correct. But it's more complex, more tragic for them than that. Our father, the bastard, had more than a passing interest in teratology."

"Teratology? Monsters?"

"Don't look so amazed, Doctor. It's more common than most of us think. Alonzo was fascinated with the old *Wunderkammern*—the 'wonder cabinets' and 'cases of curiosities' so famous and popular in the 16th and 17th centuries that became the private collections and eventually the public museums. He had a modest but growing collection of oddities, a museum of his own, a sort of travelling show."

Dan couldn't believe what he was hearing. "He *left* them joined."

Jackie Perfini nodded. "A shameful and hideous thing, I know. He had them wet-nursed by an aunt, then took them to be part of his own *Wunderkammer*. A living exhibit. But then Alonzo Perfini was a selfish and domineering man. A persuasive and charming man when he needed to be. An atheist and occultist. A would-be mystic and entrepreneur. His heroes were Giovanni Batista Belzoni, Elias Ashmole, and the Dutchman, Dr. Frederic Ruysch. These twins had caused his wife to die, he liked to believe, though it wasn't true. Maria was already very ill. Here he was with his great love of monsters, having become the father of two. Or one, depending on your viewpoint. It was destiny, something that suggested a mystical purpose. He was much taken with the notion of things being joined. The alchemical union of opposites."

"Hardly opposites, Jackie."

"Nevertheless, he left them joined to grow up like that."

"Until when?"

"Till just after puberty. They were barely thirteen. They persuaded a second cousin who was an intern to perform the 'procedure,' as you call it."

"Without your father's consent?"

"Of course. He was furious."

Dan was still trying to follow the reality that had brought Julie, Jenny, and Jackie to this point in their lives. "Where were you when this happened, Jackie?"

"I was with the show for a while as an infant, then Alonzo left me with some of Maria's relatives in a village outside Palermo before he took his troupe north. Eventually they sent me to Australia and I was raised by aunts in Melbourne. I was told my father had gone off travelling, grieving for the loss of his wife and baby."

"Baby?"

"No one knew it was twins then. The story was that it was a stillborn boy. Maria was so sick, probably even she did not know the truth. They even had a funeral—it was all a mockery. When the girls were old enough, he added them to his show, had documents falsified saying they shared vital organs and had to stay joined. Even the girls grew up believing it. I didn't meet them until they came to Australia six years ago."

"Where's Jenny now?"

"Down in Sydney, safe and happy enough. Even more shy than Julie. But missing Julie terribly."

"Can you bring her here?"

"I tried to get her to come. She wouldn't. No offence, Dr. Truswell, but she thought this place would be too much like the Perfini Chamber of Wonders and his travelling Wonder Show. She's had enough of imprisonment and disordered minds and being regarded as a curiosity. Part of one."

Dan understood her reservations. "Still, seeing her might help Julie's recovery considerably."

"My feelings exactly. But I've lived with this, Dr. Truswell. I know only too well how Jenny feels. Until Julie went missing back in June, we all had a relatively quiet life together."

"A normal life, Jackie?"

"Normal enough. Jenny was seeing someone, a young man. I could give you his number next time I visit. Julie was starting to go out more."

Dan made a few more points on his notepad. "It's difficult to know what to do. Despite what you tell me, Julie was terrified at the prospect of your coming here."

Jackie Perfini smiled. "And she would've told you I leave things, signs that I'm following her. She's done that before. Left signs I mean."

"She does it herself?"

"I'm afraid so. It's something she did during their time in the show. At first it was just a book or a stone or a flower, but then she started making things out of folded paper, clay."

"Like piling up stones or tying strips of cloth to trees."

"That sort of thing, yes. But it's just a game. She'll still come into our rooms at home and leave things. It's not serious, is it?"

"Of course not. But in her stressed condition she's made it part of her perception of you, I'm afraid. She believes you're the one doing it."

Jackie frowned, then sighed and smiled. "Well, so long as she's safe. That's the main thing now. I respect her decision to come here, though I can hardly say I'm happy about it. I'd be grateful if you'd talk to Julie about all this. See if you can get her to come home. She's had a hard life."

"Jackie, how did you find her here?"

"I called hospitals, hostels, Lifeline, drop-in centres, places like that. Had the police looking for a while. You probably got a call here. Then Jenny suggested I try looking for her under the name 'Haniver,' an alias they used in the show."

"I see. Well, I'd still like to meet Jenny. I think it's very important."

"Yes, well that's up to Julie and Jenny, isn't it?"

"I think it would probably be beneficial for both of them."

"I agree. So you speak to Julie and I'll speak to Jenny."

"How can we reach you?"

"Best I call you. I'm still deciding where to stay in the area. I can't be away from Jenny for too long."

"Can you give me a number where I can at least call Jenny?"

"Later, Dr. Truswell. I'll need to clear this with Jenny first."

It was exasperating, even infuriating, though Dan was by no means a stranger to the byzantine nature of family affairs. Institutions like Blackwater attracted the end products of crisis and despair, with the added pressures of inheritance complications and human rights issues. Jackie Perfini was giving him as much and as little as he was giving her.

"Then please call soon. We need to settle things for Julie's sake."

"All our sakes, Doctor. But Julie's and Jenny's most of all, yes. They had and still have a special connection. Jenny doesn't say much about it, but she's deeply troubled when Julie is away."

So how must she be feeling now? Dan wondered. Who's minding her?

Dan shook the young woman's hand when she stood and offered it, feeling more frustrated than he could remember. He wanted to ask more about her father's travelling show, where it went, what occurred during those crucial years, wanted to ask about her own life. But now it was *quid pro quo* and the smartly dressed young woman was heading to the door.

As soon as Jackie left him at Reception, Dan had Hans note the make and color of her car, then placed an immediate call to Jay Wendt over in Everton.

"Jay? Dan Truswell. I need Wendt Investigations do me an urgent favor. There'll be a—" Hans said a few words from the front door. "—white '94 Laser coming down the highway towards town in about ten minutes. Victorian number plate. Young female driver. Blue suit, short black hair. I need a local destination for her."

To Dan's relief, Jay was able to oblige. He replaced the receiver and leant back in his chair, told himself it was the most he could do other than talk to Julie, try to get her side of Jackie's story, find out more about Jenny from her. Later he'd phone Harry Badman down in Sydney, see if there was any background on the names Perfini or Haniver in the CIB database.

But now he had rounds to do, counselling to give, bits of his own fraying world to be brought to order. He was half an hour at it, busily trying his best to keep his thoughts off Julie's catatonia and Jackie Perfini's sudden appearance, the whole disturbing, strangely compelling sequence of events, when he was called to the phone.

"Dan, it's Jay. I'm halfway down the Putty Road. Your subject has left the Hunter Valley altogether."

"She didn't stay local?"

"She's heading for Sydney, I'd say. Flat out, too. You want me to stay on this?"

"Jay, I really need you to. This woman is the sister of a patient. We might need a destination in a hurry."

"Then I'll call a pal of mine in Windsor. Stephanie Ashburn. She can pick it up there and I'll come back. She's good, Dan. Don't worry. If necessary, I'll get someone from Parramatta to get out there as well. There'll be other traffic but we might need to leapfrog the closer she gets to home."

"Sounds like quite an operation."

"Just like the big kids do. I'll do a trace on the registration too and call when I've got something, okay?"

"Thanks, Jay."

There was no way he could return to his rounds. At 3.50 he paged Carla and asked her to bring Julie Haniver to his office as soon as possible.

When the girl was ushered in and given an armchair opposite Dan's by the French doors, she looked calm enough, though she never took her eyes off Dan for a moment, obviously expecting some fears to be confirmed.

Dan thanked her for coming and opened his notepad. He'd already decided to play it straight with her. When Carla had gone, he didn't hesitate.

"Jackie was here, Julie."

"I know."

"How do you know?"

"Peter told me."

Dammit. Peter Rait had far too much liberty, Dan decided, then retracted it. Peter had never been the enemy before, probably wasn't now. Though he'd never acted on his own before either.

"She already knew you were here, Julie. We didn't tell her."

"Peter told me that too, Doctor Dan. It's okay. I shouldn't have used the name Haniver. It was an old show name."

Thank God. Dan settled back. Julie seemed uncommonly composed and alert now, very focused indeed.

"She told me about Jenny. About the Perfini Wonder Show. About your father and his interests."

Julie nodded slightly, as if expecting it. "He couldn't help himself. Jenny keeps saying it. He couldn't help the things he did."

"Well, maybe so, Julie. But we need to know more about it. What can you tell us?" Now that Jackie's been here, Dan didn't need to add.

"We didn't have to be joined. It was only cartilage and muscle. Alonzo knew some doctors interested in *Wunderkammern*. They faked X-rays of the Lugli twins from Padua. Alonzo showed the authorities false X-rays. Jenny and I never knew."

"How did you find out?"

"It just became too much. What he did. We kept away from Italy, certainly from Sicily. Our first names were changed. We used the name Haniver. It's an in-joke. But we found we had a cousin interning in Frankfurt when we were there. When Alonzo had food poisoning and was taken in for tests, Carlo came and got us from the carnival and took us to visit. We sometimes did go out with Papa and his friends. We could walk well enough to look like we were closely arm in arm. Carlo didn't take us straight to Papa's ward. He did some X-rays of us. We didn't have to stay joined."

"Did Carlo go to the authorities?"

"Not then. It was a family thing, you see. He got two friends to help. Alonzo was away. They did the operation in our wagon."

"They what? That's burn scarring you've got, Julie. Interns with access to X-ray equipment and hospital facilities would hardly use acid or resort to cauterising wounds with flame. Do you actually remember the operation?"

There seemed a dreamlike quality between them now, almost as if her words were being recited from some false memory. "No. Jenny told me about it. I've forgotten a lot of things."

"Jenny wouldn't lie to you." He had to be so careful.

"Never. Jenny is my dearest friend. She's in my song. I'm in hers."

"Your song? I don't follow."

There was much more animation in Julie's features now. She was smiling again. "When we were young, it was our private game. We'd sing it."

"Please sing it now, Julie. Would you?"

Julie smiled and did so, in a light clear voice.

"When will Jenny come to play?
When will Jenny come to stay?
Jenny's never somewhere else,
Jenny's here with me, myself."

"Thank you, Julie. I take it as an honor."

"Jenny would sing 'Julie'; I'd sing 'Jenny'. We thought we'd have one another forever. We didn't know we could be apart. We never expected it."

"You miss that, don't you, Julie?

"Sometimes desperately, Doctor Dan. It was all there was. You made it your world every conscious moment. Washing. Going to the toilet. Even pretending to be alone by turning away from each other. Playing at separation. But I grew to hate it too. Because of Alonzo. What he did. And once Carlo showed us we were probably separable. It wasn't the same. It wasn't a necessity any longer. More like an oversight."

"So why don't you remember?"

"I was ill or something. Highly strung, they said. With bad headaches. I had to be sedated a lot. I remember that."

Dan leant back in his chair, made himself lean back, stay calm. He could no longer be sure what was truth or fiction. Perhaps he did need Peter Rait's view on this.

"Julie, after the operation, what happened to Carlo?"

"Carlo? I've put so much out of my mind, Doctor Dan, I don't know. Carlo just disappeared. Alonzo was furious. Humiliated. He tried to convince us the separation *had* been riskier than Carlo said, that he never wanted to take the chance, even claimed that he'd been misled by unscrupulous members of his *Wunderkammern* group."

"Julie, what do you mean Carlo disappeared?"

"We never saw him again. I never did. Perhaps he ran away. Alonzo said what Carlo had done had shamed him, made him a laughingstock before his peers."

The story was changing again. "His peers, not his family. Who were they again?"

"Others who owned *Wunderkammern* and traded exhibits with him. We never went back to Palermo. Alonzo finally sold off his collection and brought us to Australia."

"Did he do that in a hurry?"

"Not for three years. But then it all happened so quickly."

"What name did you use in Melbourne?"

"The show name. Haniver. He didn't want to use Perfini. He preferred the Flemish name, said it advertised his field of interests better."

"Oh? How so?"

Julie shrugged. "I don't know. Perhaps others interested in wonder-cabinets would recognise the name."

"Right. Julie, you seem to be recalling quite a bit now. Can you give me your address and phone number in Sydney?"

"Didn't Jackie?"

"No, she didn't."

"She was protecting Jenny."

"But you trust me. Can you give me your home address or phone number?"

"Doctor Dan, please understand. I need to protect Jenny too."

Which possibly explained the lies. Dan studied the earnest face, lacking only makeup to be identical to Jackie's. Something *was* dramatically different now. If not for Jackie's visit to lend an element of credibility to the whole thing, Dan wouldn't have believed any of it. He still couldn't help but feel it was some kind of hoax, or at least that layers of deception were at work, being employed to conceal what little truth there was. It was almost as if Julie had done a quick change, had managed a conspiracy so she could play both parts. Yet more than ever he had to accept the prevailing situation, not fight it, not force it.

"Julie, you believe we're genuinely trying to help you? That we want you and Jenny to be safe?"

"Of course I do."

"You and Jackie both want to protect Jenny. Jackie says that she's with Jenny down in Sydney, is that correct?"

"Yes."

"Yet you didn't want Jackie to find you."

"That's right."

"Can you explain that? Knowing Jackie is living with Jenny, knowing that Jenny misses you terribly, why would you run away from them?"

"I don't know. I just don't know."

"Please try, Julie. Why did you run away from Jenny?"

"I ran away from Jackie!"

"Why? Why would you do that? Why would you do that to Jenny as well?"

"I just don't know."

"Do you want to know?"

"What?"

"Would you like me to help you find out why you're here?"

There were only frowns now, bewilderment and uncertainty crimping her forehead, her confusion drawing out into its inevitable edge of panic. He could see it pulling at her eyes.

"H-How?"

"You remember our hypnotherapy sessions, Julie. Now Jackie's found you, I'd like to use hypnosis again. See what we can learn."

What is true, Dan told himself.

"Hypnotise me? Now?"

"That's right. We did it before, remember? It might help a lot."

"You'll find out where Jenny is."

"Not if I promise *not* to ask you that, Julie. Do you trust me about that?"

Before she could answer, the phone rang. Dan excused himself, crossed to his desk, and answered it.

"Hello?"

"Is that Dan Truswell?" a woman's voice asked.

"It is."

"Dr. Truswell, I'm Stephanie Ashburn, a friend of Jay Wendt's. I've followed the subject to a Dalloway Road address in Horsley Park. That's outside Blacktown, near Fairfield. It's semi-rural. Lots of open fields and market gardens."

"I think I know it, Stephanie. Go on."

"I've just arrived. That's 72 Dalloway Road."

"Describe the location, please."

"Large-enough property, maybe three hectares. Just an ordinary fibro cottage, a few big trees."

"Any sheds or garages?"

"There's a very large corrugated iron shed set away to the right of the house. It's seen better days but it's sturdy enough. I'd say about thirty metres by fifteen, about four metres high."

"Where did the car pull up?"

"Outside the shed."

"Not the house?"

"Right. No lights visible, but the shed has no windows on the two sides I can see. No signs of activity. What should I do?"

"You're not too obvious?"

"I'm quite a ways from the place."

"Okay. Stephanie, phone Jay and tell him where you are. I'd appreciate it if you could stay there till one of us calls."

"Let me give you my number here."

Dan wrote it down and hung up. Then, as he turned from the desk, he saw a small paper object sitting among his files. It was an origami figure of—what else?—two humans joined at back or front. But dropped there by which sister: Julie or Jackie? He couldn't know. When had either had the chance? Jackie as she left? Julie as she came in?

Without touching it, he turned back to the armchairs by the long windows, now golden with late afternoon light.

"The hypnosis, Julie. What do you say?"

She looked up at him, wide-eyed, clearly troubled by the prospect. "Can Peter be here?"

Dan didn't flinch, didn't blink or hesitate. "If you want. I know he'd like to be."

Julie nodded. Dan returned to his desk, paged Carla, and asked her to send Peter round to his office. By the time he arrived, Dan had his recorder set up and a chair positioned slightly to the back of Julie's so their guest would be out of direct sight. Peter took it with a smile and a nod, for all the world like a colleague here to observe an interesting procedure. Dan couldn't help smiling back, then set the recorder going and began.

"Peter, Julie and I decided we'd try some more hypnotherapy and thought you'd like to join us. You'll observe the usual courtesies, I know."

Peter nodded. "As silent as the Moon," he said. "Not a bird, nor the mewings of the baby stoat."

Baby stoat? Was he quoting? Dan could never be sure. But Peter settled back quietly, his eyes fixed attentively on Julie for a moment, then closed in his usual contemplative manner.

Dan positioned himself, began the relaxation recital. Julie visibly settled in her chair, actually seemed glad to give in to Dan's suggestions. Within a few minutes she had lapsed into the trance.

"Julie, tell me about the Perfini Wonder Show."

"Wonder-cabinet," Julie murmured, plumbing the years.

"Yes, the Perfini wonder-cabinet. The *Wunderkammer*. Tell me about it."

"We travelled through Europe," Julie said. "Papa took us through so many different countries. Not the big cities all that often and not all the towns. He knew where to go. The special fairs. The right estates."

"I'm sure. When did he first start showing you and Jenny?"

Julie didn't hesitate. Jenny was such a powerful reality for her. "When we were five. We were the special exhibit. He saved us till last."

"Did you enjoy it?"

"We loved it. We loved the attention then."

"Then? Not later?"

"Later it was different."

"How much later?"

"When we had turned ten. It was different then."

"How was it different?"

Julie frowned and didn't answer. Her left cheek spasmed—a nervous tic. Behind her right shoulder, Peter Rait's eyes opened wide as if in some shared sympathetic alarm, then closed again. He was trying to behave.

"Julie," Dan repeated gently, "how was it different?"

Julie was resisting, was even shaking her head a little. There was conflict, something she didn't want to face. Dan was about to put a new question when Peter broke trust and, eyes still closed, asked a question of his own.

"All the best wonder shows have a secret room, Julie. A special room. What happened in the secret room?"

Dan was silently furious but said nothing. Like Jenny, Peter was a powerful force in Julie's life. *She* had wanted him there.

Tears were rolling down Julie's cheeks when she answered. "It was where Papa took us."

Dan stayed silent. Let Peter ask it.

"To do what? What happened there, Julie?"

"He showed us undressed. He let them touch us." Despair had tightened her throat. The words were pinched, broken with sobbing now.

"He molested you? Both of you?"

Dan found they were his questions, coarsely, heavy-handedly, almost cruelly put, as direct as Peter always was, though here he was, without Phillip, coherent and focused and helping *without* Phillip Crow! The briars of unreason were blooming indeed.

Julie blinked away more tears, nodded.

Dan might not have persisted. Peter did.

"But it was your father! How could it happen?"

"We resisted. They held us down. Sometimes they tied our hands. Put rags in our mouths. We had no choice."

Dan intervened. "What about your visit to the hospital? Carlo doing the X-rays? What about your separation?"

"Carlo didn't do the separation. Carlo became a fine pair of wings. We did some of it ourselves, Jenny and me."

"What?" Dan said and, unsure of what he had heard, went back. "Carlo became what?"

But Julie was locked onto Peter's earlier question. "Papa said it was what many collectors did. Became teratophiles. There were codes, passwords, that let them into the secret rooms all over Europe. They all had them—the travelling shows and respectable homes. There were special fairs. There still are. It isn't new. The practice has been going on for centuries."

Dan composed himself. "But Carlo tried to help."

"He tried. But Papa caught him. Made him into a fine pair of wings."

There it was again, but Dan didn't bring it up then. "So how were you separated? If Carlo didn't do it?"

"One of Papa's guests in Frankfurt was a surgeon. Papa let him visit us alone. He felt very guilty after he had been with us. He took pity on us, told Jenny and me it was just a lot of muscle joining us. No arteries, nothing vital. There'd be blood, he said, quite a lot, but he told us what he'd have to do, said he'd bring the necessary instruments and drugs."

Despite the bizarre experiences of Dan's own life, it all sounded like so much fabrication again, a tall tale growing larger and more improbable by the minute: first Carlo, now this Frankfurt surgeon, Carlo becoming a nice pair of wings.

But then, like a spectre at the feast, or more a mind-reader in a high-class nightclub act, Peter was there.

"Julie, this is very important. Doctor Dan and I are finding this hard to accept. You must help us. Your Papa let this surgeon bring a bag of things into the secret room?"

"A lot of them brought bags and cases. Teratophiles are like paraphiles everywhere. Some brought masks and hoods, special costumes and things to use on us. Their cameras. Papa trusted and liked this man. Xavier Pangborn was as great an admirer of Frederik Ruysch as Papa was. Only when the pain became too much and we were crying out, did Papa break in. He and Dr. Pangborn had a terrible fight." Julie winced at the memory. Her cheek spasmed. "Jenny was in so much pain. She passed out. I had to finish the job before I passed out too."

Finish the job!

Dan made himself stay calm, focused. Things did happen violently, strangely, in life; people were capable of the most extraordinary things, acts of courage and strength, incredible perversion too, a mix of the courageous and the outrageous that did make it seem that orthodoxy and consensus were always somewhere else in human affairs.

"What happened to Xavier Pangborn?" Dan asked, warning Peter with a look.

"We awoke in a house with Dr. Pangborn and women we didn't know tending to us. Alonzo was downstairs, furious, so very angry, but also very afraid that Pangborn would tell the authorities and so was trying to be civil. The same shame and guilt that had made Pangborn help us had also led him to destroy all incriminating papers and exhibits of his own. Now he was a pillar of belated virtue. He said he'd have contacts keep an eye on us. Alonzo would never be sure who he meant and so actually made the best of the situation. He eventually sold off his own collection and brought us down to Australia."

"So you were reunited with Jackie."

Julie frowned. "It was more like meeting her for the first time really. Jenny and I were too young to remember her with the show."

"She became very taken with Jenny. Why is that, Julie?"

"Jenny has always been shy and fragile. The trauma of what those men did, the results of the separation—she took it all so much harder than I did. One of us had to cope. One of us had to be stronger."

"But Jackie came looking for you, too, Julie. Jackie cares enough for you to have searched for you."

Julie's mouth was a grim line. Her frown crushed her brow with the intensity of suffering, not merely concentration.

They should stop soon. But there was still so much to learn and Julie was so responsive, so lucid like this. He'd never have expected it. Dan decided to avoid further mention of Jackie; that was the harming stressor here.

"How did Alonzo earn his living in Melbourne, Julie?"

The frown went away; her mouth softened. "He had contacts there—keepers of *Wunderkammern* like himself. One of them gave him a job as assistant curator in a local museum."

"With a secret room no doubt." Dan couldn't help himself.

Julie took it as a question. "I suppose. It was a large public museum. There are always parts the public doesn't see."

That the brotherhood of cabinet keepers kept secret, Dan decided.

"How did he treat you?"

"Well from then on. We were with family. He found his interests elsewhere. And Xavier Pangborn came to see us."

"Pangborn did?"

"He was in Australia lecturing at ANU and Monash. One evening he stopped by. That was before he went missing."

"Went missing?" It was going wild again.

"It was a terrible thing. His wife was with him. There was a big search. It was in all the papers."

Did Alonzo kill him? Dan wanted to ask, but somehow knew Julie would have no idea. If her story were true, this terrible, elaborate, improbable tale, she had every reason to want to put it out of mind. He was probably going too far now. But Jackie had disturbed him; the case of this mysterious young woman sitting before him had opened out, blossomed amazingly. There were too many facts but not enough certainties.

It didn't stop Peter.

"Julie, what did you mean Alonzo made Carlo into a nice pair of wings?"

"Peter!"

"She isn't under, Doctor Dan. She's pretending to be in a trance!"

Dan was affronted, amazed yet convinced all at once. He hadn't wanted to believe it, but of course she was pretending; it had let her deal with experiences too difficult to face otherwise. But the illusion had to be preserved. He had to try and save it.

"Peter, listen very carefully. Trust my professional judgement here. I know for a fact Julie *is* under, and she's going to answer your question right now to prove it. Julie, please answer Peter's question."

Dan again leant forward slightly, urging the young woman with his body language to continue with the vital pretence.

And the words came in the same calm tone she had been using at the outset.

"Alonzo made monsters in the old way. Many keepers of *Wunderkammern* did. You know, fitting bat wings to the bodies of lizards, then carefully drying them to give dragons. Adding a human foetus's arms to the body of a skate. Sticking horns onto monkey skulls. The first platypus taken to Europe was regarded as such a fake. They tried to pull the beak off. Carlo was killed and dried, flayed and 'leathered.' His skin was used for wings."

Wilder and wilder, Dan thought. This can't go on. Julie improvising; Peter playing the role of a conspirator in some charade. Though Jackie *had* been real. She had been.

"Ask her about her surname," Peter prompted, leaning forward as well, playing his part, though he looked more concerned than ever. "Haniver."

"Haniver?" Dan echoed, but the phone rang. He crossed to his desk, grabbed the receiver. "Hello?"

"Dan, it's Jay. Stephanie's not answering her mobile. She was going to do a lost motorist routine. Knocking at the door, asking for directions, so she may have switched it off."

Dan kept him voice low and matter-of-fact. "Is there a problem?"

"Not necessarily. But it wasn't our arrangement. Whenever there's risk, what we call a 'nasty,' we leave our mobiles on."

"What about your back-up from Parramatta?"

"Dan, there was enough traffic going into Horsley Park for Stephanie not to stand out. I called Rick and let him go. Oh, and incidentally, the Laser is registered to a Laura Barraclough in Melbourne and hasn't been reported stolen. I'd say it's on loan."

"Okay. Jay, I'm probably overreacting badly but there's an edge to this I don't like at all. If Stephanie's run up against Jackie she may be in trouble."

"But Jackie isn't the patient."

"Correct. Like I said, she's a patient's sister and seems pretty unstable. Let me know the moment Stephanie calls in."

"Done. What do we do in the meantime?"

"You've got the number in Dalloway Road?"

"Yes."

"Call in favors, Jay. See if you can get a local squad car round there."

"You really do suspect foul play?"

"They won't find anything," Julie said from her chair by the windows.

"Hold it a moment, Jay," Dan said, turning to face her. "What do you mean?"

Julie's face was like a golden mask in the last of the sunlight. "The house at 72 is a trap. It's what's called a 'false door' in Egyptology, what the teratophile cabinet owners call a blind to throw off undesirables. But it's a trap house. Jackie will have taken Stephanie to meet Alonzo and Xavier."

"But they're dead!"

"Yes. But she knows it'll bring me back."

More and more the briars were coiling up.

"Julie, you've got to help me. You've got to explain clearly what's going on!"

"Jackie's changed the rules. She's always been concerned with connection, bringing things together, but now she's harming Jenny."

That was Alonzo with the connection thing, not Jackie! Julie was changing her story again.

"We're going to bring the police in on this," Dan said. "Listen, Jay—"

But Julie's words brought him up short. "You'll never find the house if you do."

"What?"

"If you or your friend there call the police, Doctor Dan, I swear I'll go catatonic and you'll get nothing. Jackie will never call again. Jenny will die. Stephanie may already be dead."

"What then?"

"You get this Jay friend of yours to drive us down to Sydney. I'll take you to the house. Then you can call your police friends."

"I can't do that, Julie."

"But you know you will anyway. I've got to save Jenny, Doctor Dan. It has to be this way. I know Jackie."

Stephanie never called in; her phone remained switched off. The Fairfield police found her car outside 72, found the house deserted, its lights operated by timers, found the shed locked but empty inside when they forced the lock.

This came to them in Jay's Nissan Patrol as they plunged down the Putty Road, Jay driving, Julie next to him, Dan in the back waiting for Harry Badman to return his calls.

Neither Dan nor Jay was surprised when, at 6.20, they turned into Walgrove Road and headed for Horsley Park. Of course the trap house and the real one would be close enough for convenience.

"Tell us about Alonzo and Xavier Pangborn, Julie," Dan said. "How they can be involved."

"You'll see."

Dan refused to give up. "I think I might be a better friend to Jenny than you are right now."

Julie turned in her seat to look at him. "What do you mean?"

"You're doing this because you want to help Jenny."

"Yes! Save Jenny!" Still she faced him, half-turned, eyes glittering in the dim interior.

"Why am *I* doing it?"

"Because you want to know what's going on. Because of his friend." She indicated Jay. "Stephanie."

"More than that. You know it's more than that."

"What then?"

"You want to help Jenny. But I want to help Jenny *and* Julie. Because Jenny needs to have Julie safe too, doesn't she? It can't be all right unless you're both safe."

"Yes." It was a ghostly, feeling-charged affirmation, said with a new and different emotion. She believed him, was accepting what he said. Perhaps he was earning the truth from her.

"Tell me how Alonzo and Xavier are involved!"

And Julie told them as they did 110 ks along Walgrove Road.

"Both men were interested in joining opposites, in bringing things together, the old alchemical quest. Alonzo left us joined. Xavier used us because we were. The prize of Xavier's collection, probably genuine, were two joined bodies."

"Congenitally joined?"

"Oh no, Doctor Dan. An ancient Roman punishment was to tie the condemned to a corpse, back to back, face to face, then leave you. If you weren't lucky enough to die from shock, your body was poisoned by the rotting cadaver. Necrosis took over. Xavier had acquired the preserved remains of such a wretch left like this in a cell in ancient Syria long ago. Preserved by desert heat and aridity. The bodies were unearthed in the 1700s, reached Amsterdam in the 1830s, finally made it into Xavier's collection just before we were born. The same year."

Dan thought he understood. "Xavier acquired the double corpses. Alonzo then fathered conjoined daughters not long after. He couldn't resist. He left you like that as a gesture, a living symbol of Xavier's exhibit."

"Yes." It was breathed rather than said. "That was partly the reason. He also enjoyed the notion for itself."

"Then the separation—"

"Was motivated by genuine compassion from Xavier, we believe, by outrage at something they'd done as competitive, obsessive, heartless, younger men, not just to spite a rival."

"Then—" And again Dan understood. "When Xavier went missing—"

"Yes. Alonzo avenged himself in the appropriate way. Xavier ended his days in a cellar face to face with a corpse."

"How do you know this?"

"Jackie told me."

"*Jackie!* How does she know?"

"She became Alonzo's favorite when he came to Australia. He needed to gloat. He showed her what he'd done."

"Showed her! My God!"

They turned off Walgrove Road onto Horsley Drive, then Julie directed them right into Walworth and along the crests of the low hills, the road winding its way past isolated houses with cheerily lit windows, past long intervening outlooks and swales where the land rolled away in darkened vistas, marked only by occasional, far-off, twinkling points of light, touches of civilization and sanity.

Enough touches. For other things were out there as well. The residues of madness and obsession.

"Lots of room out here, Doctor Dan," Julie said, as if answering him. "Lots of houses and sheds few people ever get to see inside of."

Lots of opportunities for secret lives, Dan thought. "What will Jackie do, Julie?"

"I don't know, Doctor Dan. But I think she wants to harm me and Jenny."

"She said she cared for Jenny. For you too."

"Sometimes she does. But she scared me. I had to leave."

You left Jenny! Dan couldn't accept that. "Julie, was Jenny already dead when you ran away?"

And is Jackie waiting to, Xavier-like, join the two of you back together? Face to face? To reunite you at last?

"Not when I left. But Jackie loves Jenny. She wouldn't harm her."

"She might to get at you. People do it all the time. Harm what they love."

"Not Jenny!" Julie said as if desperately needing to believe it. "Turn here!"

There was a street sign Dan didn't have time to read or even ask about because, almost immediately, Julie was telling Jay to pull over in front of a

large open field. No, not a field—a drab fibro house sat at the end of a driveway, a single light showing dimly from what seemed to be the living room.
To the right of the house was a large corrugated iron shed, just like the one
Stephanie had described for the place on Dalloway Road, about thirty metres by fifteen, four metres or so high, with no visible windows and none of
the double doors you'd expect for housing large vehicles in such a structure.

"There." Julie pointed, indicating the shed and the solitary door they
could see on its northwestern corner.

Jay reached for his car-phone.

"Don't!" Julie said, in a voice that actually startled Dan, so different it
was to anything he'd ever heard from her. "Please! She will harm Jenny!
And Stephanie! She probably doesn't know we're here yet!"

Jay switched off the engine. "Lives are at risk, Julie."

"They certainly will be if we don't follow her system."

"System?" Jay asked before Dan could.

"That's a *Wunderkammer* there," Julie answered. "She will have prepared
it for us."

Again Jay reached for the phone. "Someone has to know. No one's going
in there."

Dan gripped his shoulder. "Jay, it probably does have to be this way.
What's the layout, Julie?"

"She will have changed it. It's the House of Iitoi most likely. From the
Hopi legend. The maze pattern you see all over the Southwestern USA.
The Arizonan labyrinth with Death at the centre. Your journey through the
maze to Death at the centre is the journey through life."

"Julie!" Dan said, still gripping Jay's shoulder, knowing how carefully
this had to be played. "Tell us what to expect."

"There's usually an entry corridor going round the perimeter, leading
inwards. There'll be photographs, exhibits to arouse interest, *vanitas mundi*
tableaux."

"*Vanitas* what?" Jay asked.

"Displays," Dan said. "Vitrines containing exhibits. Go on, Julie."

"Definitely a maze."

"With traps? Shortcuts? You've been in there. You've seen it."

"I can't say. She will have changed it, Doctor Dan. But she wants me in there with Jenny. She won't risk harming me."

"Give us the address here, Julie," Dan said. "As we go in, Jay phones the police. No one goes anywhere till that's done."

"But *as* we go in," Julie said. "I have to be in there. Promise. Both of you."

Dan did at once. Jay hesitated, furious, then grudgingly did so, as if such oaths could hold true just by being given. There was danger here, and madness, though fortunately Jay, like Dan, recognised an essential process at work, saw that any show of force could not guarantee the safety of lives within. But a trail of crumbs had to be left for the cavalry, even if it was to be after the event. Everything on Jackie's terms, *if* they decided to go in.

"Lot 6, Jellicoe Road," Julie told them, opening her door and getting out, with Dan right behind her, determined to stay close.

Jay did too, slipping his gun into the inside pocket of his wind-jacket, his mobile in his left hand. "I want to check the address," he said, and rushed off into the night. They could hear his footsteps along the road.

"He'll call the police," Julie said, taking Dan's arm and leading him up the driveway, angling towards the shed. "We need to continue without him."

"We can't do that, Julie. His friend is in there. He deserves to be here too."

"Don't you see, Doctor Dan? If we make this difficult for Jackie, she'll make it difficult for us. He can follow. Please."

Dan tried to think it through, calculate what was to be lost or gained.

But the door was suddenly there and it opened easily when Julie turned the handle and, almost before he knew it, they were in the long 1.2-metre-wide passageway that stretched out before them, roofed and walled with sheet iron, wooden-floored, lit by single frosted bulbs every seven metres or so. The building's outer wall had been corrugated iron, but its interior was faced with sheet iron, suggesting a double wall, probably with insulating batts in between. On the inner wall of the passage were framed photographs—first, of the original eponymous twins, Chang and Eng, and of other famous conjoined siblings, then of a whole series of renowned "freaks" and hoaxes. Hanging from the roof beams, casting eerie shadows and set turning in the warm close air by Dan and Julie entering the corridor, were the shrivelled remains of false monsters. Dan saw a winged serpent-like thing the red of old blood, then a grimacing homunculus—no doubt a late-development foetus, its wizened features and oversized hands probably added by some experienced teratologist. Other dim shapes swung and spiralled further down the passageway.

From even further off, deeper within the structure, came music, the faintest strains of Prokofiev, if Dan wasn't mistaken, which lent a disturbing, too discordantly civilised edge to the whole thing, but also gave a sense of direction and destination, some kind of centre to all this.

Julie went on ahead, leaving Dan to follow. They had to complete the circuit, it seemed, follow the passage the length of the shed's long southern side, turn left along its eastern end. There were more sheet metal walls, naked bulbs, photos in dusty frames, shrivelled shapes turning overhead, then another turn left down the long northern side.

Now the photos were different. Now the pictures were of Julie and Jenny, their story told in graphic, pathetic detail: showing them first as infants, cute and normal-looking in matching outfits, then as happy little girls in identical smiling poses, then as prepubescent youngsters suddenly displayed naked and joined by their short "bridge" of flesh, just the two of them alone initially, staring wide-eyed in confusion and alarm, then attended by as many as seven figures in dark business suits, though more often one or two and always male it seemed, all but the girls masked, appropriately, with dominoes or grotesque animal and demon masks, lacquered and snouted as if denizens from a Venetian Carnivale. Sometimes the girls were shackled; other times they simply huddled together, hiding their nude or half-dressed state.

Then it changed again. Dan saw images even more blatantly sexual, and more and more often, one of the twins was shown with her hands fastened behind her and her mouth taped, while the other received the attentions of some visitor or other with what seemed increasing abandon.

"Julie," Dan said, whispered in the close air, his first words in that terrible place. "You're the one restrained, aren't you?"

Julie nodded, not turning, sobbing. "She enjoyed it! The bitch actually enjoyed it, can you believe that? I was always raped, but she *liked* it!"

"Jenny did? But you said Jenny and you."

"Not Jenny!" she cried, sobbing bitterly now, still pressing ahead, still not looking round. "Not *Jenny!*"

"That's Jackie?" Dan's gaze flicked from image to image and knew it was. "But Jackie spoke of Jenny too."

He didn't need to go on, certainly didn't need to speak what Julie so painfully knew. It was what Peter Rait had said about there being a sister. *There is and there isn't.*

There was no Jenny.

They'd both lost a sister, had both changed too much to be what they once were for each other, yet both had vivid, profoundly affecting memories of a loved one who *was* another part of them, *was* the perfect friend and sibling.

Julie didn't see her in Jackie. Jackie couldn't find her in Julie.

They'd lost each other, couldn't be it for one another, had become too different, too definitely separate, yet out of trauma, betrayal, terrible loss, had invented the one point at which they *could* connect. Preserving something of the lost intimacy, some kind of way back.

As a schoolboy in Reardon, Dan remembered that his kindergarten teacher had made a Wendy House at the back of the classroom, named no doubt after Peter Pan and Wendy—a house where the children played at being grown-ups. This was a Jenny House, everything in it a shrine to what Julie and Jackie had made between them. But playing at grown-ups. What chance had they?

Dan saw how it was. Hurrying along after Julie, rushing past those frightful images, he understood the terrible dilemma. Jackie wanted to unite with her version of Jenny—which only Julie could provide. Of course she'd wanted her back. Julie wanted to unite with *her* version of Jenny as well, but *not* with Jackie! That paradox, that crisis of opposites, had made Julie flee; the opposite pendulum swing had brought her back again into the same irreconcilable crisis.

There was only one way the sisters could ever be joined that would let them *both* join with Jenny. Peter had probably known more about it in his incredible way, had wanted Dan to ask about their pseudonym. Haniver. Now there wasn't time. Now there was only the terrible danger.

"Julie, we go back!" he cried, grabbing at her arm, but she pulled away. Dan hurried forward, went to grab at her again, but then the lights went out and a tremendous snaring weight fell on him from above. He could hear a far-off pounding as he sank to the floor.

Perhaps he lost consciousness for a few moments, Dan couldn't be sure. He found himself trying to put the world back together, found himself fighting with the weight oppressing him when the lights came on again, showed he was wrestling with a coil of heavy rope triggered to drop from above. The driving beat he could hear was probably Jay pounding at the *locked* entry door (for Jackie would have locked it behind them).

Dan finally freed himself from the tangle and stood. There was no sign of Julie, of course, nothing ahead but the passage, the stuffy dimness and turning constructs, more pictures on the walls.

There *were* traps. There *were* shortcuts and secret panels. Julie had been snatched away.

The pounding stopped. The Prokofiev was back and other sounds, far-off scuffling, thumps against the iron, muffled cries.

Dan pounded the walls a moment, crying their names, then rushed along the corridor, his footsteps ringing on the wooden floor, his hands slapping the iron. He had to get to the centre, to wherever Jackie had Julie. And Stephanie, if she were even still alive.

There was a crash and the building shuddered. Dan ignored it, continued running, bringing wind to the dead air.

Again, the building shook to an impact, a shuddering crash, this time followed by a wrenching sound.

It was Jay! Jay was ramming his four-wheel drive into the building, trying to force a way in. And again the structure shook. Beams creaked. Pictures fell and iron sheets were sprung on their uprights.

Dan wrenched one sheet away, actually pried it free and brought it clattering down, then stepped into an inner part of the corridor. One stage closer.

Again Jay rammed the building. Beams groaned, dust settled, more metal sheeting warped out from the timber. Tearing his fingers, Dan wrenched another section of wall free, revealed another inner coil of the maze. There couldn't be many more. He ran on, slewing into the walls when Jay rammed the structure a fifth time, making headway surely.

Then Dan could hear voices raised in anger, accusation, women's voices shouting, made out actual words.

"Jenny doesn't love you!"

"Jenny doesn't love *you*!"

He stopped to listen.

"Do it! Go on! I dare you!"

"Not with you! With her!"

He ran, plunging round the circuit, trying to get into wherever it was. And again the building resounded to a blow, this time followed by a shuddering crash as more outer structural supports gave way.

Dan rounded the next corner, crashed into a locked door and went spinning back, stunned by the impact.

"Julie!" he cried. "Jackie, let me in!"

Again Jay rammed the building. It was solidly made, but never meant for this sort of battering. Something had to be giving.

"He'll do it!" a voice beyond the door cried, Julie or Jackie Dan couldn't tell. "He will!"

And dazed, bloodied, pushing against the door, Dan thought they meant Jay.

When the door gave way and Dan toppled into the large central room, he saw in a glance a host of disparate things: the old-style record player, the specimen tables and cases of exhibits, the clustering of shapes dangling from the roof beams, saw the girls lying naked and joined in the shallow pit in the middle of the floor, yes, glued together front to front with the tubes of instant glue lying near them, Julie's hands tied behind her back, saw too what he had set in motion by pushing back the door, the big tub of acid even now tipping onto them.

He'll do it!

The screams and threshing about were hideous and mercifully short, and there was drumming, a relentless drumming that wasn't the blood rushing through Dan's heart and temples, that was suddenly Jay bursting into the room, eyes wide, gun drawn.

They stood in the dreadful quiet, in a near-silence of sizzling and dripping that faded even as they watched, faded to the lowest, faintest mewing of despair.

"Where's Steph?" Jay said.

"Listen!" Dan told him.

"Where is she?"

"Listen, dammit!"

And they heard it again, a dismal far-off wail, a dull thumping.

"Where's that coming from?" Jay demanded.

"There's always a secret room," Dan said, remembering what Peter had said to Julie. "Try over there, but stay clear of the pit. That's acid."

They circled the central depression where the bodies lay contorted and, yes, virtually indistinguishable now, went to one of the dimly lit corners. The mewing was louder, the dull thumping more distinct.

They discovered a catch near the ceiling, another sunk into the wooden floor, and fumbled at them, Dan with bloody fingers, Jay clumsy with desperation, but finally pulled back the panel to reveal a room lit by its single bulb.

Stephanie was on the floor, naked, gagged, strapped between the dried corpses of Alonzo and Xavier, their shrivelled heads and faces jammed against hers, their groins pressing close, front and back. Though clearly exhausted, she was jerking the hideous construct as best she could, eyes wide with sheer terror and a hysteria very close to madness.

Jackie had used false street signs, so it took the police and ambulances a while to find them at Lot 3 Dinsmoor Road, took hours of Dan and Jay answering questions at the local police station, explaining just what it was that had occurred and why.

Thankfully Harry Badman phoned in at last and vouched for them, added his verifications to those already provided by Blackwater, but it wasn't until 2 a.m. that Dan and Jay reached Everton again. Knowing how some things needed to be anchored in the mundane as soon as possible, Dan had Barbara, Mark, and Carla "debrief" them for almost another hour before sending Jay off home.

The next morning, Dan wasn't at all surprised to find Peter Rait sitting at the corner window in the library where he'd found Julie—could it be?— less than twenty-four hours before.

"I should've asked you about the name," Dan said. "Haniver."

Peter nodded and smiled. "You should have, yes. Though it couldn't have ended any other way."

"Tell me about it now."

"There used to be quite a thriving market in monsters. Many were made in Antwerp, a Flemish seaport on the Scheldt the French called Anvers. A 'Jenny Haniver' was the name they gave to such merchandise."

"These false monsters?"

"Yes, Doctor Dan. False dreams in a way. Imitations of wonder some needed to believe in so much. The sisters knew what they were making."

"They died for it, Peter."

"Yes, but it's closure, isn't it? They had already lost one another, were getting further and further apart."

"Their *Wunderkammer* was a deathtrap."

"Ah, but then, Doctor Dan, that's like the world itself. The best of them always are."

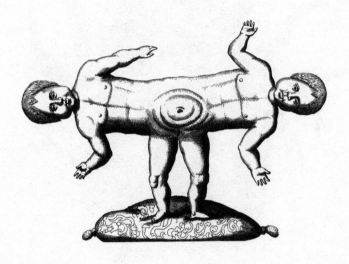

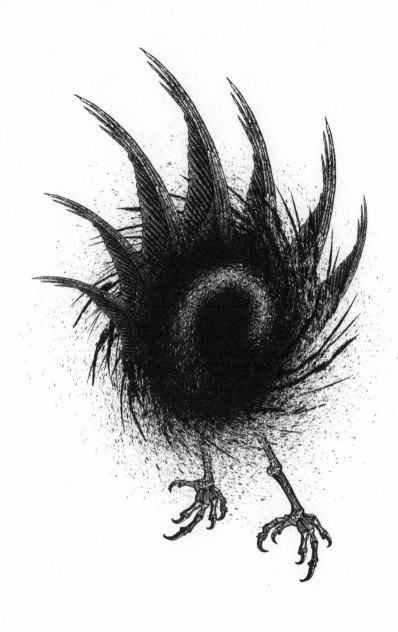

Miss Ill-Kept Runt

GLEN HIRSHBERG

*"My mother's anxiety would not allow her to remain where she was....
What was it that she feared? Some disaster impended over her husband
or herself. He had predicted evils, but professed himself ignorant of what
nature they were. When were they to come?"*
—Charles Brockden Brown, *Weiland*

Chloe comes clinking out the front door into the twilight, Pudding Pop in one hand and a dragon in the other. The summer wind sets her frizzy brown hair flying around her, and she says, "Whoa," tilting up on one foot as though anything less than an F5 twister, a tag team of grizzly bears, a fighter jet could drag her and the fifteen pounds or so of bead necklace around her neck off the ground. The plastic baubles and seashell fragments and recently ejected baby teeth bump along her chest as she tilts, then straightens.

"I told you to get in pajamas," says her father from the side of the station wagon, where he's still trying to wedge the last book and pan boxes into the wall of suitcases and cartons separating the front seat from the way-back, where Chloe and her brother the Miracle will be riding, as always.

"These *are* pajamas," Chloe says, lifting the mass of beads so her father can see underneath.

Sweating, exhausted before the drive even starts, her father smiles. Better still, the Miracle, who is already stretched in the way-back with his big-kid feet dangling out the open back door and his Pokémon cards spread all over the space Chloe is supposed to occupy, laughs aloud and shakes his head at her. In Chloe's world, there are only a few things better than Pudding Pops and beads. One of them is her older brother noticing, laughing. The baby teeth on her newest necklace are mostly for him; she actually thinks they look blah, too plain, also a little bitey. But she'd known he would like them.

"Miss Ill-Kept Runt," her brother says, and goes back to his cards.

She's just climbing into the back, enjoying the Miracle's feverish sweeping up of cards, his snapping, *"Wait"* and *"Don't!"* at her, when her mother emerges from the empty house. Freezing, Chloe watches her mother tighten the ugly gray scarf—it looks more like a dishrag—around her beautiful dark hair, linger a last, long moment in the doorway, and finally aim a single glance in the direction of her children. Chloe starts to lift her hand, but her mother is hurrying around the side of the station wagon, eyes down, and Chloe hears her drop into the passenger seat just before her father wedges the Miracle's feet inside the car and shuts the way-back door.

"Stan," her mother says, in her new, bumpy voice, like a road with all the road peeled off. "Let's just *go*."

It's the move, Chlo. That's what her father's been saying. For months, now.

Her father's already in the driver's seat and the station wagon has shuddered to life under Chloe's butt and is making her necklaces rattle when her mother's door pops open, and all of a sudden she's there, pulling the back door up, blue-eyed gaze pouring down on Chloe like a waterfall. Chloe is surprised, elated, she wants to duck her head and close her eyes and bathe in it.

"Happy birthday," her mother says, bumpy-voiced, and reaches to touch her leg, then touches the Miracle's instead. He doesn't look up from his cards, but he waves at her with his sneaker.

"It's not my birthday yet," Chloe says, wanting to keep her mother there, prolong the moment.

Her mother gestures toward the wall of boxes in the back seat. "We'll be driving most of the night. By the time I see your face again, it will be." And there it is—faint as a fossil in rock, but there all the same. Her mother's smile. A trace, anyway.

It really has *been the move*, Chloe thinks, as her mother slams the door down like a lid.

"Say good-bye to the house," her father says from up front, on the other side of the boxes. Chloe can't see him, and she realizes he sounds different, too. Far away, as though he's calling to her across a frothed-up river. But right on cue, she feels the rev, *rrruummm, rruummm*; it's reassuring, the thing he always does before he goes anywhere. She bets he's even turned around to give her his *go!* face, forgetting there's a wall of cardboard there.

Then they are going, and Chloe is surprised to find tears welling in her eyes. They're not because she's sad. Why should she be, they're moving back to Minnesota to be by Grammy and Grumpy's, where they can water-ski every day, Grumpy says, and when Chloe says, "You can't water-ski in *winter*," Grumpy says, "Maybe *you* can't."

But just for a moment, pulling out of the drive, she's crying, and the Miracle sits up, bumping his big-kid head against the roof and squishing her as he turns for a last look.

"Bye, house," she says.

"Pencil mouse," says the Miracle, and Chloe beams through her tears. It's her own game, silly-rhyme-pencil game, she made it up when she was three to annoy her brother into looking at her, and it mostly worked. But she couldn't ever remember him *playing* it.

"Want to do speed?" she says, and the Miracle laughs. He always laughs now when she says that, but only because their father does. Her father has never said what's funny about it, and she doesn't think the Miracle knows, either.

"*Play* speed," he answers, grinning, maybe to himself but because of her, so that doesn't matter. "In a minute." And he glances fast over his shoulder toward the wall of boxes and then turns away from her again temporarily.

But Chloe has noticed that his grin is gone. And when she settles onto her shoulder blades and stretches out her legs to touch the door while her head brushes the back of the back seat, she realizes she can hear her mother over the rumbling engine, over the road bumping by.

"Oh, freeze," her mother is whispering, over and over. Or else, *"cheese."* Or *"please."*

It isn't the words, it's the whispering, and Chloe realizes she knows what her mother's doing, too: she's hunched forward, picking at the hem of her skirt on her knees, her pale, knobby knees.

Knees? Is that what she's saying? No. *Please.*

"Bye, trees," Chloe whispers, watching the familiar branches pop up in her window to wave her away. The blue pine, the birch, the oak where her father *thinks* the woodpecker always knocks, the black-branched, leafless fire-trees the crows pour out of every morning like spiders from a sac. After the fire-trees comes the open stretch of road with no trees. The trees after that are ones she doesn't know, at least not by name, not to say hello or wave good-bye. Then come brand new trees.

"Please," comes her mother's voice from the front seat.

"Dad, Gordyfoot," the Miracle all but shouts.

"Right," comes her father's answer, not as shiny as usual but just as fast. Seconds later, the CD's on, and Chloe can't hear her mother anymore.

Fire-trees, Chloe is thinking, dreaming. *Fire on a hillside with no grass, in a ring of stones, but not warm enough. No matter how close she wriggles, she can't get close enough, she's been out on this mountainside with the gray rocks and gray snakes for too long, and this cold is old, so old, older than daylight, older than she is, she could jump into the fire and never be warm....*

Jerking, Chloe struggles up onto her elbows, almost laughing. She has never been camping, not that she can remember, the snakes she knows are green and slippy-shiny except when they're dead and the crows have been at them, and the only cold she's felt the last few months is the lily-pond water from the Berrys' backyard.

On the CD, Gordyfoot is singing about the Pony Man, who'll come at night to take her for a ride, and out the window, the sky's going dark fast with the sun gone. Chloe thinks it's funny that the Miracle asked for this CD, since he says he *hates* Gordon Lightfoot now. But she also understands, or thinks she does. It's hard to imagine being in the way-back, in the car with her parents, and listening to anything else. They keep the entire Gordon Lightfoot collection up there. Also, if the CD wasn't on, they'd have to listen to their mother. *Freeze. Please. Pencil-bees.*

For a while—long enough to get out of their neighborhood and maybe even out of Missouri, half a CD or more—Chloe watches the wires in her window swing down, shoot up, swing down, shoot up. It's like starting and erasing an Etch A Sketch drawing, the window fills with trees and darkening sky and the thick, black lines of wire, then *boop*—telephone pole—and everything's blank for a second and then fills up again. Gets erased. Fills up again. Gets erased. Abruptly, it's all the way dark, and the wires vanish, and Venus pounces out of the sky. It's too bright, has been all summer, as though it's been lurking all day just on the other side of the sunlight.

With the Miracle coiled away from her and his head tilted down, she can see the semi-circle scar at the base of his neck, like an extra mouth, almost smiling. Chloe has always thought of that spot as the place where the miracle actually happened, though she's been told that's just where the clip to stop blood flow went. The real scar is higher, under the hair, where part of her brother's skull got cut open when he was five years old. Of course, she'd been all of a week old at the time and doesn't remember any of it. But she loves the story. Her mother curled on the waiting room couch where she'd been ever since she'd given birth to Chloe, expecting the doctors to come at any moment and tell her that her son was dead. Her mother erupting from that couch one morning and somehow convincing the surgeons who'd said the surgery couldn't work that it *would* work, just by the way she said it. By the way she seemed to *know*. And it had worked. The pressure that had been building in the Miracle's brain bled away. Two days later, he woke up himself again.

"What?" he says now, turning around to glower at her.

"Speed, speed, speed," she chants.

He glowers some more. But after a few seconds, he nods.

"Yay," says Chloe.

They can barely see the playing cards, which makes the game even more fun. Plus, the piles won't stay straight because of all the vibrations, which frustrates the Miracle but makes Chloe laugh even more as their hands dart between each other's for cards and tangle up and slap and snatch, and finally the Miracle's laughing, too, tickling her, Chloe's shrieking and they're both laughing until their father snarls, *"Kids, Goddamnit,"* and both of them stop dead. Her father sounds growly, furious, nothing like he usually sounds.

Because he's trapped up there with Mom, Chloe thinks, and then she's horrified to have thought that, feels guilty, almost starts crying again.

"Sorry," she whimpers.

"Just…sssh," her father says.

It's the move, Chloe thinks, chants to herself. She lies back flat, and the Miracle stretches as much as he can stretch beside her.

"The Pony Man" is on again, so the same CD has played through twice, but only Chloe seems to have noticed. She's listening very closely, like the song says, so she'll hear the Pony Man if he comes. But all she hears is their station wagon's tires *shushing* on the nighttime road, which she imagines to be black and wet, like one of those oil puddles birds get stuck in on nature shows. She's fairly sure she can hear her father's thumbs, too, drumming the beat on the steering wheel, and if she closes her eyes, she can see his stain-y *Show Me!* shirt and the wonderful, white prickles around his happy mouth. He has told Chloe he's secretly a cat, and the prickles are whiskers he keeps trimmed so Mom won't know.

He's been shaving more closely lately, though. Smiling less.

Then she realizes she can hear her mother, crying now. Even the cry is new, a low-down bear-grunt, and Chloe turns toward the Miracle's back and pokes it.

"Tomorrow I'll be half as old as you," she whispers. The Miracle doesn't respond. So she adds, "The next day, I'll be *more* than half."

The Miracle still doesn't respond, and she wonders if he's sleeping. His back is hard and curved like an armadillo shell.

"Catching up," she tries, a very little bit louder, and as she speaks she glances into the seatback above her head, as though she could see through it, through the cartons to her parents. As though they could see her.

"You'll never catch up," the Miracle murmurs, just as quiet, and Chloe thinks she sees his head tilt toward the front, too.

"I can if you wait."

"Will you just go to *sleep*?" he hisses, and Chloe startles, squirms back. The Miracle's whole body drums to the road or the steady beat of her father's thumbs. But when he speaks again, he's using his nice voice. "It'll make the drive go faster."

Chloe almost tells him she doesn't want it to go faster. She likes the way-back, always has. Shut in with her brother, Gordyfoot's voice floating over and among them, her parents close but not with them, the stars igniting and the hours stretched longer and thinner than hours should be able to go. Silly Putty hours.

Chloe doesn't remember falling asleep, has no idea how long she sleeps. But she dreams of bird-feet hands. Hands, but the fingers too thin, yellow-hard. *Her* hands? *Reaching through the bars toward the frantic, fluttering thing, all red and beating its pathetic little wings....*

A bump jolts her awake, or else the *cold*, that *old* cold, she almost cries out, wraps herself in her own arms, blinks, holds on, drags her brain back to itself. *Air-conditioning, it's just her father blasting the air-conditioning to stay awake, it's not in her chest, there are no hands in her chest.* Chloe's eyes fly all the way open, and just like that, she knows.

She *knows*.

They're not my parents.

She knows because "The Pony Man" is on again, the CD repeating, *how many times, now*? She knows because her father *isn't* tapping the steering wheel, which he always does, always always *always*, especially to Gordyfoot. She knows because her mother would never let it get this cold, her mother can't stand the cold, they always wind up fighting about it on night-drives and then swatting each other off the temperature controls and laughing and sometimes, when they think Chloe and the Miracle are sleeping, talking love-talk, very quietly.

They are talking now, but not that way. And in their changed voices. Her mother's bumpy, grunty and low. Her father's a snarl. Someone else's snarl.

Most of all, she knows because her mother's eyes—her *real* mother's eyes—are *green*, not blue. She very nearly screams, but jams her fist in her mouth, holds dead still. But the realization won't go away.

They aren't my parents.

It's ridiculous, a bird-feet hands dream. She wiggles furiously, trying to shake the realization loose.

But in the front seat, the new people—the ones that were her parents—are grunting. Snarl-whispering. And Chloe's mother's eyes are green.

At least "The Pony Man" finally goes off. But the next song is the "Minstrel of the Dawn" one. Another song about someone coming.

Stupid, Chloe insists to herself. *This is stupid.* She feels around for the snack bag her father has let the Miracle stow back here, even though they've already brushed their teeth. The spiny, sticky carpet of the way-back scratches against her palms, and the engine shudders underneath her. Her hand smacks down on the paper bag, which makes a little *pop*. Chloe quivers, holds her breath, and up front, the grunting and the whispering stop.

Chloe doesn't move, doesn't breathe. Neither does anyone else in the car. They are four frozen people hurtling through the empty black. Even the CD has gone silent—because her parents have shut it off, Chloe realizes. It is so quiet inside the car that she half-thinks she can hear the cornfields passing, the late-summer stalks looming over the road like an army of aliens, an invasion that didn't come but grew, their bodies grasshopper-thin, leaves heavy, fruit swollen fat and dangling.

"Chlo?" says her not-father, in his almost-snarl.

Nearly faint from holding her breath, Chloe says nothing. After a second, she hears rustling, but whether from the corn or up front, she can't tell.

"See?" her mother whispers. "I told you. I told you, I told you, I—"

"Oh, for Christ's sake," says her father. "Five years of this. *Five years.* You can't really bel—"

"But I can. And so do you. You always have."

"Just shut up, Carol."

"He's coming."

"Carol—"

"He's coming. Face it. Face it. He's—"

"*Shut up!*"

The CD blares to life, and Chloe almost bangs her head against the seatback in surprise. Her breathing comes in spasms, and she can't get it calm. "The Pony Man" is playing again. *Why?* she wonders. *And why is she minding, anyway? According to her mom and dad, this is the first song she ever knew. The one they sang her to sleep with when she woke up screaming when she was a baby.*

Then Chloe thinks, *Shut up?* Her fingers grab so hard at the carpet that she pulls some out, little quills like a porcupine's. *When has her father ever said that, to anyone?*

And why is her mother laughing?

If that is laughing. It's mostly grunt. Panic breathing.

What Chloe wants to do, right now, is wake the Miracle. She can't believe he isn't awake already, but he hasn't stirred, still lies there with his back curved away and his scar smiling at her. If she wakes him, she knows, she'll have to tell him. Explain, somehow. And she's worried they'll hear.

Instead, she lifts herself—so slowly, as silently as she can, matching her movements to the *shush* of the tires—onto her elbows again. Turns over onto her stomach. Raises her head, then raises it more. Until she's above the seatback.

She's hoping she can see. *One good glimpse*, she thinks. *Then she'll know. Then she can decide what to do.*

But her father has packed the boxes too tight. There aren't even cracks between them. The only empty space is at the very tiptop. Pushing all the way up, Chloe straightens, and her beads *clank*.

This time, she very nearly throws herself out the back window. She's ready to. If they turn…if they pull to the shoulder and stop…she'll grab the Miracle and yank him awake, and they'll *run*.

But the car neither stops nor slows. The CD player continues to blare. The "Minstrel of the Dawn," who'll say your fortune when he comes. If her parents are talking, they're whispering so low that Chloe can't hear them. Apparently, they haven't realized she's moving around. Not yet.

Stretching, gripping her beads to keep them still, Chloe tries to get her eyes level with the opening at the top of the boxes. The little crack. But all see can see is the dark inside dome-light, the tiniest sliver of windshield, at least until a truck passes going the other way, its lights flooding the car and shooting shadows across the ceiling, but the shadows could be corn, seatbacks, surely her parents aren't that thin or that long. It's all Chloe can do to keep from burying her head between her knees in the tornado-position they taught her in kindergarten.

The words are out of her mouth almost before she's thought them or had time to plan.

"I have to go to the bathroom."

For a second, she just sits, horrified, clutching her beads.

But she had to. She needs to see. She's smushing her beads against her chest and holding her breath again, as though any of that matters now.

There is no response. Nothing at all. The car plunges on into the dark, and out her window the cornstalks twist their grasshopper-shoulders to squirm even more tightly together, denying any glimpse of field or farm-house behind them, so that Chloe's vision is blocked on three sides. The only way she can see is behind, the road that leads back to the home they've left.

"I have to go to the bathroom," she says again, meaning to be louder but sounding smaller.

This time, though, the CD shuts off, and that silence wells up from the floorboards. Chloe has begun to cry again, and this makes her angry. *It's stupid*, she thinks, *this is stupid. Or the world is a nightmare.* Either way makes her angry.

Then comes the sigh, long and explosive, from the front seat.

"I thought I told you to *go*," growls not-Dad.

"Sorry," Chloe says. "I did."

All too soon—sooner than she thought possible, and she's seen no exit sign or prick of gas station light penetrating the leafy, squirmy blackness of the fields around her—Chloe feels the car start to slow, hears the *CLICK-click, CLICK-click* of the station wagon's blinker. In her mind, she can see it so clearly, that little green triangle-eye winking at her from the dashboard. *"It's where I keep the frog,"* her father has always said, patting a spot right above the blinking turn-signal, and they'd watch it blink together, and he'd say, *"Ribbit"* in time with the clicking. Until now.

It happens all at once, the corn parting like a curtain and the station appearing, its light so bright that Chloe's eyes water and she has to look away. The Miracle mumbles and rolls over. The light sweeps across the old-mannish wrinkle on his forehead as he dreams. Chloe knows that wrinkle like she knows the frog in the dashboard, her father's cat-whiskers, "The Pony Man." A wave of affection so wide and deep rushes through her that it is all she can do not to throw her arms around her brother's neck and bury her face there.

Then, all at once, she goes rigid again. She hasn't heard any doors opening, they've barely stopped moving. But the silence has gone just that imperceptible bit more still. Her parents—*both of them*—are out of the car.

Chloe whirls just in time to see the face fill the back window, black and scarfed, too big, the doors yawn open and she can't help it, she scurries back, pinning herself against the seat and the boxes with her hands raised and her mouth open to scream.

But her mother is already gone, stalking across the blacktop toward the light, the mini-mart inside the station. She doesn't look back, doesn't wave Chloe on or call to her. But for one moment, the set of those shoulders—the stoop and shake of them—is almost enough.

That is *my mother*, Chloe thinks. *That is my mother crying.*

She is half out of the car before she realizes she has no idea where her father is. Whirling, she bangs her head hard against the top of the door, expecting him to be right on top of her, with new long arms that open like wings and bird-feet hands. At first, she still doesn't see him, and then she does.

He's at the edge of the lot, right on the lip of the road where the cornfield devours the light. Like her mother, he has his back to her, and abruptly Chloe wants nothing more than to call out, lure him here. *He and Mom have been fighting*, she thinks, rubbing the back of her head, making herself breathe. *That's all it is. It's the move, Chlo. Ribbit.*

Something red flickers in his fingers. Chloe has leapt from the station wagon and is backing across the tarmac after her mother before she realizes it's a cigarette. Fast on the heels of that realization comes another. *She has never seen her father with a cigarette before. But he's been smoking lately. That's what that smell has been.*

Stopping by one of the silent pumps, Chloe bathes in the bright light, willing herself to cut it out. Beyond her father, the cornstalks, barely visible, wiggle their leafy antennae in the not-breeze, rattle their bulgy, distended husks. By tomorrow—maybe by the next time she wakes—her family will be at their new house. By tomorrow afternoon, she will be on Grumpy's boat, the rubber boots on the red kid-skis gripping her ankles and the Donald Duck lifejacket wrapping her in its sloppy, damp embrace.

Inside the station, she spots her mother crouching by the peanut butter cheese crackers. She is in profile, but the scarf hides just enough so that Chloe can't see her eyes.

"Going to the bathroom," she says. Her mother doesn't turn.

She dawdles a moment in the candy aisle, running a finger across the silvery *Chunky* wrappers, the boxes of 10-cent Kisses along the bottom shelf. She has almost reached the bathroom when her mother says, "Need help, sweetie?"

Chloe wants to dance, turn around and race at her mother and jump into her arms. Then she does turn, and something prickly and *old*-cold rolls over under her ribs.

Her mother's face, smiling softly down. Tears streaming from her blue eyes.

"No, thank you," Chloe whispers, and shuts herself in.

The toilet has poop in it, and a mound of tissue. Chloe doesn't actually have to go. Sinking into a huddle by the door in the ugly yellow light, she tries to hold her breath, but her chest prickles and she bursts out coughing. Crying again.

She can't stay here, the smell is too much. But she doesn't want to go back out. She's terrified to think what else might have changed by the time she opens the door. Each new breath of putrid air triggers a cough, each blink fresh tears.

Run, she thinks. *Sneak past the Kisses, bolt out the door, find a way to Grumpy's.*

Except that the only place to run is into the corn. In the dark. Chloe can't imagine doing that.

And then she realizes she doesn't want to. She already knows the safest place. The only place that hasn't changed, that's still hers. She needs to get back to the way-back, where the Miracle is.

She has just gotten the heavy door partway open when she hears them. Bumpy-voiced Mom, growly Dad, whispering just out of sight in the next aisle.

"You see?" her father is saying. Halfway snarling.

Her mother sobs.

"I told you."

"You did. It's true."

"You dreamed it, Carol. And no wonder. I mean, those nights. When we both really thought we were going to lose him...."

"But we didn't," Chloe's mother whispers, her voice seeming to twitch back and forth now. Chloe's mother/changed-mother/Chloe's mother.

"Because of you," her father whispers. "Because of your unshakable hope."

"Because of *him*. Because he came. Because he—"

"Because of *you*. You saved him, Carol. You saved your son. You do see that now. Right?"

Soft sob. Silence.

Then footsteps. Chloe pushes hard at the door, but by the time she gets out and hurries down the candy aisle after them, they are already at the pumps, arms around each other, halfway to the car. Her father goes straight to the driver's side, dropping his cigarette to the tarmac. It is her mother who waits by the way-back doors and touches Chloe's hair as she climbs in beside her brother.

"Is it my birthday yet?" Chloe asks, not quite looking at her mother's eyes. She doesn't want to see anymore. Doesn't want to think.

She hears her mother gasp, glance at her watch. "Not yet," she whispers. "Oh, shit, not yet."

The door drops down, and the car starts, and up front her parents are snarling and whispering again. Chloe crouches low, curls into a ball with her knees just touching her brother's back. If he wakes and feels that, he'll be furious. But if she's sleeping when he does, he won't mind. *Sleep*, she commands herself. Pleads with herself. *Sleep*.

She dreams cold. Old-cold. Green eyes. Bird-feet hands that aren't her hands—weren't—aren't—reaching for the beating-wing bird. Straw into gold, hillsides of stone. Old stone. Grasshopper-cornstalk squeezing in the window, slithering through it, crouching over her in the empty dark with its antennae brushing her face, and its husks, its dozens of husks hard and bumping against her chest, her legs. Those hands prying into the cage, reaching through the bars. Ribs. Toward the red and beating thing.

Chloe wakes to a silent car, bright sunlight. She is flat on her back, but she can feel the Miracle's heat against her forearm. He is moving now, stretching. Out the window, there are trees overflowing with green, shading her from the brilliant blue overhead. Minnesota lake trees. Somewhere close, there's a hum. Motorboat hum. Chloe is halfway sitting up when she hears them.

"You'll see," says her father, sounding tired. But only tired. And happy, almost. Sure, in the way he somehow still hasn't learned not to be, that the worst is behind him.

He pulls open the back door, arms wide, and it's him, her CatDad with his whisker-face, and she sits all the way up—just to revel in it, just to watch it all land—and he staggers back. Staring.

Revel? That's what *it's* doing, anyway, Chloe knows. The cold one inside her. The one moving her arms, blinking her eyes. Making her watch.

Vaguely, glancing toward her brother, Chloe wonders whether she really did figure it all out, or if the knowledge just came with the intruder. The cold one with the bird-feet hands, practically dancing down her ribs under her skin in his glee. Now she really does know. She knows how this happened. She knows when the cold one first appeared in her mother's hospital room. Her mother, whose eyes have always been blue, it's this *other's* mother that confused her.

Anyway, she knows what the cold one promised. She knows what he got her mother to offer in exchange.

"Where is she?" Chloe's father is murmuring, hovering right outside the way-back door and waving his hands as though trying to clear a fogged windshield, while out the side window, her mother stands rooted, hands over her mouth, shuddering and weeping. There is something almost comforting about it, about both her parents' reaction. At least they can tell. At least she really was *her*. There really was a something named Chloe.

I'm right here, she wants to scream. *Right here.* But of course, the cold one won't let her. He's having way too much fun.

Her father is on his knees, now, just the way the cold one likes him. Murmuring through his tears. Through his disbelief, which isn't really disbelief anymore. *So delicious when they understand,* the cold one tells her, in his inside ice-voice. *When they can't stop denying. Can't stop pleading. Even when they already know.*

So pathetic, her father looks down there. Hands going still. Head flung back in desperation. Or resignation. "Please," he says. "What have you done with my daughter?"

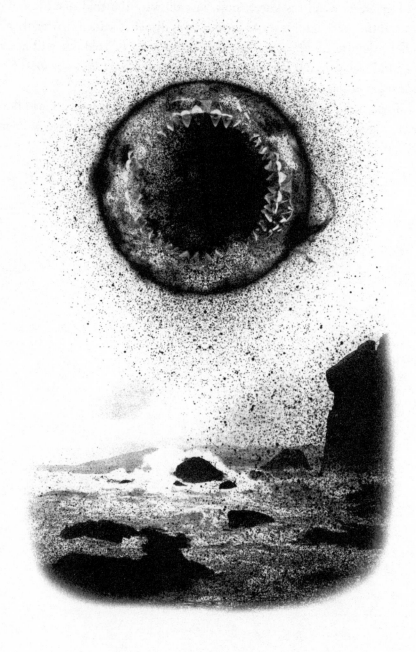

Chasing Sunset

A. C. WISE

Just short of six p.m., I'm chasing sunset fifteen miles out of Coppertown. Which is the dead fucking middle of nowhere, in case you're wondering. The road's near empty, the tank, too, but I'm running flat out, trying to put as many miles between me and uncertain doom as possible.

At least I have a few tricks up my sleeve. The briefcase riding shotgun is full of some of the baddest mojo there is—Black Goat of a Thousand Young type shit. Shit to end the world.

See, the Old Man's hunting. And, as luck would have it, he's *my* old man. He's dying and, consequently, doing his best to call me home. The prodigal fucking son.

The briefcase is my countermeasure. Fight fire with fire, they say.

And the whole world burns.

When you grow up with a head full of horror show and a father styling himself Lord of the Flies, this kind of shit makes sense. It seems reasonable to dabble with Old Gods, turn the sun into a bloody eyeball rolling its mean old gaze down the road. It makes sense to buy a plastic Baggie of mummified, freeze-dried baby squid—pre-calamari flash frying—and grind them fine enough to snort straight up your nose.

If the road jackknifes into the sky, if the angles of the desert go wrong, if the A/C pipes high, weird music, and your sweat turns mercury-thick, oozing oily beads born of the boneless bones of primordial beasts from before the world's dawn—well, it's a small price to pay. It's better than the alternative.

I got dear old Daddy's eyes, and he wants to make it literal. Look out from inside my skin, slough off the old, slip into the new, and reincarnate in a body with less miles on the odometer.

I say fuck that shit. So I run.

For now, the world is steady. I'm breathing harder than normal, but the sky is only oncoming twilight and not a color out of space. Scrub throws purple shadows, blurring past my windows. The powder-blue Caddy shimmies, but I'm keeping it between the lines. I'll run 'til it burns. If I can hit the coast, I'll be clear.

Least that's what I tell myself.

I hit the radio's scan, cycling decimal points of white noise. There's a burst of static, and my heart kicks high. I slam the brakes, but even the tire-squeal as the Caddy fishtails isn't enough to cover the wet sound caught between one station and the next. Raw meat hitting a wall. Sobbing. The buzz of flies.

Memory crowbars my skull. Light slipping through uneven boards, the just-molding scent of hay. The steady ping of blood dripping into a metal bowl. The Old Man, hair sweat tangled, eyes crimson-shot ivory. Above him, the corpse of a horse hangs head-down from rusty chains.

A warning shot across the prow.

I punch the radio into silence. Grip the wheel and roll down the window, washing desert air through the sweaty space of the car.

It's not enough.

Next time it won't be the horse, it'll be the drifter. It'll be filth-streaked flesh and barbed-wire binding, like the vines on the Hanged Man tarot card. It'll be the man's cock, painfully swollen, his eyes rolling wide, his lips silently pleading.

It'll be my father's hand, extended into a shaft of sunlight, holding a straight razor. Waiting.

Fuck.

Concentrate.

Breathe.

I ease the car back onto the road. An animal skitters through the sweep of headlights. To my jangled nerves, it looks like a hunched man. It pauses, eyes luminous, tongue lolling, and grins.

Fuck.

I flip open the briefcase, abandoning caution, and brush the blacker than black idol within.

Oiled wood, stone, whatever the fuck it is, it's cold. Even so, it burns; tacky strings of flesh pull from my hand as I jerk away. Lightning arcs between my bones. I expect sizzling drops of blue-white fire when I try to shake the sensation free.

The sky rolls over. The moon opens an eye, which is also a mouth, and howls. The sun's cooling corpse is a bloody eyeball slipping the horizon. Rotting corpse gods fuck against the sunset and carrion young drop from between their scabbed thighs.

But my Old Man still grins—teeth to stars to eternity.

Then something squiggles. And doesn't it just snap up the grinning man-beast and swallow it whole?

Cosmic distance. I'm flayed bloody and my brain's in a fucking canister screaming between cold, sharp stars.

And for a minute, the curtain tears, and I *see*.

Everything goes dark. There's no road, no Old Man. Nothing but vast deep.

I let out a shaky breath, ease back on the accelerator, snap the briefcase closed.

Score one for the Old Ones.

I keep the window down, sucking in desert night. Check the gas gauge—a sliver to empty. I risk the radio and catch a smattering of twangy country-western. It'll do.

There was no horse. No razor. No bowl catching blood.

There's just the desert night, and the horror pressed to the skin of the world. Better the devil you don't know than the devil you do.

I hope it'll be enough.

But the thing about power is it likes straight lines, the path of least resistance—from sky to tree, from father to son.

The country song fades. Silence trickles in, thick and over-sweet. I nudge the dial and nearly jump out of my skin. A voice ghosts from the static hiss-pop.

"…where he makes us go when we're bad."

Ice down my spine. I stomp the gas instead of the brake. The car lurches, shimmy dancing, spitting gravel.

Because I can see it. The shed. Little Sister—eyes big as the Old Man leads her into the dark, taking the punishment meant for me. Meat smacks the wall. Flies buzz. Sister sobs.

Shit. I slam the brakes. Door open, I bring up the gas-station burrito eaten cold miles back.

Shaking, I wipe my mouth. Desert insects sing. My clothes feel soaked-through wet; my pulse hammers, refusing to cool. I glance at the briefcase, but stop before touching it.

Some fisherman out of Providence sold it to me, Innsmouth look and all. Friend of a friend of the fucker who sold me the dime bag of freeze-dried squid on the pier.

Those squid were amateur night compared to this, just an endless walk down spiraling ice stairs into the dark and half-glimpsed shadows embed-ded in the walls.

This thing, this idol, is what lay at the bottom.

Dry-slick, but rotten to the core. How much can I take before I crack and go ha-ha loop-de-loo around the bend? On the plus side, if I end up a gibbering mass, I'm no good to the Old Man. Last resort, I guess.

I grit my teeth, trying sheer force of will. The Old Goat's kid can be stubborn, too.

Back on the road, careful-slow. The wash of headlights illumes Sister, dress stained dark, flies where her eyes should be, Daddy dearest standing behind her: *See what you've done?*

Instead of swerving, I power through. Sister and the Old Goat shred like moon-torn mist.

"Nice try, Old Man," I shout. "I never had a sister."

I hope to fuck it's true.

Now that my skull's been pried wide, Daddy dearest can pour whatever he wants inside. Still, a hole opens below my ribs, dropping my heart. This doesn't feel like a lie. I know Sister's braids, scabbed knees, jam-stained smile. Her love.

Silent picture-show memories spool across the night, pin-pricked by grub-pale stars. A black and white image of me at six: The Old Man puts out a cigarette, midway between my wrist and elbow.

I know if I cry Sister will get the punishment. That's how he breaks us. Sometimes we're strong. Sometimes.

Six-year-old me bites my lip, holds tears on dark lashes, doesn't let them fall. The smell of burned flesh reaches my nose.

When Sister peeks around Daddy's elbow, I'm not quick enough to hide my pain. Her hand goes in his, small delicacy against calloused horn.

"It's okay." The first bit for me, and the second for him. "It was my fault."

She leads him out the screen door, down the crooked path to the shed at the bottom of the garden. I don't follow. I should. I curl on the kitchen floor, six-year-old body rocked hollow by sobs. I press hands to my ears, squeeze bruised-damp lids shut, and pretend I don't hear the sounds coming from outside.

Sobbing. Flies. A wet sound like blood.

I rub the spot between wrist and elbow—a small circle, shiny and purple-pink, the color of seashells.

"Fuck."

I have to stop. I can't stop.

Even with the idol beside me, the Old Man is under my skin.

"Come home, and I'll make it stop." The words buzz through my skull. Maybe my bad mojo isn't bad enough.

Every time I step up my game he steps up his. I shoot up Innsmouth water courtesy of a needle between my toes, and he sends the rotting carcass of a horse to chase me into the briny deep. I snort powdered squidlings in a dingy motel, and after the ice shadows fade, I wake with flies crawling between my bones and my skin.

Maybe there's nowhere far enough to run.

Twilight deepens, scatter-shotting the wide night with stars. An exit sign promises gas and food. I pull off; nothing left to lose.

A lone diner shines neon. A gas station squats half a mile down the road. Scorpions clack in the dark of cactus shadows; the moon slings low, slouching over the horizon, all pale gold and bruised, rotted fruit. Right now, the idol isn't doing shit. In his death throes, the Old Man is strong.

Another memory freezes me. The scraggly-haired drifter in his roughed-up army jacket, the shadow of buzzards crossing over him. Me sweating in the bucket seat, praying my father won't stop.

The Old Man rolls down the window. "Where you headed, son?"

The bum lowers his hand-lettered sign—Sharpie on cardboard: HOMELESS VET. WILL WORK FOR FOOD. GODBLESS.

"As far as you're going, mister."

"Hop in." The Old Man pats my knee, a parody of fatherly affection. The touch keeps me from saying a goddamn word. The faint stink of old alcohol bleeding through the bum's skin fills the car. My father glances in the rearview mirror.

"You got a name, son?" Fingers dig into my leg, keeping my terror stitched inside.

"Joshua, sir."

"Well, Joshua, you're lucky we came along. Me and my boy here, we'll take you all the way."

And we did.

Shaking, I slink into the diner, smelling burnt coffee and cherry pie.

The beefy man behind the counter gives me the stink-eye; I don't blame him. I look like a strung-out junkie of the worst kind and then some. I dig crumpled bills from my pocket, showing I can pay. He grunts, jerking his thumb toward a booth way in the back.

I fork up cherry pie, red like blood. A waitress brings coffee. There are stains on her pink uniform. She cocks a hip and flashes a smile. Her whole stance is puppet-like, as though the Old Man wants me to see him make her dance.

"Get you anything else, sugar?"

I want to tell her to run. Instead, I put an involuntary hand on the table so she can see I'm not wearing a ring.

Fuck.

Wouldn't Daddy just love it if I made him a spare on my way home? Her fingers brush my arm. I watch her ass sway in her pink cotton-nylon blend uniform. She wields the coffeepot—a weapon against the dust-devil refugees washed up on her neon-lit shore.

Suddenly, I know there's a motel two miles down the road. I know her name is Sally; there's a run in her stockings that goes all the way up, and she isn't wearing anything underneath. Palms sweat on the table; I lick lips gone dry. That bare ring finger shines like a beacon, and my cock stirs despite my best intentions.

Here's the kicker: I'm a virgin. Pure as the fucking driven snow.

The son of the Fly-Lord doesn't get the luxury of love, or even consensual, mutually pleasurable relations. Humans are potential breeding grounds, nothing more.

I think about fucking Sally on the ash-stained counter. She has two kids and can barely make the rent. She's got more scars across her heart than she can count. I'll slit her throat, plant maggots in the gash, and birth flies.

The Old Man grins. "That'zzzzz it."

"No."

Teeth grit, last ditch—my hand jerks, spilling salt. I sketch a sign in the scattered grains. It glows yellow in the sick light. Sally's eyes widen and doesn't she just see the ruins of Carcosa replacing the diner's warmth?

The coffeepot shatters. I push past, scattering my crumpled bills as I hit the exit.

The night smells of a desert flower I can't name.

The moon is low gold, grinning. I'm in the car, though I don't remember opening the door. A whiff of gasoline. I'm already past the station, and the needle's thrumming on full.

The night booms over me like a tide; I smell the sea.

Maybe it's in my head, but I want to believe.

Static whispers on the radio. Sister sobs behind the electric hum. Flies buzz in her empty eyes.

"There's a place where he used to make us go...."

I stick my head out the window, drinking air. The car swerves, but I'm alone on the road. I swear I hear surf crashing. Maybe the mojo in my briefcase is good for something after all, folding distance, bringing the ocean to the desert.

What did fish-mouth say? Something about dead dreaming, and a city rising, all dripping angles, all right stars and everything else wrong.

Pedal to the metal. Tires devour asphalt, humming, almost enough to drown the static.

Sister's in the dark, where he made us go when we were bad.

And we were always bad.

Blood-tacky flies, crimson-drunk, hum in the close air. There's a dead man hanging from the ceiling, swollen cock ringed with barbed wire. There's a bloated horse, round as the fucking moon. There's Daddy, and he's sobbing. Sad. Mad. Bad. Look what we made him do.

I drive 'til I see moonlight on water.

I screech to a halt; the powder-blue Caddy's nearly burnt through. I grab the briefcase and run.

Sister always was the strong one. She never let Daddy break her. She broke herself first.

I'm almost to the edge between sand and sea when the Old Man shambles up from the dark. His shadow buzzes, blurs.

"Fooled you," he says.

I freeze. All this time I thought I was running, but I was going to, not from. Smoke and mirrors. Classic misdirection. It fools ninety percent of the people one hundred percent of the time when they want to believe. I wanted to believe.

The Old Man is stick-thin, cancer-ravaged. But his teeth are still-wicked straight, his eyes sin-dark and gleaming. Another step and I see the thing behind him.

Sister.

Her dress is stained. One hand holds a sharp bit of glass. Her lips don't smile, but her open throat does.

"A family reunion," the Old Man says. "How sweet."

A fit of coughing takes him. He spits phlegm on the sand, and it sizzles. The air smells like brimstone. It sounds like the shiver of wings.

"Whatcha got there, boy?" He points at the briefcase, wheezing.

Something in his eyes reminds me of the horse right before it was strung up from rusty chains. It reminds me of the drifter, smelling of sweat and cheap booze. He's afraid.

The Old Man stretches out his hand. No blade glints in it, but the gesture is unmistakably the same: Bend to my will, boy. Give me my due.

Fuck that.

I look at Sister.

"Forgive me?" I say.

I have no right to ask. Maybe it's my imagination, but I see the shadow of a smile.

Her words are just for me this time. "It's okay."

Faith'll jab you in the eye nine times outta ten, but sometimes when you grow up with a head full of horror show, you can't help believe.

I open the briefcase. Sister takes the Old Man's hand. Always the strong one, she holds him where sea meets sand.

The stone, wood, skin, whatever the fuck it is, burns. I cling for all I'm worth, which is shit all in the grand scheme of things if I have my way. I don't want to be the next coming of the Fly-Lord. Dying unremembered and unmourned sounds just dandy to me.

The Old Man howls with rage.

I raise the black idol high. The moon's jaundiced eye rolls my way. It shifts from sliver to full then back again, a knife-edged grin. The sky ripples, stars aligning. Something darker than dark, all dripping angles dreams its way up from the deep.

Displaced water hulks black against off-color stars. The sea, the sky—everything holds its breath. Pain flays me star-sharp, hurtles me into the dark. Cold compresses my lungs, cracks my ribs. Just before I shatter, the waiting sea falls, crashing down on Dear Old Dad, snapping his bones.

The waves retreat, oily-slick. There's nothing on the shore but me and salt-eaten footprints, fading with the tide.

A single, black spire—not skin, not wood, not stone—thrusts from the waves. Everything goes the color of a bruise. The sky melts, drips into the sea. The black needle lingers a moment, a middle finger raised, telling me how fucked I am if I dare disturb its sleep again.

Then it sinks. The cosmic eye shutters back to dreams.

I sit down hard. The tide kisses my feet. I laugh. Then I weep. I wipe tears from my eyes, and look toward the horizon where the faintest line of silver cracks the sky. Hollow, spent, I wait for the motherfucking dawn.

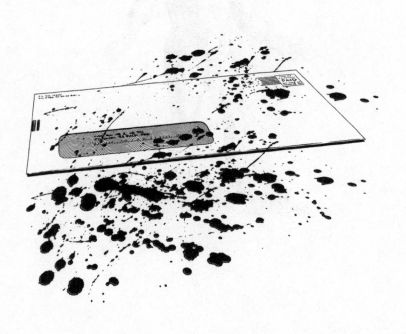

The Monster Makers

STEVE RASNIC TEM

This is all I can bear of love.

Robert is calling the children in, practically screaming it, how we all need to go, *now*. But I'm too busy gazing at the couple as they talk to the park ranger, the way their ears melt, noses droop, elongating into something else as their hair warps and shifts color, their spines bend and expand, arms and legs crooked impossibly, and their eye sockets migrating across their faces so rapidly they threaten to evict the eyeballs.

"Grandpa! Please!" little Evie cries out, but now I look at the park ranger, who has fallen to his knees, his face pale and limbs trembling, mouth struggling to form a word that does not yet exist. Because it isn't the way it is in the movies; human beings cannot accept such change so easily—at some point the mind must shut down and the body lose itself with no one left to tell it what to do. "Please, Grandpa, *now*," Evie wails, and the intensity of her distress finally gets to me, so that I hobble over to the battered old station wagon as fast as I can, which isn't very fast. Because Evie is that special grandchild, you see. Evie has my heart.

The car bucks once as Robert gives it gas too quickly. It rattles, then corrects itself. Alicia is safely in the backseat beside me, but I'm not sure if she ever left. She doesn't move as much as she used to. But it's amazing how young she looks—her long hair is still mostly blonde, even though she's about my age, whatever that might be. We agreed long ago not to keep track anymore. I've loved her as long as I've known her. The trouble is, these days I can't remember how long.

The grandkids are both on the other side of Alicia. They're small, so I can't see all of them, just four skinny legs which barely reach beyond the front edge of the seat, and the occasional equally skinny arm. They kick and wave, thrilled. Despite their fear—they have no understanding of what they've caused, or why—they're quite excited about what's happening to them. I suspect this is the way some addicts or athletes feel—something takes over you, as if it were a spirit or a god, seizing your blood and bones, your muscles—and it makes you run around or die. From this angle there's no discernible difference between Evie and Tom, but they are not twins, except in spirit. They sing softly as they often do, so softly I can't make out the words, but I've come to believe that their singing is the background music to all my thoughts.

As we leave the park I can hear the long howls behind me, the humanity disintegrating from those poor people's voices. My grandchildren laugh out loud, giddy from the experience. These changes always seem to happen around certain members of my family, although none of us have precisely understood the relationship or the mechanism. Why did the couple change but not the ranger? I have no idea. Perhaps it is some tendency in the mind, some proclivity of the imagination, or some random, genetic bullet. My grandchildren possess a prodigious talent, but it's not a talent anyone would want to see in action.

Up in the front passenger seat Jackie pats Robert's shoulder. I don't know if this is meant as encouragement, or if he even needs it. My son has always been sane to a fault. His wife's face looks worried, the skin so tight across her cheeks and chin it's as if she wears a latex mask. But then Jackie always was the nervous sort. She's not of this family; she simply married into it.

"Dad, I thought I asked you not to tell them any more stories." Robert's voice is barely under control.

They're both angry with me, furious. They blame me for all of this. But they try not to show it. I don't think it's because they're careful with my feelings. I think it's because they're somewhat frightened of me. "Telling stories, that's what grandfathers do," I say. "It's how I can communicate with them.

The stories of our lives and deaths are secrets even from ourselves. All we are able to share are these substandard approximations. But we still have to try, unless we want to arm ourselves with loneliness. I just tell the children *fairy tales*, Robert. That's all. Stories about monsters. Something they already know about. Monster stories won't turn you into a monster, Son. Fairy tales simply tell you something you already knew in a somewhat clever way."

Once upon a time perhaps gods and monsters walked the earth and a human might choose to be either one. But not anymore. Now people grow and age and die and then are forgotten about. It's the "great circle," or whatever you want to call it. It's sobering information but it can't be helped. I don't tell Robert this—he isn't ready to hear it. He loves his poor, pathetic flesh too much.

"Why couldn't you stop? What will it take to make you stop!" Robert is howling from behind the steering wheel. For just a moment I think he's about to change, expand, become some sort of wolf thing, but he is simply upset with me. Robert is our only child, and I love him very much, but he has always been vulnerable, frightened by the most mundane of dangers, as if he were unhappy to have been born a mortal human (I'm afraid the only kind there is).

Robert always refused to listen to my bedtime stories, so he's really in no place to evaluate whether they are dangerous or not. The members of our family have been shunned for ages, thought to be witches, demons, and worse. No one wants to hear what we have to say. "Your children simply understand the precariousness of it all. And this is how they express it."

"No more, Dad, okay? No more today."

Whatever my son decides to do, he's likely to keep us all locked up at home from now on. The only reason we went out today was because he knows the children need to get out now and then, and he didn't think we'd run into anybody in that big state park. Besides, it doesn't happen every time, not even every other time. There's no way to predict such things. I've witnessed these transformations again and again, but even I do not understand the agency involved.

I can't blame him, I guess. Sometimes human life makes no sense. We really shouldn't exist at all.

Back at the old farmhouse I'm suddenly so exhausted I can barely get out of the car. It's as if I've had a huge meal and now all I can manage is sleep. The adrenalin of the previous few hours has come with a cost. I suspect my food must eat me rather than the other way around.

Alicia is even worse than before, and Robert and Jackie each have to pull on an arm to get her to stand. The grandkids push on her butt, giggling, and aren't really helping.

Once inside they take us up to our room. "I get so exhausted," I tell them.

"I know," Jackie replies. "You should just make it stop. We'd all be happier if you just made it stop."

She's like all the others. She doesn't understand. It happens, but I've never been sure we can make it happen. Perhaps we simply show what has always been. Her children are learning about death. It's a lesson not everyone wants to learn.

She must think that because I'm an older man I'm likely to do foolish things. But we have such a limited time on this planet, I want to tell her, why should we avoid the foolish? I feel like that deliverer of bad news whom everyone blames.

Robert is less courteous as he guides us up the stairs, his movements abrupt and careless. He's obviously lost all patience with this—this caring for elderly parents, this endless drama whenever the family goes out. He'll make us all stay home now, planted in front of the television, transfixed by god-knows-what mindless comedy, locked away so that we can't cause any more trouble. But the children have to go out now and then. An active child trapped inside is like a bomb waiting to go off.

Periodically he loses his balance and crashes me into a railing, a wall, the doorframe. Each time he apologizes but I suspect it is intentional. I don't mind especially—each small jolt of pain wakes me up a bit more. You have to stay awake, I think, in order to know which world you're in.

By the time they lay both of us down in the bed I'm practically blind with fatigue. Almost everything is a dirty yellow smear. It's like a glimpse of an old photograph whose colors have receded into a waxy sheen. Perhaps this is the start of sleep, or the beginning of something else.

Several times during the middle of the night Alicia crawls beneath the bed. Is this what a nightmare is like? Sometimes I crawl under the bed with her. The floor is gritty, dirty, and uncomfortable to lie on. It's like a taste of the grave. It's what I have to look forward to.

I pat Alicia's arm when she cries. "At least you still have your yellow hair," I tell her. She looks at me so fiercely I back away, far far back under the bed into the shadows where I can hear the winds howl and the insects' mad mutter. I can stay there only a brief while before it sickens me but it still seems safer than lying close to her.

I wake up the next morning with my hand completely numb, sleeping quietly beside my face. I scrape the unfeeling flesh against the rough floorboards until it appears to come back to life. Alicia isn't here; she's wandered off. Although much of the time she is practically immobile, she has these occasional adrenalin-driven spurts in which she moves until she falls down or someone catches her. She is so arthritic these bouts of intense activity must be agony for her. I can hear the grandchildren laughing outside and there is this note in their tone that drives me to the window to see.

The two darlings have the mail carrier cornered by the garage. We never get mail here and I think how sad it is that this poor man will doubtless lose his life over an erroneous delivery. They chatter away with their monkey-like talk at such a high pitch and speed I cannot follow what they say, but the occasional discrete image floats to the top—screaming heads and bodies in flame. None of these images appears in any of the stories I have told them, although of course Robert will never believe this. What he does not fully appreciate is that out in the real world all heads have the potential for screaming, and all bodies are in fact burning all the time.

On the edge of the yard I spy Alicia. She has taken off all her clothes again and now scratches about on all fours like some different kind of animal. The Roberts of the world do not wish to admit that humans are animals. We may fancy ourselves better than the beasts because of our language skills, because we possess words in abundance. But all that does is empower us with excuses and equivocations.

The mail carrier has begun to change. He struggles valiantly but to no avail. Already his jaw has lengthened until it disconnects from the rest of his face, wagging back and forth with no muscle to support it. Already his hair drifts away and his fleshier bits have begun to dissolve. These are changes typical, I think, of a body left in the ground for months.

At first Evie laughs as if watching a clown running through his repertoire of shenanigans but now she has begun to cry. Such is the madness of children, but I must do what I can to minimize the damage. I make my way stiffly downstairs with a desperate grip on the banister, my joints like so much broken glass inside my flesh, and as I head for the door I see Robert come up out of the cellar, the axe in his hands. "This has to stop...this has to stop," he screams at me. And I very much agree. And if he were coming for *me* with that axe all would be fine—I somehow always understood things might come to this juncture—but he sweeps past me and heads for the front door and my grandchildren outside.

I take a few quick steps, practically falling, and shove him away from the door. I see his hands fumble the axe, but I do not realize the danger until he hits the wall and screams, tumbles backwards, the blade buried in his chest. "Robert!"

It's all I have time to say before Jackie comes out of the kitchen screeching. But it's all I know to say, really, and what good would it do to lose myself now? He would have hated to die from clumsiness, and that's what I take away from this house when I leave.

Out on the lawn the children are jumping up and down laughing and crying. There is a moment in which time slows down, and I'm heartsick to see their tiny perfect features shift, coarsen, the flesh losing its elasticity and acquiring a dry, plastic filler look, as if they might become puppets, inanimate figures controlled by distant and rapidly vanishing souls. I see my little Evie's eyes dull into dark marbles, her slackened face and collapsing mouth spilling the dregs of her laughter. I think of Robert dead in the farmhouse—and what a mad and reprehensible thing it is to survive one's child.

But of course I can't tell these children their father has died. Maybe later, but not now, when they are like this. If I told them now they might savage the little that remains of our pitiful world. In fact I can't tell them anything I feel or know or see.

"Help me find your grandmother!" I shout. "She's gotten away from us, but I'm sure one of you clever children will find her!" And I am relieved when they follow me out of the yard and into the edge of the woods.

I have even more difficulty as I maneuver through the snarled tangle of undergrowth and fallen branches than I thought I would. I'm out of practice, and with every too-wide step to avoid an obstacle, I'm sure I'm going to fall. But the children don't seem to mind our lack of progress; in fact they already appear to have forgotten why we're out here. They range back and forth, their paths cross as they pretend to be bees or birds or low-flying aircraft. Periodically they deliberately crash into each other, fall back against trees and bushes in dozens of feigned deaths. Sometimes they just break off to babble at each other, point at me, and giggle, sharing secrets in their high-pitched alien language.

Now and then I snatch glimpses of Alicia moving through the trees ahead of us. Her blonde hair, her long legs, and once or twice just a bit of her face, and what might be a smile or a grimace; I can't really tell from this distance. Seeing her in fragments like this I can almost imagine her as the young athletic woman I met fifty years ago, so quick-witted, who enthralled me and frightened me and ran rings around me in more ways than one. But I know better. I know that that young woman exists more in my mind, now, than in hers. That other Alicia is now like some shattered carcass by the roadside, and what lives, what dances and races and gibbers mindlessly among trees is a broken spirit that once inhabited that same beautiful body. Sometimes the death of who we've loved is but the final act in a grief that has lingered for years.

I think that if Alicia were to embrace me now she'd have half my face between her teeth before I had time even to speak her name.

As mad as she, the children now shriek on either side of me, slap me on the side of the face, the belly, before they howl and run away. I wonder if they even remember who she is or was to them. How only a few years ago she made them things and cuddled them and sang them soft songs. But we were never meant to remember everything, I think, and that is a blessing. It seems they have already forgotten about their parents, except as a story they used to know. The young are always more interested in science fiction, those fantasies of days to come, especially if they can be the heroes.

I watch them, or I avoid them, for much of the afternoon. Like a babysitter who really doesn't want the job. At one point they begin to fight over a huge burl on a tree about three feet off the ground. It is only the second such tree deformity I've ever seen, and by far the larger of the two. I understand that they come about when the younger tree is damaged and the tree continues to grow around the damage to create these remarkable patterns in the grain.

Their argument is a strange one, although not that different from other arguments they've had. Evie says it'll make a perfect "princess throne" for her after they cut it down. The fact that they have no means to cut it down does not factor into the argument. Tom claims he "saw it first," and although he has no idea what to do with it, the right to decide should be his.

Eventually they come to blows, both of them crying as they continue to pummel each other about the head and face. When they begin to bleed I decide I have to do something. I have handled this badly, although I can't imagine that anyone else would know better how to handle such a crisis. I stare at them—their flesh is running. Their flesh runs! Their grandmother is gone, and they don't even know that their father is dead. And they dream wide awake and the flesh flows around them.

What do I tell them? Do I reassure them with tales of heaven—that their father is now safe in heaven? Do I tell them that no matter what happens to their poor fragile flesh there is a safe place for them in heaven?

What I want to tell them is that their final destination is not heaven, but memory. And you can make of yourself a memory so profound that it transforms everything it touches.

My Evie screams, her face a mask of blood, and Tom looks even worse—all I can see through the red confusion of his face is a single fixed eye. I try to run, then, to separate them, but I am so awkward and pathetic I fall into the brush and tangle below them, where I sprawl and cry out in sorrow and agony.

Only then do they stop, and they come to me, my grandchildren, to stare down at me silently, their faces solemn. Tom has wiped much of the blood from his face to reveal the scratches there, the long lines and rough shapes like a child's awkward sketch.

This is my legacy, I think. These are the ones who will keep me alive, if only as a memory poorly understood, or perhaps as a ghost too troublesome to fully comprehend.

We try and we try but we cannot sculpt a shape out of what we've done in the world. Our hands cannot touch enough. Our words do not travel far enough. For all our constant waving we still cannot be picked out of a crowd.

My grandchildren approach for the end of my story. I can feel the terrible swiftness of my journey through their short lives. I become a voice clicking because it has run out of sound. I become a tongue silently flapping as it runs out of words. I become motionless as I can think of nowhere else to go.

I become the stone and the plank and the empty field. I am really quite something, the monster made in their image, until I am scattered, and forgotten.

Piano Man

CHRISTOPHER FOWLER

I knew I was right to hate jazz, but New Orleans gave me a reason to fear it. For years I figured it was black-sweater-and-goatee music that appealed to aged hipsters, but in the Big Easy that image is only part of the story. There are plenty of jazz-funksters and rapmasters around that town now, but you can still find bars where the music hasn't changed in eighty years. The real trouble is that old jazz can be twisted into easy listening and piped into elevators like soap bubbles that burble through the overheated air at a volume just loud enough to cloud your thoughts. A reworking of Weather Report's "Birdland" was playing in the lobby of the Marriott hotel when I arrived, and a horrible, plinky electro-version of Miles Davis's "So What" issued from the speakers as I handed my key in to the concierge.

Every city trades on its image, but in parts of New Orleans it works because they've still got the old range of religions. The *Vieux Carré* was romantic in a rundown way, although it was smaller than London's Soho and really just a few old streets of shops and bars geared around fleecing tourists, housed behind wrought-iron balustrades. And though it traded on its old movie image, the French Quarter was still kind of cool. But after I'd done it there was the rest of the place to deal with, about the most scarred-up ugly-ass concrete city I've ever seen in my life, and post-Katrina you can still see tidemarks on some buildings, warnings of what could happen again if the levees break in some other place.

It hadn't stopped raining from the moment I stepped off the plane, and the forecast predicted worse to come. Everyone was talking about how it reminded them of August 2005, just before Katrina found its full force, which was no comfort at all. But the people were friendly enough, and I was only planning to be there for a couple of days until I could hook up with Ren, the photographer who was coming down from Memphis to take me on the last leg of the trip, if he ever bothered to sober up and return my phone calls.

For a couple of days I checked out locations for good copy and moody shots, and although I quickly got tired of traipsing around with a yellow slicker dripping ice-water onto my knees, the dry hotel air made me feel sick. So, forcing myself back into the rain once more, I headed from Canal Street in the direction of Bourbon.

I was meant to be revealing "secret New Orleans" from an insider's perspective, but I wasn't an insider. I wasn't even from the same side of the country. I was working for a low-end travel supplement based out of Fresno and had, I suspect, been chosen for the assignment by my boss because I was willing to work below standard rates and leave at short notice. But I needed the cash right then, and freelance writing assignments had been pretty thin on the ground lately. I figured I could scrape by with some guff about jazz clubs and voodoo rituals, the ones that still get staged for tourists, and catch myself some good times in the process.

First I needed a funky dark-wood sawdust-floor bar with a peanut barrel, a pianist and candles in colored pots, a place where life had been restored to how it had been before the hurricane, but the coolest joints wanted to charge me a fortune for the privilege of a story, and my editor felt the bar should be paying the magazine for the free publicity. Except nobody had ever heard of the *Fresno Freedom Travel Guide* here and was like *who the fuck are you?*

But then I turned off Bourbon into one of the narrow cross-streets where the shops beneath the verandahs were smaller and darker, and found myself outside an open-fronted bar called Stormy's, where one hell of an argument was hammering. As I peered through the folding front doors into the beer-musty dimness of the bar, I saw a tall, bony old dude in a blue Zephyrs cap and collarless shirt shouting at someone who could only be an official, because he wore the kind of suit no man would ever purposely choose for himself.

"So what did you *evah* do for me, huh?" the dude shouted. "All this talk, all these promises. The last time we had a flood around here, when we was bailing out the basement trying to save th' only supplies we could lay our hands on, where the *hay-ull* were you? We couldn't even raise your damn office on the phone. Now you come in here and give me shit about breaking regulations, well you can kiss my skinny black ass before I take it down, and that's the end of it. Now you turn yourself around and get out of my bar."

"Mr. Beauregard, I have every respect for you—my father used to greatly admire your piano playing—but the fact remains that you cannot simply remake the rules on this. Now I can give you seven days to remove that thing before my boys will be forced to come in and take down."

"You ain't stepping one foot into my bar, Marchais. Your father and his pals was nothing but trouble, and all you doing is tryin' to follow in their footsteps. You come in here again, or you send any of your little butt-boys in here to do your dirty work, I'll set my dog on all of you. Now start marching."

The owner was no spring chicken but feisty as hell, I had to give him that. I got talking to LaVinna, the waitress, who told me he really was called Stormy, and he always lived up to his name. "I'll introduce you," she said, "but if he starts cursing and getting all heated up you'll have to go, because one day that vein on the side of his head is going to pop."

Stormy was riled because he'd rebuilt the bar after Katrina with his own hands, and now the official was telling him he didn't get proper permission for the work.

"What I did," he told me later, "was build a new platform out back for the piano, but to put it there I had to build a roof over it where the yard had been. Hell, it weren't even no yard, just waste ground some crazy woman across the way uses for her damn' chickens, and it ain't even legal to keep chickens around here no more, 'specially when you're killing 'em in some damn religious ritual. In the forty years we've been here we never needed no building regulations."

He took me to the rear of the bar to show me his handiwork. I guess he was pretty proud of what he'd achieved, even though it was technically illegal. The centerpiece of the new room was a piano in an upright teak case chased with silver designs, acanthus leaves, and lilies. A pair of ornate silver candlesticks stuck out above the keyboard, which was reversed from the usual layout, white notes raised out of black. It was a thing to behold, and Stormy had done the instrument justice by housing it on an octagonal stage in his covered yard.

"The piano used to belong to Warena Samedi, told me she built it herself," he said proudly. "What I want to know is, how'd Don Marchais get to find out about me rebuilding the bar?"

I'd read in a local magazine that Warena Samedi had been some kind of hot-shot voodoo priestess back in the sixties, which I guessed meant she sold potions and rag dolls to the easily fooled. The fact that she wore red leather miniskirts and looked more like a centerfold than a witch didn't hurt business, either. I didn't have too much time for people trying to perpetuate primitive black mythology, just because it suited them to believe there was something more exotic about people of a different skin color. But if she'd really built the piano and could play it like a dream, she at least had the soul of an artist.

"Maybe one of your customers saw it when he came in here, and bears a grudge against you," I suggested. "Know anyone like that?"

Well, of course he did. Everyone who owns a bar has a few enemies. Stormy thought hard for a minute and made a connection with Marchais. I got all this from LaVinna, who told me that Marchais had appointed a guy called Sam Threefinger—they called him that because he got stupid-drunk one time over in some Creole bar in Metairie and shot up his own left hand—to take down any property extensions he couldn't pull extra cash out of. Point is that Threefinger had been running a rival bar to Stormy's across the street, and they'd had a big old falling out. Threefinger knew about the piano because he was a believer, and had bought up most of the items Warena Samedi once owned. Someone had written a book about her scandalous life, and as a consequence, her stuff fetched top money from collectors. Now he and Marchais were working Bourbon as a team, shaking down owners and helping themselves to whatever they liked.

I did *not* want to mess with this. It wasn't my turf, and it wasn't what my editor wanted. But maybe some part of me, the part that had once wanted to be a real journalist and not a features hack, sparked back into life when a story fell at my feet. I told myself I'd see if it went anywhere, write it up, and then check around to find a buyer. I asked LaVinna what she thought Stormy was going to do about it, but I must have been staring too hard at her wide, deep, smooth cleavage because she told me she was ending her shift at six and maybe we should discuss it over dinner. Except that she came back to my room and we never did get that dinner.

Next morning the weather had worsened and it was hard not to think of Katrina as I fought my way up Canal Street. The NHC had pegged the little bugger swirling past the Florida coastline as a storm, not a hurricane, and weren't even going to the trouble of naming it, but they'd been wrong before. I wanted to grab a meeting with Sam Threefinger, and picked up his address on the Internet because he was using his nickname as a URL, like he was proud of it. He was running an antiques business on the side, and it didn't take a genius to work out where he was getting his stock from. I figured if he was that much of a lush I could snag an interview with him in exchange for a couple of bottles.

But he wasn't at his house. My timing was off; he was already on his way to see Stormy and make him take down his new patio. Most likely, I thought, he had designs on that piano, although he must have been pretty dumb not to think folks would put two and two together when they saw it in his store. So I retraced my steps to the bar, but the rain was sheeting off the rooftops like needles, and I'd only managed three blocks before my eyes were burning. I waited in a café as the tail of the storm hit hard and the girls on the next table started to share their memories of Katrina, how one had been forced to hide from looters, how another had her baby airlifted out without a name tag, and how she'd gone crazy trying to find it. It was all background for me; I took notes and kept quiet.

The streets didn't look like they could get any wetter so I finished my coffee and pressed on. But I'd lost valuable time. When I arrived at Stormy's, I was late again. This time the cops were already there, tying yellow plastic ribbons around the back of the bar. LaVinna came over as soon as she saw me. "I told you that temper of his would do the job," she said, shaking her head.

"What happened?"

"Sam came in here and told Stormy that he and Marchais were getting a court order to close down the bar, and that he was impounding the piano."

"I knew it," I said, "he's after that damn relic."

"Not any more he ain't. Stormy took the shotgun down from behind the bar and pulled it on him. Short version is, they got in close and the damn thing went off."

"Jesus, is he hurt?"

"He has a hole through his brain the size of a nickel so yes, I guess it pinches a little."

"You don't sound too upset."

"Listen, I liked him, I worked for him, but he was an old lech and he never raised my wages in four years. I have a little boy stuck at my grandma's house going crazy with boredom. I was about to find myself a better job. But this ain't gonna look good on my résumé." She nodded back at the mess behind her. "After the bullet left Stormy's head it went through the keyboard of the piano, then he fell back on top of it and the damn thing collapsed. The police got a blown-up body and an exploded piano back there to sort out. Now I got to stick around for witness statements instead of making tips."

I looked over her shoulder to the mess on the patio. I could see Stormy's legs sticking out from a pile of wood sticks and shattered veneer panels.

I'll be honest here, I didn't know LaVinna had a kid and it put me off seeing her again. But I wanted to flesh out the story, and she seemed the best way through it. I knew I could probably get to Sam Threefinger too, because he had the law on his side and had been attacked, and innocent parties like that were always happy to kick off about how badly they'd been treated. There's something about knowing you're in the wrong that makes you want to tell everyone you were right.

I missed something LaVinna said. "That is, if you're going to stick around for a few more days," she was saying, like she had plans for us.

"I don't know," I told her. "I got to wait until Ren gets here and do the shots, but after that I'm gone."

"Right." She gave me a cool, steady look. "But you may end up getting caught out by the storm. It ain't blown out yet." She made sure I knew what she meant.

I called Sam Threefinger but he wasn't picking up, so I left a message for him to call my cell phone. Next, I rang a few local contacts and dragged promises out of them to at least read anything I wrote on the subject; seems there was plenty of interest in any story that included mention of Warena Samedi, so I decided to do a little more research. I started online, but kept hitting the same three or four sources, so it was necessary to put in some face time with people who knew her.

Now, I don't mean to be rude, but a lot of women find God when their men leave them, know what I mean? And Ms. Samedi's friends had found religion big time. Not just Christianity, though. I met up with Tamasha Woodfall, an old follower who lived in an apartment full of plants by the river, where she sat on an overstuffed stripey sofa watching the boats, her corkscrew copper hair piled on and around her head, her beads and bangles and bracelets clattering every time she moved her arms. Her plumpness protected her from being dated to any era, but I figured the stuff in her apartment went back at least sixty years. I liked her a lot, but she was crazy as a loon.

"Warena didn't just have knowledge of the old religion, she was a living part of the process," she told me. "Come over here and sit by me, boy."

Frankly I didn't know what she meant at all, and admitted it. And I wasn't going to sit beside her either, because I could tell the old broad had wandering hands. "Are you talking about love potions, curses, stuff like that?" I had to ask.

"Oh, that's just front-of-house sales," she said, waving the idea aside. "And nobody needs love potions, they just need to get in touch with themselves and their sex-u-al-ity, you know?" She smoothed her fingers down the side of her breast, and I could see she'd be big trouble after dark and a few whiskies. It's the old ones you have to watch out for.

"So what did Warena do that other people couldn't?"

"All kinds of things. But her biggest talent? She could restore a form of life."

"You mean she could bring someone back from the dead?"

"I wouldn't use those words exactly, 'cause it's not like that. I mean, the corporeal remains stay behind and go down to the grave, bless the Lord. It was more—a conjuration."

I wasn't sure there was such a word, but gave her the benefit of the doubt. "You ever see this happen?"

"Oh sure, plenty of times."

"How did it work?"

"The usual way. There was a service, songs and prayers, a series of incantations, rituals to observe, certain powdered herbs and minerals scattered in a proscribed sequence—sometimes she used the blood of a chicken, but I think some of that was for show, you know, so the clients felt they was getting value for their money."

"And what did they get? I mean, at the end?"

"A restoration of the spirit, like I said, entirely separate from the body, but a kind of—" she watched the wide grey river for a minute, carefully formulating her words, "—essence of the departed. It wouldn't stay long, a day or two at the most, but it was most definitely visible. When my Sammy died she brought him back to me, just for a few hours."

"Sammy was your husband?"

"No, my dog, praise Jesus."

"But what was the point?" I wondered if I was missing something obvious. "Why bring someone's spirit back at all?"

"Bless you, to bring peace to those left behind, of course. How many times have you wanted someone back, just for a few moments, for one last look of tenderness?"

I realized that she was staring intently at me. "But you've never lost anyone, have you?" She made it sound almost sad.

"No," I admitted. "No one really close. I don't know much about death."

"Then you don't know about love, neither. You should testify to Christ the Lord and find the love."

The conversation closed quickly after that, but I promised to look in on her again if I heard anything more. The other woman I went to see was Missy Allbright, who was nothing like her name, and lived on the first floor of a rundown apartment out in Metairie. The stairs were dark, the room was dark, and she was dressed in black. The floor was covered in cats, some of them stuffed, and I couldn't tell which ones were alive as I stumbled through them to her guest chair.

"I'd give you some tea but I don't really want you to stay that long," she announced, seating herself opposite.

"Well, at least you're honest."

"I have to tell you no good will come of mentioning that woman," she told me straight off. "Warena Samedi—her real name was Miriam Fellowes but that didn't sound so enticing to the press—underneath that pretty hide she was a vengeful, messed-up, mean old bitch."

I remarked that she didn't look so old in the pictures I had seen.

"That's 'cause she never again let herself be photographed after she was thirty. She played with fire all her life and got old real fast. You don't race an engine without wearing down the parts."

I asked Missy if she'd read the book about Warena. "I did, and I can tell you there wasn't one word of truth in it."

"But did she really have a gift?" I asked.

"I can't deny her that, but the way she used it—well, that wasn't how we were taught."

"You have it too?"

She caught the rise in my voice. "Why is it everyone thinks she was the only one with special abilities?"

"She had good PR and prominent tits," I ventured.

That got a laugh from Missy. "Maybe you and I'll have some ginger tea."

We talked until it got even darker. I thought the storm was going to suck the windows clean out of the room. "There was only one man she ever really loved," Missy told me. "You should have heard the sweet music they made in that bar of a night. Stormy worshipped her, but he couldn't give her what she needed."

"What did she need?"

"More. More of everything. The problem was that by this time she couldn't turn it off."

"Turn what off?"

"The sex energy, the power, the darkness that channeled right through her and kept on going until she became its slave. It destroyed everything around her and it finally killed her. After she was gone old Stormy lost around a hundred pounds, like something was eating him from the inside out."

"How did Warena die?"

"She and Stormy were fighting all the time. She'd go out and stay missing for three, four days at a stretch, and he'd always take her back. Then she finally left him for good, and nobody saw her around here again. All I know about her death is what I read in the papers, but it was ugly. No one really found out the truth. The cops got a call late one night to a filthy house with a bunch of dead men in it, and the story goes she was sleeping with all of them. Of course, there was something weird right at the end. The city coroner got himself fired for incompetence, because he swore the men died after she did, even though they'd been killed with her knife and her prints were all over the handle."

"That's an incredible story," I replied. "Did the state ever follow it up and find out what really happened?"

"They had their hands full, son. Katrina hit the shore five days later."

I thought about Missy's story all the way back to the hotel, and how it fitted with Stormy's death. It seemed I was missing something, and that something was probably connected with Sam Threefinger, so that night I sat down at my laptop and did a little digging. Sam's real name was Laurent DuChamp. He'd been in a soft-touch annex of the Louisiana State Penitentiary a couple of times for fencing stolen goods, and it seemed he hadn't learned his lesson. He'd set up his antiques shop in 2002, after his last stretch. I wondered if he had approached Stormy about buying the piano before, so I called LaVinna, who told me it had been in storage for years. And that meant the first time Sam saw it after Warena's death was when it appeared on the new stage.

The thing that struck me most was how Stormy had managed to cheat his old rival by destroying Warena's most coveted possession at the moment of his demise. It was a kind of justice, but I wondered if there was more to it than that. I admit I wanted an ending; I had the material for a good article, but needed to give it a more satisfying punchline.

The next morning it seemed the storm had blown itself out, but Ren called me to say his plane had been grounded because Louis Armstrong Airport was in the eye of the storm, and the worst was yet to come, so rather than sitting around cooling my heels waiting for Sam Threefinger to call me, I decided to take a cab over to his store.

The sign on the door said CLOSED and the place was locked up tight. I cupped my hands and peered through the rain-streaked window. The interior was so murky it could have been filled with pond water. It was mainly cluttered with 1960s furniture and musical instruments, but looked as if no one had been there for days. I talked the cabdriver into taking me out to Sam's house. He didn't want to go there, complained it was beyond his working area, the weather was too bad and he wouldn't wait around for me to come back, but by this time I was getting desperate. Ren was delayed, I'd already spent my fee for the piece just holing up at the hotel, and there was no other work on the horizon. I needed to sell the story, period.

The rain was thundering loud enough to drown out the cab's radio. We came off the I-10 at Lovola, left the main strip and turned into a chain of tree-filled avenues. The house had an antebellum grandeur that seemed out of place. It reminded me of pictures I'd seen of the old Rosedown Plantation outside St. Francisville, with Greek Revival–style wings and a long verandah, only scaled down to fit a modern neighborhood—because this house was freshly painted and no more than ten years old. I rang, then knocked on the screen doors, but there was no answer. By that time the damned cabdriver had slammed into reverse and beaten a retreat from the property.

I could do nothing but circle the house and see if Threefinger was out back somewhere. Although the lawns were neatly trimmed, water was pooling fast on the grass and I was quickly covered in mud. The rear screen door was bashed in, the nets torn, the door hanging off its hinges. I tried to see inside but it was too dark to make anything out. I should have called the cops right then, but just didn't think of it. There was no one around, and I couldn't see across the street, so I went in.

The house lights weren't working but I had a lighter in my pocket. It looked like there had been a fight of some kind in the downstairs rooms; a chair lay on its side, and what I thought at first was torn-up paper proved to be broken white crockery. The rugs were squashy with blown-in rainfall. Not wanting to risk getting shot as an intruder, I called out Sam's name a couple of times, but there was no answer. I was about to leave when I heard the ceiling floorboards creak.

I figured maybe Threefinger had been attacked by someone from Stormy's who blamed him for the old man's death and wanted to make a point about it. You get that feeling about New Orleans; there are plenty of nice people, and plenty of crazies looking to get back at the world. Wherever you get old-school religion, it follows you find old-school vengeance. I wasn't thrilled about the idea of looking upstairs with no lights and no weapon, but I had no other choice. Besides, I had no personal beef with Threefinger, and for all I knew the guy could have had a heart attack. I fantasized a heroic race to the hospital, where the recovering old man would pour out his heart to give me a nice dramatic wraparound to the story.

I could smell something acrid, like burning paper that had been put out. As I climbed the stairs, the rain pounding on the roof grew louder. It was hard to see, but I could make out a long brown corridor leading to several big rooms, most with their doors open. I figured the one at the front was the master bedroom. I could see something moving beneath its windows, wrapped in a gray blanket. As I came closer, the pile shook a little and shifted backwards.

"Stay away," it suddenly warned, "don't get any nearer." The room stank of whisky. A red, puffy face emerged from the blanket cocoon and stared blearily back. Sam looked like shit. "Who the hell are you?" he asked, pushing to his feet.

I explained I'd been leaving messages for him, and wanted to talk about what happened at Stormy's. I figured he could at least give me some background to their feud, and I'd be able to give the article some shape. I had the end, I just needed the beginning, or so I thought until Sam said, "He's back," and I knew he meant Stormy, that somehow his guilt over the old man's death had manifested itself in the kind of magic the old women professed to believe in. I didn't buy the voodoo end of the deal, but it gave me a great angle.

"He's dead," I said, "I saw them take Stormy off to the morgue. What happened here?"

"Nothing." Sam had suddenly sensed he was talking to a stranger and shut his mouth. "This is private property. You should go now."

"You've had some storm damage downstairs. Back door's blown in."

"That weren't no storm, fool, it was him."

"Stormy."

"Who else?"

"Tamasha Woodfall told me that Warena could bring people's souls back from the dead, but only for a short time. If Sam's spirit returned and you think you saw him, he's gone now. It's over." Disabusing people of their notions is no way to win friendship, so I was trying to go along with him.

He gave no reply. Shuffling over to the liquor cabinet, he filled a tumbler, keeping the blanket hitched around his shoulders. "See, that's the problem, right there," he said. "Outsiders never see the full picture. You think he'd just turn up and go away again? Revenants come back for a reason, and they stay until they've done the job. Most appear so they can give the living some comfort. You get a hug like a warm breeze, they dry away a tear, then they're gone. Sam's back to do some damage."

"Why would he want to do that?"

"Don't fuck around with me, sonny. You been speaking to people, you know damn well why he's come back."

"Well, there's no one here now."

"You can't be sure, with this rain keeping up."

I didn't understand what the rain had to do with it. "Look, I'll go and I'll close the back door on my way out."

"No." Suddenly I knew he was terrified of being left alone. "LaVinna told me who you are. You want an interview, I'll be happy to give it to you, but downstairs where I can keep an eye on the place."

We moved to the front parlor, but couldn't get the power up. It really looked like there had been a fight in the room. Sam was twitchy as hell, shifting back and forth, checking both sides of the house. "He wants to give me the piano," he said, and now I knew I was dealing with a crazy man.

"The piano's gone," I reminded him.

"No, you don't understand." He held up his hand and cocked his ear. "Listen, damn it. You hear that?"

And there, behind the drumming rain, I swear I heard something like a piano being played. No, not played, *jangled*, like a cat was trapped inside it and was rolling around on the wires. "What is that?" I asked.

"So you do hear it."

But now the rain renewed its strength and the sound was lost once more. We both stood in the middle of the room listening like a pair of crazies. I knew I was being a fool, half expecting a snaggletoothed corpse to coming walking through the porch door with its arms outstretched like a character from an old EC comic, but the dark house, the storm, the crazy old man all got to me.

Then I heard it again, closer this time, a sound like a harpsichord being dropped on its side, discordant high notes and bass echoes that underscored the movement of something shifting hesitantly outside the walls. With each step there was a glissando, as if someone was dragging a piano, bumping and crashing it.

"You *do* hear that." Sam was triumphant but terrified.

"Give me your car keys, I'll get you out of here," I told him.

"They're upstairs on my dresser." He couldn't take his eyes from the front door, which was strobing with the shadows of the storm-beaten trees.

"I'll go get them."

"No, don't leave me alone!"

"Then you get them." He was spooking me now. This, I knew, was how voodoo worked, spreading its fear like a contagion, turning skeptics into believers. I followed his eyes as he turned his gaze toward each of the windows, listening. He was tracking its path around the house. The blinds were all down, but I could see a shadow passing from one bay to the next. I ran for the stairs. I found a set of Oldsmobile keys and grabbed them, then headed back, but halted on the landing. The terrible jangling was inside now. I looked down and saw that the doors I had propped shut had been kicked apart. Something had dragged itself inside. I tried to find Sam, but figured he had retreated into a corner behind the stairs.

As I came down, I looked between the banisters. I had only met Stormy alive once, and I suppose the thing below represented him. It was tall and bony, and still wore a baseball cap, but it walked as if moving on broken stilts. The piano's wires were threaded through its wasted body, and where its stomach should have been keys and cables were strung with bits of dried-out gut. Wires stuck out everywhere, through staring red eyes, elbows, leg bones and vertebrae. The fingers looked like piano keys, but it was hard to tell where meat and wood met. Warena's revival power lived on, but Stormy's spirit had been mashed with the piano in such a way that both had come back as one tortured creature. It stumped and staggered toward Sam, who was scrabbling away in a corner of the parlor, whimpering and pleading.

The strung-up keyboard fingers tore at his face and throat, wires slashing and stinging across his flesh, ripped at his soft stomach until I couldn't tell where Sam ended and the piano-man began. The whole thing was a bloody mess of flesh and wood and steel, and although it tried to pull away at the end of the attack, I could already see it unraveling and falling apart. The keys bounced to the floor, the wires lost their tautness, and the spirit of Stormy Beauregard evaporated, leaving behind a few sticks of varnished wood and the splintered remains of a man who looked like he'd been pistol-whipped with piano wire and eviscerated. And as the last of Stormy faded, I swear I heard a few chords play out in perfect harmony, before they were swamped by the drumming of the rain.

I took stock of my situation. My fingerprints were all over the house, and just in case the cops were too dumb to find me that way, I threw up all over the floor, leaving them plenty of DNA. I knew the bitches had set me up, pushing me toward Sam Threefinger, knowing that Stormy would reappear and take him down. They needed somebody stupid to carry the can, so that they would be left alone and unsuspected, free to continue practicing their damned rituals.

I'm driving out of the state on the I-10 now, trying to outrun the rolling storm, but I had to use my credit card to hire a car, and it's only a matter of time before I get hauled in for the murder of Sam Threefinger. They'll probably already have spoken to LaVinna, who'll place me in the bar near the corpse of her boss. None of it will make any fucking sense at all, but from what I heard the Louisiana police aren't going to be too bothered about that. Besides, what am I going to say in my defense, that I stood by and watched as the man whose house I had broken into tried to fight off the spirit of a half-man, half-piano? That's one piece of music that's *never* gonna play.

Man, I knew I was right to hate jazz.

Corpsemouth

JOHN LANGAN

I

I

n July of 1994, the year after my father died, my mother, youngest sister, and I went to Greenock, Scotland, from which my parents had emigrated to the United States almost thirty years before. Mom and Mackenzie flew over for a month; I joined them two weeks into their trip. The three of us stayed with my father's mother, who owned a semi-detached house set near the top of a modest hill. From the window of its front bedroom, on the second storey, you could look out on the River Clyde, here a tidal estuary, which had allowed the region to become a center for British shipbuilding for over two centuries. Two miles across, the river's far shore was layered with green hills, the Trossachs, long and sloping, the markers of geological traumas ancient and extreme.

I actually arrived a day late, because of a mechanical difficulty with my plane that was not detected until we were ready to pull away from the gate. The pilot's intimation of it in his message to the passengers caused a woman seated ahead of me to start shouting, "Oh my God, I had a dream about this last night. We're going to crash. The plane is going to crash. We can't take off." Fortunately for her—and possibly, for the rest of us—we were removed from the plane and bused to one of the airport's hotels, where we were put up overnight.

I spent part of that time trying to phone someone on this side of the Atlantic who could call my relatives overseas to let them know not to go to the airport for me. I had no luck, and passed the remainder of the night restless from the knowledge that I would have to be up early if I didn't want to miss the return bus to the terminal. I wasn't certain why I had taken the time off from the optometrists' office I was managing for this trip. Obviously, it had to do with the loss of my father, with an effort to address the gap his death had left in my life by returning to the place of his birth and early life, by spending time with the members of his family who still lived there, as if geography and blood might help to heal the edges of what remained a ragged wound. Already, though, my plan seemed off to a dubious start.

II

The sleep I managed was troubled. I fell into a dream in which I watched my father as he sat with a handful of other men in the back of a van speeding along a narrow street that ran between high brick walls blackened by age. Overhead, what might have been the gnarled branches of trees peeked down from the tops of the walls. My father looked as he had during my later childhood, slender, his hair already fled from the top of his head. He was dressed in a denim work shirt and jeans, as were the rest of the men. Although he did not look at me, I was certain he knew that I was watching him, and I waited for him to turn to me and say something. He did not.

III

Despite my concerns, I woke in plenty of time, and had an uneventful flight across the ocean, and was met at the airport in Glasgow by one of my older cousins and my mother and sister. They had checked the flight information before leaving for my original arrival, learned of the alteration to my trip, and saved themselves the earlier run to the airport. Although the ride to my grandmother's wasn't especially long, I was still feeling the effects of my night in the airport hotel (I was too much of a nervous flyer to have napped during my time in the air), and I struggled to hold open my eyelids, which felt weighted with lead. I had a confused impression of stone and steel buildings, of cars and trucks flowing around us, of a strip of blue river speeding by on my right. When we arrived at my grandmother's house, I succeeded in greeting her and one of my aunts and a couple of my cousins, but it wasn't long before I climbed the stairs to the front bedroom, assuring everyone that I just needed a little nap, and slept straight through to the next morning.

IV

Somewhere deep in that sleep, I dreamed I was standing at the picture window overlooking the Clyde. It was night, but the sky shone silver-white with the gloaming, casting sufficient light for me to see that the river was dry. Its bed was a wide, muddy trench bordered by rocky margins draped with seaweed. At points further out in the mud, boulders sat alone and in clumps. Thousands, tens of thousands of fish lay on the mud and rocks, their long, silver bodies catching the light. Most of them were dead; a few still thrashed. All along the riverbed, a great line of people walked downstream, towards the ocean. Male, female, old, young, tall, short, fat, thin: they were as varied a group as you could assemble. As was their dress: some were in their work clothes, some their pajamas; some in formal wear, some in hospital gowns; some wearing the uniforms of their professions, some stark naked. The only detail they shared was their bare feet. They trudged through mud that sucked at their ankles, that slurped at their shins, that surged around their thighs. If they were closer to shore, they stumbled on seaweed, slid on rocks. They trod on fish, kicked them out of the way. It seemed to me that there was something I wasn't seeing, a presence weighting the scene in front of me. It was waiting at the corners of my vision, huge and old and empty. Or, not empty so much as hungry. There was no sound from the crowd, but overhead, I heard a high-pitched ringing, like what occurs when you run your damp finger around the rim of a wineglass.

V

The following morning, I came downstairs to the smells of the breakfast my grandmother was cooking for me, fried eggs and bacon, fried tomatoes, buttered toast, orange juice, and instant coffee. She had insisted to my mother and sister that she was going to make breakfast for me, and that she wanted us to have some time alone. Mom and Mackenzie had removed themselves to my Aunt Betty and Uncle Stewart's house, a short distance along the road.

I wasn't certain what my grandmother wanted. While we had seen my father's parents during our previous visits to Scotland, it had seemed to me that we spent more time with my mother's mother, who had come to stay with us in America (though I didn't remember her visits). The most I had spoken to my father's mother was immediately after his death, when I had done my best to console her over the phone, assuring her that he had been suffering and was at least out of pain, and she had said, "It's like it's himself talking to me."

Now, she sat down with me at her small kitchen table and said, "Tell me about your dad, son."

I didn't know what to say. Her question should not have caught me off guard. My father had been his parents' acknowledged favorite—as one of his younger brothers had told me, their mother's golden boy. Although Mom, my siblings, and I had visited Scotland only every few years, for a good part of my childhood, Dad's job with IBM had necessitated regular international travel, to Paris and Frankfurt, and he was usually able to arrange an extra couple of days' stay with his parents. Despite his geographical distance from them, he had been able to maintain a close relationship with his mother and father; whereas myself, my brother, and my sisters knew our paternal grandparents mostly as names Dad and Mom discussed now and again. Occasionally, my father would mention his father as the source of an old song he was singing, or relate an anecdote about my grandfather's days in the shipyards, when he'd argued with his fellow workers against unionizing. He didn't say much about his mother; though his affection for her was palpable. For her to want me to tell her about him now was no surprise. Quite reasonably, she assumed that he was what we had in common, and she assumed that I felt about him the way she did.

This was not exactly the case. I loved him, fiercely, the way I had as a small child. For almost as long, though, that love had been complicated by other emotions, ones that, at twenty-five, I was nowhere near reckoning with. There was fear, of him and the temper that could ignite without warning, and for him and the heart whose consecutive infarctions during my eighth grade school year had left me in constant dread of his mortality. There was anger, at his stubborn insistence on his point of view, at his tendency to cut short so many of our more recent arguments by threatening to put my head through the wall if I didn't shut up. There was embarrassment, at the prejudices that had trailed him from his upbringing, against everyone who was not white, Catholic, and Scottish, at his tendency to point out the flaws even of people he was praising. And there was guilt (as some comedian or another said, the gift that keeps on giving), at my inability to love him as simply, as straightforwardly, as did my siblings. In the year or so leading up to his death, he and I had seemed to be moving, slowly, tentatively, toward some new stage in our relationship, one in which the two of us might be less on guard around one another, more relaxed, but his two months in Westchester Medical Center, his death, had forever kept us from reaching that place.

None of this could I say to my grandmother. Eyes wide behind her glasses, lips pressed together, she inclined ever-so-slightly toward me, her attitude one of anticipation, for anecdotes and details that would allow her son to live again in her mind's eye. So that was what I gave her, a morning's worth of stories about Dad. I couldn't not talk about his final stay in the hospital, the open heart surgery from which he had never fully recovered, becoming steadily weaker, until testing revealed that he had late-stage cirrhosis, his liver was failing, and the situation roared downhill like a roller coaster whose brakes had sheared off. But I could balance that story with others, most of them focusing on his pride in my brother and sisters. I told her about the cross-country and spring track practices and meets he picked them up from and drove them to. I narrated his help with and participation in their assorted science projects (including letting Mackenzie wake him throughout the night in order to assess the effects of an interrupted sleep schedule on his ability to perform a set number of tasks). I shared with her his delight in my brother's acceptance to medical school, and his pride in Christopher's commission in the Navy. I expressed his admiration for my middle sister, Rita, who managed a schedule that included teaching dance classes at the school at which she was a student, playing guitar with the church folk group, and working a part-time job at an optometrist's office, all the while completing high school. I considered it an achievement that, not once during our extended breakfast, did my grandmother ask about my father and me.

VI

The remainder of the day consisted of a visit to my aunt and uncle's house, a few hundred yards up the road, for a loud and cheery dinner of meat pies, sausage rolls, bridies, chips, and beans, with Irn-Bru to drink. We were joined by Stewart and Betty's children and children-in-law, and their grand-children, who were fascinated by my American accent and kept asking me to pronounce words in it. Uncle Stewart promised to drive me around to see the local sights; one of my cousins and his wife invited Mackenzie and me to watch a movie at their place; another of my cousins said that my sister and I had to come fishing with her and her dad another night. Oh, and there was a fair down by the water next weekend.... In a matter of two hours, my schedule for most of my remaining time in Greenock was arranged. I didn't mind. I had grown up without much in the way of extended family nearby; really, it was just Mom, Dad, my brother, sisters, and me. During the months after my father's death, when the flood of calls and visitors that had swept over us in the immediate aftermath of his passing diminished to a stream, then a trickle, then dried completely, I had felt this lack acutely. To be here, taken into the bosom of Dad's family, was like being gathered into an incredibly soft, comfortable blanket. I loved it.

VII

Later that night, though, as I was sitting up in bed, trying to read by the astonishing late light, I found myself unable to concentrate on my book. Had Mackenzie been awake, I would have talked to her, but I could hear my sister snoring in the back bedroom, which she was sharing with Mom. I could have checked on my mother, but even if she was awake, I was reluc-tant to disturb her with what was on my mind. It concerned my father, and his final stay in the hospital.

The morning after he emerged from surgery, the nurses propped him up in bed and gave him a pen and pad of paper with which to communicate. (He was, and would remain, intubated, his breathing assisted by a ventila-tor.) Due to the ICU regulations, only three of us could visit him at a time, so my sister, Rita, and I waited and sent Mom, our brother, and Mackenzie in first. Rita and I made small talk for five or ten minutes, then Chris and

Mackenzie came out to trade places with us. I had seen my father in the hospital before, many times, and the sight of him in his hospital gown, the top of the white ridge of bandages visible at its collar, below the trach tube, was not shocking. What was strange, off, was the expression on his face, his brows lowered, his jaw set, a look of concern tinted with anger. Rita and I crossed the ICU cubicle to him and embraced him, both of us delivering deliberately casual greetings, trying to act as if everything was fine, or was going to be fine. He returned our hugs, then turned his attention to the pad of paper propped on his lap. He took his pen and carefully wrote a sentence. When he was finished, he held the pad up for my inspection.

The line he'd written was composed of characters I didn't recognize. There was what might have been a square, except that the upper right corner didn't connect. There was a triangle whose points were rounded. There were parallel lines drawn at an angle, descending from right to left. There was a circle with a horizontal line bisecting it, an upside-down crescent, and a square whose bottom line turned up inside the shape before connecting with the line on the left, and which continued to turn at ninety-degree angles within the square, making a kind of stylized maze. I stared at the symbols, and looked at my father. My lack of comprehension was glaringly obvious. I said, "Um, I'm sorry—I don't understand what you're trying to tell me."

In response, he underlined the strange sentence several times and showed it to me again.

"Dad," I said, "I don't understand. I'm sorry. I can't read this."

His eyebrows raised in frustration. Although he was on the respirator, I could practically hear him blowing out his breath in exasperation. Employing the pen as a pointer, he moved it from symbol to symbol, as if taking me slowly through a simple statement.

I could feel my face growing hot. I shook my head, held up my hands.

He glared at me.

"Let me see," my mother said, leaning over from the other side of his bed. She didn't have any more luck with what Dad had written than had I. He was irritated with both of us—Rita refrained from looking at the pad—but his annoyance with me felt as if it had a particular edge, as if I, of all people, should understand what he was showing me.

After that, it was time to go. When we returned for the next visiting session, two-and-a-half hours later, Dad was surrounded by several nurses, all of whom were focused on preventing him from leaving his bed, which he was trying to do with more vigor than I would have anticipated from a man who had just had his chest cracked open. Mom talked to him, as did the rest of us as we came and went from the room, but though the sound of her voice, and ours, calmed him slightly, it wasn't enough to make him abandon his efforts. This led to him being given a mild sedative, then put in restraints. For the next two weeks, he struggled with those restraints daily, pulling at the padded cuffs buckled to his wrists. His features were set in a look of utter determination; if any of us spoke to him, he regarded us as if we were strangers.

My mother was afraid he had suffered a stroke, one of the possible complications of the surgery about which she and Dad had been warned. In the notes to his chart, the nurses described his new condition as a coma. Neither diagnosis seemed right to me, but where was my medical degree? All I knew was, he wasn't there, in that writhing body—or maybe, we weren't there for him, he was seeing himself in surroundings foreign and frightening. Finally, at the end of fourteen days of watching him wrestle with his restraints, one of the doctors realized that Dad might be having an allergic reaction to a drug they had been giving him (we never learned which one) and ordered it stopped. With the cessation of that drug, he returned to normal within a day. The restraints were removed, and although he only left his room for follow-up X-rays and further surgery, at least he was himself.

Those symbols, though, I had not forgotten. The most likely explanation was that they were an early product of my father's drug allergy. Had any of my siblings, my mother, asked me about them, I would have offered this rationale myself. Yet on some deeper level, I didn't buy this. He had exhibited too much focus in writing them. Had he ever been well enough to be removed from the ventilator, I would have asked him about them. Since that hadn't happened, they remained a mystery. I might be transforming the scribbling of a mind frightened and confused into a coded message of great import, but I could not forget the expression on my father's face as he showed me what he had set down.

After all, during the surgery, his heart had been stopped, and although a heart-lung machine had continued to circulate and oxygenate his blood, who could say what state he—his self, his soul—had been in for that span of time, how far he might have wandered from his body? Sometimes, I imagined him, waking from his surgery to find himself in an unadorned room with a single chair and a single door, and being told by a man in a drab suit that this was where he had to wait until the operation was completed and the doctors found out whether or not they could restart his heart. I imagined the man offering him a newspaper, its headlines the row of symbols he would copy for me.

To what end, though? I recognized the scenario I had invented, the speculation that prompted it, as magical thinking of the most basic kind, driven by longing for my father to have been involved in something more than the slow and painful process of his death. In his writing, I hoped for clues to another state of being, evidence of the place he had entered when he died.

I sat my book down on the nightstand. I eased out of my bed and crossed to the large window that gave a view of the Clyde and its far shore. In the late light, the river was the color of burnished tin, the Trossachs purple darkening to black. My father had not lived in this house—one of his mother's cousins had bought it for her after my grandfather died. But the river it surveyed had shaped his life as definitively as it had the land through which it flowed. The shipyards on its banks had brought my great-grandfather here from Ireland. A younger son of a farming family, disqualified from inheriting the farm by his order of birth, he had booked passage across the Irish Sea to find work as part of the industry building the vessels with which the British Empire maintained its quarter of the globe. Beyond that, I didn't know much about the man. I presumed he had obtained my grandfather's job in the shipyards for him, which I knew had consisted at one point of painting the hulls of ships. I wasn't sure why my father hadn't followed him in turn, unless it was because my grandfather (and probably, grandmother) had wanted something else for him, an office job, which he eventually found with IBM. All the same, Dad had courted Mom on the Esplanade that ran along the Clyde on the eastern side of town, and he kept newspaper clippings about the river that his relatives mailed to him folded and tucked within the pages of his Bible. I wasn't any closer to knowing what I expected from this trip. But gazing out at the river, the hills, felt strangely reassuring.

VIII

That night, my dreams took me down to the Clyde. A chain link fence kept me from a flat, paved surface above which cranes rose like giant metal sculptures. I turned to look behind me, and almost toppled into a chasm that dropped a good twenty feet. The gap ran parallel to the fence, to the river beyond. Maybe ten feet across, its walls were brick, old, blackened; although its bottom was level—a road, I realized when I saw a white, boxy van drive up it. At once, I knew two things with dream certainty: my father was in that van, and there was something at my back, on the other side of the paved lot. The hairs on the back of my neck prickled at it. Old—I could feel its age, a span of years so great it set me shivering uncontrollably. I did not want to see this. I shook with such intensity, it jolted me from sleep. Awake, I could not stop trembling, and wrapped the bedclothes around me. I took a few minutes to return to sleep, and once I did, it was to a different dream.

IX

Once he was home from work the next day, Uncle Stewart made good on his promised tour of the area. Mackenzie came, too. The three of us squeezed into his car, a white Nissan Micra whose cramped interior lived up to its name, and off we went. A soft-spoken man, Stewart kept a cigarette lit and burning between his lips for most of the drive. He worked for a high-tech manufacturer who had moved into one of the old shipping buildings. He was what my parents called crafty, which meant he had a knack for artistic projects. Fifteen years before, when he'd been laid off his job at the shipyards and unable to find another, he had turned his efforts to building doll-sized replicas of old, horse-drawn traveler's trailers. He'd gifted one to my parents, who placed it in their bedroom, where my siblings and I went to admire it. The detail on the trailer was amazing, from the flowered curtains hung inside the small windows to the ornaments on the porcelain horse's bridle. (He bought the horses in bulk from a department store.) Stewart had sold his trailers, first to family, then to friends, then to friends of friends, then to their friends, the money he earned helping to keep his family afloat until he found a new job.

He was also a repository of local knowledge, some of which he shared with Mackenzie and me as he steered the Micra up and down Greenock's steep streets. He showed us the house our father had grown up in, the apartment where our mother had been raised by her mother, the church where our parents had married. He drove us down to the river, to the Esplanade, and along to where a few cranes stood at the water's edge like enormous steel insects. He drove us east, out of town, towards Glasgow, so that he could show us Dumbarton Rock across the Clyde, a great rocky molar whose ragged crown stood two hundred feet above the river. A scattering of stone blocks was visible at the summit. Nodding at the rock, Stewart said, "There's been a castle of some sort there forever," the words emerging from his mouth in puffs of cigarette smoke that his open window caught and sucked out of the car. "Back when the Vikings held the mouth of the Clyde, and the islands, that was the westernmost stronghold of the British. Before that, the local kings ruled from atop it. Like the castle in Edinburgh—Sterling, too. There's a story that Merlin paid the place a visit, in the sixth century."

"King Arthur's Merlin?" I said.

"Aye. The king at the time was called Riderch. They called him 'the generous.' King Arthur's nephew, Hoel, was passing through, and he was injured. Fell off his horse or the like. King Riderch put him up while he was healing. When Riderch's foes learned he had King Arthur's nephew under his roof, they laid siege to the place. Riderch had a magic sword—*Dyrnwyn*—that burst into flame whenever he drew it, but he and his men were pretty badly outnumbered. There was no way he could get word to King Arthur down in Camelot in time for it to do him any good. It looked as if Arthur's nephew was going to be killed while under Riderch's care. So was Riderch himself, but you see what I'm saying. It would be a big dishonor for Riderch, alive or dead."

Stewart steered toward an exit on the left that took us to a roundabout. He followed it half-way around, until we were heading back toward Greenock. As he did, he said, "This was when Merlin showed up. He'd been keeping an eye on Hoel, and he'd seen the trouble Riderch was in for his hospitality to Arthur's kin. He presented himself to the King, and offered his assistance. 'No offense,' says Riderch, 'but you're one man. There's a thousand men at my front door. What can you do about a force of that size?'

"'Well,' says Merlin. The King has a point. He is only one man, and although his father was a devil, there is a limit to his power. 'However,' says he, 'I have allies I can call upon for help. And against them, no force of men can stand.'

"'Then I wish you'd ask those friends for their aid,' says Riderch.

"Merlin says okay. He tells the King he needs a corpse, the fresher, the better. It just so happens that, earlier that very day, Riderch's men caught a couple of their enemies attempting to sneak over the castle wall. He has his men bring them before him, and right on the spot, executes the pair. 'There you go,' he says to Merlin. 'There's two corpses for you.'

"'Good,' says Merlin. He has the King's soldiers carry the bodies right outside the front gate. It's going on night time, and Riderch's foes have withdrawn to their tents. Merlin instructs the soldiers to dig a shallow grave, one big enough for the two dead men. Once it's been dug, he has them lay the corpses in it and cover them over. Then he sets to, using his staff to draw all manner of strange characters in the soil. He was a great one for writing, was Merlin. If you read some of the older stories about him, he's always writing on things, prophecies of coming events, usually. King Riderch watches him, but he doesn't recognize the characters Merlin's scratching into the dirt.

"When he's done, Merlin steps back from the grave. Pretty soon, the earth begins to tremble. It moves from somewhere deep below them, as if something's digging its way up to them. Over in the siege camp, a few of Riderch's enemies have been watching Merlin's show. As the ground shakes, more of them run to see what's causing the disturbance. The soil over the grave jumps, and a great head pushes its way through the dirt. It's a man's head, but it's the size of a hut. The hair is clotted with earth. The skin is all leathery, shrunk to the skull. The eyes are empty pits. The lips are blackened, pulled back from teeth the size of a man's arm. The arms and legs of the bodies the King's men buried hang out over the teeth, the remainder of the corpses inside the huge mouth. It's a giant Merlin's summoned, but no such giant as anyone there has ever heard tell of. It's as much an enormous corpse as those it crunches between its teeth. It keeps coming, head and neck, shoulders and arms, chest and hips, until it towers above them. You can imagine the reaction of Riderch's foes: sheer panic. The King and his men aren't too far away from it, themselves. Merlin touches his arm and says, 'Steady.' He points to the siege camp and says to the monster, 'Right. Those are for you.'

"The giant doesn't need to be told twice. It takes a couple of steps, and it's in the midst of the enemy fighters, most of whom are trampling each other in their haste to get away from it. It leans down, sweeps up a handful of men, and stuffs them into its mouth. It stomps others like they're ants. It kicks campfires apart, catches men and tears them to pieces. A few try to fight it. They grab their spears and swords and stab it. But that leathery skin is too tough; their blades can't pierce it. Soon, the giant's feet are covered in gore. Its lips and chin are smeared with the blood of the men it's eaten. There's no satisfying the thing; it continues to jam screaming men into its mouth. In a matter of a few minutes, Merlin's monster has broken the siege. In a few more, it's routed Riderch's foes. Some of them flee to the ships they sailed here. The giant pursues them, smashes the prows of the ships, breaks off a mast and uses it as a club on ships and men alike.

"King Riderch turns to Merlin and says, 'What is this thing you've brought forth?'

"'That,' says Merlin, 'is Corpsemouth.'

"'Corpsemouth,' says Riderch. 'Him, I have not heard of.'

"Merlin says, 'He and his brethren were worshipped here many a long year ago. He was not known as Corpsemouth, then, but what his original name was has been lost. He and his kindred were replaced by other gods, who were replaced by newer gods than those, and so on until the Romans brought their gods, and now the Christians theirs. All of Corpsemouth's fellows went to the place old gods go when men are done with them, the Graveyard of the Gods. Corpsemouth, though, refused to suffer the same fate as his kin. Instead, he lived on their remains. If any men stumbled across him, they were his. As later generations of gods came to the Graveyard, so Corpsemouth had them, too. Down through the ages he has continued, losing hold of everything he used to be, until all that remains is his hunger.'

"Riderch watches the giant crushing the last remnants of his enemies. He says, 'This is blasphemy.'

"'Maybe,' Merlin says, 'but it saved King Arthur's nephew, and it saved you, too.' Which Riderch can't argue with.

"Once the last of the enemy fighters is dead, the giant, Corpsemouth, turns in the direction of Merlin and the King. Riderch puts his hand on his sword, but Merlin tells him to keep it in its sheath. He points his staff at the hills behind Dumbarton Rock. Corpsemouth nods that great, gruesome head, and walks off in that direction. That's the last Riderch sees of him, and of Merlin, for the matter. I don't suppose he was too upset about either."

Stewart's story had taken us all the way back to his front door. He pulled the parking brake and turned off the engine. "And that," he said with a grin, "is a wee bit of your local history."

Mackenzie and I thanked him, for the story and for the tour. While we were walking up to the house, my sister said, "Where did Merlin send the monster—Corpsemouth?"

Our uncle paused at the front door. "The story doesn't say. Maybe north, to the mountains. That's where many terrible and awful beasts were said to dwell. I'll tell you what I think. A few miles east of Dumbarton Rock, there was an old burial place unearthed in the 1930s. It was the talk of this part of the country. I remember my father speaking about it. The fellows who dug it up said they found evidence of an ancient temple there. 'Scotland's Stonehenge,' the papers called it."

"What happened to it?" I said. "Can you visit it?"

"They put a pair of apartment buildings over the spot," Stewart said. "The war interrupted the excavation, then, when the war was over, another group of scientists said the chaps who'd discovered the place had overstated its significance. There were a few rock carvings that were of interest, they said, but as long as they were removed and sent to the museum in Glasgow, they saw no reason not to build the high rises there. So the men from the museum came and cut out the pieces of rock to be preserved and the rest became part of the foundation for the new construction. My father was upset about it, about all of it, but especially about the carvings being taken away. 'There's folk put they things there for a reason,' he says, 'and yon men from the museum would do well enough to leave them be. There's no telling what trouble they'll stir.' I suppose he had a point. Although," Stewart added, "I've yet to see any giants prowling the hills. But if you ask me, that's where Merlin told Corpsemouth to go."

X

That night, I lay in bed thinking about Stewart's story, wondering what my father would have made of it. Mackenzie was sleeping over at Stewart and Aunt Betty's house, or I might have asked her. My mother was long since unconscious. I was sure Dad would have enjoyed Stewart's tale as entertainment. He was a great fan of adventure stories of all stripes, with a soft spot for horror narratives, too. Mostly, he watched them as movies and TV shows; although he might read a book like *Firefox* or *Last of the Breed*. Whenever he saw a new movie, especially if it had been on TV too late for me and my brother, he would describe it to us the next day, in a scene-by-scene retelling no less detailed than the story Stewart had told. In this way, I knew the plots to most of the Connery and Moore James Bonds, a number of Clint Eastwood thrillers, and an assortment of films focused on mythological figures, such as Hercules. He would have appreciated the way Stewart's tale blended the historical with the horrific; though he might have preferred a different, more dramatic end to the monster, blasted by Merlin's magic, say, or set alight by King Riderch's fiery sword.

I was less sure how he would have dealt with the story's pagan elements, especially the idea that gods came and went over time. I knew he'd been interested in mythology. Exploring the basement as a child, I had found stacked in the shelves near the furnace a half-dozen issues of a magazine called *Man, Myth & Magic*, whose title had appealed to me instantly but whose pages, full of reproductions of old woodcuts and classical paintings, not to mention articles written in a dry, academic language, left me confused. I'd wanted to ask him about the magazines, but had the sense that I shouldn't. There was a reason they were in the basement, after all. Plus, puzzle me though they did, I didn't want to lose access to them, which I might if he realized I was paging through them. So I kept quiet about the magazines, but I noticed that, whenever I brought up stories from the Greek or Norse myths I was reading, he usually knew them; though he tended to downplay his knowledge.

I wasn't sure to what extent this was because he was a devout Catholic, his faith fire-hardened from having grown up in a Protestant culture of institutionalized religious prejudice. He was leery of anything that might contradict the Church, his faith threaded through with a profound anxiety about Hell. Occasionally, he spoke about the Passionist fathers who visited his local church when he was a boy to deliver terrifying sermons on the fate of the damned. (I wondered if this was part of the attraction horror films had for him, their glimpses of the infernal.) The standard by which a soul would be judged after death was a source of concern, even worry, for him. We had discussed the apparition of the Virgin Mary to the children at Fatima, during which, she had told one of the boys to whom she revealed herself that he was destined to spend a great deal of time in Purgatory. While Purgatory was not Hell, neither was it a place to which you would have expected a young child to be sent. What could he have done, Dad said, to merit such a punishment? With the perspective of the last year, it had become clear to me that his questions about my church attendance during the two years I lived in Albany, his concern about my dating a girl who wasn't Catholic, were rooted in an honest desire to keep me out of Hell, whose smoky fires burned low and red in the corners of his mind.

I didn't believe my father had anything to fear from eternal damnation. I wasn't sure there was anything for him to be concerned about, one way or the other. During my youth, I had been as devout as my father. To be honest, I had loved my religion, which was full of all manner of marvelous stories, those in the Old and New Testaments, yes, and those in the lives of the saints, too. I shared some of dad's nervousness at the threat of Hell, but I grew up in the post-Vatican II Church, when the rewards of salvation were emphasized over the torments of damnation. Once I entered adolescence, however, the joys of the opposite sex became vastly more compelling than the strictures of faith. If I was hardly original in this—indeed, compared to the rest of my high school classmates, I was the latest of late bloomers—I roamed off the beaten path in my growing intellectual disagreement with the Church. I found its positions on most social matters riven by contradiction; nor did it help that so many of the men who pronounced them did so with an air of self-righteousness that set my adolescent teeth on edge. The ritual of the Mass, and its central conceit, the intersection of the numinous with the mundane, continued to speak to me, albeit, in a more figurative sense than I was sure my father would have approved. Religion in general seemed to me increasingly figurative, less a description of some ultimate reality than, at best, another human invention to help us through the struggle of living. At worst, it was another way for a small group of men to hold sway over a significantly larger group of people, politics with more elaborate costumes. Either way, it had nothing to do with any life after this one.

To be sure, I had taken comfort from the Church and its rituals during the days and weeks after Dad had died. By the following winter, though, my attendance at Mass had lapsed almost entirely. Even when my work schedule permitted me to take my mother and Mackenzie to church, I sat through the service listening with one ear, especially when the priest stood to deliver the sermon. Sometimes, I thought that I could have been a better Catholic if I lived in a country whose language I did not speak, so that I wouldn't realize the priest was summarizing a *Peanuts* comic to explain God's love for us. I missed the faith I'd had in my childhood, and I regretted its loss because it had been so important to my father, and had remained so for the rest of my family. Its loss filled me with a kind of terror, because it had taken with it my father, consigning him to a void in which I and everyone else I knew would, in the end, join him.

XI

No surprise: that night, I dreamed of Corpsemouth. I was standing on the shore of the Clyde. It was the same, twilit time I'd encountered in all my recent dreams. In front of me, the river was at low tide, exposing an expanse of waterlogged sand studded with rocks of varying size. Behind me, the Battery Park, Greenock's riverfront park, stretched flat and green. Beyond where the water lapped the sand, a wall of yellowish fog sat on the river, veiling the opposite shore. From within the fog, I heard the slosh of water being parted by something large. Goosebumps raised on my arms as the air chilled. An enormous silhouette loomed through the fog. Fear filled me like water bubbling into a glass. The fog churned at its edge; waves splashed the beach. A leg taller, far taller, than I pushed into view. The color of brackish water, its flesh was dried and wrapped around enormous bones. There were figures tattooed on the skin, but the creases and folds from its withering rendered them indecipherable. A second leg appeared, carrying the rest of the monster with it, but I didn't wait to see any more of it. I turned and ran for the edge of the park, which had receded almost to the horizon. Sand grabbed at my feet. I slipped on a rock and fell into another. When the giant hand closed on me, I wasn't surprised. I woke as it lifted me into the air, my heart pounding, relieved that I didn't have to see the old god's face, its terrible mouth open for me.

XII

The following day, my cousin, Gabriel, and his wife, Leslie, drove me, Mackenzie, and our mom to Glasgow. Gabriel was Uncle Stewart and Aunt Betty's second oldest, which made him five years older than I was. The times my parents had taken my brother and sisters and me to Scotland when we were growing up, Gabriel had always been the kindest of my cousins, willing to talk to my brother and me as equals about all manner of serious subjects: nuclear war, the fate of the human race, life on other planets. He worked for the railroad, in what capacity I wasn't clear. Leslie was an elementary school teacher; she and Gabriel had been married for eight years.

After we found a parking spot, Leslie, Mom, and Mackenzie set off for Sauchiehall Street and its assorted shops, Gabriel and I for the West End Museum, a sprawling, Victorian extravagance in red stone whose center was crowned by a selection of turrets that suggested a fairy-tale castle full of treasure. The museum, I had learned from a follow-up conversation with Uncle Stewart, was where the engraved rocks removed from the burial site east of Dumbarton Rock had been sent and were currently on display. I wasn't sure why I wanted to see them; it might have been for no more complicated a reason than that my uncle had told me about them. I hadn't shared my objective with my cousin, but he was happy to accompany me across the museum's wide, green lawn.

Inside, we traversed a large, echoing gallery to the stairs to the third floor, where the exhibit on Scotland's Ancient Cultures was located. The display was at the far end of the level. It had been organized around a half-dozen modest display cases, each of which contained a handful of relics of the country's oldest-known inhabitants. Large photographs of the Scottish countryside, each seven feet high by five feet wide, had been hung in the midst of the cases. Gabriel strolled over to a display case showing the rusted blade of an old sword. In front of a picture of a shallow brook running at the base of a snow-topped mountain, I found what I had come to see.

The only thing in its case, the piece of grey stone was rectangular, larger than I had anticipated, the size of a small table. The white lettering on the glass cover identified it as having been unearthed in 1933 on Gibbon's Farm in Dunbartonshire. The description pointed out the pairs of concentric circles visible on the stone's upper right quadrant, as well as the U-shape directly below them, which I thought resembled a horseshoe. The approximate date given for the stone was 500 CE. I crouched to get a closer look at the stone, which brought me level with its base. From that position, I noticed a series of marks in the rock. At first, I took them for the scrapes and scars left by whatever tools had been used to extricate the slab. Then they came into focus, and I was looking at a row of characters. A rough square whose upper-right corner didn't connect was followed by a triangle with rounded ends, which was succeeded by a pair of parallel lines slanting from right to left. Fourth was an approximate circle with a line through its center, a crescent like a frown fifth. Last was another square, only this one's edges failed to connect in the lower-left corner, instead turning inside in a series of right angles to form a stylized maze.

It was as if I were looking at the figures through a tunnel. Everything except that patch of rock was dark. I could hear the steady click and sigh of my father's respirator, the faster, high-pitched beep of the heart monitor, the intermittent beep of a machine keeping track of some other function. I could smell the antibacterial foam we applied to our hands every time we entered his room. I could feel the thin blanket we helped him pull up because the room was too cold. My heart fluttered in my chest. I went to stand, and fell onto my butt. I looked up, and still saw the symbols on the stone. I remembered the expression on my father's face when he showed them to me, the frustration.

Gabriel's hand on my shoulder brought me back to myself. "What happened?" he said. "Are you okay?"

"Lost my balance," I said, pushing to my feet. "I squatted down to get a better look at the exhibit, and I fell right over. I'm fine."

"So you wanted to see this, eh?" Gabriel gestured at the stone. "Let me guess: Dad told you his Corpsemouth story, didn't he? Including the part about the mysterious graveyard whose sacred stones were removed. Am I right?"

"Yes."

"You know he made up all of that."

"Not this." I nodded at the display case.

"No, but it's only a piece of rock with a couple of circles on it. There's nothing magical about it."

I was surprised by his bluntness. "I don't know," I said, "it's kind of cool. We don't have anything like this in New York."

He shrugged.

"What about the figures on the end, there?" I said.

"What do you mean?"

"These ones," I said, pointing to the half-dozen characters on the stone's base.

He bent to inspect them. "Looks like someone was playing with their penknife. What's the display say about them?"

"Nothing."

"That's your answer, then."

I was tempted to tell Gabriel about the last time I'd seen these same figures, but saying that my late father had written them on a piece of paper for me after emerging from surgery during which his heart had been stopped sounded too lurid, too melodramatic. Instead, I said, "I suppose you're right. Why don't we go see what the ladies have been up to?"

XIII

On the way to our meeting spot on Sauchiehall Street, though, past shop windows full of high-end clothes, shoes, and liquor, I asked my cousin if he truly believed his father had invented the story of Corpsemouth. "Not completely," he said. "Dad reads all kinds of books; I'm sure he's run across something like his monster in one of them. The king that's in the story, Riderch, he was real, and had his castle at Dumbarton Rock."

"But no Merlin," I said.

"Actually, there is a story about Merlin showing up there," Gabriel said. "What is it they say? If you're going to tell a lie, make sure to fit as much of the truth into it as you can manage."

"It's not exactly a lie," I said, "it's a story."

Gabriel didn't answer.

XIV

For the rest of our excursion, which ended with dinner at Glasgow's Hard Rock Café, and for the return drive to Greenock, which took us past Dumbarton Rock, those symbols floated near the surface of my thoughts. As far as I could remember, my father hadn't taken us to visit the West End Museum during any of our family trips to Scotland. Nor, as far as I knew, had he gone to the place on his own; although this was difficult to the point of impossible to be certain of. He'd never mentioned it, and he'd had no trouble telling us about his visit to the Louvre, while he'd been in Paris on one of his business trips. I asked my mother about it during our dinner at the Hard Rock, delivering my question at the end of a short appreciation of the museum. "There was a lot of fascinating stuff in it," I said. "Did you and Dad ever go there?"

A year past his death, Mom's eyes could still shine with tears, her cheeks blanch, at the mention of my father, of their life together. She reached for her napkin, dabbed the corners of her eyes. "No," she said, returning the napkin to the table. "I think I went on a school trip there—I don't remember how old I was. Just a girl."

"What about Dad?" I said. "Did his school visit the museum, too?"

"I don't know," Mom said. "They probably did, but he never mentioned it to me."

"Oh," I said. "I was wondering. Because, you know, you guys took us to a lot of museums when we were young." Which was true.

"That's what happens when you're traveling with children," she said. "No, in our younger days—BC, we used to say, Before Children—Dad and I went on picnics, or out dancing."

So perhaps my father had been to the museum as a boy, and perhaps on that occasion he had seen the weird symbols carved on the base of the rock. And perhaps his brain had tossed up that memory as his anesthesia wore off. The last perhaps, however, seemed one too many. Yes, the mind was a complex, subtle organ, and especially after a dramatic experience, who could predict its every last response? Yet this felt more like special pleading to me than admitting that something strange had happened to my father, and whatever its parameters, it had left him with a message for me written in characters I couldn't read.

XV

Back in Greenock, we dropped Mom, Mackenzie, and Leslie off at Stewart and Betty's. Gabriel and I drove back to his house, in order, he said, for him to initiate his American cousin into the mysteries of the single malt. He and Leslie lived on a steep street that gave a view of the Clyde. The houses along it sat on a succession of terraces, like enormous stairs descending the hillside. He parked in a short gravel driveway, and led me first into his and Leslie's house, to deposit her day's purchases on the living room couch, then out a pair of French doors, into the back garden. A brick path took us through rows of flowering bushes to a wooden hut whose door was flanked on the right by a large window. A hand-painted sign over the door read GABE'S HORN; under the name, the artist had drawn a simplified trumpet from whose mouth alcohol poured. My cousin opened the door, flicked a light switch within, and ushered me into the building.

To the right, a short bar stood in front of a shelf lined with bottles of Scotch, with some better varieties of vodka and bourbon to either side of them. Behind the bottles, a mirror the length of the bar doubled the size of the room. To the left, a quartet of chairs surrounded a round table. Beyond the table, a chrome jukebox stood against the wall. Posters and pennants of the local soccer team, the Greenock Morton, decorated the walls, with framed photographs of Gabriel and Leslie in assorted vacation settings among them. Gabriel made for the bar, which he slipped behind to survey his selection of whisky.

There were a couple of tall stools in front of the bar. I settled onto one of them and said, "This is great."

Gabriel glanced over his shoulder at me. "Do you think so? It's just something Leslie and me put together in our spare time."

"It's fantastic," I said.

"We like to come out here after a day at work, or if we're having friends over."

"It reminds me of a place my dad took me to," I said. "There was a guy who was a friend of his—through work, but he was from Scotland, too. One night, Dad had to go over to his house—to pick up something for work, I think—and he brought me along with him. I was thirteen or fourteen. This man led us down to his basement, which he had set up as a bar—though not as nice as this one. He passed my dad a glass of something—I don't know what it was, but Dad told me afterwards that our host had not been stingy with his booze. I had a ginger ale, which he gave to me out of one of those specialized dispensers you see in real bars, with the hose and all the different buttons on top of it. I was thoroughly impressed. The guy had been in the RAF during the war—he had a couple of big pictures of planes on the wall. The three of us sat around talking about that for an hour. I felt so grown up, you know?"

"Aye." Gabriel nodded. He had picked three bottles and set them on the bar. "I have some ginger ale in the refrigerator, but I think it's time for something a wee bit more mature." From under the bar, he produced a pair of whisky glasses, along with a small pitcher of water. He opened one of the bottles and tipped respectable amounts of its amber contents into both glasses. To each he added a literal drop of water. I picked up the one closest to me, and raised it to my nose. The odor of its contents, sharp, threaded with honey, was the smell of I couldn't count how many family parties. It was me playing waiter to my father's bartender, gathering drink orders from whichever guests were there for the latest First Communion, or Confirmation, or Graduation, and conveying them to Dad, who had opened the liquor cabinet in the kitchen and stood ready to dispense its contents. It was me returning to those guests with one or two or three glasses in my hands, delivering them to their recipients, and hurrying back to the kitchen for the next ones. It was me carrying to a particular friend a liquor my father had secured specifically for them, making sure to let them know Dad had said this was something special for them.

"Cheers," Gabriel said, lifting his glass to me.

"Cheers," I said, repeating the gesture to him.

The whisky flared on my tongue, and flamed all the way down my throat to my stomach, where it detonated in a burst of heat. Eyes watering, I coughed, and set the half-empty glass on the bar.

"You said you're not much of a Scotch drinker," Gabriel said.

"Not much as in never," I said. "Which is strange, considering it was the drink of choice at family get-togethers."

"Try sipping it," Gabriel said. "You want to be able to savor a good single malt."

"Okay." I took a more measured drink, and tasted honey mixed with something woody, almost bitter. I described it to Gabriel. "That's the peat," he said. I nodded, trying more. The flavor was not what I was used to: it filled the mouth, asserting itself as did none of the mixed drinks I'd previously had. I'd never been much of any kind of drinker, and I felt the liquor's potency before I was finished with the glass. My cousin's bar and its contents softened, their edges slightly less defined. Something inside me loosened. I said, "All right. What's wrong with your dad's monster story?"

Gabriel raised an eyebrow. "You mean Corpsemouth?"

"Yes," I said, "that. In the museum, I had the impression you were less than enchanted with it."

"Ach, it's fine," he said. "Dad's always been a great one for the stories."

"Mine, too," I said.

"That story—the Corpsemouth one—you know what it's really about, don't you?"

"A giant monster?"

"It's death," Gabriel said. "It's a way of picturing death, of representing the way death feels to us."

"Sure," I said. "It's like—there's a line in one of Stephen King's books—I think it's *Salem's Lot*—this kid is asked if he knows what death is, and he says yeah, it's when the monsters get you."

"Aye," Gabriel said, "that's what I'm trying to say."

The second Scotch my cousin served tasted less of honey and more of smoke, and something peppery. The knot within me that had started to loosen slid away from itself. Gabriel leaned across the bar and said, "So. How're you finding it, being here?"

The row of strange symbols flickered behind my eyes. "It's different than I was expecting," I said.

"It's bound to be."

"Yeah. It's funny. I thought that coming here would let me feel more in touch with my dad. Granted, it's only been a few days, but so far...."

"You don't."

"I don't."

"How could you? You didn't know him here. You knew him in America. It's okay."

"Maybe you're right. If that's the case, then what am I doing here?"

"You're with family."

"Yeah," I said. "I didn't have much of that when I was growing up, you know? It was just the six of us. It's kind of nice."

The third and final Scotch Gabriel poured was thinner, the peat combining with a briny flavor to give the liquor an astringent taste so blunt it was oddly appealing. "Thank you," I said to my cousin, speaking with the deliberation of someone whose tongue was heavy with alcohol. "I appreciate you sharing your expertise with me."

"I'm hardly an expert," Gabriel said.

"Regardless. You know what's funny?"

"What?"

"I can picture my dad enjoying the whole Corpsemouth story. It reminds me of movies we watched when I was a kid, *The Golden Voyage of Sinbad*, *Clash of the Titans*, *Dragonslayer*—these stories about heroes fighting enormous monsters."

"I suppose," he said.

"Well, you two appear to be having a merry time," Leslie said. She was standing in the open doorway to the bar.

"We were talking about monsters," I said.

"I'm sure you were," she said. "Stewart gave me a lift home. I'm not rushing you out, but he says if you want, he can run you back to your Gran's."

"That is probably a good idea," I said. "I'm fairly confident I've reached my limit for alcohol. Honestly, I think I passed it a while ago."

I thanked Gabriel for his generosity with his spirits, and him and Leslie for having squired my mother, sister, and me around Glasgow, today. "We've got to have you back for another tasting before you leave," Gabriel said.

"From your mouth to God's ear," I said.

XVI

Outside, night had fallen, the last of the gloaming retreated to the horizon. Stewart was waiting in his Micra at the end of the driveway. I lowered myself into the front passenger seat. He'd been listening to a news program on the radio; as I buckled my seatbelt, he turned it off. "And how was your education?" he said.

"Great," I said. "Gabriel introduced me to some quality stuff."

"Aye, he's a great one for the single malt, our Gabriel." He released the parking brake and reversed into the street. "Are you up for a wee jaunt?"

"Sure."

"Good man." He shifted into first and started downhill.

"Where are we headed?" I said.

"The river."

"Oh."

The whisky I'd consumed made the steep road seem almost vertical, the Clyde below rather than ahead of us. Retaining walls raced toward us and swerved right and left. The river grew larger in fits and starts, as if it were a series of slides being snapped into view. The car's engine whined and growled as Stewart worked back and forth among the gears. If not calmer, I was at least less terrified than I would have been without the Scotch insulating me.

At the foot of the hill, the street leveled and ran straight to the river. One hand on the steering wheel, Stewart depressed the car's lighter and fished a cigarette from the packet in his shirt pocket. Rows of squat apartment houses passed on either side. Stewart lit his cigarette and drew on it till the tip flared. Exhaling a cloud of smoke, he said, "Did you see that stone in the museum?"

"I did," I said.

"Not much to look at, is it?"

"I don't know. When you think about what it represents—how old it is and everything…I'm glad they have it at the museum, but it's kind of a shame they couldn't leave it where it was."

"Aye."

"The exhibit said no one's sure exactly what the symbols on it mean. Maybe images of the sun."

"They're for binding," Stewart said.

"Binding?"

"Aye, for keeping a spirit or a creature in one place. You bind them by the sun and the moon. That's why there's two sets of circles on the stone. It's a very old rite."

"What was bound there?"

Stewart shot me a sidelong glance. "I told you and your sister yesterday."

"Corpsemouth? For real?"

He nodded.

"I thought that was…."

"A story?"

"Yeah. No offense."

"There was something called up at Dumbarton Rock when Riderch was king. It was older than ancient, and it was terrible. Maybe it was summoned to help the King against his enemies. Maybe it was summoned to fight Riderch. Maybe someone was playing around and opened a door that should've been left shut. It took a powerful man to send the thing back where it belonged, and lock the gate after it. That stone was part of the locking mechanism."

"Wait. You're serious."

"I am."

"But...."

"That's impossible? Ridiculous? Insane?"

"I'm sorry, but yeah."

"It's all right. I wouldn't expect you to believe it, even with a few drams in you."

We had crossed the major east-west highway through town and come to a short road, which passed between an inlet of the river on the left, and a couple of apartment buildings on the right. Stewart drove to the end of the road, where a chain link fence sectioned off a stretch of pavement that went another twenty yards to the river. He parked the car and exited it. I followed. This close to the water, the air was cool bordering on cold. While Stewart popped the trunk, I surveyed the fence, which continued to the right, guarding the edge of a much larger paved area, which was filled with large metal shipping containers, some of them sitting on their own, others stacked two and three high. In the near distance, a trio of cranes faced the Clyde, weird sentinels looking out over the dark water. Tall sodium lights gave the scene an orange hue that made it appear slightly unreal.

Behind me, Stewart shut the trunk. He was carrying a pair of metal poles, each about a yard long, one end wrapped in duct tape. "Here," he said, handing one to me.

I took it. The pole was hollow, but heavy. "What's this?"

"Protection."

"From what?"

"Come this way." He set out to the right. I hurried after. Together, we walked the fence for a good hundred yards, until we came to a wire door set in it. The entrance was locked, but Stewart withdrew a ring of keys from his trousers, which he thumbed through until he arrived at one that slid into the lock and levered it open. The door's hinges shrieked as he pushed it in. I cringed, expecting the angry shout of a security officer. None came. Stewart stepped through. I pushed the door closed behind us, to minimize suspicion.

Keeping to the shelter of the containers, Stewart and I made our way across the paved expanse, he moving quietly, gracefully, I with the exaggerated care of someone contending with too much alcohol. We headed steadily in the direction of the river. A light mist floated around us, waist-high. This close, the cranes were gigantic, monumental. Stewart stopped, raised his hand. "Do you hear that?" he said quietly.

"What?"

"Listen."

Ahead and to our left, on the other side of a pair of stacked containers, something scraped over the pavement. Holding the metal pole in both hands, the tip low, as if it were a sword, Stewart crossed to the metal boxes. I kept a few steps behind, in a half-crouch. He moved right, to one end of the containers. The sound continued in alternating rhythm, a short scrape followed by a longer one. Before continuing to the other side of the boxes, Stewart stopped and ducked his head around for a look at whoever was there. He jerked back. Closing his eyes, he inhaled, then blew out. He murmured something I couldn't hear, raising and lowering the end of the pole while he did. As the light played up and down the metal, I saw writing on it: the symbols I had seen in the Glasgow museum, on a piece of paper in my father's hospital room. Heart lurching, I straightened. I tilted the pole I was holding back and forth, and sure enough, there were the same half-dozen characters cut into it. In an instant, I was sober, the effects of Gabriel's drinks swept away by the sensation of standing within the current of something immense and strange.

"Right," Stewart said. "There's something coming up to the end of this box. When it reaches us, I'll step out and see to it. You shouldn't need to do anything. This one isn't big. If it gets past me, though, you'll have to slow it down. Go for its legs, but mind its hands. Here we go."

The scraping was right next to us. Stewart moved out into the alley formed by our containers and one beyond them. As he did, he pivoted, slashing the pole from right to left at whatever was still hidden from me by the edge of the container. There was a heavy crunch, a sharp clang, and the pole flew out of Stewart's hands, ringing on the pavement to his right. A wooden club swung at him from his left. He ducked, but it caught him high on the shoulder with sufficient force to knock him from his feet. He landed hard.

I took a deep breath and stepped out from the container, in front of Stewart's opponent. I couldn't bring myself to strike someone I hadn't seen, but I held the pole up in what I hoped was a menacing fashion. I intended to shout, "That's far enough!" What I saw, however, stilled the voice in my throat.

It was as big as a large man. At first, I thought it was a man, dressed in a bizarre costume. Much of it was mud, thick, dripping with water. Its surface was clotted with junk, crushed beer cans, shards of broken glass, saturated cardboard and newspaper, pieces of plastic, metal, wood. Here and there, rocks studded with barnacles tumored its skin. In other spots, clumps of mussels clustered black and shining. Seaweed draped its shoulders, to either side of a head fashioned from the broken skull of a cow or horse. The lower jaw was missing, the mouth a hole gaping in the muddy throat. The thing advanced, the scraping I'd heard the debris in its flesh rasping the pavement. I retreated. The club with which it had struck Stewart was in fact its right arm, a single piece of driftwood. Its left arm was a mannequin's, wound in rusted wire and strands of seaweed.

This was not a man in a suit—which was impossible, and hurt to think. It swept the wooden arm at me. I leapt back, just out of reach. Stewart was on his hands and knees, grabbing for his weapon. I jabbed at the thing, trying to keep its attention. The wooden arm held straight, like a spear, it lunged at me. I sidestepped, swinging my improvised sword against the arm. With a flat clank, arm and pole rebounded from one another. The creature turned, whipping the wooden arm back at me. I went to duck, slipped, and fell. The arm struck the container behind me with a gong. This close, the smell of the thing, a stink of sodden flesh and vegetation, made my eyes water. Swiveling on my butt, I chopped its right leg with the pole, hammering the approximate location of its knee. The leg buckled inward, tipping the creature toward me. I scrambled away from it. Attempting to maintain its balance, it propped itself on its wooden arm, but Stewart hit its other leg from behind with a blow that sent the creature crashing on its back. Before it could recover, he brought the pole down on its head like an executioner swinging his axe. The animal skull rattled across the pavement. The rest of the thing, however, continued to move, doing its best to raise itself on its broken legs, dropping mud and bits of glass, pebbles, on the ground. My stomach churned at the sight. Ignoring the body, Stewart strode to the skull. He struck it twice with the pole, cracking it into several large fragments, which he stomped underfoot until they were unrecognizable. As if it were an engine running down, the body gradually ceased its motion.

Stewart dropped the pole and crossed to the creature's remains. Careful of its rusted wire sleeve, he caught the mannequin arm at the elbow. "You take the other side," he said.

Leaving my weapon, I did as he instructed. The wood was slimy, as if it had sat underwater for a while.

"Into the river," he said, nodding toward the end of the alleyway.

Together, we hauled the heavy form to where the pavement ended at a concrete ledge. Ten feet below, the Clyde lapped at the wall. "On three," Stewart said. "One, two, three!" I threw so hard I almost overbalanced myself into the water along with the creature's body. Stewart caught my arm. "Steady, lad." What was left of the thing struck the water with a considerable splash. It sunk quickly, leaving clouds of mud in its wake.

"What about the rest—the skull?" I said.

Stewart shook his head. "Leave it there. It's better to keep it separate from the rest."

Adrenaline lit my nerves, rendering everything around me painfully sharp. "I cannot believe I am standing here having this conversation with you," I said. It was the truth. Had Stewart said to me, "You're not. This is a dream," I would have had little trouble accepting his words.

Instead, he shrugged, turned, and started in the direction of the gate we'd entered.

I joined him. "What was that?" I said.

"Corpsemouth," he said, stooping to retrieve his weapon.

"I thought he was supposed to be taller," I said, picking up mine.

"In his proper form, he is," Stewart said. "Fortunately for you and me, enough of the old binding remains to keep him from appearing that way. What he's able to do is put together versions of himself, avatars, out of whatever's lying around. We call them his fingers."

"Who's 'we'?"

"A group of concerned citizens. We came together after the war. That was when Corpsemouth first made himself known, again, once the binding stone was removed. No one knew what they were doing. It had been too long since anything like this had happened. A couple of the founders were able to lay their hands on a few old books that gave hints of how to confront the monster, but a lot of it was learn as you go."

"I'm sure," I said. "Does Gabriel know about any of this? What about the rest of the family?"

"No, that isn't how it's done," Stewart said.

"How is it done?"

"Why? Are you interested in being part of it?"

"No," I said. "No, this was more than enough."

Stewart smiled thinly.

"Was my father part of this?" I thought of those old issues of *Man, Myth & Magic*.

"No," Stewart said. "Though I wondered a few times if he wasn't aware of more than he let on."

"Does this—tonight—does this kind of thing happen often?"

"More than I'd like."

As we walked, the mist thickened around us, rendering the shipping containers, the cranes, faint, ghostly. It didn't affect Stewart's sense of direction. He continued forward.

"What about this?" I said, holding up the pole. "Not the pipe, I mean, the writing on it."

"That depends on who you ask," Stewart said. "There's some who say that those are connected to old gods. Not as old as Corpsemouth, but not too far off. When they were young and strong, he wasn't of much concern to them. As they grew older, though, and saw themselves being supplanted by newer powers, their strength ebbed and his hungry mouth became a worry. They thought that if they gave up their divinity, the monster wouldn't want them. So they put their godhood into these symbols, and ever since, anyone who uses them has been able to draw on their power."

"Did it work? Did they escape?"

"No one knows," Stewart said. "I doubt it. Corpsemouth eats gods, but he's happy to consume whatever he can get his claws on."

Overhead, a lamp lit the mist orange. Somewhere in the distance, I heard voices, faint, indistinct.

"That's one explanation," I said. "What's the other?"

"You're sure you don't want to be part of this?"

"Is that why you brought me with you?"

"You haven't answered my question."

"Nor you mine," I said.

"Some folk say the symbols come from a fabulous city, one on the shore of a black ocean, where they were the inhabitants' most closely guarded treasure."

"That's interesting," I said, "but it's not the question I meant."

"I know," Stewart said.

Through the mist, the gate swam into view. Stewart pushed it open and walked out. I went to follow, but before I could, a shout drew my attention to the left. No more than twenty yards away, through a clearing in the mist, a white van was parked. At the sight of it, my heart knocked. I knew this vehicle, had watched it drive through my dreams. For this to be the same van was impossible, of course, but on a night such as this one had proved to be, it could be none other. I was suddenly sick with dread and grief. To walk to the van was terrifying, but to remain in place, let alone, to leave, was worse. Legs shaking madly, I stepped toward it. Stewart said something, but whatever it was didn't register.

The mist was full of yells and calls whose locations I couldn't pinpoint. Was one of those voices my father's? I wasn't sure. The mist muffled the sounds, as if I were hearing them from the other side of a thick wall. I was almost at the van. Its interior was dark. Was it empty? Half-expecting my hand to pass through it, I reached for the handle to the driver's door. It was solid to the touch, and when I pulled, it clicked and the door opened. There was no one behind the wheel. Kneeling on the seat, I leaned into the van.

It was empty. There was no evidence of its passengers left behind; although, for a second, two, I caught the faintest odor of dried sweat and laundry detergent, the scent I'd breathed whenever I'd rested my head against my father's chest at the end of the day, when I wished him good night. Then it was gone.

I exited the van, closing the door. Stewart was standing behind me. "Is…," I started, and paused, unable to utter the remainder of the question.

"Aye," Stewart said.

"Where is he?"

He tipped his head toward where the mist was thick. "Out there."

"So if I go there, I'll find him?"

"You might," he said, "or you might not. You could spend an hour searching this lot, or you could wander off someplace else, and be lost."

Without warning, I was crying, tears streaming down my cheeks. I felt every bit as bad as I had the night my father had died, when it seemed a spear had been driven straight through my chest, as if his death were a pin that had fixed me forever in place. To see him one more time, to speak to him, to tell him I loved him and was sorry I hadn't been a better son, was a prospect almost too much to bear. To fail, though, to walk away and not return, was not something I could do to my mother and sister. I turned from the van and headed for the gate.

The shouts and calls persisted. "What's happening?" I said to Stewart. "What are they doing?"

"The same thing we were."

"Corpsemouth?"

"It's not just our world he wants to break into. There are folk on the other side who do their best to keep him out of there, too."

"Can he hurt them?"

"Oh aye, he eats the dead same as anything else." Seeing the expression on my face, he added, "But your dad was always a capable fellow. I'm sure he'll be fine."

XVII

After the night's events, I did not anticipate sleeping. Almost the instant I settled onto my bed, though, my arms and legs grew heavy, my eyelids struggled to stay open, and I slid into unconsciousness. For an indeterminate time, I drifted in a blank, not unpleasant place. Slowly, a long, black cord came into view. It corkscrewed around and around, the way the cord on our old telephone had. It faded, and was replaced by the interior of the white van.

This time, it was full of the handful of men I'd seen in it a few days ago. My father was among them. All of the passengers looked worse for wear, their shirts and pants torn and dirty, their arms and cheeks cut and bruised. Dad was leaning forward, a black telephone receiver held to his ear. I couldn't hear every word he was saying, but I understood enough to know that he was saying he was okay.

With a start, I realized he was speaking to me. For the dream's brief duration, he continued to reassure me, while I said words he could not hear. The connection, it seemed, was one way. Then the call was finished, and I was awake—though not before a last glimpse of the white van, speeding along through high, brick walls black with age, carrying my father to the next stop on his long, strange death.

For Fiona

Contributors

ABOUT THE EDITOR

ELLEN DATLOW has been editing science fiction, fantasy, and horror short fiction for more than thirty-five years. She currently acquires short fiction for Tor.com. In addition, she has edited more than fifty science fiction, fantasy, and horror anthologies, including *Lovecraft's Monsters*, *Fearful Symmetries*, *Nightmare Carnival*, *The Cutting Room*, the *Women Destroy Horror* issue of *Nightmare Magazine*, and *The Doll Collection*.

She's won multiple World Fantasy Awards, Locus Awards, Hugo Awards, Stoker Awards, International Horror Guild Awards, Shirley Jackson Awards, and the 2012 Il Posto Nero Black Spot Award for Excellence as Best Foreign Editor. Datlow was named recipient of the 2007 Karl Edward Wagner Award, given at the British Fantasy Convention for "outstanding contribution to the genre"; was honored with the Life Achievement Award given by the Horror Writers Association in acknowledgment of superior achievement over an entire career; and received the Life Achievement Award from the World Fantasy Convention.

She lives in New York and co-hosts the monthly Fantastic Fiction Reading Series at KGB Bar. More information can be found at WWW.DATLOW.COM, on Facebook (WWW.FACEBOOK.COM/ELLENDATLOW), and on Twitter @ ELLENDATLOW.

DALE BAILEY's new collection, *The End of the End of Everything*, came out in the spring of 2015. A novel, *The Subterranean Season*, will follow in November.

He has published three previous novels, *The Fallen, House of Bones,* and *Sleeping Policemen* (the latter, with Jack Slay, Jr.); and one previous collection of short fiction, *The Resurrection Man's Legacy and Other Stories.*

His work has won the Shirley Jackson Award and the International Horror Guild Award, and he has been a finalist for the Nebula Award and the Bram Stoker Award. His novelette "Death and Suffrage" was adapted for Showtime Television's *Masters of Horror.* He lives in North Carolina with his family.

ADAM-TROY CASTRO's time on this Earth has included stints in customer service, a fleeting stint as a comic-book artist, and a summer spent lurking in darkness at one of the hidden safety posts in an amusement park house of horrors. As a writer, his twenty-six books include the six volumes of the acclaimed Gustav Gloom middle-grade series.

His short fiction has been nominated for two Hugo, three Stoker, and eight Nebula Awards. His Andrea Cort novel, *Emissaries from the Dead,* won the Philip K. Dick Award. Castro lives in Boynton Beach, Florida, with his wife, Judi, and an assortment of cats that include Uma Furman and Meow Farrow.

JACK DANN is a multi-award-winning author who has written or edited more than seventy-five books, including the international best-seller *The Memory Cathedral, The Silent,* and *The Rebel: An Imagined Life of James Dean.* Other publications include the short novel *The Economy of Light* and the autobiography *Insinuations.* An "unexpurgated" edition of *The Rebel* called *The Rebel: Second Chance* was published in the spring of 2015.

His short stories have been collected in *Timetipping, Visitations, The Fiction Factory, Jubilee,* and *Promised Land. Concentration,* a collection of Dann's stories about the Holocaust, is forthcoming.

He is the co-editor, with Janeen Webb, of the anthology *Dreaming Down-Under,* which won the World Fantasy Award, and his anthology *Ghosts by Gaslight,* co-edited with Nick Gevers, won the Shirley Jackson Award and the Aurealis Award.

Also forthcoming is an anthology entitled *Dreaming in the Dark,* which will launch the new imprint PS Australia, of which Dann is the publishing director, and a collection of poetry entitled *Poems from a White Heart.*

Dann lives in Australia on a farm overlooking the sea. You can visit his website at www.jackdann.com and follow him on Twitter @JACKMDANN and Facebook (WWW.FACEBOOK.COM/JACK.DANN2).

TERRY DOWLING is one of Australia's most-respected and internationally acclaimed writers of science fiction, dark fantasy, and horror and the author of the multi-award-winning Tom Rynosseros saga. *The Year's Best Fantasy and Horror* series has featured more horror stories by Dowling in its twenty-one-year run than by any other writer. Dowling's award-winning horror collections include *Basic Black: Tales of Appropriate Fear* (International Horror Guild Award winner for Best Collection 2007), Aurealis Award–winning *An Intimate Knowledge of the Night*, and the World Fantasy Award–nominated *Blackwater Days*.

His most recent books include *Amberjack: Tales of Fear & Wonder* and his debut novel, *Clowns at Midnight*, which London's *Guardian* calls "an exceptional work that bears comparison to John Fowles's *The Magus*." His website can be found at WWW.TERRYDOWLING.COM.

GARDNER DOZOIS is the author or editor of more than a hundred books. He was the editor of *Asimov's Science Fiction* magazine for almost twenty years and still edits the annual anthology series *The Year's Best Science Fiction*, now up to its thirty-second annual collection.

He has won fifteen Hugo Awards as the Year's Best Editor, thirty-two Locus Awards for his editing work, and two Nebula Awards and a Sidewise Award for his own writing. He has been inducted into the Science Fiction Hall of Fame.

Former film critic and teacher-turned-horror-author GEMMA FILES is best known for her Weird Western Hexslinger series (*A Book of Tongues*, *A Rope of Thorns*, and *A Tree of Bones*, all from ChiZine Publications). She has also published two collections of short fiction, two chapbooks of speculative poetry, and a story cycle (*We Will All Go Down Together: Stories of the Five-Family Coven*).

In 1999, Files won the International Horror Guild's Best Short Fiction Award for her story "The Emperor's Old Bones." Five of her short stories were adapted as episodes of the Showtime TV series *The Hunger*, produced by

Ridley and Tony Scott. Her next novel, *Experimental Film*, will be available from CZP in November 2015.

JEFFREY FORD is the author of the novels *Vanitas, The Physiognomy, Memoranda, The Beyond, The Portrait of Mrs. Charbuque, The Girl in the Glass, The Cosmology of the Wider World,* and *The Shadow Year*.

His story collections include *The Fantasy Writer's Assistant, The Empire of Ice Cream, The Drowned Life,* and *Crackpot Palace*. Ford has published more than one hundred short stories, which have appeared in numerous journals, magazines, and anthologies ranging from *The Magazine of Fantasy & Science Fiction* to *The Oxford Book of American Short Stories*.

He is the recipient of the World Fantasy Award, Nebula Award, Shirley Jackson Award, Edgar Allan Poe Award, Grand Prix de l'Imaginaire, and Hayakawa Award. His fiction has been translated into nearly twenty languages.

In addition to writing, he's been a professor of literature and writing for thirty years and a guest lecturer at Clarion Writing Workshop, the Stone Coast MFA Program, the Richard Hugo House in Seattle, and the Antioch University Writing Workshop. He lives in Ohio and currently teaches at Ohio Wesleyan University.

CHRISTOPHER FOWLER is the award-winning author of more than forty novels and short-story collections, including the Bryant & May mysteries, recording the adventures of two Golden Age detectives in modern-day London.

The recipient of the 2015 Dagger In The Library, his latest books are the Ballard-esque thriller *The Sand Men* and *Bryant & May: London's Glory*. Other works include screenplays, video games, graphic novels, and audio plays. He writes a weekly column in *The Independent on Sunday*. He lives in King's Cross, London, and Barcelona.

Three-time International Horror Guild Award Winner **GLEN HIRSHBERG**'s novels include *The Snowman's Children, The Book of Bunk,* and *Motherless Child,* which was recently republished in a new, revised edition by Tor. *Good Girls,* the second book in the "Motherless Children" trilogy, will be published in 2016.

He is also the author of three widely praised story collections: *The Two Sams* (a *Publishers Weekly* Best Book of 2003), *American Morons,* and *The Janus Tree*. In 2008, he won the Shirley Jackson Award for the novelette "The Janus Tree."

With Peter Atkins and Dennis Etchison, he co-founded the Rolling Darkness Revue, an annual reading/live music/performance event that tours the West Coast of the United States every fall and has also made international appearances.

He lives in the Los Angeles area with his wife, son, daughter, and cats.

BRIAN HODGE is the author of ten novels and is working on three more as well as nearly 120 shorter works and five full-length collections. His first collection, *The Convulsion Factory*, was ranked by critic Stanley Wiater among the 113 best books of modern horror.

Recent and forthcoming works include *In the Negative Spaces* and *The Weight of the Dead*, both stand-alone novellas; *Worlds of Hurt*, an omnibus edition of the first four works in his Misbegotten mythos; an updated hardcover edition of *Dark Advent*, his early post-apocalyptic epic; and a new collection tentatively titled *Echoes from the Void*.

He lives in Colorado, where he also likes to make music and photographs; loves everything about organic gardening except the thieving squirrels; and trains in Krav Maga and kickboxing, which are of no use at all against the squirrels.

Connect with him through his website (WWW.BRIANHODGE.NET) or Facebook (WWW.FACEBOOK.COM/BRIANHODGEWRITER).

CAROLE JOHNSTONE's fiction has appeared in numerous magazines and anthologies published by ChiZine, PS Publishing, Night Shade Books, TTA Press, and Apex Book Company, among many others. In 2014, she won the British Fantasy Award for Best Short Story. Her work has been reprinted in various "best of" anthologies.

Her 2014 novella, *Cold Turkey*, was published by TTA Press. She is presently at work on her second novel while seeking fame and fortune with the first—but she just can't seem to kick the short-story habit.

More information on the author can be found at CAROLEJOHNSTONE.COM.

STEPHEN GRAHAM JONES is the author of fifteen novels and six short-story collections. The most recent are *Not for Nothing, After the People Lights Have Gone Off*, and *Floating Boy and the Girl Who Couldn't Fly* (with Paul Tremblay).

Jones has had more than two hundred stories published, many reprinted in best of the year annuals. He's won the Texas Institute of Letters Award for fiction, the Independent Publishers Award for Multicultural Fiction, and a National

Endowment for the Arts fellowship in fiction. He teaches in the MFA programs at CU Boulder and UCR–Palm Desert.

He lives in Boulder, Colorado, with his wife and kids. For more information visit his website DEMONTHEORY.NET, or you can find him on Twitter @SGJ72.

CAITLÍN R. KIERNAN was recently hailed by the *New York Times* as "one of our essential authors of dark fiction." A two-time winner of both the World Fantasy and Bram Stoker awards, she has published ten novels, including *The Red Tree* and *The Drowning Girl: A Memoir.* She is also the recipient of the Locus and James Tiptree, Jr. awards. Her short fiction has been collected in thirteen volumes, including *Tales of Pain and Wonder, The Ammonite Violin & Others, A is for Alien,* and *The Ape's Wife and Other Stories.*

Subterranean Press has released a two-volume set collecting the best of her short fiction, *Two Worlds and In Between* and *Beneath an Oil-Dark Sea.* She is currently working on a screenplay, her next novel, *Interstate Love Song: Murder Ballads,* and a volume of juvenilia, "Cambrian Tales."

JOHN LANGAN is the author of two collections, *The Wide, Carnivorous Sky and Other Monstrous Geographies* (Hippocampus) and *Mr. Gaunt and Other Uneasy Encounters* (Prime), and a novel, *House of Windows* (Night Shade). With Paul Tremblay, he co-edited *Creatures: Thirty Years of Monsters* (Prime).

One of the founders of the Shirley Jackson Awards, he lives in upstate New York with his wife, younger son, and a houseful of animals.

LIVIA LLEWELLYN is a writer of horror, dark fantasy, and erotica, whose fiction has appeared in *ChiZine, Subterranean, Apex Magazine, Postscripts, Nightmare Magazine,* and numerous anthologies. Her first collection, *Engines of Desire: Tales of Love & Other Horrors,* was published in 2011 by Lethe Press and received two Shirley Jackson Award nominations, for Best Collection and Best Novelette (for "Omphalos"). Her story "Furnace" received a 2013 Shirley Jackson Award nomination for Best Short Fiction. Her second collection will be published by Word Horde Press in 2016. You can find her online at LIVIALLEWELLYN.COM.

ADAM L. G. NEVILL was born in Birmingham, England, in 1969 and grew up in England and New Zealand. He is the author of the supernatural horror novels *Banquet for the Damned, Apartment 16, The Ritual, Last Days, House of*

Small Shadows, No One Gets Out Alive, and *Lost Girl.*

In 2012, *The Ritual* was the winner of the August Derleth Award for Best Horror Novel, and in 2013 *Last Days* won the same award. The same two novels were awarded Best in Category: Horror by R.U.S.A. Adam lives in Devon and can be contacted through WWW.ADAMLGNEVILL.COM.

KIM NEWMAN is a novelist, critic, and broadcaster. His fiction includes *The Night Mayor, Bad Dreams, Jago,* the *Anno Dracula* novels and stories, *The Quorum, The Original Dr. Shade and Other Stories, Life's Lottery, Back in the USSA* (with Eugene Byrne), *The Man from the Diogenes Club, Professor Moriarty: The Hound of the d'Urbervilles,* and *An English Ghost Story* under his own name and *The Vampire Genevieve* and *Orgy of the Blood Parasites* as Jack Yeovil.

His nonfiction books include *Nightmare Movies, Ghastly Beyond Belief* (with Neil Gaiman), *Horror: 100 Best Books* (with Stephen Jones), *Wild West Movies, The BFI Companion to Horror, Millennium Movies,* and BFI Classics studies of *Cat People, Doctor Who,* and *Quatermass and the Pit.* He is a contributing editor to *Sight & Sound* and *Empire* magazines, has written and broadcast widely, and has scripted radio and television documentaries. His stories "Week Woman" and "Ubermensch!" have been adapted into an episode of the TV series *The Hunger* and an Australian short film, respectively; he has directed and written a tiny film, *Missing Girl*; and he co-wrote the West End play *The Hallowe'en Sessions.* Following his Radio 4 play *Cry Babies,* he wrote episodes for Radio 7's series *The Man in Black* and Glass Eye Pix's *Tales from Beyond the Pale.* He scripted (with Maura McHugh) the comic book miniseries *Witchfinder: The Mysteries of Unland,* illustrated by Tyler Crook.

His official website is WWW.JOHNNYALUCARD.COM. His forthcoming fiction includes the novels *The Secrets of Drearcliff Grange* and *Angels of Music.* He is on Twitter as @ANNODRACULA.

SOFIA SAMATAR is the author of the novel *A Stranger in Olondria,* winner of the Crawford Award, the British Fantasy Award, and the World Fantasy Award for Best Novel. She also received the 2014 John W. Campbell Award for Best New Writer. She co-edits the online journal *Interfictions* and lives in California.

PETER STRAUB is the author of seventeen novels, which have been translated into more than twenty languages. They include *Ghost Story, Koko, Mr. X, In the*

Night Room, and two collaborations with Stephen King, *The Talisman* and *Black House*. He has written two volumes of poetry and two collections of short fiction, and he edited the Library of America's edition of *H. P. Lovecraft's Tales* and the Library of America's two-volume anthology *American Fantastic Tales*. He has won the British Fantasy Award, eight Bram Stoker Awards, two International Horror Guild Awards, and three World Fantasy Awards. In 1998, he was named Grand Master at the World Horror Convention. In 2006, he was given the Horror Writers Association's Lifetime Achievement Award. In 2008, he was given the Barnes & Noble Writers for Writers Award by Poets & Writers. At the World Fantasy Convention in 2010, he was given the WFC's Life Achievement Award.

STEVE RASNIC TEM's latest novel, *Blood Kin* (Solaris), alternating between the 1930s and the present day, is a Southern Gothic/horror blend of snake handling, ghosts, kudzu, and Melungeons. It won the Bram Stoker Award.

His previous Solaris novel was *Deadfall Hotel*. Recently published, was *In the Lovecraft Museum*, a stand-alone novella from Drugstore Indian Press, an imprint of PS Publishing. In late 2015 or early 2016, Centipede Press will be presenting the best of his uncollected horror stories in *Out of the Dark: A Storybook of Horrors*.

Also in 2016, Solaris will present his dark SF novel *Ubo*, a meditation on violence as seen through the eyes of some of history's most disreputable figures.

A. C. WISE's fiction has appeared in *Clarkesworld*, *Shimmer*, *Apex*, *The Best Horror of the Year Volume 4*, and *Year's Best Weird Fiction Volume 1*. Her first collection will be published by Lethe Press in fall 2015. In addition to her writing, she co-edits the webzine *Unlikely Story*. Find her online at WWW.ACWISE.NET.

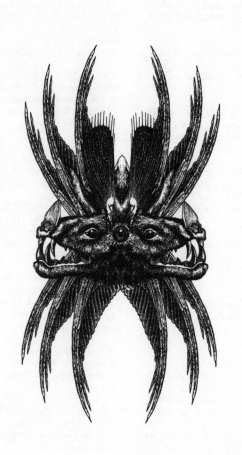